CRESCENT BEACH

A NOVEL

* * *

DAVID J MATHER

A PEACE CORPS WRITERS BOOK

ALSO BY DAVID J MATHER

ONE FOR THE ROAD

DAVID J MATHER

A young Peace Corps volunteer finds adventure and heart-breaking romance in the lawless foothills of the Andes. Set in beautiful southern Chile in the late 1960's, this coming-of-age novel paints a vivid picture of a forgotten way of life.

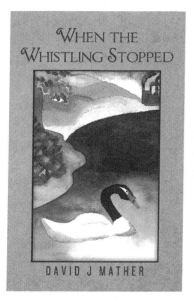

WHEN THE WHISTLING STOPPED

DAVID J MATHER

In this sequel to *One For The Road*, murder and intrigue follow a young couple's quest to expose an amoral mill owner responsible for the death of thousands of black-necked swans. The twists and turns of this eco-thriller make it hard to put down.

Crescent Beach

A Peace Corps Writers Book

An imprint of Peace Corps Worldwide

Printed in the United States of America
by Peace Corps Writers of Oakland, California.
No part of this book may be used or reproduced in any manner
whatsoever without written permission except in the case of
brief quotations contained in critical articles or reviews.

For more information, contact peacecorpsworldwide@gmail.com.
Peace Corps Writers and the Peace Corps Writers colophon
are trademarks of PeaceCorpsWorldwide.org.

ISBN-13: 9781935925743
Library of Congress Control Number: 2016931109
First Peace Corps Writers Edition, January 2016
ISBN: 1935925741

TO GRAMPA ED
WHO MADE SO MANY THINGS POSSIBLE

ACKNOWLEDGMENTS

My town of Crescent Beach is fictional and has nothing to do with the Crescent Beach on Florida's east coast; I picked the name because it is ubiquitous in Florida. Other than the Storm of the Century, all narrative and characters are fictional. However, I am deeply indebted to many native and long time residents of Florida's Big Bend area who shared with me so many details of coastal life before, during, and after the storm.

I would especially like to thank, in alphabetical order, Captains Timmy Futch, Arthur Hollenbeck, Buddy Kight, David Kight, and Johnny Squires for their expansive knowledge of the Gulf of Mexico: its wildlife, shrimping, crabbing, sports fishing, and more. I also would like to thank Tina Brotherton, Danny Hicks, Renee Futch, Mike and Maxie Puerner, Priscilla Roberts, Ray Rodriguez, and Billy Williams.

I would like to thank Janet Post for her editorial efforts, as well as a big thank you to my neighbors—Judy Barker, Allie Farrar, and Joyce Killebrew —for their always spot-on feedback. Also, big thank yous to Jill Andrews and Sue McAlary for the same, to veterinarian-extraordinaire Tom Heitzman, and to artist and friend Jennifer Brown who created the cover artwork.

Rube Waddell's novel *Twisted Justice* and Leo Lovel's memoirs *Spring Creek Chronicles* and *Spring Creek Chronicles II* were inspirational, and the regional publication *Dixie County Advocate* provided historical material, as did the three internet sites listed in the rear of the book under the section "Facts About the Storm of the Century."

Once again, the biggest thank you goes to my wife, Lindy, the reader of each and every manuscript, whose unflagging support, computer expertise, and, above all, patience with me, made it possible for this book to see the light of day.

CRESCENT BEACH

CHAPTER ONE

1993

The trooper whistled softly as he drove slowly by the blimp. Man, look at the size of that thing! Got to be at least two hundred feet by maybe fifty or sixty. The blimp was lit up by bright fluorescent lights and was secured to two-inch-thick steel eyebolts sticking out of the pavement. A steel cable ran from its bow to a massive winch mounted on an iron donkey on rails. A couple hundred feet beyond the winch was a bunker-like building with a black and tan Highway Patrol cruiser, identical to the trooper's, parked in front. A mix of antennae and meteorological equipment sprouted haphazardly from the roof, and two black sedans with the Defense Department's round insignia were off to the side.

He pulled in next to the cruiser and got out of his car. Hands on hips, the trooper stretched, then looked down and brushed some crumbs from his front. Long drive from Daytona, close to four hours. He looked at his watch. Two in the morning: hell of an hour for a meeting. The wind was gusting and he noticed an anemometer spinning wildly on the roof. Snugging his Stetson and adjusting his pistol belt, the trooper walked up to the building.

Square shouldered, six-two, around 220, the trooper had rusty red hair. His belly wasn't flat anymore because of all the riding around in the cruiser and sitting at the barracks, but he was still in good shape. He entered the building. There were no windows, and electronic equipment was everywhere. Six men, only one in civilian clothes, looked over when he opened the door. Two of them, wearing the dark blue uniforms of Air Force Able-Bodied, were sitting in front of a pair of sixteen-inch circular screens framed by a series of gauges. The trooper thought that they barely looked old enough to shave. Several clipboards hung from hooks on the walls and a maze of metal conduit and cable ran to screens, radio equipment, and gauges. It reminded the trooper of the radar room on the destroyer he was once on heading to Vietnam.

A much older State Trooper in an immaculate, sharply pressed uniform with the two vertical bars of captain, walked up to him.

"Sergeant McMillan," he said, looking over at a large clock on the wall, "you're punctual."

"Yes, sir. Long drive, though."

"I'm Captain Smathers, Cross City," the captain said, extending his hand. "Let me introduce the others."

The man in civvies was the first over.

"Detective Smart, Highway Patrol, Cross City."

The detective held out his hand. The others came up and introduced themselves: an ensign in crisp Coast Guard white, a sergeant in the black and blue of the Florida Marine Patrol, and the two young Air Force ABs. The captain wasted no time.

"Sergeant, you know this meeting is about drug smuggling, but you're probably wondering why here and at this ungodly hour."

"That did cross my mind, Captain."

"We'll get to that shortly, but first I'd like to explain a little about this area."

The captain walked over to a large map on the wall that was dotted with different colored pins. He picked up a yardstick and pointed to the Gulf Coast where it curved down from the panhandle.

"This section is called the Big Bend Area, although the Department of Tourism refers to it as the Nature Coast. The locals call it the Redneck Riviera which is probably the best description. The area both on the coast and inland is good ol' boy territory; 'lawgs,' 'hawgs,' and 'dawgs' are a way of life here, forestry is the biggest employer, and there's very little law enforcement. You especially take your life in your hands if you're a game warden. In other words, this whole area," he said, moving the yardstick in a circle, "is wild and wooly: it's like stepping into a Florida from the past."

The captain dragged the yardstick along the coastline. "We're responsible from Apalachicola here, down to Crystal River. The Gulf's nothing like the Atlantic where you're from," he said, turning back to the trooper. "Around these parts, the rule of thumb is that the water gains a foot of depth for every mile you go out; in other words, very shallow. Anywhere close in is a labyrinth of oyster bars and mud flats with hundreds of isolated creeks, little islands, marsh, and swampland to hide small craft and contraband. There are also hundreds of isolated limestone and paved roads perfect for landing small aircraft. Consequently, a very tough place to monitor.

"We've had some recent successes thanks to the blimp and the radar, especially with shipments by air. As you can see from our uniforms, it's a joint effort. The Marine Patrol and Coast Guard watch the Gulf, and we watch the roads and air. Through congressional mandate a little over a year ago, the Department of Defense, represented by the Air Force here, took the blimps over from the Coast Guard. However, this so called Tethered Aerostat Radar System has one major weakness: downtime. The blimps don't average much better than fifty percent up. Bad weather and high winds are major factors, especially during the winter, and repairs are necessary way too often. Unfortunately, the perpetrators are well aware of all this."

'Perpetrators?' Who you trying to impress, Captain? the trooper thought.

"The perpetrators seem to know when the blimp is coming down and why. Not too much happens by air if the blimp's down because of bad weather for the simple fact that the smugglers don't usually fly then either, although we have found a couple of wrecked planes, meaning some try. But the boats are another story; they'll come in any time.

"Somehow the smugglers always seem to know not only when the blimp's down for repairs, but also for how long. And that's when we get bombarded from both sky and sea. They have to be getting inside info. Everybody knows everybody around here; grew up, fished and hunted together, went to grammar and maybe high school together, worked together. Word gets around fast.

"And people here are poor, real poor; and now there's a lot of money being thrown around, more money than this area's ever seen. Most everyone who knows anything, including the local authorities, are being paid off. That is why we're meeting so late; we don't want any one to know about this."

The trooper thought, okay, but why am I here?

"We've got a plan, Sergeant, and you're the key player. About a month ago, there was a meeting of all regional Highway Patrol commanders up in Tallahassee concerning the drug epidemic. After explaining our situation, I proposed putting someone underground to find out who the kingpins are—clamp down on the activities around here once and for all. And I'm not talking about every-one with a small boat looking for some easy money; I couldn't care less about them. What we need is to get the big boys, plus find out where the distribution centers are. Your captain, Sergeant, highly recommended you for a lot of reasons. One of those reasons is that you have a unique background, especially for a law officer. Do you know what I'm referring to?"

All eyes were on the trooper.

"I think I have a pretty good idea, sir."

"Then why don't we all pull up chairs and you can tell us about it."

The two young ABs pulled their chairs over from the radar stations, while the others folded out chairs brought over from a corner. The trooper fidgeted with his necktie.

"I was born real poor in north Georgia, an area, I guess, like this one. Nobody had any money to speak of, except the moonshiners. Maybe it's the same here as it was back home where we didn't look at those run-ning contraband like they were outlaws. Hardly. They were a respected part of our community, as much as any banker or doctor, maybe even more so. Many of them were generous and their spending really helped everyone get by. Moonshine was a big part of our way of life.

"There was one family, friends of my family, that had made liquor in our area for generations. As a young boy, I began helping around the stills, lugging water, car-rying this and that, cutting and splitting wood, doing chores for them. When I was in my early teens, I be-gan to go with some of the drivers on deliveries. Those drivers were our idols: they were the Robert Mitchums from 'Thunder Road.'" The trooper looked over at the ABs. "That was a movie from before you were born." He looked back to the others. "And those boys could

drive, I mean really drive. They also were the best mechanics anywhere: they could take an engine apart and
put it back together blindfolded, 'souping' it up in the
process. I learned a lot from them.

"At sixteen I started driving. Was pretty good at it,
too. Made a lot of runs, but, at eighteen, during a long
chase, my engine blew a gasket and oil exploded out,
covering my windshield and I couldn't see. I went off
the road at over eighty. Why I wasn't killed, I'll never
know. Not even scratched, but my rig was totaled.

"I got pinched and went to jail. This was back in
the sixties when Vietnam was going full bore. The army
needed soldiers and a lot of deals were made with boys
in trouble like I was. I don't think I have to tell you that
what I'd done was a felony. The judge said if I'd serve
and stay out of trouble for two years in the army, adju-
dication would be withheld and I'd be a free man with
nothing on my record. Because of my build, I guess,
I was selected for the Military Police and stayed in the
army for eight years, six over in 'Nam, then as an instructor stateside for two. I joined the force after that, and
here I am."

The captain added, "The sergeant here is still a pretty good driver. He's had quite a few high-speed chases
in the last fifteen years and no one's outrun him yet.
Unfortunately," he said looking back at the trooper, "I
doubt if you will need those skills here. This is undercover work. Like I said, we're trying to go after the big boys,
but we don't know who they are. The runners we've arrested are lackeys, real low on the totem pole and don't
know jack shit. There is one runner, though, who does."

The captain went up to the map again.

"Jimmy Talbot from Crescent Beach, right here," he
said, pointing. "We know that he's been involved with
the smuggling from the beginning. And he's a tough
cracker. He's smart, lucky too, maybe, but real smart

and real slippery. Grew up on the water and has hunted and fished all over the Big Bend area. Knows it like the back of his hand. We believe he has been involved in every shipment that's ever come into this area by water, knows everybody from sea captains to runners to the distribution kingpins. If we could get the goods on him, I think we could get the information we need."

The trooper spoke up.

"Been my experience, sir, that if someone like that who knows something gets nabbed, a slick lawyer shows up, posts bail, and chances are he disappears, one way or another. The lost bail's penny ante in the scheme of things. Or, maybe the guy keeps his mouth shut, goes in and does his time, and has a big payday when he gets out. So how do you get someone like this Jimmy to talk? And how do you plan on 'getting the goods' on him?"

"Leverage, Sergeant, leverage. Doing what he does, you wouldn't think so, but it seems Jimmy Talbot is a real family man. And when he's not running the drugs, he's a hard-working fisherman—crabs, nets mullet and trout, and has recently begun to guide for sports fishermen. He's also a church-goer and put two of his three kids through college. He loves his family and wants to provide for them. If he's in prison, he can't do that. And I don't think he'd enjoy his family coming to see him on visiting days either.

"Sergeant, you have something else in your background that's a good fit with what I'm about to ask you to do."

"And what would that be, sir?"

"Your experience with heavy equipment. Even though you were an MP, seems you learned how to operate all sorts of equipment in Vietnam."

"Yes, sir. I wasn't one to go to bars and make friends with the soldiers I might have to bust in the chops later and throw in the brig. But I did have a few friends with the Army Corps of Engineers who let me work on roads, runways, drainage, you name it. Gave them more time to goof off, and as long as the work was done well and on time, there was never any problem. I also helped them in the garage and, truthfully, I was probably the best mechanic of the lot. If it's got tracks or wheels, I can operate it and fix it."

"Your captain says you moonlight as an operator down in the Daytona area, for 'some extra change,' I think he put it."

"Yes, sir."

"This is all good stuff, Sergeant, because we want you to pose as a retired Georgia road contractor, a good ol' boy who wants to catch fish and who just might settle in the area. Lots of Georgia people go there. We want you to hire this Jimmy Talbot, make friends, become part of the local landscape, find out as much as you can. You'll be wired the entire time and just maybe you can get the info we need. We think that your moonshining background is a fit. If we're real lucky, you'll get Talbot to say stuff we can use against him, or find out when he's doing a run and we can catch him in the act. Then, if there's a choice between ratting on the kingpins or being with his family, I think he'll choose family."

"Blackmail, in other words."

"Yes, Sergeant. Do you have a problem with that?"

The sergeant shrugged. He doubted this Talbot was the religious family man the captain had described; more likely, he was like all the other drug-dealing, coke-snorting trailer trash he dealt with on the east coast.

"He's a drug trafficker, Captain, no different from any other; he's breaking the law. No problems on my end. But I'm only forty-four years old. Kind of early for retirement, don't you think?"

"You just said, Sergeant, that it'd been your experience that convicted smugglers who didn't squeal on the big boys often got a big pay day when they left prison. We also know that the Vietnam deal the judge offered you wasn't the only one. You could have had the charges dropped if you turned state's evidence against the moonshiners. But, you didn't and went over to 'Nam. So, what's to say you weren't amply rewarded too, socked away the money, plus, when you got out of the service, you were provided with a couple of porkbelly deals that made you very successful very quickly. And the area you'll be from is one of the few really wealthy areas of Georgia. Plenty of opportunities to make good money there."

The trooper didn't say anything.

"Believe me, Sergeant, I know all this is a long shot; but, theoretically, there's a chance. And, frankly, it's all that we've been able to come up with.

"You'll have a shiny new Ford pickup with Georgia plates, Georgia bank account and personal checks, driver's license, credit cards, everything you need. We've worked up a list of references in your area of Georgia; they'll vouch if anyone checks. The next couple days you'll be staying with Detective Smart in his home in Perry to work out logistics, including giving Talbot a call to line up your fishing. The Airmen here will be your contact, the go-betweens you and me. You'll have at least a month to work this case. After that, we'll see what progress you're making. So, looks like you've got a fishing vacation on the horizon, Sergeant. Any questions?"

"No, sir, but there is one problem; no, make that two."

The captain raised an eyebrow.

"Yes?"

"I can't swim, and I get seasick."

The captain looked at him in disbelief.

"You're kidding!"

The Coast Guard officer said, "Can't help you with the swimming, Sergeant, but Dramamine, patches, or copper bracelet. Try one of those, maybe all three. My wife swears by the patches."

"As for not swimming, just wear a life vest for God's sake..." The captain paused in mid sentence. "Actually, maybe you could bring your own special vest, one we had wired. It certainly wouldn't arouse any suspicion, considering. And might be a lot easier to conceal a bug if you were out in a boat in a tee shirt or something when it warms up."

The captain stood.

"I'll talk to the FBI boys in Tallahassee to see what they can rig up. You'll also get a standard wire. I'll be in touch. Meeting adjourned."

Within minutes the trooper was left alone with the young airmen. He loosened his tie and sat heavily in one of the vacated chairs. He tilted his head back and closed his eyes. The captain didn't know it, but he was right: this would be like a vacation. Maybe not the fishing, but he was ready for a change and this area would suit him just fine. Anything to get off those freeways, away from all those dumb frigging people doing dumb frigging things. He chuckled. "Redneck Riviera," he mused out loud. Opening his eyes, the young airmen were looking at him.

"Either of you two boys been to this Crescent Beach?"

The airmen looked at each other before the taller spoke up.

"Yes, sir, gone in there several times. Got a nice bar and restaurant up on stilts looking right out over the Gulf. Good place to have a beer and watch the boats go in and out. Good grouper sandwiches, too. But that's about it. The captain's got it right: it's not like the rest of Florida, not fancy at all. Lots of run-down trailers and double-wides, and the folks look grizzled, like they've been through the ringer. Even though I wasn't in uniform, I felt real out of place. When I tried starting a conversation with some of the locals, I got nowhere. And you wouldn't believe the accents! It was like I was somewhere in Georgia or Alabama with Confederate flags flying all over the place and no blacks anywhere. I guess it's true that the farther north you go in Florida, the farther south you are."

The trooper couldn't help yawning. The other airman spoke up.

"Sergeant, sir, maybe you'd like to rest for awhile. There' re a couple of cots in the back room, and a place to wash up."

The trooper folded his hands in his lap and looked at the two young men.

"Boys, if we're going to be working together, forget that Sergeant and sir stuff. I answer to Rusty."

Chapter Two

Jimmy Talbot bent his knees to better absorb the boat's slamming into the waves. The wind was bad, but nowhere near as bad as a few hours ago. Still, his lower back was killing him, and the Gulf's February spray was frigid. Finger-numbing cold. He took a hand off the wheel and blew on it, wishing he had gloves. About the only good news was that it was too windy for the blimp to be up, no worries about the Feds and their radar tonight. That, and the wind-driven high tide enabled them to shoot straight over the oyster bars. He glanced at the lit-up Loran: right on course. Nothing coming over the radio. Just this last trip, off-load, clean up the boat, and he could crawl into a warm bed. If he was lucky, maybe Crystal would wake and they could have a little go around. He looked over to Charley, hands jammed in mismatched wool socks, hugging himself.

"Cold enough for you, Charley?"

"What'd you say?"

Jimmy shouted, "I asked if it was cold enough for you!"

Charley snorted. The boat crashed into another wave; he yelled back in his thick drawl.

"I swear, if the money wasn't so good..."

They took a pounding for another twenty minutes before they saw the shrimp boat. Jimmy didn't pull back on the throttle until they were within a hundred feet of the trawler that was lit up like a shopping center. Several spotlights in the rigging shone down onto the decks, and two Latinos were balanced on top of the cabin roof, holding poles with scrunched-up aluminum balls fastened to the ends. Several deckhands were ferrying burlap bags that had been thrown up from the holds. Each bag was imprinted with *Café Colombiano.*

Jimmy kept the bobbing boat headed into the wind as they waited their turn. Two other outboards, lashed along the leeward side, were being loaded.

"Can't believe one of them Chicanos ain't fallen overboard yet."

"Good thing, Charley. If it wasn't for those aluminum gadgets they're holding, we'd never pick them up on the Loran. And, they're Colombians, Charley, not Mexicans."

"Whatever."

One of the boats cast off and Jimmy eased up to the mother craft. Two Colombians started tossing burlap bags before he tied up. Charley quickly stacked them, each bag containing a cardboard-bound bale of marijuana weighing about forty pounds. Jimmy secured the craft. When they were loaded, Charley and Jimmy dragged a heavy tarp over the bales as another boat approached.

A tall, heavy-set American, running the show, came over as Jimmy prepared to cast off.

"That'll about do it." He nodded toward the boat idling off the trawler's bow. "They'll be able to handle the rest. Good luck, Jimmy."

As Jimmy untied the lines, he noticed two Colombians bringing out mops and brushes and bottles of Clorox. They began to lower buckets into the sea, preparing to clean up all traces of the contraband. Professionals, he thought, but still, how could they explain the false waterline painted high on the hull if they were ever stopped:

even a thickheaded Coast Guard midshipmen would realize that the false line, trademark of the smuggler, was
the method to disquise a heavily loaded boat.

Jimmy's boat was sluggish with the extra weight
and he knew the return was the tricky part: surfing
back, trying to keep a straight course without the bow
going under the running wave and keeping the wash
from coming over the stern. The tarp would help and,
thankfully, in this weather, it would be a quick trip with
the wind blowing them dead on shore.

Jimmy had worked all his life on the water, quitting
school in the sixth grade to help his father with mullet
fishing and crabbing before striking out on his own. It
was a tough life and his beaten up body was aged way
beyond its forty-six years. Hauling on nets, pulling
crab pots, being slammed around by rough seas as well
as taking the staccato punches of the bay chop, had
taken their toll. His body hurt all the time, and not
just his back; even scraping barnacles and repainting
hulls hurt his shoulders and hands, and his fingers
were swollen and painful every morning. He knew
that he couldn't keep working so hard much longer
and that was a very big reason he was running the
dope, squirreling away the money in short sections
of sealed PVC pipe in the woods outside of town. He
only hoped that the little packages of desiccant he put
in with the greenbacks were doing their job. The last
thing he needed after going through all this was for
his money to rot.

"When we going out agin to check them traps, Jimmy?"

"Not until this wind dies down…couple days, most
likely."

"Hope them octopuses don't git 'em all. Bad year
with them critters."

"If we get paid for running this stuff tonight, we can
afford to lose some lousy old crabs. I ain't about to go

fifteen miles out in seas like this if I don't got to. Those crabs just got to wait."

But it was true, getting their money wasn't a given. Lately, they were being paid one out of three, and there were fewer jobs since the blimp came in. More boats were getting caught; that or something went wrong on the distribution end, or maybe one of the drug kingpins just didn't pay up. And you didn't threaten one of those crazy, coked-up cowboys. It wasn't like it was early on; these guys had no sense of honor and might do you just for the hell of it. And you couldn't rat on them without going to prison yourself. But still, Jimmy thought, one out of three at twenty-five grand a pop for a few hours of work was still a lot of dough. Hell of a lot better than crabbing.

"You think they'll stiff us agin?" Charley asked.

Jimmy shrugged.

"Who knows, but I'm thinking we'll keep us a little security this time."

"Meanin' what?"

"We might just lose a bale. If they don't pay up, I'll find a home for it. No one's going to miss forty pounds out of forty thousand. Hell, most everybody grabs a little here and there."

Charley suddenly pointed.

"Look! There's Miss Tammy's. She left the light on for us."

Jimmy laughed.

"Shee-it, Charley. Everybody knows she put up that light because you was caught stealing beer. But I got to admit that light's a beautiful sight on a night like this!"

They watched the Crescent Club take shape. Charley took off the wool socks and blew on his hands.

"Sure wish she was open; a slug or two of liquor to warm my innards be mighty nice."

A few more lights gradually appeared; not many though, most everyone was asleep, or should be at this hour, Jimmy thought.

"What you going to do with your money, Jimmy?"

"Put my grandyoung'uns through college for one. I don't want them to work as hard as me and my daddy did."

He had two boys and a daughter. Jimmy was proud that he had put them through school, too. The eldest boy was already an officer in the merchant marine, and the other a high school biology teacher in Gainesville. His daughter, the youngest of the three, was a housewife in Tallahassee with four-year old twins. Jimmy loved those twins to death.

"And I'm going to replace this boat with one faster and more comfortable for sports fishing, without a winch always getting in the way, and one that can get out a ways quick for grouper if need be. That's the future here, Charley, sports fishing. You can bet your ass all that ban-the-net stuff's going to pass sooner or later in Tallahassee and that'll be the end of good commercial fishing. Reckon a lot of people going to be hurt by that, but the environmentalists and tourism people is too organized and got lots of money to boot. Anyway, sports fishing's a hell of a lot easier than crabbing. All you gotta do is take a couple rich fisher folk out for a few hours, bait their hooks, open them a few beers, and you make more than a week's pay. Sure beats pulling all them traps, filling them with stinky bait, then find out ten days later, just like you say, some old octopus or turtle has eaten all your profits and you wasted a trip…that and a lot of expensive gas. Money's pretty much guaranteed, and if you don't have a client, then you don't go out wasting gas neither. "

Jimmy slowed as they entered the main channel. When they passed between the dredged spoils and mounded chunks of limestone, the water calmed. Jimmy eased his grip on the wheel and the sudden lull from the heavy sea was cathartic. They idled in. With the Crescent Club off to their left, they soon entered the wide creek that split the town in half.

"What about you, Charley? What are you going to do with your share?"

Charley didn't hesitate.

"Buy me a 1964 red convertible Mustang. Fella in Chiefland's got one that's in bee-yutiful shape. If we get paid for this job, and what I got left from the others, I figure I got enough to pay what he's asking."

"Guess that's better than putting it up your nose like that white trash from the hammocks that's working this business now; but it's going to draw attention if you buy that car. People going to ask, Where's a crab fisherman get that kind of money?"

"Don't care. I'm tired of driving that old lawnmower 'round town. Folks is laughing at me. Even the kids is racing me on their bicycles every chance they git. Besides, I figure I kin drive that convertible in the parade come July with Minnie a'riding shotgun."

"You planning on being parade marshal or something?"

"Might be...why not?"

Sporadic streetlights, attached to skinny pressure-treated poles, bathed the creek in amber tones. Stilt fish houses and simple lodgings lined the shore, and a mix of bird dog and john boats with monofilament net piled in the stern were tied up at the docks. Christmas decorations still hung from the streetlights and Jimmy knew they'd stay up until the Scallop Festival in July. Now that'd be something, he thought: Charley, parade marshal. He angled the boat towards one of the fish houses.

"Get ready now, here we go."

Jimmy idled up to the dock as Charley jumped out and lashed the boat to pilings. Two men got out of a

white truck with *Spivey's Seafood* painted on the tall rear
section. They opened the back doors as Jimmy and
Charley pulled the tarp off the bales. They worked silently and quickly. The high water was about level with
the dock so they could fling the burlap sacks straight
across to the two men; it didn't take more than fifteen
minutes to load the van. Jimmy left the tarp tangled in
a corner of the stern, covering a bale. One of the men
noticed.

"Don't you think you better give us all them square
grouper, Jimmy?"

Jimmy stared levelly at the man. Charley looked
nervous.

"You got all you need. I'd get outta here quick if I
was you, Joe. Never know who's going to show up or
when."

The man shrugged his shoulders.

"Suit yourself."

As the two men drove off, Charley asked, "You sure
that was a good idea, Jimmy?"

"Joe's a regular guy. He'll pass it on maybe, but he
also knows we're the best they got. I've saved a load
three or four times when others got pinched. And it's
only one bale, and he knows we're just covering our
bets. I'll bet he's been stiffed, too. It'll be okay."

Jimmy untied the lines.

"Gotta take care of this critter."

"Want me to come?"

"Naw, less you know, the better. See you at the Club
tonight for poker. What time's it anyway?"

Charley looked at his watch.

"Four-thirtyish. Going to lighten up."

"Always does. Go get some sleep, Charley, and dream
about that fancy red car."

Jimmy reversed away from the dock and headed up
the river to the swamp. The combination of high tide

and strong onshore wind had the water extra high so he could go way up in. He knew just where he was going to hide the bale. By the time he arrived at his dock, the sun was coming up. He secured the boat and slowly walked across the street to his house, one of the few in town on stilts. He knew he should clean the boat, but he was too dang tired; later, he thought. The bedroom light came on when he shut the front door. Good, Crystal's awake. Smiling, he kicked off his white rubber boots and hung up his slicker. He sure hoped she was in the mood; there were just some things you were never too tired for.

CHAPTER THREE

Tiny was anything but. Six feet four, approaching three hundred pounds, mountainous shoulders with little flab around the waist, the man was an ox. Going to be close, he thought. The tide had turned over an hour ago and he was still a half hour out. He had gone farther south than usual on Jimmy's advice to stay clear of Crescent Beach. The last thing he needed, Tiny thought, was to get caught up in Jimmy's shenanigans and have his boat confiscated. He looked at his watch; better hurry up or I'll be plowing furrows in port. He hated to burn up even more diesel, but he pushed the throttle forward.

He was heading in after fishing three windy, frigid nights without much to show for it. Maybe four hundred bucks worth of shrimp, he estimated, not enough to break even, what with the price of fuel and all. Still, the water would warm soon and the spring shrimp crop would be there for the picking, that is, unless there was an early gumbo bloom to clog the nets. Tiny shook his head. Just like farming, he thought, all sorts of things could go wrong. But, there were the fringe benefits, too, like no boss, no time clock, sitting here drinking coffee and looking out over the Gulf. He chuckled: got me my own waterfront property with the best Gulf view anywhere. Could be a lot worse; could be a guard at one of the prisons, cooped up in a tower twiddling my thumbs, or stacking boards and breathing sawdust all day at the mill in Perry like some of the guys. No thanks. He put the boat on automatic pilot and walked aft, bringing his coffee with him. The wind was still kicking up and Tiny had kept the outriggers out for stability. He took a good deep breath, exhaling while looking to starboard. A half-mile in was a long thin line of beach rimmed with the green of cabbage palms, dwarfed live oak, and southern red cedar. Not a building anywhere. To the north he could see the Crescent Beach water tower and a few of the town's houses on stilts.   The blimp was nowhere in sight.

When Crescent Beach was about a half-mile away, Tiny put his coffee down and engaged the winch to haul in the outriggers. A few herring and laughing gulls dove for the dried bits and pieces that fell from the nets. He passed Snowy Key and entered the main channel. As the boat approached the creek, Tiny looked behind him. Sure enough, the prop was churning mud in good order, even the slight wake showed brown.   Tiny put his long hair in a ponytail as he headed towards a good-sized fish house with a concrete icehouse next to it. His hands were like catcher mitts. He eased up to the dock where a man in overalls was waiting.

"Cuttin' it close, ain't you, Tiny?" the man asked, catching Tiny's lines. The man secured the lines around two stout pilings.

"Went further south than usual, Big John."

Big John was at least a half-foot shorter than Tiny; the moniker a result of the prodigious gut that strained against his overalls.

"How'd you do?"

"Piddling, mostly bait. Got a few white fish to go with the shrimp."

Big John nodded. "Water's too cold." Tiny pulled onion bags of shrimp from the slush in the hold and started handing them to Big John. Most of the bags were tied off in yellow ribbons, some with red. Big John eyed the bags. "Mostly bait, all right, and some mediums. Don't hardly see no jumbos."

In the fish house before weighing the bags, Big John took sample pounds and counted the shrimp per pound. When he paid Tiny, he was almost apologetic.

"Mostly run sixty to seventy a pound. Don't get rich none with counts like that. Hope the water warms up soon, Tiny."

"Me, too," Tiny said, folding up the bills and putting them in his shirt pocket. He climbed aboard; he had left the Cummins idling. "Leastways, got enough to feed this thirsty gal and stake me tonight."

Big John smiled.

"That's right, Thursday's poker night. How you been doin'?"

"About like the shrimping. See you in a few."

Big John cast off the lines, and Tiny idled up the creek to his dock. Without a wasted move, he pulled smoothly up along side and quickly tied his lines. It didn't take him long to wash down the deck with the freshwater hose and load up his rusty Ford pickup with a cooler of leftover food and a few fish that had come in with the shrimp. Yawning occasionally, he drove slowly up Main Street, passing City Hall, towards his little house near the cattle gap. He noticed that the only vehicle parked in front of City Hall was Beau's golf cart. He slowly shook his head. That there councilman ought to get paid the other three's wages, Tiny thought; he's the only one does any work. Maybe I should tell him that tonight at poker. Tiny continued on, very much looking forward to crawling in bed.

Painted light blue, City Hall was a non-descript, single-story, concrete-block building. The paint had faded and was peeling in several places, and the metal roof was rust-splotched. Entering the building, there were public restrooms opposite each other in the hallway that led to the large town meeting room full of folding chairs and with an American flag on the rear wall. Under the flag were the picture windows of two offices looking out into the meeting room. Beau, tall and lanky, sat in one of the offices with legs outstretched and feet resting on a plastic chair. A pile of papers was on a large table next to him, and a thick manual lay open on his lap. His ten-year-old black lab, Skillet, was asleep by the door.

Beau was short for Beauregard, so named for the general of the Confederacy who had defended Charleston at the beginning of the Civil War. He had lived in Charleston most of his life before retiring from teaching in his mid sixties when he, along with his lovely wife Virginia, had dropped out of Charleston society and moved to Crescent Beach. When asked why he left and, especially, why he had chosen Crescent Beach, he would answer that he had tired of all Charleston's social engagements, formality, and gossip. He also said that he still enjoyed two things: fishing and drinking, and both were a hell of a lot cheaper in Crescent Beach than about anywhere else. Surprisingly, Beau and Virginia had fit right in and, last year, Beau had been elected councilman, unheard of for an outsider. People respected how he cut to the chase in town meetings, never getting caught up in the local politics and family feuds. His calm, no-nonsense approach had gained everyone's respect.

Beau was intently looking at a water plant manual and, although he was only as far as the table of contents, already his mind was rebelling. Like a frigging foreign language, he thought: what good is a doctorate in American history when it comes to something like this!

-ERC
-Maximum Day Flow
-Average Day Flow
-Peak Hour Flow
-Peaking Factors
-Fire Flow Requirements
-Pipe Size
-Velocity
-Minimum Residual Pressure

And the acronyms! **ERC—ADF—ANSI—ASTM— AWWA—DIPRA.** He looked up **ERC.** **Equivalent Residential Connection.** What gooblety-gop! He tossed the manual and his reading glasses on to the table, and ran his fingers through his wavy silver hair. Massaging the bridge of his nose, he thought, For a nickel, I'd resign and let someone else do this. But, no one else would and the water plant is desperately needed. Just taking a bath is scary with the gray to light brown water, plus all the tests show coliform. And then there's the fact that the water comes all the way from the tower in asbestos-reinforced pipes. Asbestos! Gawd almighty! Amazing that babies aren't born with three legs or seven toes! And it sure seems there's a high incidence of cancer around here—throat, kidney, esophagus, you name it. It'd be interesting to have a study done and see just how high our percentage is compared to towns with a good water system.

At least most people realize there's a problem, but still, the town vote to pursue the new plant had been ridiculously close. The naysayers said it was too expensive and pointed to old man Butterworth who's over a hundred, saying he's drunk the water his whole life, or to our good mayor who's over ninety. Virginia and I buy our drinking water, as do some of the others, but most people don't. They say if it was good enough for their daddies to drink, it's good enough for them. One reason, of course, is many can't afford it day in and day out. You'd hope that they boil their water, but who knows; certainly no law saying you have to. And how many kids come in from playing every day to take a drink from the spigot or mix up a pitcher of kool-aid?

Beau could use some help on the project, but he knew that wasn't an option. He looked over at the table. Underneath the manual was the monster's other head: all the application forms for state and federal grants, the deadline for which was looming. He sighed and picked up the manual and went back to work. He kept at it for a couple of hours, making notes and writing down questions until his stomach started growling. He looked at his watch: 11:30, time to mosey on home for a sandwich and to complain to Virginia on how hard he'd been working. Guess that comes with a wife's territory—listening to a husband bitch about his day. He looked lovingly over at Skillet who was snoring by the door. How'd he get to be so old that he snores now? Seems like only yesterday that he was a puppy and I took him to camp for the first time. I was probably rushing the gun, but I just couldn't wait to start training him. Actually, it wasn't so much training as it was channeling those wonderful instincts. We hadn't even named him yet and he was so small that I had to cobble up a pint-sized dummy that he could hold in his mouth. But what a natural: he was dropping the dummy at my feet the very first session! Beau smiled. And it was that same morning when Virginia had come up with his name: she was forking bacon onto some paper towels when she said he was as black as the skillet in her hand.

"C'mon, Skillet. Enough snoozing for today. Let's go find Sugah and see what's for lunch."

Skillet bolted to his feet and, tail wagging fiercely, waited for Beau to organize his papers and open the door. He was in the passenger seat of the golf cart in the blink of an eye, looking straight ahead. "Co-pilot all set?" Beau asked.

Skillet looked briefly over, then back straight ahead, his tail wedged against the seat so there was no tail wag. I swear that dog can smile, Beau thought as he pressed down on the accelerator. They scooted down Main Street with Skillet checking the smells and occasionally looking side to side. Beau turned left, crossing the bridge over the creek, and entered the more upscale part of town where houses ringed the crescent shaped beach. Most of the houses here were on stilts with his being the highest. Virginia was waiting for them at the top of the deck stairs. She was a slim woman with medium length gray hair that was up in a bun. She was dressed in jeans and a plaid shirt.

"My boys wouldn't be hungry by any chance?" she said, smiling down at them.

After peeing on a bush, Skillet bounded up the steps to the deck. Beau joined them and, with his arm around Virginia, the trio entered the house.

CHAPTER FOUR

Snowy Key had once been home to hundreds of egrets, giving it a white, textured appearance. Consequently, it had been called Cotton Island, but was renamed by a Yankee soldier who related to snow more than cotton. It was purchased for less than a hundred dollars in the forties by a wealthy businessman who had made a fortune with Henry Flagler bringing passenger trains down to Florida. The reason it had come cheap was because it stunk to high heaven from all the egret excrement and no one wanted anything to do with it. The birds, of course, left when the trees were cut.

The businessman built a simple fish camp that, over the years, grew into a beautiful four-bedroom cypress lodge, four feet off the ground with a deck and railing all the way around it. There was a long dock and boathouse on the inland side of the island and, inside the lodge, it was cool and dark with pecky cypress paneling, old stuffed couches, and fish mounts on most every wall. Sitting on one of those couches, watching TV and drinking beer, was Craig, the deceased businessman's grandson.

Craig was into his second six-pack when he tired of the old westerns and turned off the TV. He walked over to the window and glanced out; sun was pretty low. He didn't feel like cooking anything, so he decided to grab an early dinner at the Crescent Club before the guys arrived for poker. First, though, he'd take a little ride out to the marsh in the airboat. He went over to the refrigerator. As he reached for another beer, he could feel his gut pressing into his belt. Getting sloppy, he thought; I should try to get back into shape. He donned a wool cap and down parka, and, with beer in hand, he headed down to the dock.

It was an older airboat with a two rather than three-bladed prop that accounted for most of the deafening decibels the watercraft produced. It was powered by a prodigious V-8 automobile engine with a rusted-out muffler, and was constructed out of heavy-duty aluminum. The boat itself couldn't be simpler: rectangular with a squared-off bow and flat-bottomed with a bench for passengers below his platform seat. After putting on earphones and letting the motor warm up, Craig grabbed the stick and turned towards the marsh. The tide was going out, but that made no difference: he could go anywhere. He goosed the engine. God, he loved the power: better than riding a Harley by far! He was king of the water. He was doing close to forty when he decided to slow down because of the chop; wind's picking up again, he thought. The marsh was beautiful: amber waves of grain with sporadic white dots of egrets and herons feeding in the late afternoon sun. There was a flock of white pelicans huddled together in the main channel that ran through the marsh. He angled the airboat away from the channel into the marsh, the reeds and grass doubling over as he cut through. There wasn't even a foot of water, but that made no difference.

He set no course, had no agenda other than dinner and poker; this was a joy ride. His craft was rending temporary channels out of the marsh grass, and he didn't notice that all the birds had suddenly taken to the air. He was too busy thinking about the upcoming poker session. He probably lost more than he won, but he didn't care; the money was the least of it. It was a good time and broke up his winter routine of watching westerns or basketball on TV. Maybe the best part was giving shit to that fag realtor. Yeah, he really enjoyed that. An uncomfortable thought began to nibble at his mind, but he shook it off with a flip of his head and circled the boat around, back towards town.

As Craig approached the crescent-shaped beach, Norm was stepping out of the shower and onto the scale. One-seventy-five dripping wet, five pounds over. Should start jogging again, he thought as he toweled off, but everybody'd think he was nuts—only the sports fishermen's bored wives in their spandex did that. And they had no idea of the comments that followed them down Main Street. Nope, no jogging—not here anyway. Norm's thoughts were interrupted by the roar of the airboat. He looked out the window. Damn butthole! Although it didn't do much good, he put his hands over his ears as he walked into the bedroom to get dressed. Suddenly there was silence, and Norm's body relaxed. Pulling on a heavy sweater, he stepped out to the deck. Tide dropping fast; definitely no boats going out tonight. The sky was clear, and the orange sun real low. Five minutes or so until sunset—time enough to make a drink. He went back in and poured himself a generous Jack Daniels on the rocks. He took a sip as he returned to the deck. Not a cloud anywhere, maybe he'd see the green dot tonight. The sun was perfectly centered on the horizon, not like in the summer when it was to the north, mostly blocked by the Crescent Club. He sipped his whisky, watching the sun exit like a squished egg yolk. No green dot, just gone. Pretty boring.

Funny how life works, ending up in this backwater. Privileged upper middle class childhood, private schools, the med school grind, top-notch surgeon in a big fancy hospital, trophy wife and country club, two beautiful children, and now living alone in a cypress stilt house in a fishing village. He finished his drink. Been seven years since that life in Sarasota, four since moving here; seems like a lot more, a lifetime ago. No complaints, though, not really…well, maybe one: the damn airboats.

As if on cue, Norm heard another muffler-less engine start up, but it wasn't an airboat. He smiled and looked at his watch. The lawnmower sputtered and warmed up a bit before it headed down Main Street. Total time was usually just under five minutes, that's how long it took Charley to drive to the Club. Four-and-a-half minutes later, it was quiet again. Record time; Charley must have gone extra fast to get out of the cold.

Norm rinsed his glass before filling his pockets with quarters that he took from a mason jar. He debated putting on a jacket. The sweater was enough, he figured, and went down the deck stairs. He glanced over at the cargo elevator, wondering why he had bothered to have it installed: the only time he had used it was when he was moving in, and it was all rusty from the salt now with the gears probably frozen.

He approached the humpback bridge over the creek that split the town. On his side, most of the houses were built up off the ground along the crescent-shaped, white sand beach. They were mostly second homes owned by out-of-towners—doctors and lawyers from Gainesville and Tallahassee, successful businessmen from all over north Florida and southern Georgia. Their backgrounds varied, but they had two common denominators: money and a passion for fishing. On the other side of town, very few houses were on stilts. About half were stick-built, the others were trailers and doublewides. Most everything sat on the ground or jutted out over the water: the real part of town, Norm thought, where the fishermen, the people who worked in the fish houses, and the shopkeepers lived, a real community with a lot of activity. When he stepped onto Main Street, a little girl in a long skirt went skipping by.

"Better hurry on home, Becky, or you'll be late for dinner."

"Yes, sir, Dr. Norm. I'm on my way."

The town was tiny and so isolated that it was like living on an island. It was also full of children, two school bus loads worth, who were trucked out on limestone roads each day to the nearest school over twenty miles away. And it was as if each child had three or four moms continually watching out for them: pretty tough, Norm thought, for a kid here to get away with anything. He approached Big John's combination store and fish house. On the other side of the store, just in front of the dock, a group of men were sitting around a campfire blazing in the center of a big square made out of 2x8's and filled with sand. Chunks of limestone inside the square ringed the fire and supported a steel sheet covered with a steaming burlap bag. Big John, wearing overalls like always, was ladling water over the bag. Steam rose in the cold air. A couple of men were passing a tall bottle, and bottles of Tabasco were on top of the fish cleaning station. Big John peeled back a corner of the burlap when he saw Norm.

"How about a oyster, Doc. Got a bunch of 'em all ready."

Big John knew that Norm loved oysters.

"Absolutely, John. Thank you."

Big John placed four on a wood shingle. Nodding good evening to the others, Norm put Tabasco on the oysters. He declined the tall bottle being passed around, saying, "Boys, if I drink that stuff, I won't be able to sew your stitches straight when you get to settling arguments later."

The steamed oysters were trophies, creamy and smooth. Norm didn't turn down another four brought over by Big John. They went down just as fast, but when John reached for some more, Norm declined.

"Thanks, John, but have to go. Tonight's poker night."

"I know; from what I seen, reckon you'll be the last one there. But how about I keep a couple of dozen on ice for you to pick up tomorrow. They're real fresh, jest got 'em this afternoon."

Norm knew that Big John was still trying to pay him back for sewing up his son. The boy had run hard aground on an oyster bar and was thrown out of the boat, slicing his arm up pretty badly. It had mended just fine, but because Norm had never charged Big John, he was always trying to pay him in food. Many around here did that. Oysters, fish, crab, smoked mullet dip, eggs, wild pig, casseroles and pies from the ladies. No wonder he'd gained five pounds.

"If you have enough to spare, then sure; I'll come by in the morning."

"I'll have the coffee on, Doc."

Norm continued on to the Crescent Club, the second largest building in town. The only one larger was the assembly line fish house. The Club was also one of the very few on stilts this side of the creek and qualified as one of the three marinas because it had a hydraulic boatlift for the sports fishermen. Charley's rusty, red Toro lawnmower was parked out front next to Beau's golf cart and amongst a score of pickups. About half the pickups had big white coolers in the back; the others had cages for hunting dogs. Norm waved to the bundled-up men at the pool table on the cement slab below the bar; hard core, he thought. He climbed the stairs to the large deck where he maneuvered his way around several picnic tables to the entry door. An old Miller High Life sign, the one with the different-colored lights bouncing across it, was in a window. He laughed when he saw a new poster tacked onto the door. Crescent Beach humor, he thought. The poster had a simple drawing of a scruffy, eye-patched mutt, and read:

LOST DOG

**THREE-LEGGED, BLIND IN LEFT EYE,
MISSING RIGHT EAR,
TAIL BROKEN, RECENTLY CASTRATED...
ANSWERS TO THE NAME OF "LUCKY"**

The bar was crowded for a weekday, most likely due to the cold, windy weather. No one was paying much attention to a basketball game on the TV with the sound off. Must not be the Gators or Seminoles. He didn't see Tammy; probably out in the kitchen. Jimmy and Charley, Beau, Tiny, and Craig were already at the table, a pretty good pile of quarters in the center. Skillet, Beau's black lab, was asleep under the table. Jimmy laid his cards down and pulled out a chair for Norm.

"Running a little late, ain't you?" Jimmy said

"Couldn't pass up a few oysters at Big John's. Damn, they were tasty!"

"Almost stopped there, too, Doc, but too frigging cold," Charley said, without looking up from his cards.

"Then why didn't you put the top up on that convertible of yours, Charley?" Tiny asked.

"Very funny, Tiny, very funny. You're a real stitch, you know that? My lawnmower ain't no different from Beau here's golf cart, except his got a top."

"And is a heck of a lot more quiet and weren't made to cut grass, although judging from your place, maybe that old heap can't cut grass neither. I'm bumping two quarters." Tiny threw them on to the pile.

Jimmy said, "I'm out."

"Me, too," added Beau and Craig.

"I'm still in," Charley said as he threw in two quarters. "And," plink, plink, "I'm raising y'all two more."

Tiny looked at his cards, totally engulfed in those big hands.

"Your two, and two more." Plink, plink, plink, plink. Charley eyed Tiny, his cards, and Tiny again.

"You're bluffing, Tiny." Plink, plink. "And," plink, plink, "two more for you to stay in."

Tiny threw his cards down.

"Aw, you can have it, Charley."

"Hot diggety dawg! I knew you was bluffing!"

Charley quickly buried his cards into the deck before leaning over to rake in the quarters. A dark haired, handsome man in his mid-thirties entered the bar and came over.

"Realtor Ralph," Jimmy said. "Thought you were going to Gainesville."

"Fell through."

"What, your date stand you up? He get a better offer?" Craig asked, winking at the others. He was ignored.

Jimmy said, "Sit down, Ralph. Your deal, Beau."

Tammy came out of the kitchen carrying a tray full of food.

"Hi, boys, be right over for your drink order."

Norm's eyes closely followed her tidy figure around the room.

"You going to pick up your cards, Doctor, or watch that little bubble-butt all night?" Craig asked.

Norm looked levelly at Craig, a sturdy man with light hair and unusual eyes, like they were translucent. What an asshole, Norm thought, picking up his cards. Tammy came over.

"Jack Daniels on ice, Norm, and a coke for you, Ralph?" They nodded.

"Sissy drink for the sissy," Craig muttered into his cards.

Tammy frowned. Jimmy turned to Craig.

"That's twice. One more like that and you're cashing out!"

"Looks like you're short-handed, Tammy. Where's Minnie?" Norm asked.

"Working at the prison."

"Got the night shift," Charley said, "so she can educate herself during the day by taking crimeology courses they be offering. But she's a'fixing to be here this weekend."

"Criminology, Charley." Norm offered.

"Whatever."

Tiny spoke up.

"Be glad when your gal's done with them courses. I miss her help on the boat."

"Better not let her hear you be calling her my girl, Tiny, or there'll be hell ta pay."

"But she is, ain't she?"

"Sometimes. When she wants ta be."

Tammy brought the drinks. The men continued to play cards. The night wore on with customers coming and going, mostly talking fishing and weather. Debate was whether January or February was the worst boating and fishing month of the year. The phone rang. Most likely a fisherman's wife, Norm thought. Tammy came over.

"It's for you, Jimmy."

Jimmy walked over to the payphone on the wall. He talked for about five minutes before calling Tammy back to the phone. It was unusual for him to get a call: his wife Crystal never called him during poker night. They were all looking at him when he returned to the table.

"Got a charter—a week's worth at least. Fella called the house and Crystal told him I was here. Coming down from north Georgia beginning of the week."

"Not the best time for sports fishing, Jimmy," Tiny said.

"Told him that, but he said he's recently retired as a road contractor and he don't care if he catches a parcel of fish or not; just wants to do some relaxing." Jimmy looked at Charley. "We better go out to check them traps soon."

"Can't tomorrow; me and the Doc got a fireman function in the p.m. And still going to be blowing tomorrow anyways."

"Day after, then, Charley." Tammy was still talking on the phone. "Fella's going to rent a cabin from Tammy," Jimmy added, looking over.

Beau asked, "You boys coming to the town meeting tomorrow evening?"

"What's on the agenda?" Norm asked.

"Didn't y'all read the billboard front of City Hall?"

"No, Charley. Haven't been up there lately. What's it say?"

"Fleas," Ralph said, smiling.

"Fleas? You're kidding!"

"Nope. You know that run-down house next to the post office with the dogs everywhere?"

Norm nodded.

"Seems they all have fleas, and I mean they're FLEA INFESTED! Last month during that warm spell, the Postmistress wedged the door open and being behind the counter, she couldn't see the dogs wander in and out. Now the post office is flea ridden; the Postmistress and her baby she brings in have bites all over them, and fleas have hitched rides on the patrons, too. According to some of the ladies, the town's under siege. Say all the kids have flea bites. The meeting's to figure out what to do about it."

"That's got to be a first: dealing with fleas at a town meeting," Norm said, shaking his head and dealing the cards.

"The only other item up for discussion is a complaint from that lawyer's wife, two houses up from you, Norm," Beau added. "She's bored to death because she doesn't give a hoot about fishing and she's been jogging around town. Seems she's horrified at all the stuff in the yards, saying that it's a disgrace to humanity and that the town needs some sort of lawn ordinance."

Charley rolled his eyes. Beau looked at Jimmy, Ralph, and Craig.

"I think it'd be a good idea if the hall were full tomorrow. Nip it in the bud, if you get my meaning."

"Yeah," Craig added. "You round up the men, Jimmy, and Ralphie here will bring the ladies."

Ralph didn't say anything. Jimmy slammed down his cards.

"That's three, Craig! Think it's about time you got back to that island of yours."

Craig stood, laughing and gathering up his quarters.

"Was checking out anyway...Night gents, and," nodding toward Ralph, "ladies."

Craig paid his bill at the bar and left.

"He's a butthead," Norm said. "Don't pay any attention to him, Ralph."

"Don't worry, I don't. Believe me, I've heard worse."

Ralph had come to Crescent Beach a year or so after he graduated from the University of Florida and had opened up the only real estate office. Been here ever since. Brave, Norm thought, coming to a town like this considering his sexual persuasion. But he had stuck it out. He was very civic minded, tended the town's flower gardens, and, out of his own pocket, he put out poinsettias everywhere during the Christmas holidays. He helped with communal and church suppers, cut his real estate commissions for needy families, and was the first to help out with clean-up after a tidal surge. Ralph had a soft heart, was a model citizen, and any love affairs he had were discreet.

"Usually, he's not such a awful fella," Charley said. "But something triggers him when you're around, Ralph."

"Homophobic," Norm said.

"Homo who?"

"Means he hates, or possibly fears, homosexuals, Charley," Ralph explained.

"Craig a'scared of you? Why?"

"No idea. Ask him sometime."

"Right, and git me a punch in the kisser. No thanks."

The engine of Craig's airboat turned over, then roared, making conversation impossible.   When he could make himself heard, Norm said, "Think I'll call it a night. Looks like you're the big winner again, Charley. What are you going to do with all the money you rake in every Thursday?"

"Saving up for my convertible Mustang."

"Then, congratulations. Tonight's take might buy you a hub cap."

Norm went over to pay his bar tab and say goodnight to Tammy. Looking up from rinsing glasses, she gave him a big smile. Damned if that woman didn't turn him on. As he started out the door, Charley yelled over, "Don't forget about our event tomorrow afternoon, Doc."

"I'll be over at Big John's for coffee in the morning, Charley. Let's talk about it then."

Outside, Norm was engulfed in the roar of Craig's 450 horsepower engine. He looked at his watch. Here it was after eleven, a school night, and everybody in town had no choice but listen to that asshole. He shook his head and covered his ears as he went down the steps and headed for home.

CHAPTER FIVE

Norm backed his Subaru from underneath the house and drove to Big John's. Big John met him with a mug of steaming coffee.

"Bring your cooler?"

"In the back."

Big John fetched the cooler and Norm followed him into the insulated concrete block icehouse. A mountain of ice was on the floor. Several different colored plastic bushels were just inside, covered with burlap; Big John pulled the burlap away and started heaping oysters into the cooler.

"John, that's too many!"

Big John filled the cooler, topping it off with about three inches of ice.

"I know how much you like 'em. And you kin freeze 'em for stew later if you don't finish 'em all."

He put the cooler back in the car.

"Here, let me top off that mug and let's sit a spell out on the dock. Nice sunny morning and that wind's finally easing a bit."

The dock faced due east, the sun glorious; a few sand fleas bothered, but not bad. They sat in white plastic chairs that matched Big John's rubber boots. Norm took a sip of coffee, then tipped his head back, eyes closed, the sun turning his eyelids orange on the inside. He could hear an outboard motor faintly in the distance. Pure heaven.

"How's Johnny's arm, John?"

"Jest fine, Doc, thanks to you. Been out fishing off the bridge with his cane pole most every evening, that and catching crabs with that pole net. Ain't had him no problems."

"Glad to hear it," Norm said, with eyes still closed.

"Nice to relax a bit like this, ain't it, Doc?

"You got that right."

"With this wind dying down, though, things going to pick up fast. Everybody's fixing to git back out and I'll soon be swamped with fish and crabs."

"Feast or famine, John."

They heard Charley's lawnmower start up. Norm opened his eyes.

"Believe he's coming over here, John."

"There goes our peace and quiet, and I don't mean that lawnmower, neithers." Big John stood up. "Think I'll go hang net for awhile. Might as well be doing something useful while Charley's jawing. Help yourself to coffee, plenty of it."

Norm watched Big John uncoil a large hank of monofilament and begin tying the gill net stretched out between two posts of the dock. Big John was an entrepreneur for sure: storekeeper, fish house operator, netmaker, part-time fisherman. But wherever he was, including church, Norm had never seen him in anything but those faded blue jean overalls. He wondered if that was his only pair. And a sure sign of cool weather, like this morning, was when Big John wore a tee shirt; he was usually bare-chested. Norm spied a good-sized pile of fresh oyster shells dumped along the bank where it had been eroding.

"Looks like you all ate your share of oysters last night."

"Yep. Quite a mess. Had to hose off the dock this morning; bits of shell, Tabasco and oyster stuck everywheres."

Charley arrived.

"Be right with you, Doc. Got to git me a sody pop afore I die of thirst."

Charley walked over to the coke machine, the type you pushed a button and a bottle rumbled down the chute. He chose an Orange Crush; got a root beer. He came out on the dock.

"Dagnabit, Big John! When you going to put the sodies in where they belong! That there's like a gumball machine: you puts your money in and never knows what color's coming out!"

"Was a sale on root beer last week," John said, without looking up. Charley, shaking his head, took Big John's chair. He put his foot on a piling and tilted back, sipping the root beer. The two chair legs flexed.

"Now don't you go busting my chair, Charley. It ain't made of steel, don't you know."

"It's a wonder anyone kin live with you, Big John! Maria must be crazy, or a saint or something, what with your nagging all the time!" But Charley eased forward until all four legs were down.

"And jest what anniversary you and the missus celebratin' this year, Charley?"

"Hitching up ain't for everybody, John. As for me, I figger that the screwing you git, ain't worth the screwing you git."

"You've got that right, Charley."

Big John and Charley looked at Norm; he never talked about his marriage. But that was all he said. Big John went back to working his net, and Charley to drinking his root beer.

"Musta had me too many beers last night if'n this ol' root beer tastes good."

Charley took a last swig and pitched the bottle into the canal. Norm frowned.

"Damn, Charley! Now why'd you do that?"

"Why not? Ain't no deposit on it…and didn't you know glass is made of sand? Just returning it to its elements."

Big John looked up from his net.

"What sand you talking 'bout, Charley? That be mud in that there canal."

"Whatever."

"It's still littering, Charley," Norm said.

Charley looked at the canal.

"How's that?   I don't see no bottle nor nothing. How's that littering?"

"So, if there were a deposit on that bottle, you wouldn't have thrown it into the canal."

"Nope. Never did when there was deposits."

"He don't know no better, Doc. Charley here's jest a dumb redneck."

"I ain't no redneck, John; I'm a cracker and proud of it!"

"What's the difference?" Norm asked.

Charley didn't hesitate.

"Crackers ride horses, rednecks rides their cousins. And John here's so ignorant, bet he don't know where we got the name 'cracker,' do you?" Charley said, looking over.

Big John shrugged.

"Probably some old cowboy was eating crackers in bed and his wife didn't like it none."

"See what I mean, Doc? Big John here don't know nothing."

"How *did* they get the name, Charley?" Norm asked. Big John looked up from his net.

"Back in the early days, was more cows than people in Florida. And there was lots of cowboys who'd drive the cattle with bullwhips through swamps and such to git to the grass prairies. Them cracking whips sounded like rifles and you could hear them coming a long ways afore you ever seen them. Anyways, we was named for them cracking whips."

" 'We!' " Big John snorted. "Charley, you ain't been on a horse since your gran'daddy died, and that must have been over twenty years ago."

"Like a bicycle, John. You don't forget none. And still be my heritage."

"Charley's right. Florida was a huge cattle state, used to be number two, right behind Texas. Maybe still is, although I doubt it," Norm said. "I remember when there were a lot of ranches just inland from Sarasota, but that was before it was overrun with snowbirds. Most of the ranches are malls and housing developments now, some even waste management areas. The ranches and groves are taking it hard."

Charley stood up and stretched. "Now, Doc, about this afternoon. All the participants is getting together at three-thirty at the fire station. Then they be going out and torch that ol' cypress shed at the highway park because the county wants to build a new one outta concrete. We figure if it was a house catching fire, we'd get a call in something like fifteen minutes; that's how long we wait before coming out in the truck. We're to see how fast we can git there and put it out. Figure we should leave in the tanker at four sharp."

"You actually think we can put it out before it burns to the ground?"

"Nope, but we can squirt them big hoses for awhile, then cook us some weenies and drink us a couple beers afore the town meeting this evening."

"That's why Charley joined up, Doc. For them free suds and weenie roasts."

"John, you don't know nothing about nothing. I'm doing my civic duty, pure and simple, not like some around here who spend their time jest a'squeezing pennies."

"I'll be there five minutes before the hour, Charley."

"That's a ten-four." He stood up. "Got to git over to Jimmy's to help git the boat ready for tomorrow. Weather's going to be real good."

Moments later the whole town knew Charley was on his way somewhere. Big John went back to work on the net, and Norm closed his eyes again.

Sarasota, a lifetime ago. Beverly. Beautiful Bev. Short, athletic, blond like Tammy. But stylish, oozed blueblood class and southern charm. They were the beautiful couple; met when he was at Duke Medical, she an undergrad, number three on the women's tennis team. That's where he first saw her, on the courts. He had been captain of the Dartmouth College team in New Hampshire and continued to play socially throughout med school. The first time they teamed up in mixed doubles, the romance was on. It lasted twenty-six years.

They moved to Sarasota where he worked his way up the ladder to become a top surgeon at Sarasota Memorial. She raised the two boys while he worked crazy long hours. The money piled up, even with sending the boys to the best of private schools and owning a beautiful house on the bay with a Lyman moored at the dock and a pair of Mercedes, hers a yellow convertible, in the three-bay garage. They joined the Field Club where they were mixed doubles champs four years running. But over the years, he began to play less and less because of all the stress and the hectic pace of the hospital. He didn't want to run all over the courts in his precious free time. Fishing became his middle-age passion: grouper, kings, Spanish mackerel in the Gulf, snook in the bay. Every spring he went with some buddies down to Boca Grande for the tarpon run. He loved everything about being out on the water.

Bev hated fishing, found it boring. She stayed with the tennis and still played in the tournaments, usually winning with whatever partner she had. Everyone wanted to be her partner. And that turned out to be the problem. The tennis pro wanted to be her partner, too, but not in tennis. The kids were off to college, Norm was always at work or out in the boat, she was lonely and wanted something exciting in her life. She slept with the pro often, but Norm didn't have a clue. He shrugged off the hints from a few close friends; no way, Bev wouldn't do that. But when she had asked for the divorce, he finally got it. He asked her how long it had been going on, but she denied the whole thing. Said she wasn't screwing around. Said she was going through a mid-life crisis and now that the kids were gone, she wanted to strike out on her own.

Bev was careful. Throughout the negotiations, she never went to see the tennis pro; he knew because he hired an investigator to follow her. She continued to deny any involvement and he wanted to believe her. She had been a wonderful mother and had given him all those years. He still loved her and wanted her happy, so he agreed to a generous settlement. Maybe they'd get back together some day when she figured it all out. The day after everything was legal, she moved in with the tennis pro. That was the day he stopped loving her.

"Doctor Norm! Doctor Norm!"

Norm opened his eyes. One of the fish house workers had a hand on his arm. Must have dozed off.

"Maggie slipped carrying a crate of fish heads. Her ankle looks real bad."

Norm stood up. Big John was nowhere in sight.

"Hop in my car."

They speeded over to the big fish house where mostly red mullet roe was split out for the Japanese market. Now, however, was the slow season when the fishermen primarily brought in the ten-inch buck mullet from the creeks, that and the trash fish the workers boxed up for the crabbers' bait.   Things would change quickly, though, when the water warmed. They entered the building where a small circle of workers were looking down at Maggie Morgan, laying there with a couple of towels bundled up under her head. Norm knelt and looked at her ankle. Her foot was pointing south, instead of north like it should. He realized immediately that there was nothing he could do for her in the little clinic he had built underneath his house. She needed pictures taken and an operating room. He looked up into the faces surrounding them.

"Someone go call an ambulance."

He turned back to Maggie.

"Looks like you did a number on it. Don't dare move you. How's the pain?"

"Don't feel a thing, Doctor."

Shock, Norm knew. He noticed few beads of sweat on her forehead.

"You comfortable enough?"

"Yes, but sure would like a coke or something."

"Root beer okay?"

Maggie smiled.

"That'd be just fine."

Norm handed a dollar to one of the workers and told him to go to Big John's. The others went back to work while he waited with Maggie for the ambulance, the nearest one eighteen miles away. Hopefully it was available. As it turned out, they waited a long while.

CHAPTER SIX

Five minutes before four, Charley was nowhere to be seen. The fire station door was wide open and the tanker looked ready to roll. A few minutes later, he heard the lawnmower and Charley came racing around the corner with a case of Budweiser strapped to the hood. Norm looked at his watch. Three past. Charley hustled the beer into a side compartment and jumped into the cab.

"Let's go!" he said, turning the key. Nothing happened. Charley turned the key again. "What the....oh, shee-it!"

His shoulders slumped as he turned to Norm.

"Battery's in Tiny's shrimp boat."

"Say what?"

"His was dead last week, so we came and got this one. Damn! Forgot all about it."

He looked at the lawnmower, then at the Subaru. He launched himself out of the truck. "C'mon, Doc, notta moment to lose! Gotta get yours quick!"

Charley flung open the tool compartment looking for a crescent wrench, while Norm, resigned, opened the hood of the Subaru. Ten minutes later they were off. When they arrived at the county park, the shed was a pile of cinders. Three volunteer firemen were standing around a grill loaded with hot dogs.

"I didn't believe you, Charley, when you said you'd get here in record time," one of them said, "and, by God, you did! Got to be the slowest ever. Where you been, for Pete's sake?"

"Had us some mee-chanical difficulties with the tanker. Here," he said, handing over the case of beer, "you dig into these while we squirt them coals." The three men, cracking open beers, watched Charley and Norm pull out hose.

Two hours later, Charley and Norm, sooty and wet, eyes glazed from having downed several quick beers and their stomachs full of hot dogs, walked down to City Hall from the Fire Station. Charley's face, in particular, was sooty from where he had been scratching a bug bite. A couple of golf carts, over a dozen pickup trucks, a few beat-up sedans, and a shiny Lincoln Town Car were parked in front. Although a tiny town, almost no one, Norm thought, ever walked anywhere. They entered City Hall just as the Pledge of Allegiance was finished.

Four council members, the town clerk, and the mayor, were seated up front at a long, highly polished red cedar desk. The mayor, a skeletal old lady in a full dress, sat in the middle holding a gavel in one hand and a paper cup she used as a spittoon in the other. No one, including her, was quite sure how old she was, but she was assumed to be at least in her mid-nineties, independent as hell and still living alone. Beau was sitting to her right, a large Styrofoam cup full of scotch, Norm knew, in front of him. He nodded imperceptibly to Norm and smiled when he saw Charley.

The Mayor rapped the gavel. In a raspy voice, she said, "The meeting will now come to order. Please read the minutes from our last meeting."

The town clerk began to read. Norm looked around: good turnout. Fishermen, easy to pick out in their white boots, and their wives were scattered around the room.

A small group of the church people sat together, the women all in long skirts, the men clean-shaven and tidy. The church people made up about thirty percent of the town. Tammy was sitting about as far away from them as possible, or vice versa. The lawyer and his wife from Norm's side of town were two rows from the front. They stood out in their formality.

When the town clerk sat down, the mayor turned to the councilmembers.

"I believe the post office is the first item on the agenda."

Beau stood.

"Yes, Ma'am, and assigned to me; but before I begin, I would like to acknowledge the late arrival of two of our esteemed volunteer firefighters who, it seems, have just returned from a fire department exercise."

He looked at Charley. So did everyone else.

"How did it go?"

Charley looked like he had fought a three-alarm fire single-handed.

"Slicker than a greased pole at a fourth of Joo-lye picnic."

"I think I speak for the whole town when I say that we certainly appreciate all the volunteers' efforts on our behalf," Beau said. Polite applause. The fishermen and their wives who knew Charley well, smiled.

"Now, about the flea-ridden post office," Beau said.

Norm noticed the mayor's eyes flutter, her chin sinking to her chest. Right on schedule. Well, maybe a little early tonight. Beau looked at the postmistress.

"Ma'am, why don't you just set off a flea bomb Saturday noontime when you close? By Monday everything will be shipshape again."

"Mr. Beau, to get the money from the Government for a flea bomb, what with all the red tape, would take forever. Something's got to be done now and I'm not about to pay for it out of my own pocket! And even if we set one off, what about the week after, when those dogs come in again? Something's got to be done about those dogs!"

Others began to pop up like toast.

"What about my house? It's flea ridden, too!"

"And mine. We got fleas in all the carpets, and the kids is all ate up."

"Put flea collars on 'em."

"Who, the kids?"

"No, them dogs."

"Chain them damn dogs!"

"That's alright for you and yours, but we live close by. They've done that before and they howl all day and night!"

"Make them build a fence."

"Report them to the SPCA."

"Jest shoot the damn dogs!"

The mayor opened her eyes, spit in her cup, and banged her gavel.

"Order, order, please."

The room quieted. Virginia, Beau's wife who had been calmly knitting in the front row, raised her hand.

"Yes, Virginia," the mayor said.

Virginia, dressed in a simple wool skirt and a navy blue cashmere sweater, put her knitting aside and stood. She spoke in her long, drawn-out, cultured Charleston accent; there wasn't a single-syllable word in her vocabulary.

"I would like to make the magnanimous gesture of contributing, free of charge, a flea bomb to the United States Postal System. I think my husband's idea of setting one off Saturday afternoon, a good one. As for the dogs re-infesting the building, I suggest that the postmistress just keep the door shut and run the AC if she and her daughter are uncomfortable. I assume our government can afford that."

Virginia looked around at all the women.

"For your houses, just sprinkle some flea powder, most any hardware store sells it, on your rugs, and after a bit, vacuum. That's what I did; it works. And it's a lot cheaper and healthier than purchasing flea collars for all the kids," she said, straight-faced.

Beau and a few of the others smiled.

"As for the dogs, are the owners present?"

People looked around the room.

"I didn't think so. As a first step, I suggest that a town officer contact both the county humane society and the doggy pound. It's their job to assess a situation like this when animals aren't properly taken care of. Let them confront these people. Maybe they can take care of the problem."

Virginia sat down. No one said anything. The Mayor banged her gavel

"Do I hear a motion to do what Virginia has suggested."

"I so move," Beau said.

"And I second it," the mayor said. She glared at the councilmen. "All in favor?"

"Aye," was the unanimous vote.

The mayor rapped her gavel again. She glanced at the town clerk to make sure she was taking notes.

"So be it. Next order of business then." She looked directly at the lawyer's wife. "Ma'am, I believe you requested to speak this evening."

Norm found the lawyer's wife unattractive. Medium height and slender enough, but her dyed blond hair was extravagantly coiffed, not a hair out of place, and her face was heavy with makeup. Decked out in tailored, light-colored slacks and a light pink sweater straight out of south Florida, she wore a ring with a preposterously large gem worth a fortune if it was real and a gaudy necklace with matching bracelets. At least, he thought, she wasn't wearing stiletto heels. No one was smiling at her when she stood. She smiled nervously. Her husband was looking down at his shoes.

"Ms. Mayor, I think this town needs an ordinance to clean it up. There is junk scattered everywhere, wrecked boats, parts of old motors, piles of nets and buoys, old trucks and trailers. What lawn you can see is overgrown with weeds, and it not only looks shamefully shabby, but is a dangerous haven for rats and snakes of all kinds."

She faced the board, her confidence growing.

"I've given this horrible situation a lot of thought. The ordinance should mandate neat, well-kempt yards. The town could send letters out to those not in compliance, saying that they have two weeks to clean up their mess. If they don't do anything, then the town could hire someone to clean it up and send the property owners the bill. If they don't pay, then the town could fine them. If they still don't settle up, then the town could put a lien on their house. My husband would do that free of charge. Right, dear?"

Still looking at his feet, he nodded. She sat down to dumb-founded silence. The mayor hid a smile by spitting into her cup.

"Thank you, Ma'am. Do we have any comments by those in attendance?"

Hands sprang up all over the room. The mayor pointed to a stocky fisherman.

"Nellie…"

He stood up, taking his baseball cap off and holding it in his hands.

"I'd like to point out to the lady that the junk she is referring to is anything but. Those old motors, trucks, trailers, all those things are our source of spare parts. We can't afford to build some fancy building to store them all. Believe me, I'd like to keep my motors out of the weather, rather than under some sorry tarp. A shame if it bothers you terrible, Ma'am, but that's just the way it is around here."

The mayor took turns pointing around the room.

"We don't need no more regulations."

Charley said, "Snakes eats rats."

A heavy-set woman stood.

"If'n our town is so ugly, go somewhere else!"

The mayor banged her gavel hard.

"Now, let's keep this civil. Everyone has a right to speak his or her mind, but politely...Yes, Tammy."

"Just like you say, Mayor, we all have rights; like I have the right to run my business, which," she said looking at the church people, "I know might offend some of the people in this town. But, I have that right, just as the people of this town who own their land and pay taxes on it have the right to do what they want on it, and if that means scattering things all over the place, then so be it."

"Right on, Miss Tammy!"

" 'Atta girl!"

Norm was next.

"As you all know, I'm a newcomer, and I moved here because of three reasons. One, Crescent Beach is in a beautiful area. Two, the town is a throwback to simpler times where common sense, neighborly conduct, and tight family structure are still the way of life."

He paused, and looked around the room.

"There is one thing, though, that scares me. As Florida becomes more and more crowded, I have no doubt that the beauty of this area will be threatened. New people will come who will not adapt to the way of life here, as I have tried to do. No indeed. They will bring their own values, request controls, town doings will get complicated and require more time which the working man cannot afford. The newcomers, retired, rich, or both, will have that time and take their place on the board, and regulations will get so complicated that you'll need to be a lawyer, or hire one, to interpret them. I know this because I have seen it happen many times before. I think the town and the town council should be very careful." Norm started to sit down, but then added, "Oh, and the third reason I came was for the fishing."

The audience laughed, and there was some scattered applause. Tammy caught Norm's eye, giving him a big smile and thumbs up. The mayor rapped her gavel.

"Would anyone on the board like to make a motion to study the suggested ordinance?"

Silence. Beau stood up.

"No motion from me, but I would like to say two things. First, I, too, am a newcomer, and have been elected as one of your councilpersons. I want to assure you that Virginia and I, like Norm, have tried to adapt. We believe this town with its simple, uncomplicated life is rare. It is Florida's last frontier. Gumming it up with rules and regulations would change all that. Secondly, Madam," he said, looking at the lawyer's wife, "Crescent Beach is registered as a working Florida fishing village. If I'm not mistaken, with that classification, the State provides certain inalienable rights for its inhabitants, like having all sorts of fishing paraphernalia on their property."

Beau sat down. Virginia was nodding approval into her knitting.

"Again, do I hear any motions for studying a town ordinance governing how we keep our yards?" the mayor asked.

Silence.

"Next order of business…"

The meeting lasted another twenty-five minutes. After a lengthy discussion about how to keep dogs from rolling in the deer and pig entrails dumped by hunters, the mayor rapped her gavel one last time.

"Meeting adjourned."

Everyone filed out to a star-filled night and climbed into their vehicles. The lawyer's Lincoln was the first to leave. Tammy walked up to Norm and Charley.

"You two coming over to the Club?"

"Believe so, but we have to pull my battery out of the fire truck first," Norm said.

"How'd it get there?"

"Long story."

"Seen Tiny, Miss Tammy?" Charley asked.

"He went out at sunset. Charley, if you come over, better wash first."

Charley put a filthy hand to his face.

"Yes'm."

Beau and Virginia approached.

"Damn, Charley, you're a mess," Beau said.

"You don't got to tell me. Miss Tammy already done that."

Tammy asked, " Will you and Virginia be coming over, Beau? First drink is on me."

Beau took hold of Virginia's hand.

"Thank you, but no; we've got our tradition."

Tammy looked quizzical.

"After town meetings, Miss Virginia, here, and Beau jump bare-ass naked into that hot tub of theirs and have them a pitcher full of martinis."

"How else would you jump into a hot tub, Charley?" Virginia asked.

"Sounds like an excellent tradition to me. C'mon, Charley, let's go get that battery." Norm looked at Tammy. "See you later at the Club."

As they walked back to the fire station, Charley asked, "When you going to make the moves on Miss Tammy, Doc? She's justa waiting on you, you know."

Norm stopped dead in his tracks.

"Now why do you say that?"

"Because it's obvious. Both of you eyeing each other all the time, but neither one of you doing a thing about it."

"I didn't know I was wearing my heart on my sleeve, Charley; but, I believe you're wrong about Tammy."

"No, sir, Doc, I ain't. Minnie, she says the same thing."

They continued walking. When they arrived at the Fire Station, Norm broke the silence.

"Charley, it took me a long time to get over my marriage breaking up. It hurt a lot. And I think going through all that has done a couple things. I feel very vulnerable, scared to open myself up to any woman again. And I also think it destroys a man's confidence somehow, like he learns that he's not as important as he thought he was. Maybe that's a good thing, I don't know. But I do know that I never want to experience that kind of pain again."

"Don't know nothing about all that, Doc. But I does know it'd be a real big shame if'n you two never git together; yes, sir, a big shame…and a big waste. Now, yank open your hood and I'll get that old wrench."

CHAPTER SEVEN

The tide was right and Jimmy and Charley headed out. By the time they left the channel, the sun was beginning to rise over the marsh. They turned to look. The cabbage palms and cypress gave it perspective, a huge bright-orange ball. Almost immediately they could feel its gentle warmth as the sky began to blue.

"Never get tired of seeing that, Charley, never."

Jimmy turned and eased the throttle forward. The boat, powered by a brand new two hundred horse Yamaha subsidized by the square grouper, quickly planed off at thirty miles an hour. A breeze was out of the southwest and the sun soon played off the light chop, creating shimmering ripples of silver. Neither said a word, both enjoying the beauty of the Gulf and the solid throb of the big motor. Forty-five minutes later, as they approached the first string of white buoys with a red splotch in the middle, Charley opened one of the pungent, half-frozen boxes full of razor bellies and fish parts from the fish house. When Jimmy pulled back on the throttle, the smell of the bait was no longer masked by the wind in their faces. Charley gaffed the first buoy, hooked the line through the winch, and hauled in the cement-bottomed cypress slat trap. The trap was covered with so much mud that it was hard to see what was inside.

"We done left 'em too long, Jimmy. Look-ee at this here mess."

Charley scraped off as much muck and mud as he could, then dumped the contents onto the deck. Stuffing the bait-well full of smelly grouper heads and razor bellies, he latched the door and dropped the trap back overboard, bait-well down, as Jimmy began to head to the next buoy. Charley quickly sorted the catch. The hermit crabs, grass, mud, and everything else undesirable he threw out, along with the stone crab shells sucked empty by a fat, little octopus that was now wandering around the boat. The live stone crabs went into cardboard boxes. He ignored the octopus because it would just crawl out of wherever he put it. The large plastic tubs were for any sea bass and other good eating fish that might appear. There was a market for just about everything, even the octopus.

Jimmy glanced at the crab boxes. A few of the big crabs were really big, the crusher claws a half pound or more.

"Looks like that blow and cold weather sent us some big ones, Charley."

Jimmy slowed down and Charley hauled in another buoy and trap. When they finished with the first trap line, they headed toward the next, all the time with Charley expertly breaking off claws and throwing the crabs back into the Gulf to regenerate new ones. Occasionally he took a cutter claw too if, as allowed by law, it measured two and three quarters inches long. Most, though, were too small.

When they reached the next line of buoys, they switched jobs. It was wet, dirty, smelly, non-stop work. A few gulls appeared out of nowhere, swooping down for bits of spilled bait and discarded pieces of crab not consumed by the several octopuses now crawling around the boat. Damaged traps they piled in the stern to be repaired ashore. After visiting the third trap line around mid-day, they took a short break. Washing their stinking hands best they could, they broke out candy bars and sodas. Not wanting to taint the chocolate, they slid the wrappers down as they ate. The smell of the thawed-out fish parts had taken away most of their appetite.

"Seems to me," Charley said with a mouth full of Clark Bar, "them crabs would stand a better chance of living if'n we didn't ever take both claws. I read somewheres that ones left with a claw has twice as much chance of making it than ones without. Have an easier time feeding themselves which means they kin heal up faster."

"Maybe, Charley, but the state allows it, and those cutter claws can pay a day's gas out here. Can't take them in the Carolinas and Texas, just Florida."

Jimmy motored up to another trap line and they had at it again. They continued to work until the sun was low. The last buoy was a welcome sight, but it didn't come close to meaning the end of their day. When Jimmy pointed the bow towards shore, Charley continued to carefully break off claws, knowing that if the break wasn't clean, the crab had even less chance of healing. That wasn't the only reason he was careful. The crabs crushed oysters for a living and he wasn't about to let them grab hold of a finger. When he finished, he cleaned up much of the mud and sea grass, and rounded up all the octopuses. A proper cleaning of the boat still had to be done and then the claws had to be cooked so the meat wouldn't stick to the shell when they went on ice.

"Charley, what's that at about eleven o'clock? Too long for a manatee."

Charley had super long-range vision. He squinted, not saying anything for a couple seconds.

"Looks to me like Ralph's out exercising in that puny rowboat of his. Don't surprise me none, what with the

wind dying like it has. Believe he's a'heading in now
because he's facing right at us."

Ten minutes later, Ralph, bare-chested, shipped oars
and waved. Jimmy eased the boat up, turning off the
engine as Ralph toweled off.

"Getting your exercise, Ralph?" Jimmy asked.

"Yup, cancelled all my appointments, what there
were of them. Don't get many days like this in February."

"Purty day, alright. And you're purty far out for that
skinny li'l ol' thing," Charley said.

"Just felt so good with the sun and breeze on my back
that guess I was just sort of daydreaming and not paying
attention. Darn surprised when I realized where I was."

Ralph looked over their gunwale.

"Looks like you did alright."

"Not bad," Jimmy answered. " About average these
days. Ten years ago, would have been twice as much.
But still, not complaining, not being out on a day like
today anyways."

"You two going to Tammy's? Minnie's working there
tonight, isn't she, Charley?"

"Yep, but got a lot to do still, and I'm pretty used up."

"Charley, if you just help me unload the octopuses
and fish at Big Johns, no need to help with cleaning the
boat and cooking the claws. I know you haven't seen
Minnie all week. Crystal's already said she'd help."

Charley suddenly had an ear-to-ear grin.

"Why thanks, Jimmy, and you tell Miss Crystal that I'll
make it up to her! Tell her there's some spicy smoked
mullet dip a'coming her way. But time's awasting, let's
git a move on so I kin clean myself up."

He looked impatiently at a smiling Jimmy.

"Why look at Charley here! You'd think I just gave him
a shot of whisky! I'm skipping Tammy's tonight, Ralph;
want to be ready for my charter tomorrow morning. And
you best hurry on in, too, that sun's dropping fast."

"Have yourself a good paddle back, Ralph," Charley added, cheerfully.

"Row, Charley," Ralph corrected.

"Whatever."

Jimmy and Charley moved slowly off until their wake wouldn't bother, and Ralph began to row. It was a pretty sight, something timeless about Ralph's sleek, rich brown wooden scull knifing through the water, the smooth cadence of the oars, the workings of his upper body and thigh muscles, all bathed in the golden tones of the late afternoon sun. Ralph had no idea that he was being closely watched.

On the north side of the lodge out on Snowy Key, the deck had been built around an old live oak tree. It was here, in the shade of the oak, that Craig stood watching the scull approach the main channel. Binoculars trained on Ralph's back, Craig was mesmerized by the smooth transition of flexing muscles. When Ralph entered the channel, Craig could see his face and entire front torso, and that he wore only what looked like brief cut-off sweat pants. Handsome, no belly, svelte body, damn fine specimen. Craig couldn't take his eyes off him. He was horrified when, minutes later, he discovered he had become as hard as the post he was leaning against. At first he was aghast, then angry. He put the binoculars down on a nearby table, and strode purposefully towards his airboat. Putting on earphones, he jumped in, the engine catching on the second crank. Without letting it warm up, he roared out towards the main channel.

Ralph's tranquility, as well as the town's, was shattered as abruptly as a baseball coming through a plate glass window. The pairs of cormorants and occasional blue herons flying silently home past Ralph, low on the water and silhouetted by the setting sun, were replaced by the airboat screaming straight at him, the noise of

the props and the four hundred and fifty horsepower
engine deafening. Ralph, with a pretty good idea that
Craig was up to no good, stopped rowing and kept his
oars in the water as outriggers.

Craig roared past him, sliding by at sixty miles an
hour. He roared by again, and again, until the circle
became smaller and smaller, like a fisherman herding
mullet into a net. Ralph struggled with the oars to keep
the scull from flipping. Finally, Craig put it in neutral,
the roar reduced to a low, awkward rumble.

"When you going to get a man's boat, instead of that
fairy thing?"

"Maybe about the time you grow up, Craig! That's
about the dumbest thing you've done yet!"

Ralph started to row away, shaking his head, but kept
watching Craig closely, the man's crazy-colored eyes were
wild and he looked like he might do anything, including run him over. Craig revved the engine and turned
sharply so that Ralph received the full blast from the
prop, showering him with saltwater bb's. He took off towards the island, leaving Ralph, ears ringing, to wonder
if his hearing had been impaired. He also wondered,
what the hell was the matter with the man.

CHAPTER EIGHT

Eager to shed his wet, stinky clothes and take a shower before going to the Club, Charley cranked the lawnmower wide open. With the sun down, it had cooled off in a hurry and his eyes watered as he sped home. In a few minutes he arrived at the forty-two-foot boat that had seen better days. It looked a lot like an old Chris Craft, but was, in fact, a 1957, mahogany-hulled Mathews, perched on a rugged homemade trailer with four of the six tires flat. The boat's white paint was peeling and, although the hull had been scraped clean, it was badly in need of bottom paint. A four-inch PVC pipe along with a waterline exited a patched section of the hull and disappeared into the ground between the wheels of the trailer.

The craft was a juxtaposition: the main afterdeck was short and stubby, but the rakish roof angle of the well fenestrated pilothouse and the massive yet sleek bow made it look like it could cut through any wave. The bow was more than half its length, and three oval portholes along its graceful curve hinted to abundant cabin space below. A single strip of brown wood, milled to accept a three-quarter-inch hemp line in its center, ran the length of the boat and served as both Spartan trim and false gunwale. On the transom, Charley had painted *Stingray* in flowing letters over the original name. He walked over to an aluminum ladder lashed to the side and climbed aboard.

The boat had sat in the mud outside the main channel of Crescent Beach for over two years, sunk in three feet of water after hitting an oyster bar. According to the original lettering on the transom, homeport was Miami. Its mysterious captain, who had been drunk when he had run aground, remained aboard for a week, coming ashore occasionally in an inflatable dinghy before packing his belongings into a hastily purchased pickup and disappearing. At first, people expected him to return, but after the summer's storms, the boat listed badly and the engines were ruined. It eventually became a nightime haven for young horny fishermen and their girlfriends. Charley was one of those young fishermen and he fell in love with the boat. He began to go out alone, sometimes with a little pot, but always with at least a six-pack of beer. He'd sit at the helm looking out to the horizon or down at the various round gauges. He'd fondle the graceful chrome fixtures, open and shut all the cleverly constructed built-ins. Often he spent the night. The rich dark wood paneling glowed in the light of his kerosene lantern. It was his private yacht.

But each month the boat took more pounding and listed a little more. The spring tides and storm surges began to flood the two berths and galley. The mattresses became moldy, the paint on some of the woodwork began to blister and peel, the hardwood floor began to buckle. The boat was slowly dying before his eyes. During a full moon low tide, Charley climbed down into the bowels to inspect the damage. He also climbed down to the boot-sucking mudflat and looked at the hull. Ain't all that bad, he thought. On a tide like this, could bring me out a little generator, sump pump her, and slap on some fiberglass patches to git her ashore. Me and Tiny could tow her in.

He decided to track down the owner. It didn't take long. The owner, or more accurately, the previous owner, was a widow from Miami. After her husband died, she had been in a hurry to sell the boat because it reminded her too much of all the good times and trips they had taken together. Consequently, she took a lot of paper and a ridiculously small down payment from the mysterious captain who promptly left with the boat. She had heard nothing and received zero money from him since. When Charley explained where the boat was and in what condition, she said that he could have it. He didn't believe her until he received all the official documentation coupled with a signed hand-written note confirming the deal.

Within a week after receiving the papers, he pumped her dry and patched her up. It was after the patch job, as he was pushing his dinghy off the mudflat, that he stepped on a stingray. It jabbed him in the calf and hurt like hell. It was the first time in his life that had happened, but he knew what to do. To relieve the pain, he stuck his leg under the hot water pulsing out of his little outboard motor. It was either that or piss on his leg, he thought. He took the stinging as a sign, and it was then that he decided on the name for the boat. At high tide, he and Tiny towed it ashore. Two days later, Charley moved it to his half-lot a few blocks off Main Street, painted *Stingray* on the stern, and had lived in it ever since.

Charley passed through the wheelhouse and went down into the galley. It was a work in progress, and had been ever since he moved in. The walls were scraped bare of paint, patched and primed. He had yanked out the rusty, non-functional stove and replaced it with a couple of small cast iron, gas burner hot plates he placed on the counter next to the sink. The hot plates were only temporary, he had told himself, but that was over two years ago. He lit both burners to warm the place up. He had pulled out the old refrigerator, too, replacing it with an electric model barely big enough to accommodate a couple six-packs and a pound of burger. Pulling the lid from a tin coffee pot, he inspected the contents. No bad stuff floating on top, should heat up just fine. He put the pot on a burner. He continued on to the main berth that was big enough for two built-in bunks, only one of which had a mattress. The next berth was in the bow, where the narrow curved bunks served as storage for all his tools and building materials: beat-up skilsaw, speed square, drill, orbital sander, hammer, and odds and ends like cans with paint brushes sticking out, jars of nails and screws, miscellaneous hinges and other hardware.

He sat on his bed to take off his white boots, tossing them out towards the galley. The neighboring bunk was cluttered with clothes, an old plug-in clock radio, couple dirty cups, a few paperbacks, a ruler, some paper and plastic pens. In the middle was a cracked orange plastic tub that had been used for crabs, but now served as a hamper. He tossed his dirty, wet clothes into it and returned to the galley where he poured a cup of very strong coffee. He smacked his lips. Man alive, now don't that hit the spot!

Off the galley was the narrow head. The bathroom was so small that, standing in the middle, he could turn on the sink faucets, the shower, flush the toilet, and open the wall cabinet. There was tremendous water pressure, and soon steam from the shower filled the room. It escaped through the louvers of the bathroom door and the entire boat became as foggy as a London street. Charley squeezed into the shower. For the first five minutes he luxuriated in the soothing warmth, occasionally sipping his coffee that was perched on the sink.

He thought, Dang, been almost a full week since I last seen Minnie! Wonder if she missed me? Always hard to tell with her; don't show her cards none. But, we sure have fun! And ain't had me a drop of hard liquor since we got together; says the stuff makes me moccasin-mean and she won't put up with it. Got to admit I ain't been in a fight since I stopped. Guess I did git a little rowdy there for a spell, what with people calling me Coon-eye Charley for all the black eyes I was a'sporting.

He began to lather up. Hope she lets me visit after she's done work. Man, she sure is one hot ticket! Ought to be, I guess; done had her plenty of practice what with having gone through three husbands. But wish she'd just come here instead of me having to go all the way out to her place. Says the *Ray's* a pigsty and makes her skin crawl; but bet the real reason's because she don't want no one to know what we've been up to. Whatever. Jest as long as she stays my girl, I don't care where we go. And out at her place always gits me a little bonus like a parcel of collards or mustard greens, or maybe okra. She's about the best gardener in these here parts for sure.

He finished shaving and stepped out of the shower. He pulled out a towel and wiped off the mirror to see if he had missed any spots. Things I got to do to keep her happy, he thought, shaking his head. Like having to walk to Tammy's tonight just for her. Says its embarrassing when I come on the lawnmower. Well, just you wait, sweetie, 'til I get that Mustang; you'll be a'riding with me in style in that scallop festival parade before you know it! He threw the towel down on the sink and hurried out to get dressed.

CHAPTER NINE

Norm put down the medical journal and rubbed his eyes. Can't concentrate like I used to, he thought, and why do I try to keep up anyway? Crescent Beach doesn't exactly require being on the cutting edge of surgical procedures. I'm just a small town doctor now—like Doc in the old *Gunsmoke* reruns. He put his hands behind his head and leaned back. Let's see. And if I'm Doc, then who's Matt? Jimmy, that tough old cracker. Maybe not as big and strong as some, but tough; no one messes with him. Definitely, he's the sheriff. And Charley has to be Festus, even talks like him. Tammy, of course, is Miss Kitty. Only thing wrong with the scenario is that Kitty is Matt's girl, not Doc's.

Wonder if Charley's right? Maybe Tammy is interested in me, but where could it possibly go? Hopefully, it'd end up in bed, but then what? What would we talk about afterwards? Or anytime, for that matter. Such different backgrounds! Me from a wealthy family, lots of formal education, hers impoverished and only finishing high school. But, she's tough, capable, smart, as well as sexy as hell. She dumped that abusive husband early on and singlehandedly built up the Crescent Club. How many women do you know who could have done that? She can fish and hunt, knows all about practical things. Got to be plenty we can talk about. If there's a comfort zone beyond sex, if we have sex, it would develop or it wouldn't. But, it's never going to happen if I don't try.

He looked out the window. Almost sunset; time for a libation. Something coming in out there. He fetched his binoculars. Ralph getting his exercise. That's a peaceful sight if there ever was one; where's the camera? Be a nice telephoto shot with Ralph silhouetted by the sun, sparkles all around, cormorants passing close overhead. Be a nice present to give him sometime. He found the camera, made his drink, and took both out to the deck. As he took a sip, the sound of Craig cranking up the airboat came across the water. Norm's mood soured as Craig roared out from the island, transforming the halcyon of tranquility into O' Hare International in the blink of an eye.

He jerked his head towards Snowy Key, watching Craig gun the boat out towards the channel. Fool's not even going to give Ralph the courtesy of slowing down! The noise cut through the evening like a blasphemy. What's that man doing! Damn idiot's heading right at Ralph! What! Trying to swamp him! That son of a bitch should be shot! Craig suddenly cut the engine, and Norm felt his body relax; thank God for small favors! Hope Ralph's giving him an ear full; but no, Craig was off again. Norm covered his ears.

A couple hours later, after chilled white wine, oysters Rockefeller, a half dozen shrimp over pasta, and a salad of fresh greens, Norm headed towards the Club. A pair of white refrigerated fish trucks passed him on Main Street. The trucks came and went at all hours, transporting everything from the Gulf, including, Norm knew, square grouper on occasion. The parking lot was just about full with Charley's lawnmower nowhere in sight. Charley had gone out with Jimmy today; he must be cooking claws. Like always, a group of men in work clothes and white boots were shooting pool. Their greetings followed him up the stairs.

Most of the Formica-topped tables inside were full, a few pulled together to accommodate larger parties. The Saturday night special of fried mullet, fries, coleslaw or swamp cabbage, and hush puppies was cheap and popular, and there was a choice of homemade pies for dessert. Even though the Club was a bar, it had more of a feeling of a family restaurant, at least during dinner hours. Later on, though, most anything could happen; families were usually gone by nine, with last call at one.

There were several vacant stools at the long pecky cypress bar. The top of the bar, coated with a clear, thick plastic goop that filled all the holes, was smooth and hard as marble, so shiny that it reflected the lights on the wall, making it difficult to appreciate the rich, deep brown swirls and patterns of the wood. Garlands of lit-up plastic red peppers were draped above the shelves of bottles. Above the peppers, and in between two trophy fish mounts, was the large television tuned in to another basketball game.

Norm was surprised to see Charley down at the far end of the bar, talking to Minnie as she was drawing a pitcher of beer. Norm noticed immediately that Minnie had cut off the long thick ponytail that had come to her waist. He walked down and pulled out the stool between Charley and a stocky man eating peelers and drinking a beer.

"Now that just ain't a good enough reason to go and do that, Minnie."

"Let it go, Charley! You've told me ten times already!"

Minnie wiped the foam from the edge of the pitcher and took it to a table. She was a handsome, thin woman, taller than Charley, more about Norm's height at five-ten. She was wearing jeans and a sweatshirt with the

Crescent Club logo on it.   Charley, shaking his head, looked at Norm.

"You see what she's gone and done, Doc? All that bee-yutiful hair, gone! Just chopped it all off."

"Guess that's her prerogative, Charley. Where's the lawnmower?"

"At the *Ray*." Charley nodded toward Minnie. "She don't approve none of me driving it. Says I look silly."

Norm looked around the room.

"Miss Tammy's out in the kitchen, Doc. Maybelline didn't come in until late and they was swamped. They been frying up a storm."

Minnie returned.

"Evening, Norm. The usual?"

Norm nodded, and Minnie served him his Jack Daniels before she returned to the floor.

"So, why did she cut it off?"

"Says it was too much trouble to take care of, getting snarled all the time. That and a couple of them prison guards were a'coming on to her; thought it might make 'em pay less attention."

He took a sip of beer.

"Caught her a escaping prisoner yesterday night."

"You're kidding."

The stocky fellow eating shrimp turned towards them.

"Nope. Held him at gunpoint until the loo-tenant come out and got him."

"Maybe she'll finally get that promotion. Be about time."

"That's what I said, but she says no way. Says her and the loo-tenant is cross-threaded and he'll make sure she never gets one. Soon as she finishes that crimeology thing, she's gonna apply for a transfer to the women's prison a piece down the road."

Tammy, face flushed from cooking, came behind the bar.

"Evening, Norm. Have you two met Rusty, here?"

Charley and Norm turned towards the stocky man.

"Rusty, this is Norm, our town doctor, and Charley, Jimmy's fishing partner."

Rusty smiled and held up both hands.

"I'd shake your hands, gentlemen, but mine are a little messy right now."

"Rusty's staying in one of my cabins and is going to be fishing with Jimmy the entire week."

"You're the road feller from Georgia, then. Nice to meet you, but gotta tell you you're coming during about the slowest time for fishing. Another couple o'weeks when the water warms, be better," Charley said.

"Doesn't matter. This trip's just as much about relaxing as fishing; if I catch a few reds and trout, I'll be plenty happy."

"You don't have to worry none about that. Jimmy's the best fisherperson in these parts. If there's any out there, Jimmy'll find them."

Beau and Ralph came in with Skillet, tail wagging, close behind. Skillet trotted over to the kitchen to pay his respects to the four dachshunds that belonged to Maybelline, the cook. Beau nodded to the three men.

"Evening, gentlemen."

Charley introduced Rusty as a nearby table facing the Gulf opened up. Beau noticed.

"Aah, I see Miss Tammy held my table for me; I invite you gentlemen for some rare intellectual conversation in these parts. Rusty, I hope you will join us."

"Beau here's our councilperson. Moved down from Charleston, South Carolina, where they likes to pontificake some. He's a real polly-tishun, but don't hold it against him, Rusty; he's not really a bad feller."

"Pontificate, Charley," Norm said as they walked over to the table.

"Whatever."

When they were seated and after drink orders, Norm turned to Ralph.

"Saw Craig giving you a hard time this evening. Looked like the damn fool was trying to swamp you."

Ralph sighed.

"I swear that something's eating him; he has this spooky, wild look. I don't know what it is, but he's got a problem for sure."

"Maybe his problem is that he's just a jerk," Norm suggested.

Ralph shrugged.

"Ain't normal for him not to come in on a Saturday night," Charley added.

Minnie put their drinks down.

"Charley told me you caught a prisoner last night, Minnie. What's that all about?" Norm asked.

Minnie glanced around the room; most of the diners had cleared out. She put her hands on the back of Charley's chair.

"I was doing regular duty in one of the guard shacks along the razor wire. We're there four-hour shifts without a break and drink a pretty fair share of coffee. If nature calls, there aren't any bushes to go behind, so we women bring buckets with us."

Tammy came over to listen.

"After about three hours, I went outside to dump mine and stretch my legs. There was this ditch from some construction not too far from the fence, on the prison side, and I saw something moving. It was this round little thing, going along the edge of the ditch. Looked to me like an armadillo, but as I watched it, I noticed it was going in a straight line, and I thought, Girl, when have you ever seen an armadillo go in a straight line?"

"Now that's for sure. They're always poking around here and there, a'grubbing for stuff. They goes every which a way."

"Thank you for your expert opinion, Charley. Now would you please let Minnie continue," Beau said.

"I kept watching it for another twenty feet or so when suddenly it raised up and I could see it was a head looking around. Then it lowered and started moving again. Well, sir, I went in and got my rifle, took a bead on him, and told him to stand up or I'd shoot. Feller obliged me and I called the lieutenant on the radio. He came out lickety-split in a pickup and told me to turn my head if I didn't want to see a naked man. He made him strip right there; and I'll tell you what, it was chilly inland last night, frost looked like snow it was so thick in the morning. He made that prisoner sit naked as a jaybird on that cold tailgate while he took him back. And the lieutenant made sure he went back at a crawl."

"She's something, ain't she," Charley said, proudly. Minnie rubbed his head before returning to work with Tammy.

Rusty asked, "So, Beau, how did you end up here from Charleston?"

"Symbolism."

Ralph laughed.

"That, plus your house was the only one in Crescent Beach with a hot tub. You were an easy sell, Beau."

"What do you mean, 'symbolism?'" Rusty persisted

"Do you know what the state flag of South Carolina is?" Beau didn't wait for an answer. "A solid blue background, a cabbage palm, and a crescent moon. The color of the Gulf here on a sunny day is that exact blue. Cabbage palms grow everywhere in these parts, and a white crescent moon is the spitting image of our beach. All that seemed like sure signs to Virginia, that's my wife, and me that Crescent Beach was where we should retire. Of course, there's excellent fishing here, too. Unfortunately, though, we paid top dollar and Ralph here has been living off the commission for years."

"Now speaking of that there hot tub, when you going to throw a party and invite us all over? I can bring my rubber duckies and we kin have us a good old time."

"I don't think Virginia would be too excited about that, Charley." Beau turned to Ralph. "Virginia wants to talk with you tomorrow about this week's food distributions. We're heading up to Charleston for a few days for some quail shooting before the season closes. That, plus Virginia's got another bridge tournament."

"Hope y'all be back for poker night. I'm going to need me another couple hub caps for my Mustang."

"Rusty," Ralph said, "I can tell in five minutes if someone's going to buy a place here. People either love or hate Crescent Beach that fast, and most leave right away. Women can't imagine being here without a Publix or a hospital nearby—no offense, Norm—or no movie theater, no tennis courts or golf course, no antique shops. They've got nothing to do if they don't fish."

"Like that there lawyer's wife. Got nothing to do except put her nose where it don't belong," Charley said.

"Is that really a state statute like you said in the meeting, Beau, about inalienable rights to scatter fishing stuff all over the place?" Norm asked.

"I don't rightly know. But if there isn't one, there should be."

They all laughed.

"Now ain't that the way of polly-tishuns, just a'making up things as they sees fit."

"Weren't you worried that her husband might look into it?" Norm asked.

"Nah. I think he was there just because of his wife; he looked embarrassed as hell. Probably relieved to hear something like that so it could be put to rest."

"There goes Tiny, Charley," Ralph said, looking out the window. A shrimp boat with its running lights on was moving slowly out in the Gulf.

"Yep, said he'd be close in tonight," Charley added.

Rusty asked, "What's he fishing for?"

"Shrimp," was the chorused reply.

"Does he always go out at night?"

The others looked at each other, sharing the same thought: Rusty was a mountain boy for sure. Charley spoke up.

"Yep. Shrimps is the favoritest thing to eat of most everything in the Gulf, so they hides and buries themselves during the day with just their eyes a'sticking outta the sand. Only comes out at night. The kind we mostly got around here is called hoppers because they being so active and all, snap around real lively-like. Smaller ones that don't get bought for food is used for bait, and with all that hopping around, attract fish real good on the end of a hook. Don't know if Jimmy'll be using them tomorrow, though. Mostly, he likes to use lures, or bait fish he gets with a cast net. And he…"

The crash of a beer bottle hitting the floor interrupted Charley. A short and very drunk fisherman looked down at it dumbly. Tammy came over with a broom and dustpan.

"Sorry, Miss Tammy. Plum careless of me," he slurred. "Minnie, I'd like another if I could. Promise not to drop it."

"I'll get you another, Clem, but nothing but cans now."

Charley said, "Looks like Clem's on another bender. Don't know how he can git up in the morning, drinking the way he does."

Minnie came over to their table after putting a Bud in front of Clem.

"Another round, gents?"

Everyone nodded except Rusty.

"Not for me, thanks. I've got to go fishing tomorrow morning."

"It won't be none too early, Rusty, I kin tell you that. Tide's going to be out 'til nine, and only airboats can git in and out afore then."

Rusty looked at his watch.

"One more then, Ma'am; please."

"Ain't Minnie pretty, Rusty?" Charley asked with adoring eyes.

"Hush, Charley!"

"Well, you is, even though you done cut off all that bee-yootiful hair." He turned to Rusty. "You should o' seen it; all dark and long when she let it out. Looked so pretty spread out on a white pillow..."

"Charley!"

Charley was about to add something, but when he saw Minnie's beet red face, he looked down at the table.

"Oops," he said, in a small voice. "I'm sorry, Minnie. It's the beer talking."

Cat's finally out of the bag, Norm thought. Whole town knew that Charley and Minnie saw each other on occasion, but not that they slept together. Word would be out tomorrow, guaranteed.

Charley looked so forlorn and sheepish that the others at the table, including Rusty, couldn't help but laugh. Even Minnie smiled and patted his hand.

"It's alright, Charley."

He looked up at her, then past her. He frowned.

"Uh oh. Here comes trouble for sure. Where's Tiny and Jimmy when you need them!"

A very big man with a huge hard gut walked up to the far end of the bar. He leaned against it, staring hard at Clem who hadn't seen him walk in.

"What's the problem, Charley?" Rusty asked.

" Expect ya'll see soon enough."

"Ain't it about time for you to go on home, Clem!" the big man asked loudly.

Clem's head snapped up.

"Leave me be, Sammy. I be goin' home when I aim to."

"You got a wife and kids at home."

"Yeah, that's why I'm here."

Clem must weigh a buck thirty-five, Norm thought; his wife, Sammy's sister, half again that much, and Sammy, probably more than twice as much. In a fight, poor Clem didn't stand a chance against either one.

In a low voice, Charley said to Rusty, "Last time, Sammy dragged him down Main Street with the whole town a watching. Clem was some mad. He won't go easy this time, I kin tell you that."

"You're nothing but a sloppy, disgusting drunk; you know that, Clem?"

Clem calmly took a swig of his beer before answering.

"I am what I am, that's all I can say. Leastways, I can see my dingaling when I takes a pee."

Minnie covered a smile with her hand. Rage clouded Sammy's face. He walked purposefully towards Clem.

"Reckon I gotta drag you home again."

"You stay away from me, Sammy! I'ma warning you!"

"Ain't nothing you can do about it, little man. You're going home."

From behind the bar, Tammy said, "Sammy, don't you cause any problems. Clem'll be going home soon enough and you can settle your family problems then; not now, and not here!"

Sammy ignored her. He reached for Clem, who backed away.

"I'ma warning you again, Sammy. You stay away!"

For a heavy man, Sammy moved very quickly. In a split second, he had hold of Clem's shirt, and dragged him into a headlock, and started dragging him towards the door. Clem fumbled in his pocket and pulled a knife. Sammy didn't see it, and Clem stuck it into his thigh. Sammy bellowed with rage and quickly yanked it out of Clem's hand, throwing it to the floor. Holding Clem up by the collar, he began to pummel his face with short powerful blows. Blood was everywhere. He was going to kill him.

Rusty moved very, very fast. He pulled Clem away, which only further enraged Sammy. He swung at Rusty, which was a big mistake. Rusty stepped into the roundhouse, blocking it with his left forearm, then, with the same hand slapped Sammy twice, hard enough so his head snapped back with each blow, sunk a heavy right fist into the big gut, spun Sammy around by the left arm while kicking out one of his legs. Sammy fell hard on to his stomach with Rusty putting an arm lock on him as he fell. With a knee on Sammy's back, Rusty applied serious pressure to the arm. Sammy cried out and stopped resisting. Rusty, not even breathing hard, looked over to the table. No one said a word.

"Charley, is this man a fisherman?"

Charley nodded, speechless for once. Norm went over to Clem who was crumpled up on the floor, moaning.

"Doctor, if I were to break this man's arm right about here," Rusty said, tapping it, "how long would it be before he could haul in his nets again?"

"A couple of months at least."

Rusty increased the pressure on the arm.

"Did you hear what the Doctor said?"

"Yes, sir."

"Do you want me to break your arm?"

"No, sir!"

"If I let you up, will you leave peacefully?"

"Yes, sir."

"All right, but I want it real clear that if you don't, I will take you down again, just as fast, and I'll snap your arm like a twig. Understood?"

"Yes, sir."

Rusty let go of the man and carefully backed away. Sammy got up slowly, hand over his belly. He looked at Rusty.

"He stabbed me."

"Looked like self-defense to me. If I were his size and you came at me, I might have done the same thing. Now get out of here."

"Wait a minute, Sammy. Let me look at your leg first."

Norm cut the jeans around the wound.

"Doesn't look too bad, but it'll need a few stitches. Clean it out, and put some hydrogen peroxide or iodine or something on it. I'll come by your house later with a needle and thread."

Pressing several napkins on the wound, Sammy limped off, and Rusty returned to the table.

Beau said, "Tammy, put Rusty's beers on my tab! Damn, Rusty, where did you learn that? Never seen such quick moves."

"Was an MP over in 'Nam for a bunch of years," he said, sitting down at the table.

"If you ever want a job here on Saturday nights, you're hired," Tammy said, kneeling next to Norm and putting a couple of folded up towels under Clem's head.

Rusty laughed.

"No thanks, Ma'am. I came here for some peace and quiet. I hope it's not always like this. How is he, Norm?"

"Mostly bumps and shallow cuts. Going to be sorer than hell in a little bit, and probably both eyes are going to swell shut. But he's okay. I think Sammy would have killed him if it hadn't been for you. Could you get a few of those butterfly bandages in my medical box, Tammy?"

She nodded, and went to the backroom. There was always a chance that something like this would happen; consequently, Norm had stocked a medical emergency box that Tammy kept under lock and key.

"Thanks for the offer, Beau, but I'll take care of my check. Think I'll go get my things organized and get some sleep."

Rusty put some bills on the bar and left. Tammy returned with soap and water, antiseptic, a couple of hand towels and the bandages. She began to gently clean Clem up. Minnie sat down next to Charley and reached for his hand. Charley turned to her.

"In all the times I done spent at bars and pig roasts and such, I ain'ta never seen a man takes care of hisself like that. That there Rusty's lightning fast!"

Norm and Tammy helped Clem stand. He was wobbly, but stayed up.

"I think Clem could use an escort home," Beau said rising to his feet. "I just hope his wife doesn't take over where Sammy left off."

Beau took Clem's arm and led him towards the door. Tammy said, "Minnie, why don't you and Charley go on, too. I'm kicking everyone out of here; we've had enough excitement for one night."

"I'll stay and help you clean up, if you want," Norm said.

"You're on."

The bar cleared out, Tammy went into the kitchen, and Norm wiped off tables, put chairs up, and began to sweep. Both finished about the same time.

"How about a little brandy nightcap, Norm?"

"Don't mind if I do," he said, pulling a stool off the top of the bar.

Tammy poured the drinks. She reached across the bar, tapping his glass.

"Cheers."

They sat in silence for a while, sipping the brandy. Norm was the first to speak.

"You sure did a good job taking care of Clem, him all bloody like that."

"I can't count how many bloody noses I've wiped or sob stories I've listened to over the years." She shook her head and frowned. "Sometimes I'm ready to throw in the towel. Crap like this really gets me down. Maybe I should just leave, close up shop like the long skirts want. I hear they've even been trying to pray me out of town."

"Don't begin to think that, Tammy! This town wouldn't be the same without you and the Crescent Club. The Club's the heartbeat of the community, at least for most of it. People can get a good meal, swap fish stories, get away from the old man or old lady and relax. Where else can the tourists eat and mix with the locals if they want? You bring a lot of business and activity to this town; without you, it just might die. And certainly don't pay any attention to those ladies."

"Ladies, my foot! More like gossiping hens. I could tell you stories, but I won't. People's business is their own."

A silence followed until Norm said, "Guess Charley spilled the beans tonight about him and Minnie. And her turning bright red confirmed it, at least for me. Did you know about them?"

"Of course; Minnie's my best friend."

All of a sudden, the night was turned upside down by the roar of an airboat. Tammy frowned as she turned to look at the clock on the wall behind her.

"Bit late for that, don't you think." she said.

"Got to be that butthead Craig."

Norm walked over to a window.

"Yup. Heading for the keys full bore. At this time of night! I swear that guy is the most inconsiderate asshole I've ever met."

"He's really not so bad if he's not drinking. Maybe a bit too macho, but one on one, he can be a pretty decent guy."

"Tell that to Ralph," Norm said, sitting down again.

"Yeah, there is that."

The noise from the boat was an intrusion, like a third party. Norm finished his brandy.

"Well, guess I better be going. Should tend to Sammy."

He stood. Tammy was silent, looking at him intently. He didn't move. Charley's words popped into his head. 'She's justa waiting on you, you know...Minnie, she says the same thing.' He fidgeted.

"Damn it, Tammy, I feel like a school kid around you sometimes." Tammy still didn't say anything. Norm looked away, then back. Finally, he asked, "Would you like to do something together sometime, like go fishing or picnic or come over for dinner?"

"About time you asked me, Norm. Of course, I would. Been waiting for you to ask. Now lean over the bar." He did as he was told. Tammy kissed him lightly on the lips. "I'll look forward to it. You know we're closed Wednesdays, so make a plan. And Norm, just remember I'm not a school girl, far from it. Now go fix up Sammy."

Norm left the building, pausing at the deck railing to look out over the Gulf. Crescent moon, glorious stars. What a beautiful night! He couldn't remember such a wonderful night! He went down the stairs two at a time, oblivious to the airboat that continued to shatter the night's silence.

CHAPTER TEN

Craig turned off the TV. What a laugher, eighteen points! Those Gators are really coming into it with that new coach they got from Kansas State: they're killing most everybody these days. He walked out to the deck. Tammy's was all lit up. Funny not being there on a Saturday night, can't remember the last time I wasn't; but, Ralph's probably there. He picked up the binoculars that were still outside on the deck. Looks like a pretty good turnout, bunch underneath shooting pool. Wonder how long before one of them starts a fight and cracks a pool stick over someone's head.

That was pretty stupid this afternoon. Don't know what got into me. Yeah, you do. You know. He brought the binoculars inside, and went to the refrigerator for another beer. He opened the beer while thinking back to his senior year in high school. That's when he first realized. He attended Bolles in Jacksonville, an all male military school. Many of the students were there for one of two reasons: their dads had been military lifers and wanted their kids to follow in their footsteps, or they were wild kids who got in trouble and their parents thought sending them to a military school might bring some discipline into their lives. He was of the second variety. He had matured early, was big and strong for his age, and was not usually carded at bars. When he was sixteen, his father had given him an Austin Healy 3000, lime green with plush tan leather seats and a throaty growl. He was a B.M.O.C. and he went from one girl to another, mostly cheerleaders. His father thought nothing of paying his speeding tickets or having a drunk driving charge smothered. He privately relished that his son was the local James Dean. But when Craig knocked up one of the cheerleaders and had come to him to arrange an abortion that cost him a lot of dough, he thought maybe it was time to ship Craig out.

His senior year at Bolles, Craig was the starting guard on the state champion football team. His best buddy, Bob, was the center. They hung out a lot, occasionally double-dated with townies and secretly hit some of the bars. It had been after drinking at the bars one Saturday night that Bob had come into his room to show him his latest skin mag. He had quite a collection. Bob laid it down on the desk, and slowly turned the pages. It had everything. Naked men and women doing the deed, of course, but also women with women, and men with men. Bob didn't skip over the pages with the men. Craig had never seen anything like it.

"Where the hell did you get this!"

Bob smiled.

"Pretty wild, huh?"

"I guess so!"

"Turns me on, I'll tell ya."

"Yeah, me too. I'm hard as a rock!"

Bob looked up from the mag.

"Bet I can come faster than you."

"What!"

"C'mon, I'll race you!"

Bob unzipped his fly and exposed his hard-on. He was very well endowed. Craig couldn't believe it, but also couldn't take his eyes off Bob's erection. Bob started stroking it. He smiled at Craig.

"Better hurry up."

What the hell, Craig thought. He unzipped, and the two stroked themselves as Bob slowly turned the pages.

"You know, it feels even better if someone else does it."

Bob reached for Craig and gently took hold of him. Craig stood there, shocked; but not for long. He was right, it did feel better. Slowly, shyly he reached over to Bob. He was so big and solid. Bob acted like it was the most natural thing in the world. He kept turning the pages. They ejaculated together into a wastebasket.

It became sort of a semi-regular thing, usually when they came back from some bar, half in the bag. No one knew. And, no one would ever suspect two starting linemen on the football team. Bob led Craig down the path of male intimacy with only one tacit taboo: they never kissed. They would climax, zip up, and act as if nothing ever happened. But Craig was curious and asked where Bob had learned so much. Bob smiled.

"I was an altar boy," he said. "I was even blessed on occasion."

After Bolles, Craig went to the University of Florida. He wasn't big enough to play football there, but attended all the games in The Swamp. He also went to the O'Connell Center to cheer on the basketball team. He thought that the basketball players, with what they could do in mid air, the way they could contort and control their bodies, were the best athletes in the school. He became a big fan and would always arrive early to get a good seat in the Rowdy Reptiles section. He also watched the men's swimming team compete. It was kind of boring, but he continued to go anyway. He told himself that it had nothing to do with all the well-built guys in their Speedos.

He dated a lot of the co-eds, even after graduating when he remained in Gainesville, but nothing serious.

Just party time and slam, bam, thank you ma'am. He had no sexual contact with men. But it was always there, he knew. He took a job as a regional sports equipment salesman: Merrell boots and sneakers, Current Design sea kayaks and gear, Kelty backpacks, a lot of big brand names. He traveled all over north and central Florida. Still, no sexual contact with other men, but when he started to attend conventions farther away, like in Las Vegas, he was alone a lot, drinking in bars where everyone was a stranger, and would continue to be one. He'd be approached and, more than half drunk, he would go to some lonely man's room. As the years passed, he continued to do it, although sometimes without a single drink. He began to kiss some of them and, occasionally, might even work out with his weekend lover in the hotel weight room. Or, after sex, go to the bar with his companion and talk football. It was so easy and uncomplicated.

When his father died and left him a parcel of money, he quit his job and moved to Crescent Beach. For show, he'd occasionally have some buxom blond come over from Gainesville for a weekend, show her off at the Club, screw her, then ship her out. But he was a confirmed bachelor. Sometimes, though, when he really got horny for a man, he'd go on a road trip, telling the guys at the Club he was going camping; but he'd head straight to Atlanta where he knew of some bars.

Craig tossed his empty beer can into the trash. Try as he might, he couldn't get that picture of Ralph, so handsome with his tanned muscles rippling under a slight sheen of sweat, out of his mind. He hadn't gone to the bars in Atlanta for a long time. Maybe it was time. He cracked another beer, grabbed a pair of earplugs, and walked down to the dock. Good ride in the airboat was what he needed. Forty-five minutes later, he returned. He got ready for bed. When he pulled up the sheets,

the picture of Ralph popped up again. That wasn't all
that popped up. He didn't fight it any longer; he didn't
want to. He reached for the lubricant in his bedside
table drawer and turned out the light.

CHAPTER ELEVEN

Rusty approached the wood-framed house on stilts. A boat with an aluminum winch and sporting a big shiny Yamaha engine was tied up to a dock across the street. The boat was spic and span with a half-dozen rigged fishing rods stuck in holders attached to the console. A couple of large coolers were in the stern. It was about nine-thirty, a cool, bright sunny morning. Rusty, wearing an Atlanta Braves baseball cap and dark glasses, had a bright orange life vest in one hand and a plastic bottle of sunscreen in the other. Jimmy appeared at the railing of the open porch deck of the house.

"You must be Rusty. Come on up for a cup of coffee; tide's just turned and we gotta wait a little for the water to come in."

Rusty climbed the stairs and shook Jimmy's calloused hand. So this is Jimmy Talbot, a shade under six feet, wiry with sinewy arms and skin sun-cured like leather. Captain was right, he thought, this man's seen his share of hard work

"You didn't need to bring that life vest; got plenty stowed on board."

"Can't swim a stroke, Jimmy, and I'm a big guy. Wanted to make sure I got a vest that can keep me up, and this one I know works; tried it out in a motel pool on the way down."

Jimmy shrugged.

"Where we'll be going, doubt if the water would come up to your neck. Pretty shallow most everywhere these parts."

A woman who was almost as tall as Jimmy, and possibly outweighed him, stepped out on to the deck.

"This here's my wife, Crystalline; but everybody calls her Crystal."

Crystal was big boned with flesh in all the right places. With those wide hips, Rusty'd bet she could pop out babies without batting an eye. Her loose brown hair hung almost to her waist and her eyes were a striking blue-gray. He found her very attractive.

"A pleasure, Ma'am. Crystalline, now that's an unusual name."

She smiled.

"My mama and daddy never got around to naming me formal-like for a long time, although Daddy kept calling me Sparkles because he said my eyes sparkled when I smiled. Mama, she said that was a ridiculous name, but got her a dictionary and looked up words that meant the same thing. Hit upon crystalline, and there you have it."

"Reckon I agree with your daddy."

"Whoa there, Rusty; you a lady's man, too?"

Rusty looked at Jimmy.

" 'Too?' "

"Heard you can take real good care of yourself."

"Word travels fast around here."

Crystal laughed.

"You can say that again. How about that coffee, Rusty?"

"Please."

"Cream or sugar."

"Just black, Ma'am"

Jimmy and Rusty sat down. They looked out to the Gulf.

"So you're a road builder."

"Was. Just retired a little while ago."

"At your age! Some people got it made."

"I worked real hard and fast, Jimmy, for quite a few years. I'm about wore out."

"You plan on retiring in these parts?"

"Don't know; maybe. I might look around some, but, right now, I just want to relax and fish."

"How much fishing have you done?"

"Not much, mostly fresh water, and…and there's something else you should know."

"What's that?"

"I get seasick."

Jimmy laughed.

"Can't swim and get seasick. Why in tarnation do you want to go fishing instead of," he looked at Rusty's hat, "going to a ballgame or something?'"

"Baseball season hasn't started yet for one thing. But, I've got stuff to take for the nausea, and, damn it, I want to go saltwater fishing; so, I'm going fishing. Simple as that."

Jimmy smiled.

"I get seasick, too."

"No way!"

"Yup, but only way out in deep water where it rolls. I tend to puke if I go out for grouper. But in close, it's more choppy-like. For some reason, I don't have a problem with that, and I wouldn't be surprised if it'll be the same for you."

Crystal came out with the coffees.

"Now don't that beat all, Rusty, having a fisherman husband who gets seasick!"

The men drank their coffee; Crystal went in to make their lunches. When she brought them out, she looked out over the water.

"Looks like the tide's about ready, Jimmy."

Jimmy looked out. "You're right. Here I go drinking coffee and yakking and not paying attention."

"How can you tell from here?"

"See that skinny stick a ways off to the left?" Jimmy asked.

"Yeah."

"If there's no oyster bar showing around it, water's deep enough. Time to git a move on."

"Wait, Jimmy, let me get your sweet tea."

She returned with a large thermos.

"Thank you for the coffee, Ma'am."

Crystal smiled.

"There'll be more of it tomorrow. Good luck."

The two men boarded the boat. With the Yamaha purring, they cast off and headed out to the Gulf. Rusty noticed a few good-sized black and white shore birds with bright orange beaks on some of the oysterbars. He could just hear their whistling over the idling engine: it sounded like the second half of whistling at a pretty girl.

"What are those?"

"Oyster catchers. Pokes around for crabs and sea worms and such."

Jimmy pushed the throttle forward and the boat planed off nicely. Their wake became a series of gentle curves as they threaded the mudflats and oyster beds. Rusty raised his voice.

"There's some more of those skinny sticks. Are they marking oyster bars, too?"

"Yep, tear hell out of a boat if you don't pay attention. Pretty much know where they all are, but a storm can change things and you get fooled sometimes."

After twenty minutes, they approached the mouth of a creek. Jimmy cut the motor and raised it up before reaching for a long pole lashed to the side of the boat. He poled towards the creek until they gently went aground.

"Far as we go. By the time we're done, tide will be a lot higher and we'll be able to motor out."

"Guess you weren't kidding about it being tough to drown around here. What are we going after, it being so shallow and all?"

"Reds."

"But they're big, aren't they?"

"Hope so," Jimmy said as he baited a hook with a snapping shrimp. "Don't usually use live bait, but I got an idea that you're pretty green with all this. Might as well start with the basics. This here's a hopper like Charley told you about."

"So that's how you knew about last night."

"Yep."

"I enjoyed meeting him and the doctor and the others. Nice bunch of fellows."

"Yep, they are. And don't get fooled none by Charley. Might come across with his miserable English as some dumb cracker, but no flies on that man. He pays attention, knows stuff that surprises you. And he's a damn fine waterman who can shrimp, oyster, and crab with the best of them... But, Rusty, lookee here," Jimmy said with a shrimp in one hand and the hook in the other. "You stick the hook in near the tail here, through this tough part so it'll hold, curve it around and come up through the back again. Although he's cinched up pretty good, he can still snap to attract fish. And this here reel is called a Zebco. Doesn't cast real far, but far enough. There's a hole over yonder, in close to the right side of the creek," he said pointing. "That's where you want to cast it...you do know how to cast?"

Rusty nodded.

"Used a rod and reel like this for bass up north."

He threw over to the hole, putting it almost in the middle.

"Nice cast. Now give it a twitch every little now and then."

Rusty twitched it, and the water exploded. His rod bent way over.

"Keep the tip up...that's it...play with him a little, let him tucker himself out."

It took a full ten minutes before Rusty landed the redfish. Jimmy measured it. He smiled up at Rusty.

"Twenty-three inches. Nice fish."

Rusty was ear to ear.

"Dang, Jimmy, dang! What a beauty! And first frigging cast!"

"And some mighty fine eating to boot," Jimmy added as he unhooked the fish and threw it into a cooler. Rusty caught two more, one of which they threw back. Jimmy told it to put on some girth and length and he would see it next year. Rusty, who had had a couple cups of coffee before going to Jimmy's, had to pee. He asked Jimmy the procedure.

"Just hang it over the side. It'll help reduce the salinity."

When Rusty zipped up, he asked, "You ever take women out fishing?"

"I haven't been guiding all that long, but yeah, some."

"What do you do if they got to pee?"

"Depends. Women is different. I had one who'd just squat off the stern, but that's rare. Mostly they have to have the men on board turn around, and for me to have the motor idle in neutral. That ways no one can hear their tinkle. Guess that embarrasses them. There was one lady who said she had to go ashore which, considering where we were, would have been a real pain in the butt. But, you got to be obliging in this business, so I said no problem. As we headed towards the nearest island, I told her to be mighty careful of all the moccasins and rattlers. Well, sir, she changed her mind in a hurry and ended up holding it for the next two hours."

Rusty laughed. The tide, he noticed, had come in just like Jimmy said it would. Jimmy lowered the motor.

"Let's go introduce you to some speckled sea trout. Not as much fun to catch, but a real pretty fish, and pretty darn tasty, too."

They headed straight out, and then south, following the coast for a few miles. Jimmy slowed down for some fishermen banging on the side of their boat."

"What are they doing?"

"Herding mullet into the net. They put the net in a big circle, with them on the inside. They make a racket to scare the fish into the net as they draw it in. Fish get hung up and then they shuck them out into coolers. But the water's still too cold: most of the good-sized mullet are a ways further out." They watched the fishermen for a few minutes. "Don't hardly seem worth it," Jimmy said as they pulled away. Jimmy resumed speed and course. In ten minutes he stopped and threw out the anchor.

"This area's got a grassy bottom and if there are any trout around, it'll be here."

Rusty continued to use live bait with success. In an hour they had caught half a dozen, varying from twelve to twenty inches. After throwing the sixth into the cooler, Jimmy rinsed his hands in the gulf.

"What say we see what Crystal packed us today?"

"You're on; I'm starved."

They opened the boxes. Fried chicken, homemade slaw, bread and butter pickles, and a brownie each. The two men ate quickly; both boxes were bare when they finished.

"That may have been the best cold fried chicken I've ever eaten," Rusty said.

Jimmy smiled.

"Crystal's a mighty fine fryer. She's always in demand to cook at the church suppers and the like. Got her an excellent reputation."

Jimmy looked at his watch and checked the bait bucket.

"Think we've about fished out this area. Aren't as many as I hoped. We got enough bait left to try one other spot. It's on the way back."

He pulled up anchor. It wasn't long before they came around a point and could see Crescent Beach way off. The water tower and blimp stood out.

"Is that a blimp, Jimmy?"

"Yep."

"For what. Pretty strange spot for a blimp."

"Smuggling."

"Marijuana?"

"That's what they say."

The Yamaha droned on smoothly. Rusty said, "Guess that figures…"

"What do you mean?"

"Oh, the new pick-ups around town, parked in front of houses that really aren't more than shacks. Sort of like where I grew up in the mountains of north Georgia. Lots of moonshine running up there. You could usually tell who was involved because he'd have a brand new pick-up or tractor or something. Owe my start in the road business because of moonshine."

"That right," was all that Jimmy said: end of conversation. An hour or so later, after catching another four trout, they headed in. At the dock, Jimmy noticed how effortlessly Rusty handed up the large coolers. Full of fish and ice, they weighed plenty. Strong man, he thought. He began to filet the fish. Soon the dock was surrounded by a dozen hungry pelicans.

"Just like chickens in the mountains, the way they fight over scraps," Rusty said, as he watched the birds.

He took a turn at the fileting. "Jeez, this isn't as easy as you make it look, Jimmy." He was having a hard time holding on to the slippery fish, and his filet was all hacked up.

"Takes some getting used to." Jimmy began putting filets into plastic baggies. " I'll put these in the freezer for you to take whenever you want."

"If every day's like today, no way I'll ever be able to eat them all."

"Whatever you don't want, we'll keep for Crystal to fry up for the church camp benefit. Have a fish fry at the beginning of the summer with all the proceeds going to kids who can't afford it. Raises a lot of money. Like I said, when Crystal's cooking, people come from all around."

They left the dock.

"You going to the bar tonight, Jimmy?"

"Yep, usually go for a couple of beers after sunset."

"Then I'll see you there. And, Jimmy, thanks. I really enjoyed today."

"My pleasure."

As he walked away, Rusty thought that he really had enjoyed the day. He also thought that Jimmy and Crystal reminded him a lot of the folks back in his Georgia mountains.

CHAPTER TWELVE

Outside the greenhouse, the sun was low and the temperature falling; inside it was warm with an organic, moist-dirt smell.

"I've got to call Minnie to make sure she knows what to do," Virginia said to Beau, while tending to one of her hanging orchids. "And I'm going to take the golf cart over to talk with Ralph about the food delivery."

A very knowledgeable horticulturist, her side of the greenhouse was full of prized and healthy flowers like the tall bright mums that defied gravity, the irises of all different hues, and her delicate, exotic orchids. Before Crescent Beach, she and Beau had lived outside the Charleston city limits in the antebellum home that had been in her family for over a hundred and fifty years. The brick walkways lined with azaleas, the large greenhouse full of rare species, and the scattered arbors and gardens were legendary. Virginia led a tour one Sunday each month, except in the spring when the azaleas were in bloom and the tours were daily. She worked as hard as the two gardeners in her employ and met with them Monday mornings for scones and tea when they put together the week's schedule. Considered a bit eccentric by the blue-blood Charleston social circle, she was forgiven for the dirt under her cut-short fingernails.

When Beau officially retired from teaching and they decided to move to Crescent Beach, Virginia had sold the house cheap to her younger sister so that the estate would remain in the family. It wasn't long before her sister had let one of the gardeners go, and over the last few years the gardens had declined and the tours ceased. Virginia knew how much work, time, and money were involved to keep everything up, but it bothered her to see the shabbiness encroach little by little. She resisted the urge to visit more often and jump back into the mix. Beau told her to let it go, that it was her sister's responsibility now. Virginia acquiesced, but, still, it was never easy when she returned, and she knew the next few days would be difficult.

Beau stopped weeding and arched his back. His side of the greenhouse was all about vegetables: greens, tomatoes, peppers, even artichokes. Beds of cold-weather vegetables were scattered around their double lot along with his lemon, lime, and grapefruit trees. He turned to Virginia.

"Charley's been lobbying pretty hard to get in that hot tub of ours. Even wanted to bet taking a hot tub against a ride in his Mustang over a poker hand the other night."

Virginia smiled.

"And, you said?"

"I said, 'What Mustang?'"

"Poor Charley. Do you think he'll ever get one?"

"He swears he's got one lined up."

"But, where's he going to get that kind of money?"

"These days, Sugah, most anyone around here might come up with a wad of cash. Even Charley. He and Jimmy go out at night on occasion and, judging by the weather, I don't believe it's for crabbing or fishing."

"Hear no evil, see no evil, speak no evil. Maybe we should tell Minnie it'd be okay to use the tub when she house-sits. Then you-know-who would be over in a second."

"That'd be fine, Sugah, long as he showers first." Beau wondered if Charley really had any little rubber ducks; anything was possible with Charley. Beau wiped his hands on the back of his jeans and looked at his watch. "I better go start packing the Caddy."

He left the greenhouse and was immediately met by Skillet who had been patiently waiting outside the door. The pair climbed the stairs and entered the living room where Skillet trotted over to his beanbag bed, circled it once, and plopped down. Beau surveyed the room as he washed his hands in the bar sink. Couch, two easy chairs, big TV, several windows, some oil landscapes on the walls, and tall bookshelves filled mostly with hard-bound American history books. A dozen or more of Virginia's bridge tournament trophies rested on the top shelf.

Beau had taught history for more than twenty-five years at Clemson University, his specialty being the Civil War. He had mostly enjoyed it, although in the latter years he began to find the life of academia sheltered, unreal, even boring. He had tired of interacting with his pompous, pipe-smoking colleagues, wearing their tweed jackets with worn leather elbow patches during the winter and their linen suits during the warmer months. There were no calluses on their hands, and when a fuse tripped, they called the electrician, or when a faucet leaked, a plumber. When he wasn't teaching or helping Virginia at home, he went on fishing and hunting trips where he met all sorts of people, many of whom were contractors, farmers, cement men, and the like. Unlike his colleagues, these men were hands-on. When an outboard motor didn't start, they'd tinker with it until it did. If a pipe burst on a cold morning at a hunting camp, they'd fix it in minutes. Beau felt useless and in-significant as he watched them take care of things. That was one big reason why he loved Crescent Beach. Talk about hands on! People made their living harvesting nature's bounty. It didn't get any more real than that. Okay, he thought, maybe there was a lack of higher education and plenty of prejudice all around, but there was so much more. There was such useful, practical knowledge that had been passed down through the generations: mother to daughter, father to son, like cooking, mechanics, foraging the woods, carpentry, boat building. Knowledge he had never been privy to. If a problem came up, any kind of problem, they figured out a solution and rolled up their sleeves and took care of it. If something broke, they fixed it. If there were no tool to fix it, then they would make one. And it certainly wasn't an easy life; just looking at those weathered, hard-lined faces spoke volumes. But there were many rewards, like the pride of making a sea-worthy boat, building a house, installing a roof that didn't leak, making a net to catch fish, providing for your family with your hands.

Beau walked over to the living room closet where he removed a false panel and pulled out a beautifully etched twelve guage double-barrel shotgun from the gun safe. Skillet jumped up and, with tail wagging and paws skidding on the hardwood floor, raced over to the door. Beau laughed.

"Not yet, Skillet. Tomorrow."

Skillet stayed at the door, looking back to Beau as he cracked the gun and held the side-by-side barrels up to the light. Clean as a whistle. He placed it in a hard leather case; Skillet was still at the door.

"Go on now, Skillet. Go lie down. We're not going anywhere today."

Skillet moped over to his bag. He didn't even circle it, just plopped down. Beau pulled out a large cooler for the five pounds of claws he had gotten from Jimmy. Nice house gift for Virginia's sister, he thought, and such a bargain: fraction of what stone crab cost in Charleston. He grabbed a bottle of scotch from the bar and stuffed it into the open suitcase Virginia had left on their bed. He snapped it shut and carried it down to the Caddy.

The 1990 Coup de Ville had low mileage and was in cherry condition: it was used only for the grocery store, doctor appointments, and, of course, road trips like to-morrow. Beau glanced towards the corner of the carport and saw that Virginia had left in the golf cart. Once a week a truck from the Piggly Wiggly grocery store deliv-ered perishable or outdated foods to Virginia's church, and she and Ralph made distributions to the poor and older people in town and out in the country. They al-ways used Ralph's little Toyota pickup because Virginia thought it would be a slap in the face to show up in the big Cadillac: people already had a hard enough time ac-cepting charity, let alone from some rich bitch in a shiny Caddy.

Beau uncoiled a hose and mixed up some soapy wa-ter in a big bucket. He began to wash the car. He was toweling it off when Virginia returned from Ralph's.

"Again, Beau? I swear, you're going to wash the paint right off that car."

He began drying the trunk.

"It had limestone all over it from that rain a couple of…" He slammed his shin against the trailer hitch. "Ouch! God damn it! Now Sugah, you…" He closed his mouth and shook his head. Virginia stifled a laugh. How many times had he done that? And she knew that he blamed her for distracting him.

"I swear, Beau, when are you going to put a bright colored tennis ball over that hitch?" she asked sweetly.

"You must have banged yourself fifty times at least!" She looked out over the Gulf. Sunset wasn't far off. "Dear, why don't I uncover the hot tub while you make us a pitcher of martinis. Sun's going down soon and looks like it might be a good one."

Beau never stayed angry long. How could he with this woman who was the absolute love of his life? In fifteen minutes he had the pitcher of martinis made and, in their bathrobes, they descended to the hot tub which was up off the ground and discreetly walled on three sides by a jasmine covered trellis. In another month and a half, the jasmine would flower and they'd breathe its sweet perfume, but for now it was a thick green screen. The open side faced the Gulf where the sun was barely visible because of all the clouds. Skillet climbed up to his rug-covered perch along side the tub while Beau and Virginia disrobed. Settled in, side by side, Beau poured the drinks, putting two olives on a toothpick in Virginia's. They touched glasses and took a sip.

"Retirement's not so bad, huh, Sugah?"

"We are very fortunate, Beau. We should never forget that." She took a thoughtful sip of her martini. "I feel guilty that Ralph's delivering the food without me tomorrow. He said no problem, of course, and that he had enlisted Crystal to fill in for me. I swear that man's a prince. This community is very, very lucky to have him...and he's a hunk, too."

Beau turned to look at her.

"A hunk?"

"Well built. When I rang his doorbell, he didn't come to the door right away; probably didn't hear me because of the music that was blasting. So, I rang it again, and, finally, out he came wearing a bathing suit and one of those basketball T-shirts. If he had any more muscles, Beau, I swear he'd pop. I never realized it."

"Guess you've never seen him out rowing his scull."

Skillet started licking his balls, loudly enough so Virginia glanced over.

"Skillet, stop that!"

Skillet looked up, tail thumping. Beau smiled.

"You know why he does that, don't you?"

Virginia rolled her eyes.

" 'Because he can.' Old joke, Beau."

Chuckling, Beau reached for the pitcher and replenished their glasses. The sun went down; some color, but not a lot.

"I'll give it five or six minutes to brighten up," Beau said.

"I agree."

In ten minutes, the sky was on fire. The jasmine walls, like blinders, focused their view on a solid block of mixed gold, red, and blue hues. For the next twenty minutes, it was breathtaking. By the time it faded, the pitcher was empty and Skillet was asleep. Virginia shifted a little and closed her eyes, luxuriating in the warm bubbly water. Beau looked at her. How he loved her. She was still beautiful at sixty-two, even with her silver hair. Her breasts bobbed in the hot tub; the sight never failed to excite him. He stretched out. He was a tall man, six feet three, large boned, and, now, with a large boner.

"Could I have one of your olives, Sugah?"

Virginia opened her eyes, and pulled the toothpick out of her glass. She turned and held it just in front of his mouth. One of her breasts pressed into his arm. He bit off one of the olives, she ate the other. As she turned to drop the toothpick back into her glass, her free hand inadvertently grazed Beau's erection.

"My, my," she said, turning back to gently caress him. "You know, dear, Ralph may be a hunk, but I doubt very much if he has a hunk like yours."

Beau put an arm around her shoulders and pulled her close. His voice became professorial. "You know what Teddy Roosevelt said, don't you, Sugah?"

"What's that?"

"'Speak softly, but carry a big stick.'"

CHAPTER THIRTEEN

"Hot diggety dawg!" Charley exclaimed as he stuffed a thick wad of bills into his jeans' pocket. "I'ma off to Chiefland, Jimmy," he said, doing a little jig. "Next time you see me, I'll be a'driving that old Mustang. Called the feller last night and he's going to have her a'waiting for me."

Jimmy couldn't help but smile, seeing Charley so lit up.

"Taking your lawnmower in for trade, is he?"

"Now don't you go making fun of my lawnmower, too. It's been a right handy piece of equipment."

"How are you getting there? Minnie's at the prison and I've got Rusty coming. And Crystal, she's out delivering church food with Ralph."

"Tiny's taking me down."

The two men saw Rusty walking up the street, life jacket under his arm.

"I swear, that man don't go nowheres without that life jacket," Charley said.

"Charley, don't you go off on some road trip with that new car. Blimp's coming down directly and we got a shrimper on its way. We're going out again soon."

"That's a ten-four."

Rusty came up to them.

"Morning, Rusty," Charley said with a toothy grin. "Reg'lar beauty of a day!"

"And a good morning to you, Charley. You seem in good spirits."

"Sure am. Yep, that's for sure…Well, reckon I'll be moseying along. Good luck fishing. Later, Jimmy."

Charley almost skipped down the road. Rusty turned to Jimmy.

"What's up with him?"

"Finally getting that car he's always talking about."

"That Mustang! What, just get an inheritance or something?"

Jimmy shrugged.

Drug money, Rusty knew. New pickups, outboard motors, boats, and now a pricey antique Mustang in this backwater town. Jimmy motioned towards the dock.

"Boat's all set and lunch's in the cooler. Let's get a move on; we're going down the coast a ways and I want that tide still coming in."

A few minutes later, they were heading out the main channel. When they passed the last channel marker, Rusty looked back towards town.

"Still say it seems odd to see a blimp in these parts."

"Take a good look because it'll be down by the time we get back. You probably won't see it up again for at least a week."

"Why? Weather's fine and all."

"Got electrical problems."

Jimmy put the throttle down three-quarters and began threading the oyster bars as they headed south. How the heck did Jimmy know that? Rusty wondered. The decision to lower the blimp had only been made late yesterday afternoon, and he had only learned about it when he had checked in with the ensign this morning.

They passed several creeks emptying into the bay. Jimmy described the attributes of each. When they approached a long, narrow beach fringed by cabbage palms and small live oaks, he took off his Ray Bans.

"Pass me them binoculars for a second, would you, Rusty?"

He trained them on a boat that was pulled up on the beach.

"Well, I'll be. About damn time!"

Jimmy was smiling.

"What's up?"

"That's Norm and Tammy. They been eyeballing each other for months now, but neither one of them's been brave enough to make the first move. But something's going on now for sure; looks like they're getting ready to have themselves a little private picnic."

Jimmy reached for the aerosol air horn below the controls and blasted it a couple of times. Norm and Tammy looked up and waved briefly before turning back to the picnic basket Norm had packed. The wind had recently shifted and was coming out of the east. What breeze there was brought the no-seeums out of the woods.

"Not such a great idea to come here," Norm said, brushing his hand back and forth in front of his face. "You don't have any bug stuff by any chance?"

Tammy, also brushing at the sand fleas, shook her head. Norm shut the basket.

"Come on. Let's follow Jimmy and Rusty toward the Keys and anchor off Bird Island."

They jumped into Norm's Carolina Skiff and were soon cruising in Jimmy's fading wake. They sat together on the wide, cushioned bench behind the controls, the sun in their faces, and the rush of air taking the itch out of the bug bites. Tammy ran her fingers through her hair. They didn't say anything until they reached Bird Island where they anchored in the eight feet deep channel a hundred yards off shore. The water was clear enough to see the bottom, and the trees on the island had a hodgepodge of noisy sea birds sitting in them.

A colony of white pelicans was on the beach. Norm opened the basket, announcing its contents.

"My fried chicken. Some of Maybelline's coleslaw, some crackers and Charley's mullet dip, sweet and sour pickles, chips, and some brownies I also made for dessert. And you have your choice of sweet tea or white wine to wash it down."

Tammy smiled.

"You went all out."

"Aw, shucks."

"This is a celebration. White wine for me."

Norm filled their plastic cups, then tapped hers.

"Here's to having a good time together."

"I'll drink to that and also to this weather: I'll bet it might even reach eighty today."

After sipping her wine, Tammy pulled out her shirttails and tied them in a knot, exposing her flat midriff. Hell of a figure, he thought: maybe not too bow heavy, but more than a handful was a waste anyway.

"Good job on the chicken, Norm," she said wiping her mouth with a paper towel. He agreed.

"Not bad, but doesn't hold a candle to Maybelline's. Don't believe anybody can cook chicken or fish like she can, except maybe Crystal. People drive thirty miles just for her fried mullet...Maybelline, what a name to be saddled with. How do you suppose her parents came up with that one?"

"Chuck Berry fans."

"Right, the song."

"1955, his first single."

"More like '56, I'd say."

Tammy wiped her mouth again.

"Nope."

Norm looked at her. Pretty, and pretty damn sure of herself. He stuck out his hand.

"Want to bet?"

"Sure. If I win, you treat me to a candlelight dinner at your place, and vice-versa."

They shook, but Norm didn't let go of her hand. He drew her to him.

"Sealed with a kiss," he said. It was a long kiss. When they surfaced, Tammy was starry-eyed. She smiled at Norm.

"I like bets like that: they're a win-win."

The boat wasn't particularly comfortable: the only places to sit were either behind the wheel or in the fixed fishing chair in the bow. After lunch, they continued to share the seat behind the wheel. With the full sun and heat of the day, the gentle lapping of the water, and their full stomachs, the conversation lulled. Norm's eyelids were fluttering when Tammy suddenly put a hand to his cheek.

"What do you say we go skinny dipping?"

Norm's eyes flew open.

"Ahh," was all he managed to say.

Tammy's hands were already on her shirt's top buttons.

"Tammy, the water might be seventy degrees at best!"

She started unbuttoning.

"I'm not having you go to sleep on me during our first date. C'mon!"

Off came the shirt, then the sexy black bra. She turned away from him to remove her slacks and the skimpy panties that matched the bra. She climbed up to the gunwale, and neatly dove in. She smiled up to his shocked face.

"I told you I'm not a schoolgirl, Norm. Water's just fine. Jump in."

Norm quickly shed his clothes. Like Tammy, he turned his back to her, then jumped off the other side. It had been quite awhile since he had been with a beautiful naked woman, and he didn't want her to see that he was already aroused. The cold water took his breath away, and quickly shrunk him back to normal. He swam around the boat.

* * *

Ralph was bent over, puking into the ditch alongside the road. When nothing more came up, he staggered over to the passenger side of his pickup.

"Do you mind driving, Crystal?"

"Not at all." She dug into her purse. "Here."

Ralph took the handkerchief, and wiped his mouth. "Thanks."

As they pulled out into the road, Ralph, still pallid, said, "If only I hadn't asked what it was."

They had been delivering food to an old woman who lived with her grown sons in a weathered-gray cracker shack in the woods, way down at the end of a narrow limestone road. The house was surrounded by tall longleaf pine and a lone, very large Magnolia tree. Sawtooth palmetto grew in clumps everywhere under the pine. Wearing a gingham dress and long apron, the woman came out of the cabin, wiping her hands on a towel. Ralph went around to the rear of the truck to fetch a box of food.

"Why, thank you kindly, Ralph," she said, as she examined the contents. "It's always a treat to get some store vittles from y'all."

She looked up at the sun.

"Have y'all eaten dinner yet, because if you haven't, you gotta set down with me. I had all the fixin's laid out for my boys, but seems Tommy and Butch done stood me up. They went'a hog hunting this morning and my guess is the dogs caught a scent. Sure hope one of them dogs don't get tore up again; I'ma running out of things to give Dr. Norm for all of his patching. Anyways, I'd be mighty proud if you'd take my boys' place at the table."

The woman wouldn't take no for an answer. They
dutifully followed her into a good-sized dining room,
maneuvering around wicker baskets full of garden
vegetables before sitting down at a large oak table.
The old woman uncovered a large platter of swamp
cabbage, a bowl of sweet potatoes, and some sort of
lunchmeat in a gelatinous mix that Ralph didn't recognize. After thanking God for this bounty, the woman filled their glasses with sweet tea and served them.
Ralph loved swamp cabbage and sweet potatoes. He
eagerly dug in. When his mouth was clear, he said,
"This swamp cabbage is delicious, cooked just right,
nice and tender."

The old woman was pleased and smiled. Ralph was
always surprised how good her teeth were. Must be good
well water, he thought.

"Goes by a different name up north, don't it?" the
old woman asked.

"Yes, Ma'am; hearts of palm, they call it. But usually
it's served raw in salads. They consider it a delicacy and
get a good price for it. " Ralph began eating the meat
conglomeration. Pretty darn good, whatever it was.

"We used to eat it every day when that old scoundrel
of a husband of mine was around. About the only thing
he was good for was to cut them cabbage palms. Never
could keep a job with the mills or logging crews. Butch,
guess he's a chip off the old block because he brings
some home most every day. Even sells some on occasion. If you ever be needing any, Ralph, just you let me
know."

Everyone knew Butch. He was the younger son and,
like his father, was an infamous n'er do well. He was a
loud-mouthed redneck who had never held a job more
than a few days. If he had any money, he spent it on
beer. Hunting seasons and hunting licenses didn't apply to him, and he would cut the heart of palm out of

someone's front yard tree rather than walk fifty feet into the woods. The game warden had tried for years to catch him, but without success.

The old woman noticed Ralph's plate was almost empty. "It's good to see a man with an appetite, Ralph. Help yourself," she said, passing the plates of food over. "Yep, about the only thing that worthless husband liked to do was drink his cane and corn liquor." She looked over to Crystal who nodded. "Crystal here knew him well enough. He used to raise hell in town when he had a dollar or two. When I laid down the law about his drinking, the miserable cur, bless his heart, left me and the boys. And they was just little tykes back then."

When she paused to take a sip of sweet tea, Ralph asked, "Ma'am, what kind of meat is this?"

"You never had headcheese before, Ralph?" she answered.

He looked down to his plate.

"Headcheese?"

"Yes, sir. From a razorback my sons kilt a week ago Sunday."

"So, pork then; but it's so creamy. I'd think a wild pig would be leaner," he said before taking another forkful.

"Them's the brains makes it like that."

Ralph stopped chewing.

"Brains..."

"Yep, and the eyeballs."

Ralph slowly put his fork down.

"It's quite a production, I kin tell you that. Got to first saw that old head in half. Tommy done that for me. Then you gotta boil it for hours until the brains, lips, eyeballs, ears, tongue, everything's just falling off the bone, so's to speak because, of course, it being the head and not a bone. Well, come to think of it, guess it is a bone. Anyways, it's the pig's skull's and feets' natural gelatin that makes it sorta jelly-like. Add some spices, put it in that there mold hanging on the wall yonder, chill it, and your all set."

Ralph's fork remained on his plate.

"What's the matter, Ralph?" the old woman asked.

"Guess I filled up too much with the cabbage and sweet potatoes, Ma'am."

Crystal reached over and took his plate.

"Can't let this go to waste," and she quickly ate everything. Ralph watched her in sickening awe.

When Crystal and Ralph left the houses, they hadn't gone very far before Ralph pulled over to puke. When he caught his breath, he looked over to Crystal.

"And you ate all of it, and half mine, without batting an eye!"

"Ralph, I was born in Perry and have lived in Crescent Beach most all my life. I don't know how many times I've eaten headcheese. I thought hers was delicious."

"Truth is," he said climbing into the truck, "guess it didn't taste too bad, but picturing all those ingredients like eyeballs and lips made…Oh God…"

Ralph jumped out again but only got two feet from the car before he was sick again. Crystal looked away as he retched several times. He got back into the truck. After a mile or so, he said, "Now you don't have to go tell Jimmy about this. I'd never hear the end of it at poker if you did."

Crystal smiled mischievously.

"Maybe, maybe not. How about you making me one of those flower arrangements you're so good at?"

"Crystal, that's blackmail!"

"Take your choice."

He didn't have a choice.

"Irises or lilies?"

"Both."

Ralph sighed and shook his head, but he was already arranging the flowers in his head. He loved arranging flowers, and Crystal knew that. After awhile he reached for the clipboard and looked at their list.

"What do you say we take the limestone road back through the swamp when we're done with the deliveries? Only three more."

"Don't believe that's a good idea what with the rain we had last week. Takes the water awhile to find its way to the Gulf and there's a good chance it's just getting to the road now. I don't have to tell you that your truck doesn't have the best clearance or four wheel drive."

"Oh, it'll be fine. I've gone through plenty of times with water over the road."

After the final delivery, Ralph, feeling better, took the wheel. In a few minutes they were on the limestone road that, although always rough-going with the potholes and washboards, was only a third the distance back to Crescent Beach.

"I love this road," Ralph said, as he looked out at the cypress knees and trees in the swamp. "Always something to see if you pay attention, and I don't mean the beer cans. All sorts of birds, gators, coons, otters, even a panther if you're really lucky. April and May are my two favorite months out here: the wildflowers, especially those irises in April, are spectacular. Even the huge thistles are pretty and the butterflies love them.

"But the beer cans are an eyesore," he continued, shaking his head and turning to Crystal. "I'll never understand why people just chuck them out. I mean," he said waving a hand expansively out the window, "surrounded by all this beauty, how could you? Such a violation! Last time I rode my bike out here, I counted over a hundred. I'll bet I've picked up over a thousand the last couple of years."

They came up to the first overflowing culvert. Ralph got out and looked.

"No prob; plenty shallow and hard bottom," he said, as he climbed back into the truck. Crystal was silent.

They continued on, passing through three more shallow rivulets slowly eating into the limestone. The swamp water widened, narrowing the road, and scattered small groups of white ibises and snowy egrets were feeding, mostly on the eastern side. They spooked and flew in front of them a ways before veering off to the swamp.

"I told you no problem, Crystal, less than a mile to go."

Crystal still didn't say anything. They came around a bend, and Ralph slammed on the brakes.

"Damn, looks like a lake out there."

"You might want to turn around now, Ralph."

"But, we're so close! It can't be that bad. I'll check it out."

Wading birds were everywhere. Ralph removed his shoes and socks while Crystal put her hands behind her head and leaned back. He waded in about a hundred feet, the water barely above his ankles. He returned to the truck.

"Piece of cake, Crystal. Hard as a rock. We'll just go slow."

"Ralph, do you have a chain?"

"Sure, behind your seat."

"Good. We'll need it to get pulled out. If the water is in the road this far away from the culvert near the highway, we're going to have problems."

"Oh, you're just a worrywart. We'll be fine."

Ralph drove slowly, creating a wake. Almost imperceptibly, the water deepened. They could see the highway off in the distance now, but the water was at least eight inches high. Ralph kept looking down, outside his window.

"Maybe you were right, Crystal; but, there's no way we can turn around now."

Suddenly they hit a good-sized, hidden pothole. Ralph floored it, and the front wheel just pulled out, but then the rear drive wheel dropped in and the truck stalled. Ralph got it started again, but they couldn't get out. Ralph gunned it, causing the tire to madly spin, digging the hole deeper and spraying water everywhere.

"You keep doing that, Ralph, and you'll have your motor underwater too."

She was right. He sat there for a minute, weighing options; they didn't have many. He knew he'd have to wade to the highway to find someone to pull them out. Embarrassed, he asked, "Crystal, could you scooch up so I can get that chain out?"

As she leaned forward, she said, "Too bad we don't have a fishin' pole. I'll bet there are some hungry catfish around."

"I just hope there aren't any moccasins."

He laid the chain on the hood and started to wade towards the highway. Crystal stuck her head out the window. "Make that two flower arrangements, Ralph."

Two hours later and ten dollars poorer, Ralph drove across the cattle gap at the edge of town. Crystal and Ralph were silent as they passed Ralph's house and continued on down Main Street. When they approached Crystal's house, they could see a boat slowly coming in from the Gulf. Two men were in the stern, and the cowling was off the motor.

"Isn't that Jimmy's boat?"

Crystal nodded.

"Look's like he's had his problems today, too," she said casting a meaningful glance at Ralph who had been eating humble pie since getting stuck.

Out in the boat, Jimmy replaced the cowling, and turned to Rusty.

"Damnation! Brand spanking new and giving me problems already! " He spat in the water. "And the last thing I feel like doing is to trailer this boat all the way up to the marina in Perry."

"I don't think you need to, Jimmy. Believe all it needs is some tinkering with the carburetor; it's just a mite out of whack. These new engines are great, but more finicky than the old ones. Give me an hour or so and I'll have it purring like a kitten."

"You know all about outboard motors?"

"Any motor that burns gasoline or diesel, I can fix. Remember how I told you about growing up in the mountains where there was a lot of moonshining?"

Jimmy nodded.

"Guess it doesn't matter none if I talk about it now, seeing's as it was so long ago. I was one of those runners. I know as much about motors as you do about fish. Had to. If a motor wasn't running right, it could mean jail time. So, how about you get us a six-pack from the store? I always work up a good thirst when I'm tinkering."

Twenty minutes later, Jimmy was cleaning their catch on the dock and watching Rusty. They both had an open beer. A small pile of tools was on top of the cooler in the stern of the boat, and Jimmy had set up a large fan to blow the sand fleas away. Rusty's bright orange life jacket lay between them.

"So, you were running moonshine," Jimmy said, after tossing a fish carcass out to the pelicans below the dock. There was a mad scramble. "What was that like?"

"Exciting, really. And fun, that is if you liked to risk your life at a hundred twenty, a hundred thirty miles an hour. You made awful good money and some good friends, too. And you learned how to drive and work on cars, that's for sure.

"I had an old beat-up Ford Fairlane that looked like maybe it could go sixty. But we souped her up with four barrels and bored her out so she could do a hundred and forty easy. Had her decked out with extra leafs so she'd ride high with a heavy load of 'shine' in the trunk and backseats. Made an awful lot of trips with that old girl."

Jimmy thought about the false waterlines painted on the shrimp boats that brought in the bales.

"But then the feds started using planes with infrared cameras, and that was the beginning of the end."

Jimmy thought about the blimp.

"That why you got out of it?"

Picking up a tiny screwdriver, Rusty shook his head.

"Nope. Got busted."

Jimmy waited for him to continue, but Rusty was concentrating on adjusting a jet in the carburetor. When he put the screwdriver back down, Jimmy asked, "What happened?"

"Was being chased, and I was going at a pretty good clip when my engine blew a head gasket and oil sprayed all over the windshield. Couldn't see and went off the road. Lucky I wasn't killed, but they nabbed me." He picked up the screwdriver again and looked up at Jimmy before turning back to the motor. "It didn't turn out too bad though because the judge made me a deal: serve two years in 'Nam, and I'd be a free man. I served six over there as an MP.

"Some of the guys back home were real lucky. They were never nabbed and they put all that driving experience and tinkering to good use. A bunch of them became stock car drivers and mechanics, following in the steps of my godfather, Junior Johnson; he was one of the first in the Winston Cup Series, and I believe he was just about the best NASCAR racer there ever was. Of course, I'm a bit biased."

Jimmy's mouth dropped. He was an avid race fan.

"You mean *the* Junior Johnson!"

"The same. Like I say, he was my godfather. He about taught me everything I know. We'd go out on back Georgia roads and race some, sorta. I never beat him, of course, but I learned a hell of a lot. And, honest to God, a couple times I swear I was right on his bumper when we crossed the finish line. But, then again, maybe he was just being nice and all…There, all set. Let's take this baby for a spin," Rusty said as he snapped the cowling back on. Looking over the stern, Rusty said, "Looks like you beefed up this transom some and got some brackets on the motor that sure don't look factory made."

Jimmy, filet knife poised in mid air, was still trying to digest that this man was the godson of Junior Fucking Johnson! Almost in a daze, he looked down towards the transom and motor.

"Yeah, I had it adapted some so I could disengage the hydraulic motor lift. If we're running fast after a storm or something and the channel's shifted and we hit hard, that motor will flip up. Not the best thing to happen, but at least the prop and lower unit shouldn't get all stove up and that extra thick transom should hold." Jimmy tossed the last filet into the cooler and grabbed a couple fresh brews. "Let's go check her out."

Rusty undid the lines. Once outside the channel, Jimmy pushed the throttle to three quarters. There was no hesitation. He opened her up, and she was as smooth as silk, no vibration or missing whatsoever. Rusty guessed they were doing over forty.

"Damn, Rusty. You got it running better than it ever has." He shook Rusty's hand. "That just earned you a dinner for starters. What say we head back and see what Crystal can whip up? Then let's us open a bottle of rye. I want to hear more about you and Junior."

Rusty smiled.

"Sounds good to me, Jimmy."

CHAPTER FOURTEEN

Beau looked up from his cards and noticed Skillet sitting in front of the wide-open kitchen door, looking in with his tail sweeping the floor behind him.

"Skillet, quit flirting with those hot dogs and get over here where you belong."

Skillet got up immediately and returned to his spot underneath the table. Norm, Rusty, Jimmy, Tiny, Ralph, and Craig, intent on their cards, shifted their legs to accommodate him.

"Yours to open, Rusty," Beau said.

He threw in two quarters.

"Fifty cents to you, Jimmy."

"I see that, Beau."

He tossed in the coins, with the others following except Ralph who threw in his cards.

"No guts, no glory, Ralphie," Craig said.

"I've got nothing, Craig, and I like to start out with something. I'm not a bluffer like you."

Blowhard's more like it, Norm thought. The game was five-card draw, and no one bumped the bet.

"I'll take two," Rusty said. "Where's Charley tonight?"

"Washing the Mustang. Expect he'll be over directly. He wants to show her off. Three, Beau," Jimmy said.

The others drew one each.

Virginia's words echoing in his mind, Beau said, "He better be careful or he'll wash the paint right off that car."

Rusty upped the bet.

"A buck to stay in."

Jimmy dropped out, as did Tiny and Norm. Craig smiled at Rusty, and said, "Your buck, and three more."

Beau threw in the four dollars, and Rusty his three plus three more. Craig folded. Norm laughed and said, "Guess Ralph was right, Craig."

Beau put his three dollars in and called. Rusty laid down his cards.

"Full house, queens and eights, Beau."

"That beats me; full house, nines and sevens."

"Oh, Lord! He's done it again, Beau," Tiny exclaimed pushing out his chair and standing up. Tiny had a very acute sense of smell. It took the others a full five seconds to realize an Alpo fart was wafting up from beneath the table.

"Pee-yuu!" Ralph exclaimed and left the table.

Norm, wondering how Tiny could possibly be a fisherman with such a sensitive sense of smell, also got up. Beau was soon the only one in his seat; the others were at the open window. Beau looked under the table.

"Don't you pay them any attention, Skllet," he said, giving the dog a pat. "You're just doing what comes natural." A steady thump, thump, thump came from under the table.

"Here comes Charley," Jimmy said. "And he's got the top down."

Charley tooted the horn a couple times as he parked the fire engine red Mustang directly below the street-side deck. Everyone in the bar stepped out for a look. He revved the engine once before turning it off and looked up at the crowd, proud as punch. Charley draped an arm over the passenger bucket seat.

"Well, boys, what'cha think of my new rig? She's a beauty, ain't she?"

Tiny went back to the poker table to grab his full bottle of beer. He returned to the edge of the deck, elbowing a couple men out of the way.

"What I think, Charley, is that new rig of yours needs to be christened." Tiny put a thumb over the bottle and began to give it a good shake. Panic painted Charley's face. He quickly started the car and flung it into reverse just as Tiny removed his thumb. To hoots of laughter, a torrent of beer arched towards the convertible as the tires squealed. Tiny missed, but just barely. Charley was hopping mad.

"That ain't a bit funny, Tiny, notta bit! This here interior is gen-yoo-wine leather. You could have ruined it, know that!'" he said from out of range and putting up the top.

Tiny had tears in his eyes. He stopped laughing long enough to say, "I just wanted to scare you a mite, Charley. Believe me, I wouldn't of let your 'gen-yoo-wine' leather git wet. We gotta live here in this same old town and you're my friend. I was just having some fun. Now git on up here so you can win some gas money for that beauty, and she is a beauty, make no mistake."

The crowd, once they stopped laughing, agreed with Tiny: she was a beauty. Charley, basking in their compliments, made his way up to the deck. When he sat down at the poker table, he was proud as a peacock.

Beau said, "Charley, Skillet and I took a ride past the *Ray* this morning and your yard looked like a gopher had gone beserk. Holes and piles of dirt everywhere. What's that all about?" When Charley hesitated, Beau continued, "Now, don't go telling me that Skillet was responsible: he's been with me ever since we got back from Charleston."

Charley avoided Beau's eyes.

"Trying to locate my septic tank. Had me a heck of a time."

Tiny snorted.

"Right, Charley. Everybody knows you got a straight pipe to the canal."

"Used to be one," Charley countered.

"My bet's that you buried something when you was drunk and you couldn't remember where. And I'm also thinking it kinda odd that the next day after all your digging, I take you to git yourself that fancy automobile."

Charley shrugged.

"It's a free country, Tiny. You kin think what you want."

The sun had gone down and Tammy turned on the lights. When she took drink orders at the poker table, she placed a hand lightly on Norm's shoulder. Everyone noticed. She left to fetch the beers, and Charley smiled at Norm.

"Well, I'll be doggoned, Doc. Here I'm away for only a day and you done made the moves on Miss Tammy! Why I..."

Charley was interrupted by a cacophony of squeals and barks from the kitchen. It sounded like a boarding kennel. Skillet sprung up, banging his head hard enough on the table to spill Norm's drink.

"Easy, Skillet; it's jest them hot doggies going for their walk," Charley said.

Maybelline appeared at the kitchen door with four straining dachshunds on leashes. Skillet, peering out from under the table, greeted them with a muted woof and a slow tail wag that thumped against Charley's thigh. One of the dogs, hackles raised, growled at Skillet.

"That's Mean-ey. He's the ornery one," Charley explained to Rusty. He pointed at the others. "Them there is Eeney and Miney. They're the two little girls, though hard to tell, them being so fat. And that one who's about to pee on your chair is Moe. He's dumber than molasses."

Maybelline took offense.

"Eenie and Miney are plump, Charley, and Moe's not dumb. He just takes his time doing things."

"Eenie, Meeney, Miney, and Moe?" Rusty said, disbelievingly.

"Who's on first?" Norm quipped.

"Who's on first, Doc?" Charley asked.

"Old joke, Charley," Norm answered.

Rusty stood and stuck a hand out to Maybelline. He towered over her. She was maybe five one, or two, and as round as her dogs. In fact, Rusty thought, she kind of looked like them.

"Ma'am, I'm Rusty. I want to thank you for the excellent victuals you've been feeding me these last few days." He looked down at the dachshunds. "And mighty fine looking animals you got there. Had them long?"

"Why thank you, Mr. Rusty," Maybelline said, and sat down in Rusty's chair. Beau shook his head at Rusty, and Jimmy leaned back and folded his hands across his chest.

"They're a hundred percent purebreds, unlike all the other mongrels here in town."

"I beg your pardon," Beau said.

"Other than Skillet, that is. Eenie and Meenie here are brother and sister. Got them from a breeder in Gainesville in eighty-nine...or was it eighty-eight? No, it was eighty-nine, I'm sure of it. Anyway, that makes them youngsters still. Eenie was the runt of the litter which I'm thinking is why she's always been so sweet. You're a regular sweetheart, aren't you Eenie," she said, bending down to pet her. "Now, Meenie always been a little cantankerous, I don't know why, but he is. Still, he's a good dog, and he's a good watchdog. No one comes up to the house without me knowing it. Why just three nights ago he started barking like heck at someone at about two in the morning. There's been a bunch of petty thievery lately, mostly fishing poles and such. Joe Cherry and Amos Butler both lost batteries two weeks ago. Taken right out of their boats, too! And according to the sheriff's deputy, they don't even have a lead. I got some ideas about who's responsible, but I don't think I'll make it public just yet. But, getting back to whoever it was came by my place the other night, he skedaddled thanks to Meenie."

Rusty, politely standing, shifted his weight from one foot to the other. He looked over at Jimmy who shrugged.

"Now, Miney and Moe are brother and sister too. They come from a litter of six that I had to drive up to Tallahassee to get.   And don't pay no mind to Charley, here, Mr. Rusty. Moe is not dumb, he just is real careful-like, cautious, you might say, and takes his time doing things. And Miney might be the best one of them all, not that I play favorites, mind you. She…"

Tammy, setting three beers down on the table, said, "Maybelline, I think Moe really has to go outside."

Moe had stopped sniffing the table leg and was backing up to it. He raised a leg in slow motion.   Charley stamped his foot and scared him enough so he lowered it, still in slow motion.

"Really, Maybelline," Tammy repeated, "I do think Moe's got to go outside, plus Minnie's got the kitchen by herself and I'm too busy at the bar to help her while you walk your dogs," she added.

"Oh, all right, Miss Tammy." She gave Charley the evil eye as she untangled the leashes and dogs. "Charley, that wasn't very nice to scare Moe like that."

"Was that or clean up a puddle of pee, Maybelline. Was jest saving someone a messy job. Don't worry, I like Moe good enough, even though he's 'tarded some."

"Retarded, Charley," Norm said.

"Whatever."

Maybelline looked at Norm.

"He's not retarded, Dr. Norm."

Norm held his hands up.

"I didn't mean…"

"Come on Maybelline," Tammy said. "Time's a'wasting."

When Maybelline stood, the leashes snapped taut and she was quickly pulled to the door. Beau said, "I swear that woman should have a chariot."

"Ben Hur," Norm said.

Beau looked gratefully at Tammy. "Thanks, Tammy. We owe you one." Rusty sat back down. "Rusty, way it is here, you never ask Maybelline a question, never, no matter how simple, unless you got at least half an hour to kill…Now, who's damn deal is it anyway?"

The men played several hands. When Maybelline returned to the kitchen, Minnie came out and stood behind Charley, placing her hands on his shoulders. Charley, with a shit-eating grin, looked around the table.

"See what happens, fellers, when a man gets hisself a fancy car. The women is all over him. Can't help it. Guess I'll just have to give this lovely lady here," he said giving Minnie's hand a pat, "a ride under the stars to-night when she's done work, and, what with the wind in her hair, she…"

"When you're finished waxing eloquent, Charley, the bet's to you," Beau said. "Minnie, I want to thank you again for taking care of the house while we were away."

"No need to thank me, Beau. And those quail! We cooked 'em up last night. They were delicious."

"I'll raise you fifty cents," Charley said. "Hardly a mouthful each, and I had to spit out a little lead time to time, but tasty enough, I'll grant you. Did you find the present I left you?"

"Yes, Charley."

Charley waited a couple beats.

"And?"

"I'm glad to hear it was a present."

"Why's that?"

"Because Skillet found it before we did and I imagine it doesn't look much like it did when you left it. And it doesn't float any more, either."

"Dang!" Charley said.

"I'll raise Charley's bet by another fifty cents," Rusty said. What are we talking about here, gentlemen?"

"My rubber ducky. Had it for a long time, too. Was my favorite. I left him on top of Beau's hot tub." Charley looked back to Beau. "And was hoping maybe I might visit him from time to time."

Beau didn't say anything. Craig threw in his cards.

"I'm out. Bet you have some rubber duckies, too, Ralphie." Craig said before draining the last of his Bud.

Ralph ignored him. Charley said, "I swear, Craig, the more beers you have the more attention you pay Ralph here. Don't you ever git tired of giving him shit?"

"Watch your language, Charley," Minnie said as she returned to the kitchen.

Craig paid no attention to Charley.

"Don't know why you're in real estate, Ralphie. Seems to me interior decorating be more up your alley."

Ralph smiled thinly at Craig.

"I don't believe I'd make much money around here doing that."

"Then I guess you'll just have to stick with your flower arrangements. Excuse me, gents, while I grab me another brew."

"The pot's yours Jimmy. About the biggest tonight," Beau said.

Jimmy raked in the pile of quarters and dollar bills. Ralph asked him, "Did Crystal say anything about our food delivery yesterday?"

Jimmy looked up from stacking the quarters.

"No, why?"

"Oh, nothing. Just curious. Was a long day."

There was a commotion over by the bar. A fisherman cleared a table of the plates and bottles, and two burly fishermen sat down opposite each other. Bets were being made. Craig stood there watching with a fresh beer in his hand. Rusty looked questioningly at Ralph.

"Arm wrestling. You can almost set your watch by it, usually begins around nine, nine-thirty. Big sport around here. You just hope it doesn't turn into fisticuffs."

Rusty looked at his watch. Nine-forty. Voices and laughter picked up by the bar. The match didn't last long. The taller fisherman was soon holding and flexing his right forearm. The other man, much shorter but built like a fire hydrant, was treated to beers. Craig returned to the table.

"Have you ever arm wrestled, Ralphie?" he asked as he sat down.

"Nope. And don't plan to."

"That figures: man's game."

Craig always managed to piss Jimmy off at some point during poker nights. Tonight was no exception.

"I got twenty dollars here says Ralph can beat you arm wrestling, Craig," Jimmy said, slapping down a bill in the middle of the table.

Everyone at the table was surprised, especially Craig. Craig took a swig of beer, thinking why not—it'd be an easy twenty. But then he remembered how fit Ralph had looked out on the water. Might not be so easy, and the bar was jam-packed; it'd be a disaster if he lost. And Jimmy wasn't one to throw away his money. Craig laughed.

"I don't think Ralphie here would be up for that,"
he said.

Ralph backed him up immediately.

"Craig's right. Put your money away, Jimmy. I don't
want to arm wrestle anybody."

Norm was watching Craig closely. He reached into
his back pocket for his wallet. All he had was a ten and
a five.

"I think Craig here looks a little nervous," Norm said
in a loud voice. "Maybe he's bluffing again. I'll put fifteen on Ralph."

They were drawing interest from the bar and soon
the table was surrounded. Bets were made, most everyone wanting to bet on Craig. It was soon impossible for
either to back out. A crowd formed around the table,
even Maybelline came out to watch. When the table
was cleared off and the pair given space, Charley finally
joined the betting.

"I figger Jimmy ain't hardly ever wrong. I got me ten
bucks to put on Ralph."

A fisherman took the bet immediately. Craig and
Ralph locked arms. Norm thought Craig looked nervous. Jimmy gave the signal to begin. At first it seemed
even, with no man holding the advantage. Craig gave
everything he had. God, he thought, he just couldn't
lose; how could he ever face the men in this town! He
soon began to sweat.

Ralph's face was a mask. Maybe he was straining, but
it sure didn't look that way to Norm. That's what Jimmy
thought, too. Jimmy was sure that if Ralph lost, it would
be because he would let Craig win. Craig was big, but no
where near in the shape Ralph was. For his part, Ralph
didn't know what to do. He could tell right away that he
could slam Craig's arm down in an instant. But, what
a loss of face for Craig. True, Craig had treated him
poorly, but, still, he was a human being and Ralph knew

it would crush him to lose. He thought again about all the shit he had taken from Craig, and unconsciously applied more pressure, causing Craig's arm to slowly go down.

No mistaking it now, Norm thought; Craig's eyes were round with surprise and fear. Rusty was watching with interest. He had made a lot of money arm wrestling in bars over in Vietnam and had never been defeated. He hadn't done it for the extra cash, or for the ego. Rather, more importantly, he did it for the widespread reputation that came with winning. When he had to break up fights in bars and haul soldiers off, they usually went peaceably rather than mess with him.

Ralph was thinking, what about my friends? They've bet on me, they're expecting me to do my best. I wish Craig were stronger so I could lose legitimately, but he's not. Just got to make it look good. He eased up and Craig pressed to an advantage. The crowd noise picked up; they sensed the end was near. Craig looked surprised. Ralph let him get very close to winning. With his hand almost down, Ralph looked around the table. Jimmy, silent, was looking him straight in the eye; their eyes locked. Jimmy knows, Ralph thought as he looked away. Slowly, Ralph increased the pressure. There was no hesitation or wavering, just a slow swing of the arms until Craig's arm was flat down on the table. For better or worse, it was over. Ralph looked up at Jimmy. His eyes were smiling. Craig was rubbing his forearm, and looked close to tears.

"One heck of a match, Craig! I thought you were going to break my arm." Ralph, unnecessarily supporting his right arm with the other, reached across the table to shake Craig's hand. "Guess someone had to win."

Craig shook his hand. "Congratulations, Ralph. You wupped me fair and square."

"I wouldn't call it that," Ralph said good-naturedly, but Craig was already out of his chair, heading towards the bar. Ralph watched him while the others settled their bets. He saw Craig ask Minnie for a Jim Beam on the rocks; he had her leave the bottle on the bar. Bad idea, Ralph thought.

Charley counted the ten singles before folding them and stuffing them in the front pocket of his jeans.

"Guess all that paddling done you some good," he said to Ralph. "Craig ain't no humpty. Maybe some day you might be ready to take on Tiny here."

Both Tiny and Ralph laughed.

"Don't think you'll ever have to worry about that, Tiny," Ralph offered.

Charley informed Rusty, "Tiny's the champion in these here parts; fisher people from Apalachicola to Crystal River done took him on. No one's beat him, ever, and that's why he got that name for his boat. In fact, no one's even got him to raise a sweat."

"And no one ever will," Tiny said, confidently.

"Pretty sure of yourself, huh, Tiny?" Rusty asked.

Tiny shrugged his shoulders.

"No reason not to be."

"I used to arm wrestle some in the service," Rusty said.

"That so?" Tiny was looking a little more closely at Rusty. "How'd you do?"

"I've never been beaten either."

"You're not thinking of challenging me, are you?" Tiny asked, surprised.

Rusty shrugged.

Charley said, "Rusty, I wouldn' get any such notions. Tiny here has broken arms afore. I'd hate to see your fishing career get cut short afore you rightly begun."

"No offense, Rusty, but you're a good guy, and Charley's giving some good advice. And you don't get good advice from Charley every day, so you should pay attention to it," Tiny added.

Jimmy recalled all the times over the last few days Rusty had effortlessly lifted heavy stuff. Usually, any man, even Tiny, would have to brace himself when hoisting coolers packed with close to a hundred pounds of fish, but Rusty didn't. And, how about when Rusty lifted his big Yamaha to get it in a better position to work on? And those full gas tanks he lifted up over the tailgate with one arm like it was nothing? No mistake, he was strong, real strong! But was he strong enough? Tiny was a man-mountain, a freak. Never been beaten, and he had gone against every bruiser around. Like Charley said, never even worked up a sweat. But, still... What the hell. If he bet twenty on Rusty and lost, he'd still be even. Jimmy addressed the room in a loud voice.

"Gents, I think we got another match here tonight, and it just might be a doozy." To the table he said, "I'm putting the twenty bucks I won with Ralph on Rusty here against Tiny."

Charley said, "Jimmy, that's plum crazy. No one can beat Tiny, and I mean no one. You're throwing your money away, and if you want to do that, better I take it than someone else. You're on."

Norm said, "No offense, Rusty, but I'm putting twenty on Tiny, too, that is if anyone will bet against me."

Looking at Tiny's arms and shoulders as he stripped to a tee shirt, Rusty said, "Don't blame you a bit, Norm."

"What we have here is an unknown quotient," Beau said, "and we just might all be in for a surprise. I'll take that bet, Norm."

A crowd soon formed again around the table. Only a couple more bets were made because it was hard for anyone to bet against Tiny. One exception was Sammy, the large gutted fisherman that Rusty had put down when he was beating up his brother-in-law. He bet on

Rusty. Rusty noticed and nodded to him. Sammy raised his beer in response. Tammy stood next to Norm and Beau in front of the circle while Ralph stood at the outside. Maybelline came out of the kitchen again to watch. About the only person not around the table was Craig who was off drinking alone at the bar, staring at the TV.

Rusty and Tiny locked arms. Tiny said, "Good luck, you'll need it."

"We'll see. Good luck yourself."

Jimmy gave the signal to begin. Both men flexed and pushed. The room was dead silent. The air soon seemed to thicken with their effort.

"Back off, everybody. Give them room," Jimmy demanded.

Their arms remained vertical for a minute or so as they measured each other. Tiny, with a mildly surprised expression on his face, said "Not bad, Rusty, not bad at all." With his left hand, he took a swig of beer, showing off to the crowd, most of whom laughed. Rusty was silent. Tiny put the beer down. "Guess it's time to get down to business."

Rusty's arm began to lower. Tiny was smiling confidently. Rusty closed his eyes, fiercely concentrating, willing the whole of his being into his arm and shoulder. This man was strong, stronger than anyone he had ever faced in 'Nam, faced anywhere. But he couldn't doubt himself. Just concentrate, don't give up. Remember that childhood story, the little train. I think I can, I think I can…Slowly, very slowly, Rusty's arm came up until both arms were vertical again. He opened his eyes and looked at Tiny.

"You're sweating, Tiny," Rusty said. Tiny didn't answer. He too was concentrating, looking serious for the first time, maybe even with a tinge of concern. It fueled Rusty. Sweat began to course freely down Tiny's face. His arm began to lower.

"Someone wipe my face!"

Charley went to the bar for a towel. "Well, I'll be danged," he said, returning to mop off Tiny. "Never thought I'd see the day. Tiny, looks like you're in for a tussle alright.

Tiny remained silent. Beau spoke up with emotion.

"What we have here, gents, if I'm not mistaken, is the ancestor of some great Scottish warrior. And you can bet, Tiny, this man will never give up."

But neither would Tiny.

"I'm Scottish, too, Beau," Tiny said, grimacing. With incredible effort, he brought the arms even. Both men were breathing hard. The match had been going on for ten minutes, maybe more, but it seemed like hours to the two men. Even the audience felt drained. The pair continued to struggle.

Ralph looked over to Craig who was staring into his empty glass. He reached for the bottle of Jim Beam, filling the glass half way before taking a slug. Ralph suddenly wished that he had let Craig win; obviously drunk, Craig looked crushed, so vulnerable. Ralph's heart went out to him. At that moment, Craig looked over and their eyes met. For a long moment, Craig's eyes turned soft, doe-like, lonely, before he looked away. It jolted Ralph as if he had stuck a fork into an electrical outlet. He knew that look, had seen it plenty of times. It explained everything. Craig had let his guard down for an instant. Now, it all made sense: Craig was closet gay, and probably hated himself for it.

The match continued in absolute silence. An incredible match. A stalemate. Ralph watched Craig stumble up to Tammy and give her some bills, then weave his way to the door. No way, Ralph thought, should he drive that airboat home; but no one was paying attention, everyone was riveted on Tiny and Rusty. Ralph walked out to the deck above the dock. Craig's airboat was below, tied to a deck support post. Craig appeared below, lurched aboard, and fumbled with his keys. He climbed up to his perch, and after a few tries, got the key into the ignition. With ear protectors more or less in place, he turned over the big engine.

At the poker table, Rusty and Tiny were still at it though it was obvious both were beginning to tire. Both men had been so valiant, Jimmy thought, that there shouldn't be a loser. When he spoke to the two men, his voice sounded extra loud in the silence.

"I think most everyone here would accept a draw. What do you say?"

Several in the audience grumbled.

Tiny spoke.

"Nope."

Rusty smiled at Tiny.

"Ditto."

The audience cheered as the two men's arms shook with renewed effort. Suddenly, Craig's airboat roared as Craig gunned it. BAM! A terrific jolt shook the building. Glasses and bottles fell off tables and shelves, people lurched, everyone wondering what the hell had happened. But, Tiny and Rusty, locked in like two old snapping turtles, kept at it. Except for Skillet who was commanded by Beau to stay, the two men were deserted as everyone rushed out to the Gulfside deck.

Tammy, fearing the worst, was the first to reach the deck where she arrived just in time to see Ralph launch himself over the railing. She ran to the railing. Craig's airboat was semi-submerged, upside down with its stern line still tied to one of the restaurant's deck posts. Ralph was in the water, looking anxiously around. The dredged channel was only six feet deep, but deep enough. He went under and found Craig first try, and pulled him up. Tammy screamed for Norm. He was at her side almost immediately and he saw Ralph dragging Craig back to the dock. Craig's head was bleeding profusely. Norm flew down the stairs, yelling over his shoulder, "Tammy, get my medical box!"

Tammy sprinted to the backroom, pulling out her circle of keys as she ran. Box in hand, she passed Rusty and Tiny with only Skillet patiently watching them. Arms still wavering, Rusty and Tiny were at a stalemate, each applying only minimum pressure while resting up for another offensive. The door slammed behind Tammy.

Tiny asked, "You want to go see what all the excitement's about?"

"Nope."

Tiny smiled.

"Ditto."

Rusty tried an offensive. Tiny countered. Their arms were even again.

"Nice try."

Rusty shrugged. Time was moving real slow. He asked, "You going shrimping tomorrow night?"

"Yup. Been running real good around the Keys."

Tiny's turn to mount an offensive. He took Rusty down a couple inches before Rusty could counter. Stalemate again.

"Nice try."

Tiny's turn to shrug.

"That's where Jimmy and I went yesterday. Had real good luck, too."

"Hope you realize that with Jimmy it ain't so much about luck."

"That's what everybody says, and we caught a parcel of fish, that's for sure...So, you going back to the keys tomorrow night?"

"Maybe, maybe not."

"Why not, if they're running good and all?"

"In these parts, sometimes there are things going on you gotta avoid if you want to stay healthy and not lose your boat both. And I'm not talking just about the weather. Always best to check around afore you go out."

Tiny tried another offensive. Got nowhere.

"Jimmy tells me you used to run liquor up in Georgia."

"Yeah, I did, but that was a long time ago."

As Rusty started another offensive, Tammy arrived at the dock. Craig was vomiting. Norm gently turned him over when he was done puking. There was a horrific gash on his forehead. Norm wondered, with all the Jack Daniels he had drunk tonight, if he could stitch in a straight line. But, that was the least of it. Besides almost drowning, Craig had been seriously concussed.

Tammy, ever his nurse these days, applied pressure with a bandage to Craig's forehead while Norm gingerly checked for broken bones. He manipulated his neck first. As he poked and prodded, he asked Ralph, "What happened?"

"He forgot to untie the stern line and it had a lot of slack. When he took off, the line held after it played out, caused the boat to flip. Craig was launched and bounced off the corner of the bow. That must have been where he cut his head, the damn fool."

Craig was woozy, but conscious.

"Where do you hurt, Craig?"

"That you, Norm?"

"Craig, how many fingers am I holding up?" Norm asked, holding three.

Craig concentrated.

"Three."

"Good. Now, where do you hurt?" he repeated.

"Head mostly, right shoulder."

"Can you stand up and walk?"

"Don't know. Jesus, my head hurts!"

Norm looked around.

"Charley, can you and Sammy help him upstairs? If he can't walk, carry him. I'll be right behind you."

"What about that?" Charley asked, nodding at the upside down airboat.

A couple of men volunteered to tow it over to the public landing, but only if they were given a full report on Tiny when they returned.

"Charley," Tammy said, "ask Minnie to put a couple of tables together and have Craig lie down on them. And make sure she covers them with plastic first. Damn place is turning into a regular hospital," she muttered.

Business had never been so good on a Thursday night, mollifying Tammy somewhat as she tended her patient upstairs, over in a corner. Word was out, and even some of the women came in to have a soft drink and gawk. Charley made sure Norm had plenty of space to work. After tying the last knot and snipping the thread sticking out of Craig's forehead, he looked over to Tiny and Rusty. He shook his head: they were still at it. Regular three–ringed circus, he thought: arm wrestling, basketball on TV, and Dr. Kildare.

Jimmy squeezed through the circle of spectators around Rusty and Tiny, and sidled up to Beau in front. Skillet was safely tucked between Beau's legs. Jimmy watched the match for a minute or two before he suddenly reached over the table to push against Tiny's arm. There was minimal resistance. Both Rusty and Tiny yelled, "Hey!"

"What in tarnation you think you're doing, Jimmy!" Tiny exclaimed.

"You two are so tuckered out, you're weak as kittens. Hell, Tiny, even I could whup you right now."

"That'd be the day!"

Jimmy reached into his pocket.

"Here's that twenty, I put on Rusty. I'll put it on me now if you'll call it a draw and arm wrestle me."

Jimmy started rolling up his right sleeve. Tiny didn't say anything. The crowd didn't either: the match was getting pretty boring, and a new match between Jimmy and Tiny might be more entertaining.

"Or maybe, as you Scots like to say, you're a wee bit chicken-shit, Tiny," Jimmy added.

Tiny looked at Rusty.

"It'd be pretty easy money," Tiny said.

"Would buy us a bunch of beers," Rusty answered.

"I've worked up a powerful thirst."

"Me, too," Rusty agreed.

"What do you say, then?"

"Alright by me. Like I say, I'm pretty thirsty."

"Want a rematch?"

"Nope. You?"

Tiny smiled.

"Nope." Tiny's eyes narrowed a fraction. "We both let go when I count three?"

"You got my word."

Tiny counted. When they released, both arms flopped down on the table.

"Now I know what Atlas looked like when Hercules took the world off his shoulders," Beau commented, shaking his head. "A heartfelt congratulations to you both; hell of a match," he said, and began to clap. Others joined in.

Tiny stood up. Flexing and rubbing his arm, he said, "Give me a couple of minutes, Jimmy."

"You got all the time in the world, Tiny, because I forfeit," Jimmy answered, dropping the twenty on to the middle of the table. The crowd moaned. "I figured this was about the only way for you two snappers to let go, and the way I figure, I've come out way ahead. I stood to lose a day's pay if Rusty here can't hold up a fishing pole tomorrow morning."

"Jimmy, you're one cagey guy," Rusty said, picking up the twenty with his left hand. "Come on Tiny, I'm buying."

"Yeah, with my money," Tiny said.

Stepping up to the bar, Rusty looked around the room.

"Never a dull moment in these parts, huh Tiny?" Rusty said.

Tiny shrugged.

"Almost as good as a Saturday night." He turned to Minnie. "A Bud for me and my pal, here," he said, slapping Rusty on the back.

After Norm put Craig's arm in a sling, he and Tammy started cleaning up the mess of bandages, gauze, towels, and equipment. Craig, mostly sober, awkwardly pushed himself up off the tables.

"Can anyone give me a ride out to the island?"

"You can't go out there, Craig," Norm said. "You've been concussed. You have to stay where someone can check on you and be able to contact me if need be." Norm turned to the crowded bar, raising his voice. "Anyone got an extra bed for Craig here?" No one volunteered. Many looked away, or at their feet. You reap what you sow, Norm thought. He looked over to Tammy who was looking at him. They had planned on his coming over after the Club closed, and the last damn thing he wanted was to babysit this knucklehead. Norm tried again, "Anybody?"

"I've got an extra room."

Norm turned around. It was Ralph. Of all people, he thought.

"Well, I'll be a skun coon," Charley said, shaking his head. "The way he's treated you and all, Ralph. Don't that beat everything! I hope you know, Craig, that it was Ralph here fished you outta the drink. He's a gen-yoo-wine hero: he done saved your life."

Craig, hanging on to the table with his good arm, was speechless. He had no memory of what had happened. He looked at Ralph, then away, then back again. The room had quieted. Craig, teetering as he hung on to the table, began, "Ralph, I..." but didn't say anymore; he couldn't because he suddenly turned and puked onto the table. Norm rushed to him as the crowd collectively groaned and looked away. Tammy sighed. At least, she thought, the table Craig threw up on was still covered in plastic.

CHAPTER FIFTEEN

Beau sensed he was being watched. He opened an eye. Immediately came the thump, thump, thump of Skillet's tail hitting the side of a bedside chair.

"Oh, come on, Skillet. You were out as late as I was. Go on back to bed."

Beau turned over. Thump, thump, thump.

"Sugah…"

Virginia had her eyeshades on.

"Forget it, Beau. He's your dog."

Beau turned over again. The thumping continued. He couldn't stand it.

"Alright, alright, hold your horses, Skillet."

As Beau slowly extricated himself from the covers, Skillet ran excitedly to and from the bedroom door. Beau pulled his bathrobe off the chair, lashing it as he walked towards the front door. Skillet was out like a shot, making a beeline to the neighbor's front lawn where he sniffed out the absolute best place to take a dump. Vigorously raking his rear legs when he was done, Skillet was ready to go. Funny, Beau thought, how male dogs were so macho when it came to peeing on things, leaving their scent and staking out territory, but when it came to pooping, they looked every bit as self-conscious as a human. He shut the door and returned to bed.

Skillet was off. First stop was Norm's where he looked up to the deck. No movement or greeting. He continued over the humpback bridge to Main Street. Next was the big fish house. If he was lucky, he might find something to roll in, or a cat or two to chase. Right off he spied a big fat gray cat that he knew was easy pickings. He had chased it plenty of times and, although he could easily catch it whenever he wanted, he never did. It was all about the chase. Today was no exception. Barking loudly, he chased it for about a hundred feet until the cat, terrified, scrambled up a cabbage palm. Skillet walked around the base of the tree a couple times before he peed on it, then continued on to the post office. Distracted by the cat, he never noticed the pile of fish scraps, perfect to roll in which would have sent Virginia running for the hose.

Several mangy brown dogs were chained next door to the post office. Skillet, just out of their reach, sauntered around, leaving his scent wherever he could. The dogs went ballistic, howling and barking and running at Skillet as far as their tether allowed. Skillet ignored them, reveling in his freedom. Eventually, an unshaven and disheveled bare-chested man in white boots and jeans came out and yelled at Skillet. Skillet took his time to walk away until the man made motions of picking up a stone. Then Skillet, tail between his legs, hightailed it to safer ground.

Next was Maybelline's house, situated smack dab on a slab at ground level. Skillet walked up to the low picture window and looked in, knowing there was a good chance that one of the dachshunds was looking out. Sure enough, Meenie was on guard. He immediately jumped off a chair and began to bark. Eenie, Miney, and Moe were by his side in a heartbeat, but it was only Meenie that barked. The girls wagged their tails and Moe stared at Skillet like a cow watching a train go by. Soon the front door opened.

"Good morning, Skillet." Maybelline looked at her watch. "Running a little late this morning, aren't you? Understandable with all the goings on last night."

Skillet came up, tail wagging. Maybelline put a hand in each of her front two pockets.

"Which one?"

Skillet looked at her, then at the pockets. He went up to the left one, then the right. He returned to the left, and sat down, looking at her. Maybelline laughed.

"Right you are. You never miss!" Lowering her voice, "I wish Moe and Meenie were as smart as you," she said, as she dug the doggy cookie out of her pocket. "Now, don't you go telling them I said that." She handed Skillet his treat and gave him a pat on the head before returning inside.

Skillet devoured the cookie and continued on his way to Charley's where, if he was around, Skillet knew it would mean at least another cookie. After looking curiously at the red Mustang parked alongside the boat, Skillet stopped in front of the ladder leading up into the *Stingray*. He barked a couple of times. Nothing happened, but Skillet was patient. He barked again. Nothing. On his next volley, he heard some shuffling around inside the hull. He began to wag his tail. In a couple of minutes, a very sleepy Charley peered down over the poop deck railing.

"Morning, Skillet. Mite vocal this morning, ain't you?"

Skillet continued to wag his tail.

"Now you just gotta wait a minute for me to git things together. Was a late night last night; but, you know that already with you being there and all. Pretty exciting though, weren't it? Now, wait right there and I'll be bringing you your treat directly. While you're at it, why don't you fill in some of them holes. Then maybe we can go over to Big John's for me to git a cup of java. Whatcha think, Skillet?"

Skillet barked once and ran around in a circle a couple of times.

"Okay, be right there, Skillet."

Within ten minutes, Charley was on his lawnmower with Skillet trotting happily along side. They pulled up to Big John's where Big John and Rusty were sitting out on the dock. Both had a cup of coffee in their hands. Charley helped himself to the coffee as Skillet greeted Rusty and Big John. Skillet followed Big John over to a glass jar near the cash register where he was given another treat.

When Charley, coffee and plastic chair in hand, joined the trio, Big John said, "Just help yourself to coffee, Charley. Don't even think of ever asking."

Charley was unfazed.

"Thanks, don't mind if I do."

He took a sip.

"Aah, dang that sure tastes fine." Looking at Rusty, he asked, "How's your body, meaning your shoulder and all, this morning?"

"Body's fine, but my head's another matter. Lost count on how many beers I drank with Tiny. Man, can he put them away!"

Skillet put his head in Charley's lap. Charley scratched his ears.

"Look at 'em, Rusty, best friends. Weren't always that way, kin tell you that. Took Charley about a year to forgive old Skillet here."

"Yeah, and was about a year that Miss Tammy had me at hard labor, what with all the fish I had to supply her with, not to speak of the mullet dip and soft shelled crabs. She had me running all the time on account of him," Charley said, looking down affectionately at Skillet and continuing to scratch his ears.

"What are you two talking about?"

"Was because of Skillet here that Miss Tammy caught me red-handed swiping some beer."

Rusty sat back in his chair.

"Do tell, Charley."

Charley stopped scratching Skillet's ears, and Skillet decided to mosey out on the dock to bask in the sun.

"It was back before I pulled out the *Ray*. It was sunk in the bay, but not all the way. The cabin and everything was still high and dry, and I used to take me some women out there to git laid. I also went out there to spend the night alone, drinking and playing with the controls, just imagining what it'd be like to live permanently aboard her. You gotta understand how much I loved a'setting there looking out over the Gulf. Anyways, round about then, I was in between jobs and didn't have no money…"

Big John interrupted.

"Didn't have him a job because back then he'd git in fights with everybody he worked with."

"Not everybody, Big John. Just them folks who was too big for their britches."

"Don't think Charley ever won one of them fights; he was always walking around town like a tattered up old tom cat."

"So where do Skillet and Tammy come in?"

"I'm gitting to that, Rusty. If Big John here can keep hisself from buttin' in, I'll tell you." He looked fixedly at Big John. "Like I says, I was broke and I wanted in the worse way to go out to the *Ray* and drink me some beers. So, I thought I'd a'borrow me some from Miss Tammy's storeroom…"

Big John snorted. Charley glared at him.

"You gonna let me tell the story or not!" Charley looked at Rusty. "So I jimmied the lock some and went in. Man alive," he said shaking his head, "I can still re-member all that beer, floor to ceiling. Miss Tammy had just got a big shipment in, I seen the truck pull out that afternoon. Anyways, I left the door open a smidgeon, and was shining my light on all them cases, trying to make up my mind which one to grab. Turns out, Skillet here was making his evening rounds and he gits a whiff of me inside that storeroom. So he sets down right there outside the door and don't move, his tail just a wagging full bore.

"Dang if'n a church lady wasn't taking her evening stroll about then and saw Skillet. She thought it a mite peculiar and she stopped by Miss Tammy's house to tell her. Tammy came by to investigate and caught me inside with nothing but egg on my face. But she didn't turn me in. We made a deal that I was to give her a portion of whatever I caught for as long as she said. Like I says, that went on for a year. She got herself a hell of a deal, I'll tell you that. I'd have been 'a way better off going to jail for a couple of months and picking up trash along side the highway."

"Darn, Charley, I didn't know you were an outlaw."

"Weren't so much that, just that I had me a powerful thirst back then and I weren't thinking too straight."

"That's been known to happen with alcohol, Charley. I could tell you plenty of stories from 'Nam…"

Just then there was a loud ringing like a schoolmarm's bell. Immediately Skillet jumped up and ran out through Big John's wide-open store door, skidded around the corner, and made a beeline towards the humpback bridge.

"What's up with Skillet?" Rusty asked as he followed him with his eyes.

"Dinner bell. Miss Virginia's done made him his breakfast." Charley paused. "Skillet's more than a dog to them two, more like a grandyoung'un they never had, if'n you ask me." Big John nodded, one of the few times he agreed with Charley.

Skillet scrambled over the bridge, galloped past Norm's, and clambered quickly up the stairs to the deck where Virginia was waiting patiently.

"Hope you're still hungry, Skillet, after all your pan-handling," she said. Skillet had no problem. He wolfed down his meal as Virginia stood there watching.

CHAPTER SIXTEEN

Balancing the tray in his left hand, Ralph knocked on the bedroom door.

"Come on in, Ralph. Been awake for awhile."

Ralph entered the dimly lit room. Although a bright sunny morning, the curtain was still drawn because of Craig's concussion.

"How's the bod'?" Ralph asked, handing the tray to Craig.

"Shoulder's much better," Craig said, raising up an arm. "But still got the headaches and dizziness."

"Norm said that's to be expected, part of the 'post concussion syndrome.' Said it could last a month or more. Are you sleeping all right? Any insomnia?"

"Nope, like a baby; like a baby who's getting fatter all the time with your cooking," Craig said, while looking down at the scrambled eggs, toast, bacon, and grits with a pat of butter melting on top. He reached for the cup of coffee. "That shrimp scampi you made last night was the best I've ever eaten, bar none."

Ralph smiled broadly.

"I love to cook, but I don't usually make the effort when it's just me."

Craig looked at Ralph while he sipped the coffee. He put the cup down.

"Ralph, I feel like such a shithead. I am so sorry for the way I've treated you all this time. I just wish there was something I could do to make up for it...I really do."

Ralph shook his head. He sat down on a far corner of the bed.

"Don't worry about it. I'm just glad it's behind us." Ralph looked at his watch. "Norm should be coming sometime soon to check on you, although it's still pretty early for him to be out and about these days."

" 'Cuz he's shacking up with Tammy?"

Ralph stood, smiling.

"Yeah. And I'm happy for him, for both of them. Now, eat your breakfast before it gets cold. I'm going to work out for awhile."

Craig finished the breakfast. Nothing wrong with my appetite, he thought. He started to get up to take the tray out, but the room started spinning. He put the tray off to the side and lay back down. He soon dozed off.

He dreamed he was out on his airboat on a beautiful sunny day, heading towards a bright white sandbar out in the Gulf. He could see a single coconut palm sticking straight up in the middle and, as he approached, he noticed Ralph's scull was beached at the far end. Ralph was standing under the tree, wearing a bathing suit and the top half of a tuxedo. His hair was as dark as the tuxedo and he was very tan. In front of him was a table with a linen tablecloth and two settings. Off to the side of the tree, there was a smaller serving table with a silver domed cover on top.

As Craig idled his boat up to the sandbar, he noticed that he, too, was dressed in a bathing suit and tux. As he walked towards the table, Ralph bent to light the pair of tall candles on the table.

"Don't light them, Ralph; not yet."

"What do you want to do then? Arm wrestle?" Ralph asked, smiling. Craig thought Ralph looked handsome.

"Very funny, Ralph. You know the answer to that. But, I'll leg wrestle you."

"You're on, but not with these fancy duds," Ralph said, extending his arms and looking at the sleeves of the tux. He walked over to hang the tux, tie, and shirt on bright brass hooks Craig hadn't noticed on the palm. Craig did the same.

They lay down, opposite each other on the warm sand.

"We'll lift our leg up three times," Craig said. "On the third, we hook them. Whoever pulls the other guy over, wins. Okay?"

"You got it."

"One, two, three!"

They hooked, and Craig, the heavier of the two with his football lineman's thick legs, easily flipped Ralph over where he lay half on Craig and half on the sand. Ralph, laughing, slowly rolled off Craig to the starting position, saying, "Two out of three?"

"Sure."

They locked legs again with the same result. When they untangled and stood up, Ralph said, "Geez, didn't give you much competition. That wasn't even close."

They walked over to their shirts and jackets. Craig was about to put his on when Ralph said, "Wait a minute. You're all sandy. Turn around."

Craig did as he was told, and Ralph brushed off his shoulders, back, and the backs of his trunks and upper legs. When Craig started to repay the favor, he woke up with a headache. Crazy ass dream, he thought. Noticing he had an erection, he briefly fondled himself. Well, at least that still works.

When the headache subsided, he looked over at the clock. Almost ten-thirty. Norm still hadn't come, and the tray was still on the side of the bed. He tried standing again, making sure to hang on to the headboard.

Hallelujah, no spinning! He picked up the tray and slowly headed towards the kitchen.

He passed through the living room paneled in rich-brown pecky cypress, the wood creating a warm, den-like atmosphere. Ralph had a number of oil paintings on the walls, mostly old Florida land and seascapes with cabbage palms and egrets, and sunsets over the Gulf and marsh. It was the Florida that was disappearing fast. Craig suddenly thought, Maybe that's what I can do, buy Ralph another oil painting, a really good one. It would cost, but so what—I've got plenty of money. And what price do you put on saving your life?

Craig put the tray down by the kitchen sink, the farthest he had walked in three days. He heard a faint clanging from the other end of the house, and felt strong enough to go investigate. He came to a door part-way open. Ralph was inside, back to him, doing curls with a dumbell in each hand. He was in a tank top and those same cut-off sweatpants Craig had seen him wearing in the scull. Craig didn't say anything, just stood there watching Ralph do his reps, muscles flexing in a slight sheen of sweat. His eyes were trained so fixedly on Ralph that he didn't notice the mirror on the far wall. Ralph was watching him as well.

Ralph did more reps than usual before putting the weights down on a bench and picking up a towel. He turned while mopping off, feigning surprise to see Craig standing there.

"I heard you when I brought the breakfast tray to the kitchen and came back to check it out."

"That's fine Craig, just so you're careful. Any dizziness?" Ralph asked.

"So far, so good. Man, I knew you had some sort of a gym, but nothing like this. Hell, Ralph, you could open up a health club; I mean, look at all this stuff: nautilus, weights, stationary bike, Nordic track, parallel bars, rings, rowing machine." He turned back to Ralph. "No wonder you wupped me. I didn't stand a chance!"

"What do you mean? It was close, nip and tuc, you just about…"

"That's bullshit and you know it. You could have flattened me anytime."

Ralph didn't say anything. Craig laughed.

"But I'm sure as hell glad you didn't. I know you didn't want to embarrass me, Ralph, and I appreciate it."

Ralph didn't know what to say. As it was, he was swimming in the liquid light blue of Craig's eyes. Unique, really. Beautiful. As striking as Crystal's, he thought.

"I should try to get in shape, too."

Ralph surfaced.

"You can work out here anytime, Craig. Be good for all this to be used by someone other than me. And I don't have to be here either; the door's never locked."

"I don't think I'm disciplined enough to do it alone."

"Then together, if you want; when you're better. I do this three times a week, plus I try to bike or row when the weather's nice and I'm not showing property."

"Oh, shit, Ralph, I'm getting dizzy again."

Swaying, Craig put his arms out for balance. Ralph quickly grabbed one and draped it over his shoulders, holding on to it with his left hand. He put his right arm around Craig's waist, and slowly, gently, walked him back to bed.

* * *

It sounded like a loud, angry hornet buzzing around the room, unsettling and annoying. Norm opened his eyes. Tammy stirred. "Damn airboat," he said. "At least it's not Craig joyriding. Probably low tide and someone's getting oysters." Norm got out of bed, naked except for a pair of socks. He pulled the curtains back and looked out. "Yup. Low, low winter tide."

"Called a tong tide," Tammy said, yawning and stretching her arms.

"How's that?"

"For the tongs the commercial oystermen use when they go out."

Even though Tammy's house was ground level and on the other side of a tiny little town park full of stunted but beautiful live oaks, she had a very nice view of the Gulf. It was indeed a low winter tide with the mudflats and oyster bars exposed seemingly to the horizon. The maze of narrow channels through the flats looked like the veins on a hand. Only an airboat could get out in such a tide. Norm let go of the curtains and walked back to the bed. Tammy was looking at his feet and began laughing softly. Norm looked down, then back to her.

"So, I'm not a furnace like you. My feet get cold in the night, and if they do, I can't sleep," Norm said, climbing back into bed.

Tammy snuggled up to him.

"But socks, Norm?"

She worked her way down under the sheets, and removed his socks. She straddled his feet. This left her head near Norm's manhood, a fact that did not escape him, and he became aroused...again.

"Well, well; what have we here?" Tammy asked. She moved up. I do believe your feet are warm enough; it's another body part I'm concerned about now."

They made love for the third time since one-thirty in the morning. When they finished, Norm looked at his watch. It was almost nine-thirty. He yawned before putting an arm around Tammy, who put her head in the crook of his shoulder.

"I should go check on Craig," Norm said, but didn't move. He was about as content as he had ever been.

"Ralph would call if there were any problems."

"Suppose so," he said, before drifting off to sleep.

He woke to the smell of rich coffee. Tammy was standing at the foot of the bed, barefoot and dressed in a terrycloth bathrobe, watching him. She had a cup of hot coffee in each hand. She sat on the edge of the bed and handed him his cup. "Bless you," he said. They softly clinked cups before taking sips.

"Can I cook you up something?"

"No thanks, I really should go check on Craig." He felt around for his socks under the sheets with his feet. When he had them in hand, he got out of bed. "And I should get my car out of here. It's just giving everyone something to talk about." He walked over to the clothes he had flung on a chair. "Especially the church people," he added.

"Actually, you're probably giving me some respectability, being the town doctor and all. Most of them think I'm a jezebel that sleeps with every man that comes into the bar."

"You got to admit, a lot of them try."

"Sure, but they don't get anywhere." She looked him directly in the eyes. "It's been a long time, Norm, a very long time since I slept with anyone."

"Ditto, but you sure fooled me."

"Just what do you mean by that?"

He smiled disarmingly.

"Like riding a bicycle. You're one hot mama in my book, lady. And I have a confession. I've never done it three times in one night before."

Her smile was ear to ear. She put the mug of coffee down and sashayed up to him, twirling the tie of her bathrobe.

"Want to go for four, big boy?"

Norm slipped into his shoes and, feigning fear, walked quickly towards the door. Over his shoulder, he said, "I'd love to oblige you, Missy, but I took an oath and duty calls." He stopped in the doorway and turned towards her. "See you tonight?"

Tammy smiled.

"Of course. Say hi to Ralph and Craig."

Tammy watched Norm drive away before getting another cup of coffee and sitting down at the little table with a view of the Gulf. She looked at the thermometer attached to the window frame outside. Thirty-eight degrees. Brrrr. But, bright and sunny, a blue, blue sky. A beautiful, terrific morning. She took a sip of coffee. Heck, she thought, it could be blowing a gale with horizontal rain and it'd still be a beautiful morning.

Can't believe Norm and I are an item. So different from Bobby. Wonder if he's still in prison. Such a loser, but, so was I for hooking up with him in the first place and running off to Georgia to get married. But what girl knows what she's doing at seventeen? Just wanted out. Jacking deer with Daddy, eating swamp cabbage every night, and wiping the mouths and butts of four brothers and sisters for years: not a lot of fun. Mama was the one having all the fun, somewhere, wherever she ran off to. Daddy didn't bother to look for her. Said she was a tramp and good riddance.

Who could blame her? Five kids, cooking, washing, no money, no new clothes, no socializing, no movies, no nothing. No wonder she took off. But that put it all on me with Daddy pulling me outta high school after she left. Daddy started to refer to us as a team, him and me, a unit who had to do everything together to make it all work. I knew it weren't right when Daddy began sneaking looks while I was dressing, but I didn't really mind because it let me know I was growing good in all the right places. But when he began touching me, I had to leave pronto, and Bobby was the ticket.

Bobby and me had a real fine time for awhile, riding around in his pick-up drinking and mud bogging, and going to dances in bars when I was old enough. We had some pretty wild nights alright, but that was before he started drinking hard liquor. That stuff made him real mean. How many times did he backhand me in the pickup coming home from a bar? Don't know how I stuck it out for so long, what with all the stories to explain the bruises, then the lies to the doctor who wired my jaw that one time. Bobby felt bad about the jaw and stopped drinking for a spell—even brought me McDonald's strawberry milkshakes every afternoon after work. But it all ended when Bobby was flat out drunk and hit me with a roundhouse for talking to some guy sitting next to me in a bar. A trooper was called in, and Bobby punched him, too. Knocked him flat out cold. A big mistake, and most likely he's still paying for it. At least, sober in prison, he didn't contest the divorce.

Thank God there were no children. Never knew why, me or him, but it was a blessing. Never would have gotten my GED. No way I could have afforded the time if there had been kids. Norm's got two sons somewhere. Never talks about them much, and I've never seen them visit. Wonder why?

Tammy finished her coffee, put the cup in the sink, and walked into the living room to begin her daily ritual.

"Good morning everybody," she said, surveying the four cages, one in front of each wall. "Sorry I'm a little late today, but I'm sure you understand." She started pulling off covers. Birdsong instantly filled the room. She unlatched the little door of the parakeet's cage first, and put her finger out. "Morning, Huey," she said to the baby-blue parakeet who jumped onto her finger. She put her hand to her shoulder, and Huey jumped off, chirping in her ear. Immediately, the green cockatiel with her slicked back yellow head feathers and the rouged cheeks began squawking. "No reason to be jealous, Henrietta. You'll have your turn soon enough." She didn't dare let them both out at the same time; Henrietta would be all over Huey in a flash.

The pair of zebra finches and the pair of lovebirds couldn't care less about being let out. They flew back and forth in the long horizontal cages that had cost her a small fortune. In between flights, the finches sang their beautiful songs. She freshened all the little water containers before going to the cupboard to sort out their different foods. Huey flew off her shoulder onto the countertop to supervise. Tammy had to keep gently pushing him out of the way.

The whole operation, including socializing with the birds and giving Henrietta her fair share of shoulder time, took up the rest of the morning. She never begrudged the time or expense. They were her friends, her buddies through thick and thin. They, as well as a few predecessors, had gotten her through some very tough times. Suddenly, there was a bird chirping sound from the kitchen. Her pets immediately stopped whatever they were doing and cocked their heads. Tammy looked at the bird clock on the wall. Noon. Time to go to the Club.

* * *

Rusty was sitting on a bench near where the creek flowed into the main channel. He had a pair of binoculars around his neck, and the bench faced west where the low sun bathed his face in a warm glow. He was thinking that there were certainly tougher physical jobs in this world than his when he heard a diesel start up. Without turning around, he knew it was Tiny preparing to go out. Tiny had been bustling about with buckets, coolers, and ice for an hour already, and the tide was about right. When Tiny's boat slowly idled out the creek, Rusty turned to wave. Tiny waved back and put the boat in neutral.

"When you going to come out and help me, Rusty, instead of bird watching or whatever you're doing? Shrimp are starting to show themselves and I could use me some help real bad. And if we do good, the pay ain't so bad neithers."

"Maybe later in the week, Tiny. I still got a couple of days left with Jimmy."

"Keep me in mind, then."

"I will for sure. Good luck."

Tiny waved and Rusty watched the boat as it gurgled out the long channel. Tiny cleared the markers and headed due west into the setting sun. Rusty trained the binoculars on the boat. He smiled when he read *Never Been Beat* on the transom. The boat was not much bigger than a dot when it turned South. Rusty watched it until it disappeared. Must be going down to the Keys again. He looked at his watch. Time to check in.

Rusty walked up the street to the tiny general store where there was a pay phone out front. The store was a simple concrete, one-story affair that sold an assortment of snacks, hardware, and fishing supplies. Charley had told him that if you ever found what you actually needed, it was like winning the lottery. But there was plenty of beer, cheap wine, chips, slim jims, hot sauces, and pickled eggs. He went in to get change for a dollar. That turned out to be a mistake.

When he came out, Maybelline, wrapped up in her dogs' leashes, was just dialing. He sat down on a plastic chair by the front door. Judging from the nearby coffee can full of sand and cigarette butts, he figured it must be where the one employee took her breaks. Maybelline began to chat away. Fifteen minutes later, Rusty looked at his watch. It was beginning to get dark. Rusty stood and purposefully walked back and forth in front of her. She smiled and waved, but kept on talking. It was obvious that he was waiting to make a call, but she seemed oblivious. It was another fifteen minutes before she hung up.

"That was my daughter. She's always asking advice about her children. Should she buy pampers or cloth diapers, what to do about rashes, how long to nurse, when to give them solid foods; it just goes on and on."

Rusty smiled politely as he stepped up to the phone. "Yes, ma'am. I'm sure it's real complicated. Good thing she's got you," he said lifting the phone.

Rusty was wearing a tee shirt. She looked at his biceps "Now that sure was something last night, Rusty; surely was. You're almighty strong, I must say. Anyone that can take on Tiny like that!" She couldn't take her eyes off his arms.

"Maybelline, I really do have to use the phone."

"Oh, don't mind me. You go right on ahead. I'm all done."

He brought the phone to his ear. She continued to stand there.

"Er, Maybelline, this is kind of personal. I'm calling my girlfriend."

"Oh, where is she?"

"Georgia."

"Why ain't she here with you?"

"Doesn't like to fish."

"Do you ever get lonely?"

"Of course. Everyone gets lonely sometimes."

Maybelline was looking hard at his arms again. Oh God, he thought.

"I really do have to make this call, Maybelline. And like I say, it's kind of private."

Maybelline smiled coyly.

"I understand completely. I guess I wouldn't want a handsome hunk of a man standing next to me if I was calling my boyfriend." She started to sort out the leashes. When she had the dogs all pointing in the right direction, she said, "Now anytime you might like a cup of coffee or something, you just come on by the house, Mr. Rusty…and I do mean anytime! It's two houses down past Miss Tammy's." She looked at her watch. "Time to go to work." With that, she gave him a final coy smile and walked off, her round rear end swinging back and forth. Rusty started to dial, but stopped when Maybelline turned around.

"Mr. Rusty, just want you to know that I'm the one makes your bed every morning. Come by around ten, in case you was curious."

"I didn't realize, Maybelline. You've been doing a fine job. I'll make sure to leave you a big tip when I leave."

Maybelline smiled and batted her eyes a couple of times.

"That'd be nice, Mr. Rusty. Believe I'd accept your tip anytime you want to give it to me." Rusty didn't know how to answer that. "Did you hear that there's going to be a big Valentine's hoe down at the Club next weekend? Miss Tammy's hired a band, and she's going to roast a pig and have a fish fry and all. And although it ain't really Valentine's Day, it'll be close enough. Sure hope you come." She gave him another big smile before allowing herself to be pulled away by the dachshunds.

Lordy, he thought, as he watched her sashay down the street. He waited until she was out of earshot, then began to dial again, thinking Crescent Beach must have the only public rotary phone in the country.

"Ensign Thompson."

"Rusty here."

"Yes, sir…er, yes, Rusty."

"Just checking in. Nothing much to report from my end except I'm getting to know everybody and making some friends."

"I've got nothing new here."

"Okay, tell Detective Cross that I'll check back in a couple of days, same time." Rusty heard Charley's lawnmower heading his way. "That's it. One of those friends is heading this way now, got to go."

"Yes, sir."

Rusty hung up the phone. He thought of what he had told the young ensign, that he was making friends. He realized it was true. Charley came up.

"Where's the Mustang, Charley?"

"Don't like to use it much for in town activities. You heading to the Club?"

"Yup. About dinner time "

"Then climb aboard. I'll give you a ride."

"Only if you keep her under sixty, Charley."

"I'll do my best."

CHAPTER SEVENTEEN

The highway to Perry was straight as an arrow with very little traffic. It seemed to Rusty that there were more turkey buzzards than cars and most every driver they passed waved. The land on both sides of the highway had been recently cleared with deep, dirty gray furrows running all the way to the faint, even tree line in the distance. Here and there were tall, thick piles of tree trunks and slash ready to burn.

"This all used to be oak before the timber companies moved in," Tiny said. "Now, slash pine everywhere." They slowed for a few buzzards that flew up from feasting on an armadillo. "That's their most favorite food, even more than deer. And they don't seem to like dog meat much at all. Dogs is still used to hunt deer in these parts, but they're clueless when it comes to highways because they live most their life in cages, pens, or chained. During November and December you might see half a dozen Walkers laying long side the road between Crescent and Perry."

The traffic picked up considerably when they turned north on to Hwy 19. They followed a log truck freighted with a load of tree length slash pine secured by a single strap and with a red rag nailed to the end of a log. A rotten smell wafted into Tiny's pickup.

"What's that god-awful smell!" Rusty asked.

"Buckeye Pulp Mill, largest employer here in Taylor County." Tiny shook his head. "I knows how important jobs are, but here we be, miles from the Gulf, and them sons-a-bitches are killing my shrimp."

"How's that?"

"Dumping bad stuff into the Fenholloway River which takes it down to the Gulf. Done killed miles of sea grass. No one does nothing about it because only money talks up in Tallahassee."

Tiny pulled into an Exxon station on the outskirts of town.

"First stop, Rusty, three hundred gallons o' diesel. Be a whole lot simpler if we had us a fuel dock in Crescent like they got in Steinhatchee and Apalachicola." Tiny climbed out and unscrewed the cap of his bulk tank. As the tank filled, he stuck his head in the window. "I figure with all the costs, fuel, food, and ice and such, not including any of my time, I gotta catch me five hundred bucks worth jest to break even."

On the way to buy groceries, they passed several more gas stations, a couple of which doubled up by selling used tires. Rusty counted four fast food joints before they pulled into a Winn Dixie, kitty corner to a WalMart.

"Not much of a town," Rusty said, getting out.

"This is jest the strip. Real town's off thata way about a mile or so. Got a courthouse, library, some nice old buildings on Main Street. But it's dead. The strip done killed it. Nothing much there except bondsmen and lawyers going in and out of the courthouse."

After buying and loading plastic bags full of sandwich makings, they were back on the highway when Rusty asked, "How'd you get in the shrimping business?"

"Because Daddy was, and I grew up a'helping him early on like Jimmy did with his daddy mullet fishing.

Inherited the boat when Daddy drowned in January, twelve, no, thirteen years ago."

"What happened?"

"We was heading home, trying to git outta a sudden storm with squalls so heavy that you couldn't barely see nothing. The wind was driving the rain sideways and the waves whipped up something fierce. I was at the helm when Daddy went astern to secure some rigging. A boom broke free and musta knocked him overboard. I didn' even know it, concentrating on the sea like I was. When I did, I radioed in and turned around which weren't easy. Turned on all five of them five hundred watt lights the boat's got, but with them waves I didn't see him nowheres. I looked until I was about outta fuel."

"Never found him?"

"Coast Guard did. Daddy had found hisself a crab buoy and hitched himself to it with his belt. Don't know if he drowned or if it was the cold water. Don't take long when it's a below fifty like it was."

Rusty shivered.

"Possum run over your grave?" Tiny asked

"Just can't imagine, Tiny; all alone like that in that cold water."

" Anyways, don't matter none, he was dead. Whole family took it hard, especially Mama. She and Daddy's families been in Crescent since about the beginning when no one hardly fished; cutting cedar for pencils and harvesting salt from the flats was the way of life back in them days. Mama and Daddy grew up together, paired off early, and lied about their ages so they could git hitched right off. But Mama smoked a couple packs of non-filters every day and it caught up with her not too long after Daddy drowned. Took her pretty quick. But it was when Daddy died that the family busted up. My two sisters and brother left lickety-split, and I ain't heard hide nor hair of 'em in years and don't have no clue

where they ended up at. Left me to take care of Mama;
I was the baby of the family." Tiny looked down at his
bulk and smiled at Rusty. "Kinda hard to imagine that,
ain't it?"

They were silent the rest of the way in. When they
crossed the cattle gap, Rusty said, "I can't swim."

Tiny smiled.

"I know that. Everybody in town knows you don't
go nowheres near the water without your bright orange
life jacket. But, that's a good thing, Rusty. If Daddy
had been wearing something bright like that, maybe
I'da found him. And," he added, "where we're going
is a mite deeper than fishing off them oyster bars with
Jimmy."

Tiny set Rusty to pumping fuel from the truck while
he put the food away in the galley. After checking the
rigging, he said, "Guess we're pretty much shipshape.
Tide'll be right in a few hours; why don't you try to grab
a little shuteye, then git your life vest and what all you
need, and I'll meet you at Big John's about four or so.
Ice is the last thing on the list."

Life jacket on, slathered in sunscreen, full of
Dramamine, and carrying a plastic bag with a change
of clothes and toilet articles, Rusty climbed aboard. He
carefully ducked and angled into the cabin that served as
galley, double bunk berth, and pilothouse. Only a thin
plywood wall separated the galley and sleeping quarters
from the wheelhouse, and there was a rough cut-out
in the wall over the galley sink so food could be passed
forward. When he was bending over to throw his bag
under the lower bunk, his butt banged into the cabinet
below the sink. Two big men in this space? Good luck!
Going to be dancing around each other, Rusty thought.
Couple countertops, but no tables. Guess you eat in the
wheelhouse or standing up. He could barely squeeze
into the head when he checked it out, and wondered

how the hell Tiny managed? Maybe this wasn't such a good idea. He angled back out to help with the ice. It took thirty baskets to fill the hold, each basket, he estimated, weighing a good fifty pounds.

"You take the usual number, Tiny?" Big John asked.

"Yup, fifteen bars worth."

Big John wrote it down in a little notebook he took from his shirt pocket.

"When you going to git one of them rigs that kin blow ice like they does in Apalachicola, Big John, so I don't have to break my back every time? "

"About the same time you buy yourself a new boat. Good luck," he said, as he untied the lines and tossed them to Rusty. Tiny eased the trawler to the center of the creek. When they entered the main channel, they were heading due west into a low sun.

Eight miles out, Tiny turned south. Rusty was standing next to him in the wheelhouse, a steady throb from the engine.

"How fast can she go?"

"Eleven, maybe twelve knots with the wind behind us; we be cruising at about eight right now. Even though she's got a four hundred horse Cummins, boats like this got what's called a displacement hull, made for pulling, not speed; the *Never Been Beat* is a working girl for sure."

"Guess I know why you didn't want a rematch arm wrestling, Tiny."

"Oh yeah? How's that?"

"Didn't want to change her name."

Tiny laughed.

"Fat chance! How you doin' anyways?" Tiny asked.

"What do you mean?"

"Stomach ok?"

"So far, so good. Took some stuff. Guess I'm not the only one; I hear Jimmy gets seasick."

Tiny laughed.

"Never woulda made a shrimper, that's for sure."

"Jimmy seems to be doing alright taking guys like me out and crabbing, what with a brand new boat motor and late model truck. And Charley buying that restored Mustang. That must have cost a pretty penny."

Tiny snorted.

"Don't think it was from crabbing that bought them things. They got their hands in other stuff."

Rusty looked out over the water.

"Was kind of thinking that myself. Around here reminds me of growing up in north Georgia."

"How's that?"

"You always knew who was in on the moonshining by what was parked in his front yard."

"Guess it be about the same around here."

"What about you, Tiny? Your truck looks like it's got two hundred thousand on it, and," Rusty said, looking at the mended nets, peeling paint, and raw fiberglass patches, "this boat's no spring chicken. Don't you want to get in on it?"

"Nope, don't interest me none, even though one load in a boat like this would bring in a small fortune, for me anyways. But it ain't worth it. If you git caught, besides going to prison and locked up inside day and night, they take everything, like this old boat. This forty-three-foot hunk of wood and fiberglass is more home to me than Daddy's house. Besides, I got most everything I need," Tiny hesitated, "though, maybe I could use some cash for a IQF."

"What's that?"

"Refrigeration system I could run aboard with my generator. Flash freeze everything and no more shoveling and lugging ice. I'm out here three, sometimes four days; would make my product much more fresh when I git 'em in, better than have them just sitting on ice. Even the bait. If I leave it in a IQF extry long, it freezes extry hard. A lot of them tourist fishermen perfers 'em like that to live ones: says they hold together better on the end of a hook.

"But, no matter. Lookee out there," he said waving at the horizon, "at that old sun setting down. Onliest thing that compares to that is when it comes back up again. Like I says, I got most everything I need... except for dipping these here nets," he said, standing up. "Time to git 'em wet. Them shrimps get real active-like when the sun sets and I wanna make sure they feed us, not something else."

Tiny put the boat in neutral, and went astern. Rusty followed and watched him unfurl the rigging and extend the booms with hydraulic winches. Didn't take long before the nets were in the water. Tiny returned to the wheelhouse to put the boat in gear and Rusty hoisted himself up on the sorting table and watched the last of the sunset. The weather was warm and partly cloudy. The light coming from below the horizon began to play on the clouds, at first a shimmering yellow hue that gradually changed to orange with red highlights. The whole western sky was soon lit up.

Tiny joined him.

"See what I mean. Ain't that pretty?"

A few moments later, Rusty turned to look back at Crescent Beach. He could see it just well enough to make out that some lights had been turned on and that the blimp wasn't up.

"Blimp's down."

"Yep, electronics went phooey. Going to be down for awhile."

Rusty had checked in with the ensign two days ago and he hadn't mentioned any problems with the blimp. How the hell did Tiny know? He looked west again. Spectacular. After awhile, Rusty realized no one was steering the boat. Wasn't going fast, but still. Tiny seemed to read his mind.

"Put her on automatic pilot, if you was wondering. First drag will be a short one, hour or so; want to check and see how clean the bottom is in these parts. If there ain't too much gumbo and dead sea grass and such weighing the nets, we'll drag for at least every two, two and a half hours. Want a hot dawg or something?" Rusty shook his head. "Reckon I do, and more than one, but there's one last thing to do first. Gimme a hand." Tiny handed him a bucket with a rope, and had one of his own. They brought in buckets of seawater that they dumped into the hold. Tiny explained, "Making a slush with seawater chills the shrimps better than just ice, sorta like what salt does when you make ice cream."

Buckets put away, Tiny went into the galley. Rusty sat back down on the sorting table. He was still there when Tiny came out eating a hot dog.

"Guess it's about time I showed you the ropes," Tiny, said between bites, a bright ketchup and mustard ring around his mouth. Rusty was glad the Dramamine was working. "If you look behind you, there's two openings on the back of that table I made, and there's a basket underneath each opening. That's where we drop the shrimps. First hole, there to the left, that's for all the bigger eating shrimps. The teenie weenie guys we call bait goes down the other. Big John sells them to the fishermen.

"When the baskets is full, we pull 'em out and put the shrimp in onion bags. I ties off the bags with a red or a yeller ribbon, with the red for eating. Then we throws 'em in the slush, and starts over. The fishhouses buy 'em according to size, the bigger they is, the more money. But they don't go a measuring each and every one. They takes sample pounds from the sorts and count 'em. Twenty ta twenty-five shrimp to a pound, for example, means they're jumbos. When they figures out what we got, then we get paid by the pound."

About an hour later, although still twilight, Tiny throttled down and turned on the bright lights above the rigging. "Here," he said, handing Rusty a pair of white rubber boots. "Believe these'll fit okay. Gits mighty slippery and they grip good. Otherwise, you'll be on your butt in no time, a'wearing them sneakers." He opened a locker. "And here's a bib, too."

Tiny swung in the nets and brought the drop bags just in front of the sorting table. As Rusty put the bib and boots on, he couldn't believe that he, a State Trooper who had seen his share of hair-raising life and death situations, was excited as a little kid on Christmas morning to see what was to come out of the nets. Tiny undid the triple slip knot and a mix of translucent shrimp, shiners, thick strands of green snot-like algae grass, a few fish, and a single small stingray poured onto the deck. Tiny shook and cleaned the drop bags, retied them, swung the nets out again, and entered the wheelhouse.

When he returned, the first thing he did was to grab a broad aluminum shovel and carefully scoop up and drop the stingray overboard. He threw most of the fish back except for a whiting and two flounder that he put in a cooler. He kicked the shiners out the scuppers or threw them overboard with the shovel. "By-product," Tiny said, looking over his shoulder. "People say us shrimpers destroy everything. That's bullshit. Maybe twenty percent of our catch is guys like these," he said, picking up a handful of pinfish, tiny shrimp, and other odds and ends of the fish world, "and we throw probably ninety percent of 'em back." Tiny put a shovel full of shrimp on either end of the sorting table for them to go through.

Pulling out the green algae from the two piles, Tiny said, "This green stuff's what we call gumbo, though ain't got nuthin' to do with the gumbo I'll be making tomorrow. Other than maybe Maybelline's, I figures my seafood gumbo's about the best anywhere."

"Hope my appetite improves by then, Tiny."

"Y'all be losing out if it don't." Tiny took a handful of the green stuff and threw it overboard, shaking his head. "But this here gumbo's a royal pain in the butt. Not bad now when the water's just warming up, but in the summer it gets thick-like; takes hold of the needle grass and clogs our nets as we drag. Intead of water passing through and letting us git the shrimp, it makes our net so solid-like that you can't even see through it and it just pushes everything off to the side; like dragging a big board behind us!"

"What causes it?"

"Reckon fertilizers and such that the farmers use. They even fertilize the plantation pine around these parts. All that stuff gits in the groundwater and run-off and eventually finds itself in the Gulf. You also got them phosphate mines that puts their stuff in the rivers. When the Gulf water gits warm, like I say, it jest takes off. Got a big fancy name for it, yuter-something-cation. Good news is it ain't like the runoff from the Buckeye pulp mill we passed this morning. That stuff's poison, kills everything."

Tiny began to separate and throw the shrimp into the openings. His hands were a blur. He was on his second shovel-full before Rusty had done half his.

"Dang, Tiny. I feel like I'm in slow motion, watching you."

Tiny laughed, his hands a blur again. "Ain't my first rodeo." He looked at his watch. "Bottom appears clean enough so we'll pull for a couple hours next time, though I'm gonna have to swing her around in about a half hour because we'll be running outta grass and approaching a bank where I don't want them nets to git fouled."

The routine never varied, just the amounts of shrimp, dead sea grass, and species of critters that came out of the bag. Rusty felt like he was on a stage with all the bright lights shining down on him; it was dark everywhere else. He helped Tiny empty the baskets into the onion bags and watched him tie them off. Tiny explained that he kept a tally of eating versus bait by counting the number of rings on the baskets to where the shrimp leveled off. "I figgers about five pounds per ring," he said counting. "This basket's got somethin' over twenty pounds of bait."

At three a.m., with only a candy bar in his stomach and after yet another generous dollop of Dramamine, Rusty could barely keep his eyes open.

"You're about asleep on your feet, Rusty. Why don't you go git some shuteye. I kin take care of all this. Just one more pull anyways."

"Don't know why I'm so tired, Tiny."

"The stuff you're taking is doing it. Go on now, git!" As Rusty stumbled off, Tiny called after him, "Bottom's mine." Rusty nodded. He fumbled with his bib, boots, and life preserver, and stowed them before entering and, fully dressed, climbing up. He was asleep the moment he closed his eyes.

The radio woke him. Rusty opened his eyes and didn't recognize the ceiling less than a foot above his head. Where the hell was he? He turned and saw the clock on the galley wall. Oh yeah, Tiny's boat. The clock said a little after five. There was more static from the radio. Tiny went into the wheelhouse.

"Tiny, you read me? Over."

Tiny reached for the mike.

"I read you, Jimmy. What's up? Over."

"Switch over."

"That's a ten four."

There was a little more static. Jimmy's voice came in again.

"You there, Tiny?"

"Yep."

"Rusty, too?"

"Yep, but he's conked out. Musta drank hisself at least a full bottle of Dramamine."

Rusty could hear Jimmy chuckle into the radio.

"Better him than me."

"Think you'd be just fine, Jimmy: so far, ain't been rollin' much at all."

Jimmy turned serious.

"Tiny, might want to chipmunk."

"Ten four, Jimmy." Rusty heard a switch click. "All set. What's up?"

"Where you fishin' these days?"

"South. Not too far from the Keys."

"Got a shrimper heading in that direction, going to come in right around the Keys in a few days or so, depending on the weather. If I was you, I'd plan on fishing north next week."

"That's a ten four, Jimmy, thanks. Sure is a coincidence that them shrimpers come in when that old blimp's down."

"Yeah, sure is. How's Rusty doin'?"

"Just fine, he's a trooper alright."

If you only knew, Rusty thought.

"Say 'hey' to him for me. How's the catch?"

"Middling, but we got another couple days still."

"Coming in for Tammy's party?"

"Wouldn't miss, it."

"Then see you there."

"Best to Crystal."

"That's a ten four. Good luck. Over and out."

Tiny switched off, and Rusty closed his eyes as he passed through the galley. Shipment coming in next week; big chance to nail Jimmy, catch him red-handed and end this charade. His eyes popped open. Be mighty handy to know what frequency Jimmy used. Rolling awkwardly out of his berth, he climbed down. Damn if he didn't still feel groggy as hell. He went into the pilothouse. Frequency should be on the one fifty range, but it was set at 166.666. Had to be Jimmy's. He returned to the galley, wondering if he should go help Tiny. Nah, he was supposed to be asleep. As he got comfortable again, he was nagged by the thought that most everybody he had met, including Jimmy, were good, hardworking people, upfront and forthright; where did you find that these days? And as poor as they were, who could blame them if they wanted some extra money to take better care of their families and provide a few frills in their simple lives? What real harm were they doing by running the marijuana? It took him longer than he thought to get back to sleep.

He woke up to the rich smell of coffee and no engine noise. Tiny was looking at him, sipping from a mug. Rusty glanced at the clock. Nine o'clock! Damn, some crew he was! He quickly sat up and rapped his head against the ceiling. Tiny laughed.

"Don't know what your hurry is. We're anchored and everything's shipshape. Can you handle some coffee and breakfast?"

Damn, if he didn't feel pretty good, even though he hadn't taken any Dramamine for—he did the arithmetic—close to six hours. Rusty nodded.

"I'll git outta here so you can git organized." Tiny took a mug out of the drainer. "Here."

A short time later, Rusty emerged to a beautiful sunny and, more importantly, calm morning: the Gulf sparkled everywhere he looked and there were gulls and pelicans floating astern, preening and waiting for scraps. Tiny, sitting on a gunwale, watched Rusty take a good pull on his coffee and look around the boat. It was indeed shipshape, even the deck was swabbed clean.

Rusty opened the hold; it looked like there was about the same number of yellow ribbon bags as red.

"About even, eating and bait," Rusty said.

"Not really. Heck of a lot more of them little guys in a bag than big ones. But, that's to be expected early spring. Shrimps live for a year and a lot of these is new ones. As the water warms up, they'll git big quick, shedding shells and making new ones to fit; just like a blue crab."

Tiny stood up. "Think you can handle some scrambled eggs alright?"

"Believe so; can I help?"

"Pretty tight quarters."

Rusty nodded.

After breakfast, Rusty said, "I got the dishes."

"Good, and I got the lower bunk."

Tiny was asleep and snoring before Rusty had the coffee cups in the drainer. When he finished the dishes, he went aft to throw the scraps overboard, pleased that he felt fine even though he still hadn't taken anything. The seabirds fought over the scraps like chickens in a barnyard. He hefted himself up onto the sorting table. The sun felt great on his face. Eyes closed, he smiled into it, thinking this is the life. Sure beats riding the interstates and sitting at the barracks. What the hell was he doing with his life, anyway?

How he hated interstate duty! A trooper was always first on the scene to clean up the mess—mutilated bodies with blood everywhere, lives destroyed. And it was usually the result of something stupid and unnecessary: careless drivers, drunk drivers, drugged drivers, falling asleep at the wheel. Then there were the late night speeders. You never knew what to expect and always had to be careful...always! Could be a drug dealer with dope in his veins and a gun under the dash. Or some crazy who might shoot you just for kicks. The high-speed chases were different. Those got his juices going, but they were few and far between; plus it usually wasn't pretty when they ended. He pictured that young blond flying high on coke who was decapitated at a hundred and twenty miles an hour when her car flipped over and hit a guardrail.

You had to form a shell to protect yourself from all that; just like the crabs. But this last week or so, he actually felt like he was shedding that shell. He felt more relaxed, at peace; he was enjoying himself, the people, and his surroundings even though he was undercover. Maybe in another life he could have been a fisherman, a shrimper, or a crabber. Live in a community like Crescent Beach. He had the body for a fisherman's hard work, that is, if he could solve the seasickness problem. Maybe some day, when he retired, he could find an area like this one and work part time as a mechanic to keep busy if he couldn't fish. He'd enjoy that; no shell required.

The sun was making him sleepy. He didn't go back to his bunk because he'd disturb Tiny, plus he didn't know if he could stand his snoring. Rusty took his life preserver off. Using it as a pillow, he stretched out on the sorting table and, like Tiny, was soon asleep.

He woke to Tiny staring at him again, a big grin on his face.

"Rusty, you should have covered up some: you're about as red as the ribbons I tied on them bags."

Rusty put a hand to his cheek. He could feel the burn. Had forgot all about putting on sunscreen.

"While you been snoozing, I been making us some killer gumbo. Be ready soon."

Tiny returned to the galley, leaving Rusty to slowly, stiffly get on his feet. He put his life preserver back on. He felt his face again; with his fair complexion, he'd be paying a price tonight. Tiny returned with a large bowl of creamy gumbo in each hand. He handed one to Rusty.

"Damn, Tiny, this is good! What's the green stuff? Okra?"

"Yep, and there's some of them flounder and whiting and shrimps we caught. Don't git much fresher."

Rusty's appetite was back. He inhaled the gumbo.

"Plenty more where that came from, but might want to take it easy. Weather says the winds suppose to pick up a mite and we might git some rain. Might take some of your stuff if you ain't already."

"Think I got it wupped, Tiny," Rusty said.

"Suit yourself. Just hope you don't go feeding them seagulls following the boat."

Rusty stood up.

"Get you another bowl?"

"Nope," Tiny said, putting his down on the sorting table. "Later. Going to digest a bit while I mend that starboard net. Musta hooked on a piece o' coral or somethin'."

Rusty was halfway into his second bowl when he said, "You know, Tiny, there's something I can't figure out."

Tiny looked up from the nylon net, needle in hand. "What's that?"

"If Jimmy and some others are bringing stuff in by boats, there must be all sorts of radio communication. Why the hell doesn't the Coast Guard pick up on that and bust them?"

Tiny put down the needle.

"Let you in on a little secret. There's a guy lives near a little hole-in-the-wall town called Panacea who has him a business of doctoring radio equipment. He goes around to yard sales, dumpsters and such, and finds him old radios and TV's. Takes out transistors and other parts he kin use. Man's a regular Mr. Wizard. And it's all legal. There's about a kazillion frequencies out there and he rigs fishermens' radios so they gots their own special channel. I got me one. Cost me five pounds of shrimp."

"Why do you need one; I mean, if you're not involved and all?"

"I ain't no runner, but I ain't no angel neithers. There's some places you're not supposed to fish and there's usually more shrimps in them places than anywheres else. But, big fines if'n you git caught. So we shrimpers kinda let each other know where the authorities is at. That plus sometimes you want to call in to port to Big John or somebody to tell them what you're bringing in and when and how much. Now, if I got me a good rich spot, I don't need no one else a'dragging it too."

"I'd still think the Coast Guard could flip frequencies around until they stumbled on to one they'd want to listen to."

"Maybe. That's why we got scramblers, too. Just hit a button and though you kin hear the person you're talking to jest fine, for anybody else tuning in, sounds like a pair of chipmunks squabbling. Scrambler cost me ten pounds of shrimp." Tiny went back to mending.

"If I ever hear someone talk about some 'dumb old fisherman,' I'm going to laugh in his face," Rusty said. "There ain't no flies on you boys, none at all."

Tiny finished mending, and swung the net out. He secured the rigging, before turning back to Rusty.

"If'n you really got that seasickness beat, should consider coming up to Apalachicola with me sometime. Kin fish day or night up there because they got a different kind of shrimp lives in them waters, the white ones. And when we come in to port to sell the catch and fuel up, there's lots of bars and oyster houses. One place in particular kin fix you up a plate of oysters in about a hundred different ways. And just down the street's a bar right over the water. Not much more than a shack, but

got good cold beer and there's always a few girls looking for a little fun for the price of a couple drinks. Yep,
Apalach is a fine place, alright." Tiny started to do a
little jig and began singing. His jig wasn't much more
than a shuffle, and he was way off tune. "Got some crazy
little women there and I'ma goin' to git me one." He
suddenly stopped and asked Rusty, "You play checkers?"

"Been known to."

"We got some time to kill afore headin' out. Wanna
play some?"

"Sure, but gotta warn you."

"What's that?"

Rusty smiled. "Never been beat."

"That so?"

Two hours later, heading out towards the sun, good-
sized waves crashed against the bow. Tiny was alone in
the pilothouse because Rusty, a light shade of green, was
in the stern feeding the sea gulls.

CHAPTER EIGHTEEN

"What's the temp, Doc?" Charley asked
"Not quite two hundred."
"Dying down some."

Charley pushed himself up off a white plastic chair and joined Norm in front of the large trailer-hitched, steel pig cooker. Nearby, the pool table was covered in plastic and had a thick piece of plywood on top. Over a dozen picnic tables had been trucked in and set around and under the Club. Charley rummaged through a pile of firewood until he found a few pieces that hadn't been split. Norm held open the firebox door, enabling Charley to rake the coals and throw the wood in.

"Why those, Charley?" Norm asked, taking off leather gloves and laying them down on his chair next to Charley's.

"Round ones take a little longer to catch good, but then puts out more heat, plus they smoke more in the beginnin' which makes piggy here taste better. Of course, that's just my perfessional opinion."

"How many hogs do you think you've cooked over the years."

"Dern if I know. A parcel of 'em for sure. And afore I was cooking 'em, my daddy was, and my gran'daddy afore him. Back in them days, never used to be all them hunting clubs and such along the highway to Perry as they is now. All that land was woods, bee-yutiful oaks everywhere, and no 'keep out' signs nowheres. I believe a fox squirrel could go clear to Perry without ever stepping on the ground there was so many trees. Me and my gran'daddy could shoot us a razorback whenever we needed meat. And if we caught us some iddy biddy shoats, we'd mark 'em to harvest later."

"'Mark them?'"

"Yep. We'd catch 'em, cut notches outta their ears, and if'n they was males, cut 'em. Ours was three notches on the left ear; was like branding 'em. People would know our mark and respect it, just like we'd respect theirs. No one, well, almost no one would inteshally shoot…"

"Intentionally, Charley."

"Whatever; inteshally shoot 'em if they saw it was marked. And if'n they did, they'd bring us over the hog, gutted o' course. Sort of a code, you might say."

"Sounds like a pretty good system."

"T'was."

They could hear furniture scraping the floor above them.

"Sounds to me like the girls is organizing for the dance tonight."

"That and about a hundred other things. Tammy came over at five this morning."

"Done beat me, that's for sure; I started this here fire around six."

Norm began thinking how busy Tammy had been tending to details: she was all business, and this made two days running he hadn't woken up in her bed. He'd be glad when the Valentine Day's party was over.

Minnie, coffee pot in hand, came down the steps.

"Refill, boys?"

She filled both their cups.

"What time's it, Minnie?" Charley asked.

"Approaching eleven."

" Good, in another hour we kin switch over to beer."
Minnie rolled her eyes at Norm.

"You ever wonder, Doctor, why Charley here is trying
so awful hard to become the town drunk?"

Norm didn't say a word.

"This here's demanding and hot work, Minnie,"
Charley said from his chair, "and Miss Tammy said it'sa
part o' the deal. Besides, it's plain downright un-Ameri-
can to roast a hog without drinking some beers!"

Minnie shook her head as she returned to the restaurant. Charley asked, "How things going with you and
Miss Tammy, Doc?"

"No complaint so far, Charley, none at all. How
about you and Minnie?"

"Ain't no road that don't got some bumps in it,
but it's them blind curves when you got no idea what's
a'coming is what gits me. I love that woman to death,
but she kin git mighty ornery sometimes."

Tiny pulled up, parking his truck in the shade of a
live oak across the street.

"Right on time, Tiny. Thanks," Norm said, as Tiny
walked up. "Tiny's taking my place, Charley. I'm going into Perry to get Tammy a box of chocolates for
Valentine's. Want me to pick you up one for Minnie.
Or a card?"

"Nah."

"Charley here's a regular ladies man, ain't he, Norm,"
Tiny said.

"You mind your own business, Tiny!"

"Might help straighten out some of those curves you
were talking about, Charley," Norm said.

Charley shrugged. Norm smiled.

"I'll pick you up both."

"Whatever…Tiny, your timing's pretty good. In
about an hour, we start gitting some free beer from Miss
Tammy."

Norm left the two good friends jawing away. As he crossed the humpback bridge, a pickup slowly rumbled up Main Street from the cattle gap. The truck sat up extra high with oversized tires, was covered with mud, and a chained pit bull sat behind the rear window on top of a dented and rusty toolbox. From his vantage point, Norm could see the truck's bed was full of swamp cabbage. It was Butch coming in to get a little beer money.

The pickup stopped in front of the Crescent Club. Charley and Tiny watched Butch get out and swagger over. Everything about him was medium: height, build, length of dirty blond hair. His eyes, though, were small dark beads, flicking around. He wore cowboy boots, jeans, wide belt with a large western style buckle, a faded denim shirt, and a dirty Stetson.

"Guess that cut-out o' yours, Butch, makes you feel like you got a big bad-ass V-8 under the hood instead o' that puny little old six," Charley drawled.

"That truck can go places a coon dog won't, Charley."

"That's because a coon dog's got hisself more sense."

"Butch, you driving for Steinhatchee agin?" Tiny asked.

"Most likely."

"Can't wait to see what dirty tricks you got up your sleeve this year," Charley said.

"Charley, you and Jimmy ain't never gonna win; might as well git used to it," Butch countered.

Charley stood up and walked over to the truck, making sure he was out of reach of the chained pit bull. He glanced at the dog.

"Morning, Hero. Kill yourself anything today?" No tail wag. The dog stared at Charley as he looked into the bed of the pickup. "I see you been visiting the state parks today, Butch."

"Fuck you, Charley. Tiny, Miss Tammy upstairs?"

Tiny shrugged.

"Ask Charley. I just got here."

Charley walked over to check the cooker's thermometer, taking his time to answer.

"Yep. She, Minnie, and Maybelline is upstairs working their tails off, something I know's kinda foreign to you. And I'ma guessing Miss Tammy don't need no trespassed cabbages because she got her menu all set for tonight."

"I think I'll just go see for myself, asshole."

Butch climbed up to the restaurant.

"Why you go pitching his sucker in the dirt all the time?" Tiny asked.

"Because he's a low down no-good that gives us rednecks a bad name, that's why. I didn' like him none when we was kids, and I don't like him none now."

He and Butch must have scrapped twenty times over the years, Charley thought, but one still stuck in his craw. Must have been about ten, he recalled, when he, Butch, and Butch's older brother, Tommy, were taking turns plinking with Butch's daddy's pump 22 at some cans on top of a fence. The rifle had just been reloaded and it was Butch's turn when a mocking bird landed in a tree and started singing. Butch shot it, knocking it out of the tree and it began flopping all around with Butch laughing and saying what a goddamn good shot he was.

"Now why'd you go and do such a fool thing?" Charley had asked.

Butch, still laughing, poked at the bird with the barrel. Each time he propped it up, it would flop over, weakly peeping, its beautiful songs a memory.

"Put it out of its misery, Butch!"

"What are you so upset for? Just a damn bird."

"Yeah, and you're just a damn idiot," Charley said, pushing the 22 aside and going to his knees. He picked up the mockingbird and, tears in his eyes, wrung its neck. Butch turned to his brother.

"Lookee at the crybaby, Tommy. Jest a goddamn sissy, ain't he?"

Charley lunged, tackling Butch, luckily the 22 falling harmlessly away. They rolled around in the dirt, but when Charley began getting the best of Butch, Tommy took his brother's part and pulled Charley away, holding him with his arms pinned behind him. Butch came up and sucker punched Charley who went crazy and broke away from the much bigger Tommy, which pissed Tommy off. Tommy and Butch had then kicked the shit out of Charley.

Less than the time it took Charley to baste the pig, Butch came down the stairs and jumped back into his pickup. He revved the engine as Charley yelled over, "Told you, numb nuts!" Butch slammed it into gear and laid a patch as he drove away. A couple of blocks later, he slowed down to work the streets, selling the hearts of palm. He had few takers and he figured that he'd probably have even less with the people across the creek. But you never know, he thought as he crossed over. Norm passed him, heading out to Perry. He shook his head at Butch who was pointing at the palm hearts. A couple of houses later, Butch saw Beau raking leaves in his front yard. Skillet was closeby, watching Beau. When Butch pulled up, Hero started barking ferociously, the chain snapping like a whip as he lunged towards Skillet. Skillet barked back causing Beau to immediately throw down the rake and grab Skillet's collar. Butch got out of the truck and held up a heart of palm. He made no move to settle his dog.

"Want any swamp cabbage, Mr. Beau?" Butch asked. Hero kept lunging towards Skillet, his mouth beginning to froth. Beau could barely hear him with all the barking. He was curt.

"No. Glad you have that animal secured, Butch," he said, dragging the struggling and barking Skillet back towards the house.

Butch flung the cabbage back into the truck. "Don't blame you none, Hero, and we know you'd tear him apart if I'd let you." He walked around to the cab. "Goddamn uppity rich people," he muttered.

It was a beautiful late afternoon, no wind and warm for February, when people started arriving. Tammy, with a rebel-flag-decorated money pouch around her slender waste, was the greeter and money taker. Crystal and Maybelline were operating the fish fryer, while Norm and Minnie were all set to dole out sides of baked beans, slaw, rolls, and hush puppies. A tall igloo of sweet tea sweated at the end of the table. It was understood that because church people and children would be present, no alcohol would be served. It was also understood that people could bring whatever they wanted to drink as long as it was masked in cups, and that the dance upstairs in the Club would be a different story.

Charley, a little in his cups, was whetting his knife when the reverend and his wife arrived. Tammy was glad she had picked up all the beer cans scattered around the pig cooker. The reverend and his wife, Sarah, watched Charley slice up the pig. His knife strokes were steady and sure; each piece fell away in uniform thickness and there was no hacking or wasted moves. He was a pro.

"Well, Charley," said the reverend, "I see you're a man of many talents."

"Yes sir, Reverend. Can do lots of things."

"Except go to church on Sunday," the reverend's wife added.

"Now, Sarah," the reverend said. "Don't…"

"It's okay, Reverend; that's the truth alright. I jest don't cotton much to sitting inside somewheres on a nice morning and listening to someone pontificake, no offense meant. But, it don't mean I don't got my own beliefs."

"I'm glad to hear that, Charley; that you believe in something," Sarah said with raised eyebrows. "And just what are some of those beliefs?"

"Guess you don't beat around the bush none, do you, ma'am?"

Crystal, Norm, and Minnie, heads down, seemingly concentrating on their duties, were all ears. So was Tammy who was pointedly looking up the street towards several tidily dressed people walking in their direction. Charley worked on the pig for a few slices before looking back at Sarah.

"Now don't git me wrong, ma'am, and I don't mean to insult you in any way, but you asked me a question, and I'ma going to do my best to answer it. I believe there's something higher than us for sure, but I don't call it God, and I don't rightly know what to call it. I also don't think whatever it is gotta be in our image as you folks say. Seems to me there's lotsa beliefs around this world, both now and long afore us, of all kinds. And I don't know how anyone can say this one's right and this one's wrong. That don't make no sense to me; I just don't believe people will go to hell if their beliefs differ.

"But what does make sense to me is the natural order of things, how everything works together, connected-like. I believe there's a something higher all right, and that higher whatever it is, is what puts everything together. Like I say, I don't got no clue as to what's the right name to put on it, but maybe Mother Nature's about the closest. That's my God, I guess, my religion. It's just so amazing to me, it truly is.

"But I think the church is real important too, to teach us the difference between right and wrong. There's nuthin' worse than some person who knows better, but does bad. I ain't got no patience for that, and what's more…"

"Charley," Tammy interrupted, " I think the reverend and Sarah and the other people here might like some of that pig you been cutting up before it gets stone cold."

Charley hadn't noticed the others. Neither had the reverend and his wife. Sarah was staring at Charley with her mouth half open.

"Jeez, I'ma sorry, Miss Tammy. Here's I go justa spouting off and neglecting my duties. Reverend and Mrs. Sarah, ma'am, why don't you git yourselves a plate over yonder. I'll save you some of this here," Charley said, pointing with his knife at some strips. "It's the loin and that be the best part."

Two lines quickly formed, one for Charley, the other for Crystal and Maybelline. People kept arriving, some on foot and by boat, many in cars, but mostly in pickups. Beau and Virginia, minus Skillet, arrived by golf cart. Every picnic table was soon full, forcing some of the younger men to eat standing up. No woman or old person had to stand. Many of the diners were from town, of course, but there were also ranchers, farmers, and backwoods folks, as well as a few from Perry. The dinner was a huge success.

By the time Tammy turned on the lights underneath the restaurant, most of the church members had gone home. There were still some people sitting at the picnic tables. The men, most of whom were working toothpicks, looked like they could lift hundred pound sacks of feed all day long. But fried food and barbecue were staples in this part of the country, consequently not a flat stomach in sight and belts with big western buckles were cinched low to accommodate the bellies that hung over. A few, Norm noted, were nothing short of prodigious. As soon as Norm cleared off the pool table, a foursome, beers in hand, began playing. The band arrived and went upstairs to set up. Norm tossed the paper plates and other flotsam he had collected into the lined garbage cans and took a last look around. Satisfied, he climbed the stairs up to the restaurant where there was not an empty table and standing room only at the bar. Earlier in the day, Tammy had pushed together two tables and reserved them for the poker regulars and their families.

Tammy had gone all out with decorations, and Norm wondered if maybe their romance had played a part. He hoped so. Swags of red paper hearts and white doily-like connectors were draped around the windows and along the top of the walls, and a large red cardboard heart covered the TV behind the bar. Heart-shaped balloons were all over the ceiling and each table, covered with a heart-shaped tablecloth, had a small bowl of different colored, hard heart-shaped candies in the center. The band was set up at the far end of the room. Everything, including the band, was financed by the cover charge. Because of the pig roast and fish fry, the kitchen was closed and only packaged snacks would be sold. Maybelline was tending bar, aided by several waitresses Tammy had hired for the event so that she and Minnie could party with everyone else, or so she hoped.

Norm wanted to whistle when he saw that Tammy had changed into a clinging, sparkly-red single piece outfit. Where had she gotten that? Certainly not in Perry, a paper mill town with as many second hand and used tire stores as fast food restaurants. Mail order? She was holding on to a chair at their table, her back to him, giving instructions to a young waitress. She had the curves of a mermaid. Minnie, Beau and Virginia, Jimmy and Crystal, Ralph, Craig, Rusty, and Tiny were seated, along with Big John who wore a clean red tee shirt under his overalls. Big John was flanked by his wife Maria and their teenaged daughter. The chair next to Minnie was empty.

"Where's Charley?" Norm asked as he sat down.

"Norm, you missed a fine instance of our democratic principles in action," answered Beau. "We took a vote, with the overwhelming majority here deciding that Charley was unfit to sit with us until he cleaned up."

"Which, of course, was understandable," Crystal interjected, "considering he'd been stoking fires all day, then cutting up a whole hog. He had to be prodded some before he'd leave, though. As for me, I couldn't wait to shower and get rid of all the grease."

"Don't forget the beers he drank today," Minnie added. "Good chance for him to sober up."

"Heck, Minnie, weren't that many," Tiny said.

Tammy sat down next to Norm. When she reached for his hand under the table, Norm wished he could bottle what he felt. The band started out playing a sixties number; only fitting, Norm thought, with their long hair and tie-dye shirts. The band was composed of a lead and a bass guitar, drummer, electric piano, and a sexy sequined lady lead singer shaking a tambourine. They followed the first number with a long, low melody while the lady singer introduced the band members.

A Johnny Mathis song from the fifties was next. Women around the room began pulling their husbands and boyfriends to their feet. Beau and Virginia were the first out, comfortable in each other's arms. They were soon surrounded. Tammy snuggled up to Norm, as well as Crystal to Jimmy. Much to Melissa's delight, even Big John allowed Maria to pull him out to the dance floor where he engulfed her. Rusty paired off with Minnie, but they hadn't danced long before Charley, showered, shaved, and hair plastered down, cut in. Rusty graciously gave way while Minnie gave Charley an approving look.

"Heck of an improvement, Charley," she said. "You're almost presentable."

Charley pulled her in close and they were soon cheek to cheek, with his arms around her waist and hers resting lightly on his chest. Tammy and Norm were almost as wrapped up. When they returned to the table, Minnie found a little heart-shaped box of candy and a card with her name on it.

"What's this?" she asked, looking around. Tiny looked over to Norm who was smiling at Charley.

"Beats me," Charley said, deadpan. He looked accusingly around the table. "Someone here messing with my girl!"

Minnie opened the card. Her mouth dropped open.

"Why Charley!" She hugged him and gave him a big smacker on the cheek. Charley beamed as she moved her chair closer to him.

"Always said Charley here was a real ladies man," Tiny announced to the table.

A slow dance began.

"Charley?" Minnie said.

"Yes, Ma'am," he said, standing up and pulling out her chair which surprised her and everybody else.

"You might add, Tiny," Virginia said in her best Charleston accent, "that Charley can be quite the gentleman." She turned to her husband. "Dear..."

"With pleasure, Sugah," Beau said, making sure he pulled out her chair, too.

Rusty noticed Crystal look at Jimmy who shook his head.

"Jimmy, do you mind if I ask Crystal to dance?" he asked.

"I don't mind, but she might."

Crystal smiled at Rusty.

"Be mighty pleased, Rusty," she said, standing up.

He led her out to the floor next to Minnie and Charley who were already tangled up. As they started to dance, Crystal asked, "What do you think of our little town, Rusty?"

"Like it. Even though I grew up in the mountains nowhere near the Gulf, Crescent Beach is a lot like it was there, back when things were a lot simpler."

Crystal laughed.

"Guess that's a good description of us around here, 'simple.'"

"I meant that as a compliment."

She pulled her head from his shoulder and looked at him. Damn how her eyes sparkled, he thought.

"I know you did, Rusty."

"I like the people, too."

"Ralph says that you're meeting with him to look for a house, or maybe some land to build. You thinking of moving here?"

"Just kicking tires right now, I guess."

"You're certainly making some friends, Jimmy included. He doesn't usually take to somebody as quickly as he's taken to you."

"That's probably because of Junior Johnson."

She laughed. "That could have something to do with it. Has he told you about the CB 250, yet?"

"Nope. What's that?"

"Imagine you'll find out soon enough," she said, cryptically, and returned to his shoulder.

As they continued to dance, Rusty couldn't help thinking he was living a lie. Lying all the time, making friends based on lies. And his job description—snitch. No other way to put it. And Crystal felt good in his arms, their bodies fit well together. Great, now he's coveting another man's wife! Congratulations, you've come a long way, partner. Still, he couldn't help thinking the dance ended too soon.

The band's selections were balanced throughout the evening, about as many slow tunes as fast, with a little blue grass and country western thrown in. Norm and Beau were the only ones at the table drinking hard liquor. Virgina was sipping amontillado sherry while Craig, Ralph, and Big John's daughter Melissa were drinking cokes, and everyone else was drinking beer. By the time the band took their break, there were empty bottles scattered all over the table. Tammy, seeing how busy the waitresses were, began gathering them. Minnie stood up to help.

"Appears you don't dance much, Tiny," Rusty said.

"Nope. I crushed enough feet in my day; don't need to crush no more."

"Haven't seen you out on the dance floor none neither, Craig, and I know you can dance good," Charley said. He looked around the room. "Seems to be quite a few unattached heifers scattered around."

"Don't think I'll chance it, Charley. Still having dizzy spells."

"And that could continue for awhile, or stop tonight," Norm said.

"Not so bad now, Norm. Not like a couple of days ago. Planning on going back home tomorrow; I've imposed myself long enough on Ralph here."

"Been no bother, Craig; have enjoyed the company," Ralph said.

"Got to say, sure seems to me that little old bump on your noggin done knocked some sense into you, Craig. You been mighty civil to Ralph here for a change."

"Charley, wouldn't you be 'civil' to a man who saved your life, and then took care of you until you were on your feet?"

Ralph looked down and fiddled with his coke. Craig changed the subject.

"Rusty, Jimmy says you're a good mechanic."

"Been known to tinker some, yeah."

"Could I hire you to get my airboat running?"

"I'll take a look at it. Sure."

"Knew it was too good to last," Norm muttered, as he reached for his drink.

"Don't worry, Norm; Ralph's convinced me to sell it and buy a skiff to run around in. But I won't get anything for the airboat if it's not running first."

Norm smiled broadly.

"Craig, you've made my day!"

"Won't hardly be the same around here without you rawdawging out in the marsh somewheres, scattering all the birds and a'running over their nests," Charley said.

They were interrupted by Tammy at the microphone.

"Folks, when the band comes back, there's going to be a fast dance contest with prizes for the top three contestants. Our honorable mayor and town clerk, as well as Maybelline over yonder behind the bar, will be the judges. If one of them taps you on the shoulder, that means you're out and should sit down. Last ones out on the floor will be the winners. First place will win a very nice fishing rod and reel donated by our store here in town. Second is a fry-o-later big enough to cook a turkey whole, donated by Perry Hardware. Third place is dinner for two here at the Club. They're nice prizes, so I'm expecting to see y'all come up here and do your best. Good luck!"

People started to choose partners. At the table, Rusty asked Big John's daughter if she wanted to give it a go. The others paired up as usual except for Norm who begged out. Ralph took his place. As the band tuned up, the floor filled up fast. The mayor, the town clerk, and Maybelline stood together a little off to the side. The mayor had her cane in one hand and a plastic cup in the other. The three conferred as people started to dance. It didn't take long for the judges to make their decisions and the crowded floor quickly thinned out. Minnie and Charley, Rusty and Big John's daughter, and

Big John and Maria were among the first to be tapped on the shoulder by the mayor's cane. By the end of the number, only six couples remained, among them Beau and Virginia, and Ralph and Tammy. The band started up again.

The beat accommodated several styles of dance. Beau and Virginia jitterbugged using precise and complicated twirls, never missing a beat or flubbing a move. Beau would twirl her into him, lock arms, they'd dance as one before he'd fling her out again, and then, somehow, they'd lock into a mutual twirl, before Beau would spin out of it and start twirling Virginia around and around, her feet a blur. Why Virginia didn't get dizzy mystified Norm. They looked like they had done it a hundred times, then realized that they probably had.

Three of the couples dodged each other as they two-stepped all around the dance floor. People that had remained standing rather than return to their tables, backed up to give them space. Like Beau and Virginia, their steps were perfectly orchestrated and they, too, never missed a beat. Rusty was surprised when he recognized Sammy, the large gutted fisherman he had thrown to the floor on his first night in town, was one of the dancers. For a big man, he was very light on his feet and surprisingly gentle and precise swinging his partner around.

But it was Ralph and Tammy who wowed the audience. It wasn't so much a particular style as much as it was an erotic event so enticing that all eyes were soon on them. The judges conferred. Three couples were eliminated and sat down to scattered applause. Maybelline tapped Sammy and his partner next, but made sure they remained standing up front. Third place. The town clerk walked up to Beau and Virginia, leaving Ralph and Tammy to dance out the number. Someone brought out a chair for the mayor. Ralph, lithe and lissome, was all over the floor, seemingly in another world while provocatively circling Tammy. Suddenly, the lead singer stopped the music. No one, including the rest of the band, seemed to know why. Ralph had his back to Tammy and he looked frozen in time, leaving his arms upraised. A windup toy suspended. The singer quickly conferred with the other band members. Ralph, arms still upraised, didn't move. Tammy looked curiously at him, then back to the lead singer.

The band started up again and Norm recognized the song immediately: a Bee Gees number from *Saturday Night Fever*. Ralph's arms dropped and he spun around, head tilted, looking hard at Tammy. He was someone different. Suddenly his arms were pointing at her. Tammy stared back, slowly beginning to gyrate in place, teasing. Norm was riveted. So was Craig, although he was watching Ralph, not Tammy. Ralph exploded with moves, arms pumping up and down while strutting from side to side of the dance floor, thrusting his lower torso out repeatedly every time he turned towards Tammy who now looked like she was doing her best to wiggle out of her tight red outfit. He shot imaginary arrows at her as he worked his way closer, then would back off and begin again. But he was getting closer each time, zeroing in. When he was a few feet away, with perfect timing and arms outstretched, supplicating, he slid on his knees to her. He stopped a few inches from her waist where she took his head in her hands just as the music stopped. There was a stunned, absolute silence, then shouting and applause. Even the musicians put down their instruments to clap.

The mayor put down her cup and got up out of her chair to award the prizes. When Ralph and Tammy received theirs, the audience clamored for more, but without success. After awhile the hubbub died down.

Beau, holding out Tammy's chair, bowed.

"Tammy, my dear, you were positively and wonderfully lewd and lascivious. Scintillating!"

Virginia drawled, "Heavens, Ralph. I do believe you and Tammy may have redefined the genre of 'dirty dancing.' Where on earth did you learn how to dance like that!"

"Y'all musta spiked Ralph's drink," Charley said, looking at Craig.

Ralph turned to Charley with a crooked smile.

"Music, Charley, that's all. It can take me over like that. Can't explain it, just is, or, at least, sometimes is."

"But your steps and moves, Ralph, like a professional," Virginia said.

"Studied dance at the university. Thought I might try to make a living at it, but that didn't last long. I'd have starved. But I still practice some as part of my workouts." He looked down and pulled out his shirt. "Can raise a sweat real fast." Virginia recalled that day before going to Charleston when a sweaty Ralph came to his door, toweling off with loud music in the background.

"Do you want the rod or the reel, Tammy?" Ralph asked. She shook her head.

"All yours, Ralph. You're the man!"

Ralph turned to Crystal.

"Think that church camp could use a nice fishing pole, Crystal?"

"I imagine," she answered with a smile. "Mighty fine of you, Ralph."

"And mighty fine flower arrangements you gave my wife," Jimmy added. "What was the occasion?"

Ralph barely hesitated.

"Just a thank you, Jimmy, for Crystal helping me with the food delivery last week."

"And Miss Tammy here can sure shake a leg...and about everything else at the same time," Charley said. "Now I knows you didn't learn that at no university."

"Bar dances in my younger days, Charley." She looked at Norm. "Sometimes it didn't go over too good with my ex."

The lead singer announced a ladies' choice. Not more than a couple seconds later, Rusty felt a tap on his shoulder. He turned. Maybelline. Rusty forced a smile and graciously stood. Maybelline barely came up to his stomach. As they walked out to the dance floor, Beau asked the table, "Did you ever hear the one about the seven foot basketball player who was dating the four foot cheerleader?" His only answer was Virginia rolling her eyes and shaking her head. "He was nuts over her." Tiny and Charley guffawed, Big John's daughter didn't get it, and Big John didn't explain.

"C'mon Beau, ladies' choice."

"Yes, Sugah."

Big John and his family were the first at the table to call it a night, followed by Craig and Ralph. Beau, getting up slowly, announced that he already was stiffening up from all the dancing and needed to get into the hot tub. Charley, a short time later, announced that he and Minnie were going to take a ride in his convertible and look at the stars. When Rusty stood up to leave, Tiny asked, "Where you going? Scared Maybelline's going to corral you again?"

Jimmy asked, "Rusty, you doing anything special tomorrow?"

"Nope," Rusty said. "Nothing more than catch up on some sleep. That shrimping business takes it out of you."

"Wouldn'ta been so much coming out of you if'n you had took your stuff early on," Tiny put in.

"Don't remind me. What's up, Jimmy?"

"I was hoping I could maybe enlist your help before you got all tangled up in fixing Craig's airboat. Don't want to explain right now except to say it's sort of a town project, but I guarantee it's right up your alley. How about me picking you up around eleven, and afterwards you could eat Sunday dinner with us. My daughter and the twins'll be there."

"We're having fried shrimp for the grandyoung'uns; it's their favorite. Think you can still eat shrimp?" Crystal asked.

"Long as they're cooked. Thank you, Crystal. I'll look forward to it. See you at eleven, Jimmy."

When the band finished playing, the Club had thinned out considerably. Jimmy, Crystal, and Tiny left after last call, and Norm remained to help Tammy and the others clean up. When the Club was empty, Tammy and Norm sat down for a nightcap.

"Long day," Norm said.

Tammy sighed.

"Glad it's over," she said.

"Me too."

"And, thank the Lord, no fights," she added.

"Most likely due to all the women present," Norm said, as he reached behind the bar and pulled out the heart-shaped box of candy he had stashed. "Be my Valentine?"

"Aw, that's sweet, Norm." She opened the box and carefully selected a piece, delicately biting it in half, eyes on his. "Milk chocolate and caramel, my fave," she said as she fed him the other half. She stood and walked around behind him. Bending over, she put her arms around his neck and kissed him lightly on the cheek. She cooed into his ear, "My place or yours, Valentine?"

CHAPTER NINETEEN

"Ensign, tell the captain to have someone monitor the radio frequency, 166.666. It'll probably be scrambled most of the time, but might give a heads up: the closer to the drop, probably the busier it'll be. I'll report in as soon as I know anything more. And, Ensign…"

"Yes?"

"I've been wanting to ask you ever since I met you. Have you started shaving yet?"

"Very funny, Rusty, you're a card. I'll relay your message."

Chuckling, Rusty hung up and started walking back to his cabin. Robins everywhere. There had been a few around, but now, just overnight, the town was being overrun. They were eating the palm and cedar berries, crowding the puddles from the rain a few days ago, making a racket, and shitting dark purple all over everything. Must be a couple thousand of them. He had never seen anything like it. He looked at his watch; Jimmy should be along any minute. He hurried back to his cabin.

Jimmy was punctual. Rusty commented on the robins as he climbed into the cab of the truck.

Jimmy said, "They're a little late this year and lucky to find any berries at all; seagulls already been working them trees pretty good. Robins are heading north I suppose, although they don't rush none: having themselves too good a time socializing and getting drunk on them berries."

A few miles past the cattle gap, Jimmy asked, "You heard anything about the CB 250?"

"Only that I was told you'd be telling me about it." Jimmy looked over curiously. "Crystal, when we were dancing." Jimmy nodded and looked back to the road.

"Crescent Beach has got an annual stock car race. First weekend in March and it's a very big deal, ain't just some mud bogging event. People take it real serious-like. Got a two-and-a-half mile course that's a mix of curves in the woods and one kick-ass straightaway. Anything goes and cars get banged up pretty good, especially on the curves. Only about half that enter make it through to the end, regular demolition derby. Usually get more than twenty entries representing towns from all over: Steinhatchee, Crystal River, Apalachicola, Perry of course, even sometimes from the bigger towns like Gainesville and Tallahassee. Cash prizes and trophies for the top three drivers, and the town that wins gets to keep the special five foot high trophy for a year, although it usually ends up in a sponsor's store or bar. Get more than a thousand spectators. Crescent Beach ain't never won and, to add insult to injury, Steinhatchee won last year with someone from our town driving. But, I'm hoping this year might be different. We've dumped quite a bit of money into our rig and I'm hoping it'll pay off. I want that trophy in City Hall real bad. So that's where we're headed, out to the hunting club where the track and our car is."

"Who's your driver?"

"Me."

Jimmy slowed and turned left onto a limestone road. Several miles later when they came around a corner, Jimmy turned on to a narrower limestone road and stopped at a gate with a sign that read:

No Trespassing
Black Hawk Hunting Club
Members Only

"Mind opening it, Rusty?"

As Jimmy drove through, Rusty saw that the entry road was still surfaced in limestone, although it was hard to tell because it was covered with live oak leaves. Rusty shut the gate and they drove through a long tunnel of low oak branches. A half-mile later, they emerged into a gigantic clearing. The track was on the far side of the clearing, fenced off with a wide gate between wooden grandstands and a large booth on stilts.

"This is the straightaway, almost three-quarters of a mile long. It's called the Crescent Beach 250 because there are a hundred, two-and-a-half-mile laps. Barring any major problems, the race usually lasts between five and six hours. Cars kin git going pretty good here on the straightaway." Jimmy turned and pointed to the booth on stilts. "The judges will be up there."

The tall page wire fence might keep animals and people off the track, Rusty thought, but no way could it stop a car. Jimmy turned the truck around and headed past a complex of weathered gray shacks set one cinder block high off the ground and each with a little porch rimmed by a bark-covered railing. The largest building, Jimmy explained, was the main hunting lodge and the rest were cabins for the members. A BBQ area with picnic tables and a large smoker extended along one side of the lodge.

"There's no hunting this time of year which makes this whole thing possible. Including the practice runs and working on the track and all the organizing, we're out here most of a week. The hunting club makes out like a bandit because we pay 'em a lot of money. We make enough from admission, entry fees, and food to swing it, although ain't much more than break even on our end."

They pulled up to what looked like a long equipment shed with several closed-in bays. Jimmy stopped at the last bay where he unlocked the double door and swung it open. Inside was a seventies vintage, fire engine red Plymouth Barracuda with the number 666 painted on the sides and roof. Rusty recalled all the sixes in Jimmy's radio frequency. The car body looked like it had been straightened out with a sledge hammer after being body slammed a couple of times. Local business names were painted all over it: **CRESCENT BEACH CLUB**, **THE STORE, BIG JOHN'S FISHOUSE**, *NEVER BEEN BEAT SHRIMP*, **DAVE'S STONE & BLUE CRABS, TALBOT'S FISHING GUIDE SERVICE**, even **CRESCENT BEACH CITY HALL**. Scattered around the car was an assortment of car jacks, tires and rims, gas cans, boxes of motor parts, and toolboxes. On the vertical plank walls were some simple shelves and calendars with half naked girls that advertised different motor oils and auto parts. A bright blue driver's suit and helmet hung from nails.

"Bet six is your favorite number?"

"Yeah, how'd you guess?"

Rusty shrugged. He walked slowly around the car, crouched down and looked underneath. Standing up and putting a hand on the trunk, he said, "1971 Hemi 'Cuda, Dana 60 rear axle. Ladder bars front and rear. Guessing maybe the 426 Hemi."

"Not bad. How'd you know it was a '71?"

"Only year they had gills on the sides and four headlights. I might never have gotten nabbed if I had had a car like this, though it looks like it was borrowed a couple of times by the Dukes of Hazzard."

"Told you that anything goes in this race. And you're right about the 426."

"Can I take a gander?"

"Help yourself," Jimmy said, opening the hood. Rusty looked it over, very clean.

"You've been taking good care of it," he said, wiggling the throttle cable. He looked up. "Jimmy, why am I here?"

"Because of your skills. Need you to be in the pit crew: make sure she's tuned up and ready, and to be here if there's some sorta problem. Last year, if we had somebody good in the pit, might have won. Good chance anyway. I figure with your experience…"

Rusty nodded and shut the hood. He didn't say anything as he walked slowly around the car again.

"You'd get a cut of the prize money, although it ain't a whole lot."

"Not worried about money, Jimmy." He continued to walk around the car. "What do you use for fuel?"

The question surprised Jimmy. He shrugged.

"Highest octane we can get."

"Ever think about arming it with a tiny pump that could shoot nitrous oxide into the carb when you punched it coming into the straightaway? Give it quite a jolt and easy to do. Equipment's still stock, just special fuel."

"Dang, Rusty, you gotta be in the pit crew!"

Rusty laughed and stuck out his hand. Jimmy quickly took it.

"Of course I will. Would enjoy it. How about we walk that track?"

Jimmy locked up. They walked to the gate below the elevated booth.

"Cars go in this direction, enter the woods there, and come out yonder," Jimmy said, pointing back to the far end of the straightaway. They passed through the gate. Rusty estimated maybe five cars could run abreast in the straightaway. The road abruptly narrowed when it entered the woods. Three abreast would be a squeeze.

They soon came to a fairly tight S curve with a couple exit trails that led to small clearings.

"What's the story with those," Rusty asked, pointing towards the clearings.

"This race is as much about surviving as going fast. As I said, regular demolition derby. Ain't that many rules, but a few for safety, mostly being the race flags just like they got in Darlington or Daytona to slow you down or stop the race. We probably git more yellow flags than Bristol Speedway. And ain't no push-starting stalled cars allowed anywhere on the track. We got two Pettibone loaders with winches, one stationed in this area and one on the backside before the straightaway. They pull out any rig can't go no further and git 'em outta the way pronto. I expect you seen all them scars on the oaks and pine as we been walking?"

Rusty nodded. "Seems they been kissed once or twice. Looks like the main skid trail of a logging operation around here."

"A lot of the fans watch from the woods here, at the hairpin clearing, and on the other side. Some climb up in the oaks to watch; that is, if there ain't too many chiggers in the Spanish Moss. We got some guys, track marshals is what they're called in the big races, stationed with the Pettibones. They got walkie-talkies so the tower knows what's going on, and vice-versa. If'n there's a bad collision anywhere, they kin wave the caution or stop flags."

"What do you do if someone gets hurt?"

"Good news is that no one goes like a bat outta hell in these sections, and we got a fast squad and ambulance from Perry out here for the whole race. Those guys all want the duty, draw straws for it. We've got Norm, too, of course; he's on our fire truck squad. Charley, though, got permanently kicked off race duty because he had him one too many beers a few years back and went to spraying every well-endowed young woman in a tee shirt within range. The girls didn't seem to mind it none, but when he sprayed a young church filly, the shit hit the fan. So, Charley helps in the pit now, although mostly he sits and watches the race and drinks beer. Anyway, so far we've been lucky; nothing much serious has happened in the way of accidents."

The turquoise water of a flooded limestone quarry appeared on their right. They followed it until the water ended and the track turned sharply.

"This is the first hairpin," Jimmy said. "Got another right before you come out of the woods."

The sun was bright on the limestone; Rusty wished he had brought his sunglasses. They continued on the backstretch which had a much longer S curve. Finally, after the second hairpin, they exited the woods, coming into the far end of the straightaway.

Rusty said, "Imagine you can get that 'Cuda up pretty good here."

"Yep, maybe a hundred and twenty or so before you got to downshift like a sonofabitch."

Rusty nodded; about what he had guessed.

"I like that nitrous oxide idea of yours, Rusty. Maybe later this week we can rig it. But, as for right now, I've worked up a pretty good appetite from all this walking and," he looked at his watch, "the twins got to be home by now. Let's head."

The two little boys were running around the deck when Jimmy and Rusty arrived.

"Grampa, Grampa!" they screamed as they ran down the steps. Jimmy scooped each in an arm. They were identical. "When you taking us fishing, Grampa?" they asked in perfect unison.

Jimmy hugged them before lowering them back to the ground.

"That depends on when your grandma's planning to feed us. First, I want you to meet a friend of mine. Rusty, this here is Luke," he patted one on the head, "and Matthew. Boys, say hello to Rusty."

The boys immediately stuck out their hands.

"Nice to meet you," Luke began.

"Mr. Rusty," Matthew finished.

Rusty laughed.

"Likewise," he said.

The boys turned to grab Jimmy by the hand.

"C'mon, Grampa, let's, " Luke said.

"find out from Grandma," Matthew finished.

Rusty laughed again.

"LSMFT, Rusty."

"Lucky Strike Means Fine Tobacco?"

"Nope. Luke Starts, Matthew Finishes Talking; that's their way."

Crystal came out on the deck wiping her hands on an apron. She was followed by a young woman with similar features, but with dark hair and eyes like Jimmy's.

"Rusty, this is our daughter, Rachel."

Rusty tapped his ball cap.

"Pleasure, ma'am. Fine looking boys you have here."

Rachel smiled.

"You men, wash up. Dinner'll be on the table directly," Crystal said, then added, "and that means you boys, too."

Luke asked, "Grandma, do you have both tartar…"

"and cocktail sauce?" Matthew added.

"Yes, boys. Now hurry up."

On the center of the table was a large platter loaded with golden brown fried shrimp. Luke and Matthew started to fill their plates the moment they sat down.

"Now hold your horses, boys," Jimmy said. "Let me say grace, first."

When he finished, Matthew slopped half a jar of cocktail sauce on his plate, Luke half a jar of tartar. Rachel said, "Luke, Matthew, it would be nice if you had some shrimp with your sauce." Rusty thought the difference sauces a good way to tell the twins apart, at the table anyway. He looked from Crystal to Rachel, and back to Crystal again. Definitely mother-daughter, but Rachel's eyes were nothing in comparison.

After pecan pie, Jimmy pushed his chair back and patted his stomach. The boys asked to be excused and rushed off to get their fishing poles from Rachel's car. When Crystal and Rachel stood up to clear, Rusty said, "I'll do the dishes," and began to get up. The women wouldn't allow it. Instead, they brought coffee to him and Jimmy. A few minutes later, Crystal came back into the dining room.

"Sounds like someone's calling in on the radio, Jimmy."

Jimmy sighed and threw his napkin on to the table.

"On a Sunday, yet," he said. Just then the boys burst back into the room, ready to go.

"Rusty, can you entertain these varmints for a minute or two while I go down to my shop?"

"You two ever do any bronco riding?" Rusty asked, getting down on his knees. The boys looked at each other. Rusty whinnied and bucked a couple of times, and scrambled around the room on all fours. He came back up to the boys. "Climb aboard, if you dare."

The boys looked at each other again. Luke, of course, was the first on, grabbing hold of Rusty's collar. Matthew climbed up behind him, locking his arms around his brother's waist. Rusty took off, the boys screamed with a mix of dread and excitement. Crystal and Rachel rushed in, but laughed when they saw Rusty buck and shake and make like one heck of a clumsy horse. Matthew lost hold of his brother, and in desperation grabbed on to

Rusty's shirt, pulling it out from where it was tucked in, but saving himself from falling off.   Rusty kept galloping around. He was already out of breath by the time the women returned to the kitchen.   Rusty made one final buck, rearing way up.   When he felt the boys begin to slide off, he put his arms behind his back to stop them. In the process, the top three buttons of his shirt popped, exposing his chest and, without realizing it, the bug.

When he faced the boys to see if they were okay, the boys asked, "What's that, Mr. Rusty?"

Rusty looked down, and immediately whipped his shirt closed.   He looked to the kitchen; both women had their back to him, one washing, the other drying. "Some old horses got bugs; like me. Guess I'm just a buggy old horse. Do you think you could go ask your grandma for a couple of safety pins?" he asked, tucking in his shirttails with one hand and holding the shirt together with his other.   When they returned with the pins, they heard Jimmy coming up the stairs. The boys rushed to the door. Jimmy took each by the hand.

"Grampa, Grampa! We rode a bucking bronco!" Luke exclaimed.

Jimmy laughed. "I wondered what all the commotion was."

"And he's all buggy!" Matthew added.

Jimmy look puzzled. Rusty, stomach churning and attaching the pins, said, "Not like your grandpa, no flies or bugs on him. You boys are pretty darn lucky to have about the best fisherman in all of Florida for your grandpa; that's what I think."

The boys started pulling on Jimmy.

"Yeah, c'mon Grampa…"

"Time to go fishing!"

They pulled him out the door. Taking a deep breath, Rusty followed.

CHAPTER TWENTY

Rusty looked at his watch. A little before midnight. Two hours he'd been sitting on the unlit porch of one of Tammy's vacant cabins that had a view of the main channel. Tide was low enough, he thought, so Jimmy had to go out this way. Maybe he'd been wrong. Maybe Tiny had just wanted to try shrimping to the north for a change. But Jimmy had warned him to go north this week. And the weather had been good, and was holding. And Jimmy said he didn't have time today to install the nitrous oxide pump on the Barracuda. No, Jimmy must be going out tonight, tomorrow at the latest. Imagine I'll get an earful if I'm mistaken, that is, if the captain even had the time to effectively mobilize on such short notice.

He looked out towards the Gulf. So different here, and yet so much like where he grew up. Everything and everybody connected. The moonshine had kept the economy going back home, the marijuana here. New Ford pickups from Perry, new outboard motors from the Big Bend marinas, boats being built, homes with shiny refrigerators and freezers full of store bought groceries, some gaudy new furniture, new washing machines out on the porches, families going out to eat. Was the smuggling really such a bad thing?

Momma and Daddy had worked so damn hard, her taking in laundry, him at the sawmill during the week

and tending the plot of tobacco on weekends. Raised
hogs like everyone else. How many times was he sent
out to fill sacks with acorns for the pigs, or go bring the
sheep down from the balds to hand shear so they could
stuff a new mattress. Lord, how that wood smoke smell
in his clothes would make him nauseous after smoking the hams and bacon around the clock! But, when
things were going well with the stills, Momma would get
tips; people were a lot freer with their money. When he
started driving, they never had it so good. But when the
raids shut down the stills, the economy would shrivel up
again and it was back to hand to mouth.

So what if people here in Crescent Beach benefitted
from the pot, what harm was there in that? It wasn't
like they were trafficking in cocaine; now that was bad
stuff, or worse yet, heroin. Hell, booze was worse than
pot anyway, caused way more problems. Like in 'Nam.
It was the drunken soldiers that got in fights, pulled
knives, sometimes service weapons. On account of alcohol, people were beat up bad, or cut up, or even killed.
About the worse thing the potheads ever did was break
into the PX when they had the munchies.

And here he was, on the outside looking in again,
just like in 'Nam. Back home he had been a part of
the whole, a cog of the wheel. In 'Nam, he was the police, the law, avoided by most of the soldiers. Sure he
was damn lucky not to have to go out on patrols, see
his friends blown apart, but MPs were an entity to their
own with no real camaraderie. Yeah, they hung out together, but there were only a couple guys he would call
friends. Many were macho assholes, reveling in their
small time power. Others were wearing blinders, just
wanted to be cops when they got out, eat donuts and
grow bellies until their pensions after thirty years. With
his skills he should have been in the motor pool, that
would at least have made him a part of the wheel. But,

funny the way things turn out, here he was, still a cop, still on the outside. He liked these people in Crescent Beach, and they seemed to like him. He felt like he was making some real friends, but it was all a lie, lies to everyone, even to a pair of four-year-old twins, just to get the goods on Jimmy who was a damn good man. The more he thought about it, the ripples of guilt grew into a wave of shame.

He stood up abruptly and walked towards the water. There was a foursome playing pool, otherwise not too much going on at the Club. It was a Monday night after all. The only noises were the occasional night herons from the marsh, a hoot owl way off, and suddenly a complaining blue heron close by. It was the heron that gave Jimmy away. Rusty soon heard the outboard motor, and there was Jimmy's boat heading slowly out the channel, all running lights off. The pool players didn't look up. Although it was still too dark to make them out in what light was cast from the Club, he could see two silhouetted men and that the winch was no longer attached to the side. He watched the boat disappear into the darkness. After checking for pocket change, he purposely strode towards the little store. The street was deserted and there were no lights anywhere near the payphone. He picked up the receiver and dropped a quarter in the slot, but didn't dial. He stood there looking down the silent, empty street. He started to put the phone back in its cradle, but couldn't. Reluctantly, he dialed. "Ensign, Rusty here. Inform the captain that Talbot just left for the Keys."

Jimmy kept the boat at a snail's pace until he was well beyond the last channel marker. After turning south, he pushed the throttle almost all the way down, and the boat quickly planed off at close to forty miles an hour. Neither he nor Charley said a word as they headed towards the Salt and Pepper Keys. The tide was going out with only a slight chop. They made good time. In a little over an hour they could see the shrimper's lights close in off the western side of the keys and screened from shore by an island. Other off-loaders were there. Jimmy eased off the throttle and idled into line.

"Don't like it," Charley said.

"What?"

"Just got me a bad feeling; don't know why. Had it all day."

"Last time you had a bad feeling, the shit hit the fan. Hope you're not putting a hex on us."

"You and me both."

The shrimper crew was fast, bales were flying into the smaller boats, and soon there were only two boats in front of them. They pulled up to the mother ship and Charley started packing bales. When he had the first course in, suddenly a man jumped down from the cabin roof, a walkie-talkie in his hands. "Dump 'em!" he screamed. "It's a bust! Highway's crawling with cops!" He yelled to the helm. "Pull out!"

Bales were flung overboard as the shrimper's idling twin diesels were goosed into action. A helicopter with a spotlight appeared slowly rising up above Snake Creek. Jimmy immediately put the boat in gear and the throttle all the way down, speeding southeast and hoping to put a couple of the islands between them and the mouth of Snake Creek. When they passed between two of the islands, he could see several boats, two with powerful spotlights, powering out the creek. He saw a couple of flashes. Jesus, someone means business! Looking back, the helicopter was almost over the fleeing shrimp boat, bathing it in light. Bales bobbed everywhere in its wake. Good chance they wouldn't be seen, but you couldn't be sure. Everyone had infrared these days. Jimmy had his infrared binoculars hanging from his neck.

They lost their cover when they passed the last of the islands, but Jimmy had put a pretty good distance between them. The boat was going flat out with Jimmy dead reckoning and Charley keeping an eye on the two boats, most likely Coast Guard.

"Shit, Jimmy, one of them's turning our way...Yep, he's after us. Should I start pitching?"

Jimmy immediately turned towards shore.

"Hold off, Charley. The bales ain't slowing us much, and we're fucked if they catch us with or without 'em. We'll just see how good those boys know these waters."

When he approached the shore, he turned to follow it south. Every now and then he checked for landmarks through the night vision binoculars.

"That there's a fast boat, Jimmy. I do believe it be gaining on us."

"That won't help them much in a few minutes, unless it's an airboat."

Charley squinted at the boat, holding up a hand to screen its spotlight.

"Don't appear to have that 'figuration, Jimmy. And appears to be much bigger."

"Good. Then probably got a deeper draft than us."

Jimmy turned and entered a creek.

"Jimmy! They'll trap us up here!"

"Not where we're going."

They went up the creek at full speed. Jimmy took a right fork. Farther up, he took another right where it quickly narrowed to less than twenty-feet. Only then did he cut it back to half throttle. He looked at his watch, judging the tide. The creek narrowed even more.

"Unhook the motor lock on the transom." There was another fork up ahead. "You get it all right?"

"That's a ten-four."

Jimmy brought out a spotlight from under the controls.

"Charley, we got another split coming up. Take this and shine up ahead on that little creek to the right."

Charley did as he was told.

"Jimmy there's oysters sticking up on both sides."

"Yeah, but right there in the middle is mud; nice, soft mud, and water's deeper on the other side. We're going to thread the needle. Just keep the light on that creek and hang on to something!"

Jimmy pushed the throttle all the way down. The trees and bushes were a blur.

"Jesus, Jimmy!"

"Hang on Charley!"

When they hit the mud, the motor flung up hard just as Jimmy cut the throttle, but the engine still revved loudly. They sliced through the mud for about forty feet before stopping. Jimmy turned off the motor, and jumped over the side and waded in front of the boat. He looked back at Charley.

"Only gotta push her six feet or so and she'll be free, and so will we. C'mon, let's git her off quick, but watch out that this muck don't suck your boots off."

Charley jumped in. It wasn't easy, but they pried her free. No sign of the other boat. They didn't hear anything either.

"Think maybe they chickened out when it started getting shallow," Jimmy said, checking the transom and prop. "Either that, or they're waiting for us to come out again. Probably called a chopper, too. Good news is that the transom held up real good. Worth every goddamn penny I put into it."

Jimmy started the motor and put it in gear. When the boat moved forward with no apparent problems, Jimmy's smile was ear to ear. "Guess we didn't damage her too bad."

Charley sat on the gunwale, boots dangling in the water, washing the mud off. He shook his head in disbelief and admiration.

"Damn, Jimmy, I thought you was plum crazy. What now?"

"Now we mosey, Charley, mosey real slow down this creek before we cross over to another, then another. They're the only ones around here that have enough water for us to get back to the Gulf, and we'll be way south by that time."

Jimmy shined the spotlight above their heads.

"Now ain't that a pretty sight, Charley. Look at them oaks. I doubt we'd get wet in a rainstorm, let alone some chopper finding us. And we ain't in no hurry neither, not now, not by a long shot. We're going to unload these bales and cover them up somewhere, although I don't believe there'll be too many folk coming to these parts any time soon. But you never know. Then we're going to work our way down to Cedar Key where we're going to buy us some new peeler traps from Tommy Cherry who's going to tell anyone who asks that we'd been drinking with him for a spell and we spent the night. And we're going to take those traps home, and if anybody asks, you and me were just on a business trip to get us some traps." He smiled. "Totally legit and Crystal's going to write off the whole thing as a business expense. I only wish I had a bottle of Rye right about now...Nope, that's not all; got me another wish, too."

"What's that, Jimmy?"

"I wish that if you ever get one of those bad ass feelings again, you tell me before we leave Crescent, not after."

CHAPTER
TWENTY-ONE

Crystal was out on the deck, staring at the Gulf. Her back was to Rusty who approached on foot.

"Morning, Crystal. Jimmy around?" Rusty asked at the foot of the stairs. Crystal jumped. "Sorry, didn't mean to startle you. Just came over to see if Jimmy wanted to install that switch we talked about." He knew Jimmy wasn't around. Boat was still gone. Good chance he was in jail. Crystal turned to him. She looked worried. Made Rusty feel like shit.

"Jimmy's not here. Don't know where he and Charley are. Been out all night." She looked beyond him. "Oh, Lord."

Rusty turned. Two State Patrol cruisers slowly pulled up and parked on either side of the house. Rusty knew they were blocking the road so Jimmy's truck couldn't leave. Two serious looking troopers got out, both of them young, tall, white, and wearing Ray-Bans. One was stocky with heavy shoulders, the other rail thin.

The thin one looked up and asked Rusty, "You Jimmy Talbot?"

"Nope."

The stocky one turned to Crystal. "You Mrs. Talbot?" he asked.

"That's right," Crystal replied.

"Where's your husband?"

"Out crabbing," Crystal answered. If they're looking for him, then he couldn't be in jail, Rusty thought. The troopers came up the deck stairs without an invite.

The thin trooper said, "We know your husband's a drug runner, Ma'am, and," he consulted a small notebook, "he left here around midnight last night to meet up with a shrimp boat loaded with marijuana."

Great, Rusty thought. You damn idiot, why don't you just announce there's a snitch in town!

"I think you better tell us where he is."

"And I think I told you; he's out crabbing."

"Don't get smart with us, lady, or we'll take you in to Perry!"

"For what?" she asked incredulously.

"For withholding information, for wising off to a police officer, for aiding and.abetting, for…"

"Trooper, quit trying to intimidate Mrs. Talbot," Rusty said.

"And just who the hell are you?" the same trooper asked.

"A friend."

"Well, friend, mind your own business!" He turned back to Crystal.

"So where is he?"

"Crystal, they're out of line. You don't have to answer. They seem to have forgotten that they are public servants and that their job is not to go around threatening innocent people, especially a law abiding woman who is at her home and who has not invited these two dolts onto her property."

"You think you're some kind of lawyer or something, bub?" the thin one asked.

"No, Skinny, I don't. But I can call one, and so can she. Either way, I believe we can get you reprimanded. Like I say, you're way out of line!"

"That so? Maybe we should take you in for questioning, being a 'friend' and all of Talbot," Skinny said. The other trooper moved in behind Rusty.

"Now don't go doing anything boneheaded, Pudgy," Rusty said. Crystal put a hand on Rusty's arm. He looked at her, felt protective of her.

"Don't get into any trouble on my account, Rusty. I'm okay."

"Too late," 'Pudgy' said, as he grabbed Rusty's wrists and slapped a cuff on, but only one. Rusty broke free and faced off. Crystal stepped between him and the two troopers. She put a hand on each of his arms.

"Don't give them an excuse."

Rusty nodded. 'Pudgy' cuffed the other wrist. "Come on, tough guy. We're going for a ride." The troopers started to lead Rusty down the stairs.

"Officers, if you want to talk to my husband, I expect he'll be here directly," Crystal said, looking out to the Gulf. Jimmy and Charley were headed in with a tall pile of traps lashed in the stern of the boat. "Like I told you, he's been crabbing."

The troopers put Rusty in the back seat of one of the cruisers. They were none too gentle. They followed Crystal down to the dock. A short time later, Jimmy and Charley idled in.

"Morning, Officers. Looking for somebody?" Jimmy asked. Charley was fiddling with the lines, eyes averted from the troopers.

"You Talbot?"

"Yep."

"Where you been all night?" 'Pudgy' asked.

"Setting traps, then getting some new ones in Cedar Key."

"Kind of a funny time to be doing that, wouldn't you say?" 'Skinny' asked.

Jimmy shrugged.

"Just taking advantage of the good weather."

"Didn't happen to visit a shrimp boat off the Keys on your way, by any chance?" 'Skinny' asked.

"Nope. But saw one all lit up. Told Charley here that it was a strange time and place for a boat like that, and we better stay clear. Said, probably some funny business going on. Sure enough, wasn't much later that we saw all sorts of lights both on the water and up in the air. Luckily we were already south of them by then, but we hightailed it to Cedar Key anyway. Didn't want no trouble."

"I see. You have any problem if we look your boat over?"

"Help yourself, but ain't going to be easy with all them traps."

Jimmy and Charley traded places with the troopers.

"Jimmy, they got Rusty in the backseat of one of the cruisers."

"What! What for?"

She looked evenly at the troopers as they were poking around the boat. Charley was glad they had Cloroxed it at Cedar Key.

"No good reason I can see," she answered. "Except maybe standing up for me."

The troopers got off the boat. 'Skinny' asked, "You got anybody that can vouch for you in Cedar Key?"

"Yep."

Skinny pulled out his little notebook. Jimmy didn't say anything. The trooper sighed.

"Who, Talbot?"

"Crabber by the name of Tommy Cherry." A sheepish expression on his face, Jimmy looked at Crystal, then back to the troopers. "Hopefully he'll remember okay.

Drank us a bit o' whisky last night. Tommy's not hard to find, everybody in Cedar Key knows Tommy."

"Don't think it'll do us much good staying here any longer," 'Pudgy' said to the other trooper. 'Skinny' put his notebook away.

Jimmy followed 'Pudgy' over to the cruiser with Rusty in the back seat. When the trooper opened the door, Jimmy said, "Just call us when they're done with you, Rusty, and I'll come pick you up. Don't imagine they'll be givin' you a ride back."

"Thanks, Jimmy. I'll do that. Shouldn't be long."

Jimmy and Crystal watched the cruisers pull out.

"Jimmy," Crystal said.

"Yeah?"

"They knew when you left last night."

"That a fact?" He looked thoughtful.

Rusty was wrong. It took three and a half hours before Captain Smathers even learned that Rusty was being held in the Perry jail, then another three hours for the captain and his men to finish processing all the people arrested in the bust. When the captain was finally able to get to Perry, he had Rusty brought into a private room. Rusty made it clear he was pissed.

"What a goddamn bonehead move, telling her that they knew when Jimmy left in his boat!" The captain noted that Rusty said 'Jimmy,' not 'Talbot.' "They might as well have spelled it out that there's a snitch in town! Damn idiots!

"And I thought we had some sort of code for ethical procedure. Those two morons blatantly tried to intimidate and threaten Crystal. And me! What bull shit! It's because of troopers like them that we get a bad rap. Whether I'm a trooper or a private citizen in this case, I want those two boneheads reprimanded."

"I'll talk to them, Sargent. I also want to congratulate you on the information you sent us. Quite a catch last night: couple ton of contraband, shrimp boat and crew, couple fish trucks, and some runners. We'll see if anybody turns evidence. So far, no such luck."

"How'd Jimmy get through, anyway?"

"Like I said early on, no one knows the waters like him. Went up a shallow creek, and it just swallowed him up. Boat chasing him went aground, but once they got off, they still waited around the mouth until morning. Called in a chopper, too, to look for him. Man just disappeared."

Rusty smiled; that's Jimmy. The captain looked at him closely.

"You all right, McMillan? Maybe you're getting a little too close to these people."

Rusty shrugged.

"Don't know. Maybe. Do know that those troopers have jeopardized me."

"You want out?"

Rusty thought about that. Probably the best thing. Somehow, though, didn't seem right. After a long pause, he answered.

"I'm getting real close to Jimmy and a few of the others. They're starting to talk to me as if I was one of them. Especially with the race coming up, I'll…"

"What race?"

Rusty told him about the CB 250 and pit crew, shrimping with Tiny and the radio frequencies, eating meals as if family with the Talbots. The captain listened intently.

"Sergeant, why not stick it out for another couple of weeks and see what happens."

Rusty vacillated. Finally, he said, "All right. Just hope it's the right move…Now can I call Jimmy and get the hell out of here?"

"Nope. I think you should stay overnight. More credibility. Might help mend any damage my men may have done. You can call Talbot tomorrow." The captain got up and opened the door. He called over to the desk. "Sergeant, take this man back to his cell. I think he should cool his heels overnight; maybe teach him some manners."

CHAPTER TWENTY-TWO

"Where ya off to now, Butch?"

"Steinhatchee, Maw."

She looked up from the chicken she was plucking.

"Lordy, why ya going all the way over there? Can't ya find enough excitement around these parts?" She didn't give him time to answer. "Tommy going with ya?"

"Nah, he's cutting firewood."

"Don't he need help?"

"He kin handle it."

"You didn't say why you're a'going over there."

"Didn't give me no chance."

"Well, answer me, boy!"

"Work on the race car some."

'Work' sounded good to her.

"That's nice. Now don't ya be late for supper."

"Yes, Maw."

Butch, with no intention of returning for supper, put a machete and his faded yellow Poulan chainsaw with slack chain and no muffler into the back of his pickup. Hero, chained to an iron stake, looked at him.

"Sorry, Hero. You're staying here. Going to be out late."

He climbed into his pickup and headed. After a couple of miles, he turned on to the limestone road through the national wildlife refuge rather than continue on the roundabout paved highways. Wasn't much difference time-wise, but way too much traffic on the highways to cut cabbage palms, and he could use a little cash, ten bucks wasn't much of a stake. There was a restaurant in Steinhatchee that would buy any palm hearts he brought, no questions asked. He sat back and rolled down the window; felt damn good to be on the move again. Been spending too much time on the porch, he thought; about time I got out and saw how the tinkerings going with the Charger, then drink me some beers and shoot some pool.

Other than for a couple broad bends, the bright white road could have been drawn with a ruler. It bisected a mix of live oak, slash pine, cabbage palm, and red cedar whose green tops contrasted with the naked gray branches of sweet gum, cypress, and maple. Dark spiked air plants stood out here and there on bare branches, and the fat red buds of the soft maple looked ready to burst. But Butch didn't notice any of these things; he only saw the cabbage palms. He stopped over a dozen times, each time turning off his truck and carefully listening for any traffic before starting his chainsaw. The Poulan shattered the silence; it was even louder than his truck with the cutout. Soon there were scattered fronds and sliced up trunks here and there along the road, and a pile of palm hearts, covered by a tarp, in the back of the pickup. The forest service likened such indiscriminate slaughter to the killing of elephants for their tusks.

He approached the new concrete bridge across the river to Steinhatchee. Although ten years old, it seemed new to Butch because he could remember its predecessor: the single-lane swing bridge built out of wood. The new bridge was tall enough for any boat to pass under, and wide enough to have pull off lanes. At the highest point, he pulled over. He liked looking out to see who was in town and where all the action was. The view was similar to Crescent Beach with its strip of fish camps lining both sides of the creek, although the river here was a lot wider, maybe as wide as a football field was long. There were never more than a couple shrimp boats in town which was crazy, considering that the river had at least six foot of water, even at low tide; but that was because of the feud between shrimpers and crabbers, he thought. Unintentionally, the shrimpers had kept snagging crab traps in their nets which didn't make the crabbers too happy. The crabbers retaliated with tricks like sinking barbed wire with concrete blocks in the grass flats to tear up nets. Most of the shrimpers got tired of it and left, moving to Crescent Beach and other towns more friendly.

He looked up river and could see Rick's Restaurant; almost immediately his stomach started to growl. He started up the truck and wound down to the street that followed the river. Twenty minutes later he was sitting at a small round table in the bar that overlooked the river, drinking a beer and waiting for a grouper sandwich. The barroom was Holiday Inn plush, with heavy red curtains, red table cloths, thick red shag carpet, red cushioned chairs and barstools in front of the long leather padded bar. Behind the bar was a long line of liquor bottles up against mirrors that extended to the ceiling. Large TVs were in two corners. The natural pecky cypress paneling was the only clue that you weren't in a motel lounge off an interstate someplace. On one of the paneled walls was a collage of fishing photographs, mostly of proud anglers holding their trophy catch. There was one photo in the center that was twice the size of others. It showed Butch holding up a five foot tall racing trophy. The trophy itself was behind the middle of the bar, flanked by the liquor bottles.

Out on the river, a pair of crabbers was returning in the late afternoon sun. The boats were small and beamy, each with a little plywood cabin in the bow and a winch in the stern. Normally, the restaurant's customers oriented themselves so that they could look out the big windows at the river, but not Butch. He sat where he could look at the trophy and his picture. He was taking a sip of beer when the kitchen door opened and his waitress passed by, carrying food out to the main dining room. She was dressed in a tight navy blue *Rick's Restaurant* tee shirt and designer dark jeans with white curly cue stitching coming up from the leg seams and circling the cheeks of her butt. He wondered how long it took her to squeeze into the pants. Everything jiggled as she walkled except her platinum blond hair, a chubby Dolly Parton with the same pair of attractions. He watched her return to the kitchen.

He smiled at her when she brought him his sandwich.

"Haven't seen you here before."

"Only my second week," she answered.

Butch stuck out his hand.

"Name's Butch, but maybe you already know that."

They shook. He didn't see any ring.

"I'm Darlene. Now why would I know your name?"

"What with you passing my picture on the wall yonder fifty times a day, thought you might."

She looked over at the wall and back to Butch.

"So it is. I didn't notice. What's the trophy for?"

Butch looked incredulous

"Never heard of the CB 250!"

"Nope."

"It's an automobile race and about the biggest thing in these parts since sliced bread."

"So, I guess you won it."

"Yep, beat about forty drivers. Was some race, I'll tell you."

She smiled again, flirting.

"Maybe you can tell me about it sometime, but I," she said, looking over her shoulder towards the kitchen, "better get back to work. Still earning my stripes and all, if you know what I mean."

"Maybe you'd like to go the race this year as my guest: it's coming up real soon. About a million people come to watch and there's barbecues set up everywhere and lotsa partying afterwards."

"When is it?"

"First Saturday in March."

"Can't. Gotta work Saturdays." Darlene smiled again. "Maybe some other time."

"That's a ten-four. Could you bring me another beer, Darlene?"

"Sure thing."

Dang, he thought. Might be worth pursuing that little filly. He left a good tip, something he never did, but he looked at it as an investment: tip for tits. Just outside town, he turned into a small limestone parking area in front of a Quonset hut. The end of the building was wide open. Two men were standing in front of a bright yellow, late seventies Dodge Charger. Like Jimmy's, it was covered in sponsors' names. The two men were carefully lowering a motor with a chain fall that was suspended from a steel I-beam running the length of the building. Tools were scattered everywhere and the two men barely looked up when Butch swaggered in. When they had the motor positioned, one of the men scooted under the front of the car on a creeper. The other began to wipe his hands on a rag.

Butch, thumbs hooked around his gaudy belt buckle, walked around the car. Right away he noticed the new rear panel to replace the one he smashed last year. He looked into the cockpit and tapped the roll bar. "Just git her back from the machine shop?" he asked.

The man with the rag said, "Yup, and none too soon with practice week coming up."

All entries could trial run the racecourse the week before the event. The man on the creeper spoke up. "Ain't fair that Crescent Beach gets to keep their car out there and practice three hundred and sixty-five days a year if they want."

"But they don't," Butch said. "I'd hear 'em if they did. I live pretty close as the crow flies and I'd know if Jimmy was out there. Besides, hunting club wouldn't allow 'em."

"I hear they've been putting some money into their rig," the other mechanic said.

"Don't know about that, but do know Jimmy's a good driver, not as good as me, but good; bears watching for sure."

From underneath again, "They'll be gunning for you, Butch, and not just because you won last year."

"Whatcha mean?"

"I mean there's been lotsa complaints how you drive, especially out in the woods. People say dirty tricks."

"And what do the rulebook say?" Butch asked.

"Ain't no rulebook, Butch. You know that," said the mechanic scooting out and getting up.

"Then what's them crybabies bitching about? If'n there ain't no rules, then anything goes. Let the best man win, is what I says."

Neither of the mechanics said anything. Butch swaggered around the car another time, the heels of his cowboy boots clicking on the mirror finish slab.

"Reckon I'll mosey back to town and find me a game of pool with some sucker fool enough to take me on. You two grease monkeys keep up the good work and git my chariot ready. Ben Hur here is gonna hit the road."

With his back to the men, clicking his way out, Butch waved his hand before he disappeared around the corner. The creeper mechanic said, "Regular piece of work, ain't he."

"Piece of something, anyway," the other answered.

Butch shot a few games of pool and won some money, leaving the bar just in time to get to the package store before it closed. After he bought a couple six packs, he tallied up his money. Forty-six bucks and some change. Not bad considering he had started out with a ten spot, eaten a couple of sandwiches, drank he didn't know how many beers, and left that blond waitress a good tip. Not bad, not bad at all.

By the time he hit the limestone road, he was feeling pretty good. No more houses or camps, just his headlights on the white limestone outlined by the dark ditching roadside; lonely country. He turned the cassette player up, John Denver blaring out. Butch joined in at the top of his lungs. "Rocky Mountain high, Colorado. Rocky Mountain high." He never remembered any of the lyrics, so swigged beer in between. Was having hisself a good old time, he thought as he pitched an empty out the window and reached for another beer. He stopped to take a piss. Leaning against the truck, head tilted way back, he looked up at the stars. Nothing special to him, he saw it like this all the time. But, with the absence of city and suburbia, the stars would have dazzled most anyone else. He heard a barred owl way off. Another answered. As he gathered himself in, he glanced down the road. "Son of a bitch," he said softly, not bothering to zip up. He slowly reached into the cab for his rifle hanging behind the seat. A doe had stepped out on the road not more than two hundred feet away. He had a hard time steadying the rifle, the barrel was all over the place. He rested it on the doorframe. When he cocked the rifle, the doe must have heard because her flag went up. He hurried his shot, quickly pulling the trigger just as she leaped. She disappeared.

Butch jumped into the truck and floored it, stopping at where he judged she had left the road. He got out and looked around, saw a couple of crimson spots on the limestone. Son-bitch, hit the whore, he thought proudly. Rifle in hand, he approached the brush, but stopped when he saw the hedge-thick palmetto. Snake territory. He spread the palmettos in a couple of places with the rifle barrel. Hell, deer's probably a mile from here by now. Ain't gonna git me snake bit for a little bit o' meat, no way. He climbed back into the pickup and cracked another brew. He looked out to the palmetto while taking a slug. Nothing moving, no noise. He started the truck, turned the cassette up again, and was gone.

Butch was singing to his tapes when he realized it was probably less than a mile to the two humped sections where the new culverts were. He put the can of beer between his legs, and pressed down on the accelerator. If he went fast enough, he could get all four wheels off the ground. He hit the first one at seventy-five. Was one hell of a bump, but the next one, he knew, would be better. He didn't realize that the bump had dislodged the chain saw and that it was rattling around in the back of the pickup. He took a slug of beer and pressed harder on the accelerator, all the way down. He hit the next culvert at over eighty. All four wheels came off the ground; when he came down his wheels skidded in the newly worked material. He fishtailed hard at eighty miles an hour.

"Yahoo, mama!"

Even drunk, he got it under control. Damn, he thought, that was a good one. Man, can't wait for the 250; he'd whip 'em all again! He reveled in the memory of last year's victory. By the time he reached his mother's house, he was pie-eyed drunk. Bouncing off furniture, he weaved his way to his and his brother's room. He didn't realize until the next morning that his chainsaw had bounced out of the truck.

* * *

"I never knew there were all these trails," Craig said, standing next to the fat tire bike. "And so close to town."

"There's a whole network, mostly used by hunters and loggers. The majority dead end at the Gulf, but with the tide running out now, we should be able to do a loop," Ralph said. "This is my first time out since hunting season opened last November; I don't come anywhere near these trails during hunting season."

They started off on their bikes. When they came to a hundred foot section where the trail had been worked over by a number of pickups and four wheelers, Craig stopped.

"You got to be kidding me, Ralph! That's sugar sand; impossible to peddle through."

"I told you today was about aerobics, and I know there's no way you'd dance to music in the weight room."

"Got that right!"

Ralph laughed.

"So this is taking the place of the dancing; just peddle as far as you can. Secret is to go fast, try to stay on the matt of leaves and pine needle on the edge, and try to keep your butt back, over your rear tire for traction. At the same time lean forward to distribute your weight over the length of the bike. Here, watch me."

Ralph pedaled like a madman and almost made it, just ten feet shy.

"Damn," he yelled back in between gasps for breath. "Almost!" He pushed his bike the rest of the way. "Your turn."

Like Ralph, Craig got a running start, but barely made it a third of the way. He pushed his bike up to Ralph, breathing hard.

"That's the hardest stretch. Only pine roots to bounce over the rest of the way to the Gulf," Ralph said.

Craig looked at the palmettos, thick and waist high, on both sides of the trail.

"What about snakes?" Craig asked.

"Not out much this time a year; lot more active when it warms up. Armadillos, though, plenty of them.

They mounted and rode off. Sure enough, a quarter mile later, there was an armadillo rutting around through the grass and leaves on the side of the trail, clueless to their presence.

"Watch this," Ralph said, laying his bike down. He quietly walked up behind the armadillo, reached down and plinked its tail like he was shooting marbles. The armadillo jumped up as high as it was long, and scurried off into the palmettos. Both Craig and Ralph laughed.

"Not a very nice thing to do, but I can't help it," Ralph said, still laughing.

When they arrived where the marsh met the Gulf, Ralph pointed down the coast. Way off was Crescent.

"Damn! We've come a long ways," Craig said.

"This is where we ride through the marsh to connect up to another woods trail back. Couldn't do it with the tide any higher. Try to go around the puddles, salt will raise havoc with the gears and chain." Ralph pedaled at a snail's pace. "I try my best not to hit the fiddlers, but it's almost impossible not to, no matter how slow you go. But, going this slow and trying to dodge them is also good balance exercise."

Scattered fiddler crabs, large claw upraised, ran away from their front tires as the two men followed the low tide trail that curved around the edge of the woods. Ralph grimaced every time he heard a crunch. Fortunately, he thought, they were missing the mass of crabs that was moving like a brown blanket off into the marsh reeds. Occasionally they could hear odd chortles of birds calling to each other.

"What are those, Ralph?"

"Clapper rails. Nest in the middle of the marsh."

Craig thought how many times he had roared through marsh with his airboat without a thought as to what might live there.

Ralph turned on to a trail at the edge of the woods and they were soon surrounded by oak and pine again. They saw two more armadillos and a very shy fox squirrel before they reached the paved highway. With the home stretch in sight, Craig said, "Race you!"

"You're on!"

They took off, Ralph in better shape, lighter, but Craig had those piston thighs. They arrived at Ralph's house, neck and neck. Craig was wearing gray sweat pants and gray sweatshirt with the sleeves cut short. Damp sweat marks ringed the neck and pits. Ralph in sweatpants and tee shirt, looked fresh.

"Tie," Craig said, extending his hand.

"Agreed," Ralph said, laughing. They held the handshake longer than normal, or so it seemed to Craig. "One last thing for today's workout, then shower, and back to weights tomorrow."

"What's that?" Craig asked, wiping his brow."

"Five minutes of jump rope."

"You're kidding. Haven't done that since...since I don't know when. Five minutes; that all? " Craig said, following Ralph into the weight room.

"Think you'll be surprised how hard it is."

Ralph handed Craig the jump rope. Putting one hand on Craig's shoulder and pointing with the other, he said, "Just be careful of the ceiling fan." He looked over at the clock. "I'll time you. Start when you want."

"Let me practice first." After a few attempts, Craig got in the rhythm. He stopped. "Okay, here I go."

At twenty seconds, he was breathing hard. At forty-five, sweat was pouring out of him. He stopped at just under two minutes. He handed the rope to Ralph, too winded to say anything.

Ralph said, "There's a reason prize fighters include this in their training." He looked at the clock, five minutes to five. He started. It was obvious right away that Ralph wouldn't have a problem. Craig sat down on a weight bench, duly impressed. At three minutes Ralph began to show off. He switched from using both feet with half jumps in between, to alternating from one foot to the other, then began crossing the rope, finally straight jumps with no stutter jumps, the rope a blur. He stopped at four minutes, Craig was about to ask why when Ralph immediately did the same routine, but with the rope swinging backwards until five o'clock. At least, Craig thought, he's breathing a little hard and finally sweating. As Ralph was hanging the rope on the hook on the back of the door, Craig said, "Ralph, you are something else."

Ralph turned around, smiling.

"Craig, you'll get there if you keep working at it. I haven't been doing this just for a week or two, or a month; I've been at it consistently for a couple of years. Just takes commitment." He put a hand firmly on each of Craig's biceps and gave a squeeze. In a tough guy tone, he said, "Stick with me, big guy, and work out regular, and no one will ever kick sand in your face again." Ralph dropped his hands. "You have a change of clothes in your rucksack?"

Craig didn't answer immediately. Ralph's hands on his biceps had him flustered. He was thinking how many times they had been touching lately; not normal, at least not between guys. His body began to feel fuzzy, a neon wave coursed through his body. Ralph was waiting for an answer.

"Sorry, Ralph, was spacing out. Yeah, everything but a towel. Forgot that."

"No problem. Follow me." Ralph led him to the guest bathroom. "I'll go get a towel off the line. Got some fresh, sun-dried ones out there." He shut the door behind him.

Craig couldn't get the touching out of his mind. He took off his clothes. He looked down. He wasn't totally hard yet, but extended. A knock came on the door. He grabbed his pants and held them in front of him. "Come in," he said.

Ralph stuck his head in smiling, holding a neatly folded towel out. When he saw Craig naked, holding his pants shyly in front of him, he blushed.

"Oh, I'm sorry, Craig..." he said, turning his head. Craig made up his mind in an instant.

"Ralph..."

"Ralph turned. Craig had his pants to the side. Ralph couldn't help looking down. Craig was three quarters hard now. Ralph looked up into those beautiful eyes.

"Would you like to shower with me, Ralph?"

Without taking his eyes off Craig's, Ralph put the towel down and nodded.

* * *

Even though it was only early afternoon, Norm and Tammy were in bed. They couldn't get enough of each other. They had finished making love a while ago and Norm was fiddling with one of Tammy's bangs. He thought she was asleep, but he was wrong.

"What are your sons' names?"

"John and David," he answered.

"How come they never visit?"

Norm stopped playing with her hair and put his hands behind his head.

"Different kids, different reasons."

"Such as?"

"John, he's the eldest, followed in my footsteps, I guess. Went to Duke medical school like I did and finagled his way back down to Sarasota to do his residency. He's been here once and hated it right off the bat; he thinks it's the last place someone with my skills should be. He couldn't understand what I was doing here, except maybe hiding, he said. I think his words describing Crescent Beach were something like 'a back water pit.' He loves about everything I don't."

"How does he get along with his mother?"

"They're friendly, but I think Bev lost a lot of respect from both my sons when they found out she'd been messing around with the tennis pro while we were still married."

"Tennis pro, that's who she left you for?"

Norm nodded.

"Damn fool," Tammy said. Norm smiled.

"As for David, he's never been here. He dropped out of Evergreen College which is sort of a hippy type school in Oregon that's very environmentally oriented, and moved to Alaska to build a homestead in the outback. Lives off grid and the only vehicle that can get in to where he lives is a four-wheeler in summer and a snowmobile in the winter. He learned how to fly and now he's a bush pilot taking wealthy people in to sporting camps. He likes to fish and hunt, so I'd think he'd like it here okay. I hoped he might visit during the winters, but he hasn't so far. He doesn't have much money with his work being so seasonal and the high cost of living up there; he says he can't afford the airfare and is too proud, I guess, to accept a freebie from me. So he just hunkers down and lives simply with his girlfriend who's a yoga instructor. Never met

her. I'm thinking of flying out this summer to see them.
Any interest in going?"

"Nope, too much going on, what with scalloping and
the fishing."

Norm was silent for a spell.

"One thing did surprise me last time I was together with
my boys. You'd think with our medical backgrounds, I'd
have a lot more to talk about with John; but the opposite
was true. Even though his life has closely mirrored mine
both socially and professionally, I can't really relate to
the hospital grind and Sarasota life anymore. I guess all
that lala land lifestyle of south Florida is behind me for
good now."

"Norm, probably half the people here would swap
their life for that lala land."

"I don't believe that for a second."

"Of course they would! People are stuck here. It's
a hard, backbreaking life for most and they'd trade it
in a heartbeat. But they don't have a choice because
they don't have the money and education, or the background to consider any sort of change like that.

"Hell's bells, I'd opt in a second for sitting around
the pool sipping piña coladas with little umbrellas sticking out of fancy glasses, go to the beach or maybe hit a
few tennis balls at the club like your wife, mosey down to
the nearest Publix to buy a filet or a key lime pie."

"Come on, you're not serious? What about all the fishing and hunting around here? Wouldn't you miss that?
What about all the traffic, concrete, parking lots, fenced
off properties, signs to 'keep out' everywhere down there?"

"All that's nothing compared to busting my butt at
the club, trying to collect on peoples' accounts, wiping
bloody noses and paying the bills for all the busted up
chairs and tables. Or trying to get help to show up ev-
eryday during scalloping and hunting season, or having
to pull the entrails out of a hog or a deer, all the time

being eaten alive by bugs. Ain't a very tough decision, Norm. Believe me, you and Beau and Virginia ain't normal to leave the lives you had."

Picturing Tammy in the Sarasota scene didn't exactly perk him up. Maybe they really were too different, didn't have much in common; maybe he'd been kidding himself and it was just about the sex. He sure as hell hoped not because he knew relationships like those were usually short lived. Tammy must have picked up on his mood. She snuggled and changed the subject.

"Ready for the big race?"

Norm snorted.

"Right! My favorite! Right up my alley! Amateur NASCAR day creating every type of fucking, excuse my French, pollution there is: squealing rubber tires, exhaust fumes, consumption of gasoline, oil, and other petroleum products. I'd rather attend an airboat convention. And what beats all is that I'm the damn doctor responsible for patching up the drivers and drunk spectators!"

Tammy laughed. She knew Norm was just getting warmed up; she put an arm on his to calm him down.

"Nothing gets me more revved up than that damn race. The only year I enjoyed it was when Charley was squirting girls with the hose. The way they paraded around, they loved it as much as the men did. A damn shame that didn't become a tradition."

Tammy lifted the sheets up and looked at her chest.

"Guess I wouldn't have drawn no crowd."

"No, probably not, because you wouldn't have been there long enough. I'd have dragged you off into the woods somewhere if I'd seen those beauties." Norm looked over at the bedside clock, then back to Tammy. He took the sheets out of her hands and pulled them down. Arching his eyebrows like Groucho Marx, he said, "Still got an hour 'til you go to the club..."

CHAPTER TWENTY-THREE

Although just partially visible in the headlights, Jimmy knew that the trees in the Old Town hammock were giants compared to those around Crescent Beach and on the road to Perry. Some were over a hundred feet tall and many were two to three feet in diameter. And the hammock was a regular warren of limestone roads. There hadn't been a clearing of any size for miles, only patches cut out here and there for campers, trailers, and doublewides, all of them rust buckets and lookalikes. Be damn easy to get lost.

Jimmy also knew that the hammock was a lawless maze of meth labs, marijuana growers, down and dirty drug dealers, people hiding out for any number of reasons. It would take a hell of a lot to get the local police to chance coming out here, and Jimmy didn't blame them; he wasn't too happy to be here himself. But it was a command performance; he had been called on the radio, the message loud and clear. The Colombians were upset with the latest loss and a kingpin had suddenly showed up from Miami to take charge. He wanted to meet with everyone that wasn't in jail, and Jimmy was no exception.

Jimmy knew he was close when he saw the rusty barbed wire fence with the no trespassing signs. He turned into a driveway not much more than a packed down trail and stopped in front of a metal tube gate. When he stepped out of the truck, two stocky Latinos, each holding an Uzi, stepped out from behind trees.

"Hands on thee hood, *amigo*," one said, pointing with the gun. Jimmy did as he was told. The man frisked him as the other searched the truck. When they were satisfied that both were clean, the first man pulled out a walkie-talkie and began to speak in Spanish. "You, Jeemy?" he asked. Jimmy nodded. The man put the walkie-talkie away and motioned for him to drive through.

The road was narrow and rough, pockmarked with potholes and crisscrossed with thick roots. Looking in his rear view mirror, Jimmy could just make out that the gate had been closed and the men nowhere in sight. He drove slowly, bouncing his way for a quarter mile or so before entering a clearing with a ramshackle cabin and barn. His headlights shined on a new, limestone-coated Lincoln town car with Florida plates parked off to the side of the barn. He parked in front of the cabin between two pickups, one a late model Ford and the other a beat up Chevy he recognized. He estimated the cabin to be half the size of the barn, maybe sixteen feet by twenty-four.

The Chevy had its tailgate down. A man was sitting on it. It was Joe, the man who had driven the fish truck the last time he and Charley had off-loaded the bales in Crescent Beach. Jimmy walked up to him as two more short, stocky men with Uzis appeared from the shadows. The bright white light coming from one of the cabin windows played off Joe's face; it was a mess. Jimmy wondered why Joe wasn't in jail: he must have been at the scene of the bust with his fish truck.

"Jesus, Joe! What happened? Police do that to you!"

"Not hardly." Joe was visibly upset. "Jimmy ..." He stopped when the two men came up to either side of Jimmy.

"Come," one of them said, taking Jimmy's arm, "*El Espantoso*, he eez waiting."

Jimmy looked back at Joe as the two men escorted him to the door. Jimmy thought he mouthed, Be careful.

Jimmy was several inches taller than the two Hispanics who were at best five-five or six. They wore dark sneakers, dark pants, and dark, lightweight long-sleeved shirts. Their dark hair was long and slicked back. They said nothing as they opened the door for Jimmy and followed him in. Jimmy looked around the room as he was being frisked again. The cabin was lit by two hissing Coleman lanterns and had a total of six small windows, two to the front, two to the rear, and one on each sidewall. A sink with a plastic bucket full of dirty plates was against the rear wall between the two windows. A knotty pine counter in front of the sink had a cooler and Coleman stove on it. An open plastic garbage can next to the counter had old pizza boxes sticking out, and a beat up aluminum ladder led to a loft above the counter. Jimmy could just see the edges of mattresses poking out. Other than a couple of plastic chairs near the front windows, the only furniture was a large old desk in the center of the room. Its oak veneer was peeling, and a man wearing a peach colored Guyabera shirt sat at it, pulling off little pieces.

Jimmy didn't think the man was tall, but he wasn't sure because of the desk. But he looked strong with very broad shoulders and a bull neck. His black hair was thick, slicked back liked the others, and his face was acne scarred. If Jimmy had a single word to describe the man, he would have said, wide. He also looked tough.

The top buttons of the Guyabera were unbuttoned, revealing a bright gold chain and cross that contrasted with his swarthy but hairless chest. The man stopped picking at the veneer and smiled up at Jimmy. Gator smile, Jimmy thought.

"Ahh, Señor Jeemy," he said, looking at his watch. "You are on time. We have not met, but I know about you. You are a very good waterman."

Jimmy shrugged.

El Espantoso folded his hands and looked at Jimmy. After a brief silence, he said, "Two days ago my men followed your instructions and picked up the bales you hide. That is goood. But they were the only ones I get back; I lose much money and that is bad. It upsets me." He turned to the man to Jimmy's left and nodded toward the counter. *"Cuatro lineas, cabro."*

The man slipped the strap of the Uzi over a shoulder and walked up to the knotty pine counter. Jimmy watched him pull a plastic baggy from his shirt pocket. In it was a good-sized white nugget. The man shaved off a liberal amount with a razor blade and began to chop it into four lines as thick as Tiny's fingers. When he was done, he handed *El Espantoso* a rolled up bill and returned to stand next to Jimmy. *El Espantoso* stood and walked to the counter. He was very short, maybe five-three in his pointed black boots. His shirt was bunched up from sitting in the chair and Jimmy could see a gun nestled between his back and belt, the handle looked to be gold and silver.

El Espantoso snorted one of the lines, half up each nostril, and remained with his back to Jimmy. When he returned to the desk, his pupils looked like saucers.

"Señor Jeemy?" he said, offering the bill as he sat back down.

"No thanks."

"*Si*, that is what I have been told. You do not do the *cocaina* or the *marijuana*. That you are a family man.

That is very goood." He held the bill out. One of the men stepped forward and took it. Both men snorted a line. Not very sanitary, Jimmy thought.

"That's a nice pistol you have," Jimmy said.

"Yes, eet eez," *El Espantoso* said, bringing it out and fondling it. "Eez a Beretta 92, made especially for me." Jimmy had been right. The tooled grip as well as the trigger and trigger-guard were gold. The barrel and hammer were etched silver. "Eet can hold twenty rounds and eez very powerful."

Jimmy knew about Beretta 92's. They were nicknamed 'cop killers' because their bottleneck bullets could pierce Kevlar vests. *El Espantoso* placed the gun on the desk.

"Señor Jeemy, I am not very happy. I would like to be in my home right now with my own family; not," he said, looking around the room, "here in theez peez of sheet *cabina*. But it is necessary for beezness." *El Espantoso* sighed. "I have lost much money, and not just for the *marijuana* and boat. There eez much overhead when something like theez happens; money for the lawyers, the judges, the police, and also the money to keep everyone quiet. I do not like paying for all theez.

"Two things I learned have also upset me, and that eez why you are here." He held up a stubby finger. "First, how do the police and the Coast Guard know so much, eh? They were waiting, even though the bleemp, she was down."

Jimmy shrugged again. *El Espantoso* continued.

"I have learned that the police received a call several days before, telling where the boats would come een. And they received another call to tell when you left your *pueblo* for the shreemp boat. I am theenking, Señor Jeemy, you have a spy in your *pueblo*. What do you think?"

"I don't know about it being someone from our town, but it's pretty damn obvious that the police got the heads-up. Been thinking about that ever since my wife told me a couple state cops came by to hassle her the morning after the bust, before I got back. They said the same thing, that they knew I had left town around midnight. But if there's a snitch, you got me by the short hairs. Don't got a clue. Living in my town is sorta like living on an island where there ain't no lawmen and few rules. People know what's going on, but mind their own business; sorta live and let live."

El Espantoso ran his finger over the gun handle. Jimmy noticed the silver letters spelling Arias on the gold handle; *El Espantoso* must be a nickname.

El Espantoso asked, "No ideas, Jeemy? No workers move in, new fishermen from other towns? Somebody with money troubles?"

Jimmy laughed.

"Most of the town's got money problems; but, like I say, there ain't no snitch that I can think of."

El Espantoso stood and held out his hand to one of the men. "*El billete.*" The man handed him the rolled up bill, and *El Espantoso* walked over to snort half the last line. Good Lord, Jimmy thought, doing lines like that, probably high-grade stuff to boot, the guy's a regular cokehead! *El Espantoso* returned to the table. He pulled a suppressor from his waist high shirt pocket and methodically attached it to the pistol. Pistol in hand, he walked around the room, taking aim at various objects in the cabin. No one said anything. The silence was long and loud. Finally, Jimmy broke it.

"What's the second thing bothering you?"

El Espantoso turned, his face hard, all pretense of friendliness gone. He walked back to the table and faced Jimmy.

"You reeped me off, Jeemy."

"I what!"

El Espantoso looked at the two men.

"*Agarren a los brasos, muchachos!*"

The two men shouldered their weapons and grabbed Jimmy's arms. Jimmy didn't struggle; it would have been futile. Instead, he asked in a cool voice, "What the hell's going on?"

El Espantoso backhanded Jimmy. The slap was like a gunshot, Jimmy's cheek burned and blood began to drip from his nose.

"I ask the fuckeeng questions, *huevón,* not you!" Eyes crazy with coke, *El Espantoso* put his pistol up against Jimmy's temple. Jimmy stood perfectly still.

"You stole a bale of weed from me. You remember that, *conyo?*"

This crazy cokehead's going to shoot me over one lousy bale when I save him half a boatload? Jimmy couldn't believe it. He forced himself to remain rock steady.

"Yeah, I remember," Jimmy said.

"Why?"

"Figure we were owed. My helper and I hadn't been paid nothing for two jobs."

"You fuckeeng saltwater cowboy, I do the feeguring around here, not you!" He cocked the pistol.

Jimmy managed to remain outwardly calm. What else could he do? Crystal's face flashed through his mind.

"What would you have done if you was in my place?" he asked.

"Not fuck with mee!" *El Espantoso* shouted, his face furious, finger tight on the trigger. But he didn't shoot. He suddenly pulled the pistol away and began to walk around the cabin again. The two men continued to hold Jimmy as *El Espantoso* did a full circuit.

"What do you theenk, Señor Jeemy, if word gets around that any *peon* can steal from me, eh? That eez not good, I lose respect and I soon have more *problemas*. You have set a bad example." He held the pistol down by his side. "You are a feesherman, no?"

Jimmy nodded.

"*Muchachos, agarren las manos por las munecas y pongenlas duro encima del escritorio!*" The two men grabbed Jimmy's wrists and flattened his hands on top of the desk. *El Espantoso* smiled his gator smile. "You right or left handed, Jeemy?"

"Right."

El Espantoso walked up and calmly pressed the suppressor against the middle of Jimmy's right hand. He looked up at Jimmy.

"It eez lucky for you that you saved the *marijuana*. Because of theez, I will not keel you."

El Espantoso squeezed the trigger, it wasn't loud, but fire burst out the sides of the suppressor and the pistol kicked up. The bullet went through Jimmy's hand and the thick desktop, lodging in the wooden floor. Jimmy screamed and tried to pull away, but the arms of the stocky Hispanics were like a vice. Sweat broke out on his brow. With a kerchief, *El Espantoso* slowly removed the suppressor and put the gun away. He walked over behind the counter and returned with a thick roll of paper towels that he tossed onto the desk.

"*Suelten lo,*" he said, and the two men let go of Jimmy whose legs had buckled. He kept from falling by holding on to the edge of the desk with his left hand. Forcing his legs to obey, he managed to stand upright. Leaning against the heavy desk, he reached for the roll of paper towels, tearing several pieces off with his teeth that he wrapped around his gushing wound; the powder burns were as painful as the hole in his hand. He looked at *El Espantoso*.

"You son-of-a-bitch!" he hissed through clenched teeth. The two men started to grab him, but *El Espantoso* shook his head.

"Like I say, Jeemy, you are lucky.   Now get out of here, and tomorrow you will take one of my men to the bale, no? And in case you have other ideas, remember I know you are a family man and very proud to be an *abuelo* for such fine *mellizo* grandsons.   They leeve in Tallahassee, no? That is not so far away. *Adios,* Jeemy."

Blood had already soaked through the layers of paper towels. Jimmy's eyes, cold as ice, were locked on *El Espantoso's* until the two men led him out of the cabin. Joe was still on the tailgate. He saw the bloody paper towels wrapped around Jimmy's hand, but didn't meet Jimmy's eyes as Jimmy walked to his pickup. Jimmy drove out to the limestone road. The gate was open with the two goons nowhere in sight. He didn't stop until twenty painful minutes later when he was on Highway 19 at the center of Old Town which wasn't much more than a hardware store, small super market, café, and two gas stations. More of a pit stop than a town. He wanted to wash his wound, but everything had been closed for hours. He pulled into the gas station with the outdoor payphone and turned off the truck.   Pulling the soggy paper towels away, he found the wound still heavily bleeding. Dark, almost black blobs of blood covered the towels.   He squirmed out of his long sleeved shirt, and with the help of his teeth, fashioned and tied a tourniquet.   Fumbling for change, he walked up to the payphone and called Crystal.

"Hey Babe," he said when she answered.

"Jimmy, it's late! You okay?"

Crystal knew he was meeting with the Colombians. She always worried when he met with them.

"I'm fine, on my way home. Got a little favor to ask."

Jimmy didn't realize his voice sounded strained. Crystal knew right away. She was silent.

"You there, babe?"

"What happened, Jimmy?"

"Nothing much, but I wonder if you'd go wake up Norm. I'm in Old Town, so I'll be awhile. But I'll need some patching up when I git there."

"You going to tell me what happened?"

"Yeah, Babe, later. But you might tell Norm that I accidently shot myself cleaning a pistol, right in the middle of my hand, just to let him know what's coming. Burned pretty good, too. Oh, and you might just make sure he knows my blood type."

"Oh, Jimmy!"

Jimmy was getting a little woozy; he leaned back against the phone booth. He said, "Don't worry none, just a scratch. I better go. Call Norm, now."

"Yes, Jimmy."

"Good girl. See you in a bit."

Jimmy hung up the phone and undid the tourniquet. He tied it again, tighter this time, and went back to his truck. He headed north on the highway, deep in thought.

That fucker! Okay, bad things happen in this business, I know that, I knew that. You take your chances. And I can understand the discipline thing and setting an example for someone ripping him off, even the shot in the hand. I understand about the respect thing, although that's just another name for fear. But for that motherfucker to threaten my family, that's stepping across the line, way, way over the fucking line! And him who talks about family! He may be one tough motherfucker with a bunch of fucking goons to protect him, but if he thinks he can frighten me, be his boot licker, he's dead fucking wrong. He's made a big ass mistake underestimating us crackers, underestimating me! And, he's in our neck of the woods now, not fucking Miami. Threatening the twins! Son of a bitch!

But he might be right about the spy, a snitch in town. How else would the cops know when Charley and I left to make the run. But who? Known everybody forever. Sure, don't get along great with everybody, like Craig sometimes, or Butch, couple others, but I don't believe they'd ever...well, maybe Butch, he'd rat on his mother for a case of beer. Nah, he's too dumb, too dim a bulb. His life's about coming into town to play pool or sell his cabbage, be a hot shot on the track, nothing else. Nah, not him. And everybody knows that the dope money gets spread around, people is generous with it; why would someone rat and screw it up for everybody? For money of course, paid informer, but I just can't see anyone I know doing that. And no new workers in the fishhouse, no new crabbers or shrimpers.

One thing's for sure, though: I'm fucked for the race. Ain't no way I can muckle onto that wheel and shift, not with this damn hole in my hand. Just hope it don't get infected, that's the real worry. And crabbing, too. Shit! Gonna put a lot a pressure on Charley and Crystal, that's for sure. Gotta find 'em some help. Maybe Rusty. He went out with Tiny, said he enjoyed it, except for puking his guts out the second night. Jimmy laughed. Better him than me. But coming into an important time of year now; now's when we can make a little dough what with the crabs beginning to shed and all. Hell, don't take more than one hand to separate them shedders out in the shed. At least I kin help with that.

Shit, where am I anyway? How many times have I driven this highway and here I don't know where I am. Did I miss the turnoff? Jimmy shook his head, trying to clear the webs. Getting confused, I am. Loss of blood, that's why. Calm down now, son. Concentrate. He wiped sweat from his brow. There, up ahead, that motel billboard, means I'm still a couple miles from the turnoff. He concentrated hard, determined not to miss it. He relaxed some when he turned onto the Crescent Beach road.

Now where was I? Oh yeah, Charley's gonna need help, and with the water warming up, most everybody's gonna be busy. Maybe Rusty, bet he'd help us out. Good shit, Rusty. Put that nitrous switch into the rig and all, part of the pit crew. "Rusty!" Jimmy exclaimed out loud, thumping the wheel with his good hand. Rusty! That's who can drive the car. Probably do a hell of a lot better than me anyway, what with his experience. Whoa, there, Jimmy! Watch where you going! He yanked on the wheel. Two feet over the yellow line, you were. Why not take a break and pull over and check the old hand?

Jimmy pulled over and turned on the cab light. He didn't like the color of his arm. He loosened the tourniquet; better let her breathe a bit, he thought as he kept steady pressure on the bullet wound. He noticed the tips of his fingers looked a little blue. He looked in the mirror. Same for his lips. Been losing too much blood. Good thing Crescent's just down the road. He waited a few minutes then retightened the tourniquet before setting off, his thoughts all over the map. Rusty kept popping into his mind. Crabbing, arm wrestling, fishing, shrimping with Tiny, maybe driving in the race. Rusty sure has got around in the short time he's been in town! Hell, because of the arm wrestling, he's about a legend, knows most everybody and everything going on. When he crossed the cattle gap, suddenly a thought slapped him in the face as hard as *El Espantoso's* hand. Eyes wide, he recalled the Colombian's questions. Rusty's a newcomer, the only real newcomer in town. Could he be the one?...Nah...nah, not a chance. But the thought nagged him the rest of the way to Norm's.

CHAPTER TWENTY-FOUR

Charley gaffed the first buoy and winched the trap up to the boat. Hoisting it aboard, he pulled out a few small crabs and put them into a white plastic crate. He inspected the large crab in the bait well.

"Looks fit enough," Charley said. "This here crusty guy is what we calls a jimmy. He gits all them little she-crabs to come visit, and they're so horny and all, they stand in line a'waiting their turn. Don't know exactly what he does, puts out a smell, does a little jig or something, maybe even makes some sorta noise, but whatever it is, they likes it. Think I'll give him a little something fresh to munch on, though he mostly don't have his mind on eating." Charley put chopped chunks of fish in the bait well and dropped the trap back overboard.

"Then all these are females?" Rusty asked.

"Maybe."

Charley turned them over to inspect their abdomens.

"Got us one male. Lookee here. See this here design underneath looks like a boner. That's a jimmy." Charley picked up another, tracing its undersides with a finger. "The female here has more of V like a crotch. Purty easy to tell, plus the tips of the jimmys' claws is blue and the she-crabs wears a bit of red fingernail polish on hers." Charley dropped the crabs back into the crate and handed Rusty the gaff. "Here, you take the next one. Just pull in the buoy and wrap the line round the spool here until the trap's aside, unloop the line, and haul her in. Once you git the hang of it, we don't needs to stop and dawdle none like we is now."

Charley went up to the bow and headed to the next buoy. Rusty pulled it in without a problem and hoisted up the trap. He turned to smile at Charley who smiled back as he came astern.

"You're a natural, Rusty."

Rusty threw out the muck and seaweed that had collected in the trap before dumping a few more crabs into the crate. One of the crabs was extra large with a few barnacles on his shell. Charley carefully picked him up and put him in a separate container. Most of the others were about three or four inches long.

"This here ugly one be a good recruit to jimmy up any trap where the stud looks sick or done died. Seems the uglier the jimmy is, the more the she-crabs comes a'running. You done good, Rusty, and you're all set; throw her back."

Rusty quickly got the hang of it, only asking Charley about the state of some of the bait jimmies. They took turns, alternating the buoyed lines, occasionally waving to other crabbers they passed. While at the helm, Charley liked to gab on the radio. Man, how he can chatter, Rusty thought. No problem with seasickness today, thank God. Maybe he was like Jimmy: close in was no problem. He looked out over the calm water. Odd. No horizon, the gray sky and water were one. Looked kinda eerie. Although his hands and forearms and the stern of the boat were a stinking mess, he felt clean, alive, as much of the big picture as the gulls following the boat, or the crabs he dumped from the trap. Part of the chain. The solitude and the peace of it all. There was no bull shit.

But, of course, it wasn't always like this. Could be freezing cold, fierce squalls, lost traps, wind and waves, no crabs when the price was high, low prices when they were around. Jimmy said it seemed the price of gas always went up during 'sorry' crabbin. Watching Jimmy get out of a chair said a lot about the constant pounding, the beating a crabber took. Jimmy couldn't stand talking in one spot for long, he'd have to sit down or move around. That, or seize up. Who could blame him for running the dope, trying to get money to build up his guiding business, have it a little easier, a future after working so hard for so long? He and Charley were the only ones he knew clever enough to escape the bust the other night, and what does Jimmy get for a pay-off: a bullet hole in his hand. At least that wound must've had something to do with the smuggling because he sure as hell didn't shoot himself cleaning a gun, like he says.

Rusty kept pulling traps, continuing to think about Jimmy. When Charley was finally off the radio, he asked, "How's Jimmy's hand, Charley?"

Charley slowed the boat so they could talk.

"Doc says it's got infected some. Don't surprise me none what with him getting it wet all over trying to get them germy tanks cleaned up fer the peelers. Crystal's some rip shit at him, tell you that!"

"He really shoot himself, Charley? Can't believe Jimmy'd be that careless."

"Just between you and me and these crabs here, ain't no way; but that's all I got to say about that except maybe Jimmy's mighty pissed off at somebody, and son, believe me, you don't want Jimmy pissed off at you." Charley motioned him over. "Come on, your turn at the wheel, Rusty. Only two more lines to go and we head in."

"How many traps are there?"

"Twelve lines of eighteen traps. You do the 'rithmetic; something over two hundred."

Rusty whistled.

"Not a bad day's work, I'd say."

"Just think if'n we didn't have no winch like in the old days. Now that was a day's work alright." Charley laughed and shook his head. "I remember working once for a poor crabber outta Steinhatchee. Was years ago when I was a drinking my share of liquor and I'd be god-awful hungover. Got me the idea of dumping some of the bait overboard when the captain weren't looking, so we'd have to quit early. Captain weren't the brightest bulb and it worked a couple a times; but then the birds done give me away. Got me fired right quick." Charley smiled. "But since I got together with Minnie, done mend my ways. Now, let's git them last ones and head on home."

The return trip took just under two hours. Jimmy, faced flushed and hand bundled up in clean white gauze, met them at the dock; Crystal was watching from the deck. As Charley and Rusty eased in, Crystal yelled down, "Now don't let Jimmy do nothing, Charley!"

"That's a ten-four, Crystal," Charley yelled up. He turned to Jimmy. "Now you heard her, just you git! We kin take good care of all this. Rusty here's proved hisself a right expert crabber."

Crystal came down to the dock and stood next to Jimmy as Rusty and Charley began to unload the crates.

"We done good today, Jimmy. Reckon going to be round the clock baby sitting all these sallies," Charley said.

"And once you git them in the tanks, Charley, you and Rusty go git some rest and something to eat. I'll be taking the first shift," Jimmy said.

"The hell you will, Jimmy Talbot! Didn't Norm say you're to keep that hand dry and elevated. You'd have it soaked again quicker than Charley here can drink a beer. And you should see your face, plum red. You got

a fever and should be in bed! Now git!" Crystal said, tak-
ing him by the shoulders and pointing him to the house.
Jimmy went. Charley smiled as he handed a crate up to
Rusty on the dock.

"That there," Charley said nodding toward Crystal as
she followed Jimmy up to the house, "be the oniest person I know kin order Jimmy around like that. He don't
ever mess with her, no how, no way." He handed up another crate. "Smart man, that Jimmy," he added.

Five hours later, Rusty was getting his first peeler les-
son from Charley who had a sally in his hand.

"She starts busting out here in the back," Charley
said, pointing to the crab's soft body bulging out of its
shell. "The guts stay, but she sheds her lungs and gits
new ones that fits her better. She bleeds a little, but you
can't see it none because it's clear. But if'n you feel the
edge of this tank, it feels a little bit greasy. That's from
the blood and the crab wastes and all." He dropped the
crab back into the tank and pointed to another tank full
of oyster shells. "That's why that tank over yonder is full
of shells. As the water travels around from tank to tank,
water passes over them shells which gots algae on 'em.
The algae cleans everything up as it feeds on the ammo-
nia and such from the crab's messes. Got a swimming
pool pump to change out the water from time to time."

Charley returned to the first tank.

"Now when the she-crabs shed completely, you gotta
move her to a tank that jest holds ones totally shed. If
you don't, the sally here becomes bait fer the others because she can't do nothing; can't defend herself, can't
even swim none. Sometimes she gets hung up some gitting rid of her shell; sorta like a calf that gits tangled up
at birth. But we don't call no vet nor nothing; we just
pull her for ourselves to eat later. When this happens,
sometimes means tanks needs some freshening up with
some new sea water. Best between sixteen and eighteen

percent salty. Even got us a heater to keep the water in the low to mid seventies when it's cold around here."

"Damn, Charley, lot to this business."

"That's fer sure, and that ain't the half of it." He walked over to the last two tanks. "These here is all the ones done shed good. But, you gotta watch 'em close. You want 'em to git stronger, but you can't wait too long. Their shell grows back pretty dang quick, and if'n you run a finger over one and feels like sandpaper, then that's been in the water too long. You want 'em soft and squishy, sorta like a sponge, and you pull 'em when they kin support their arms up and move around some." Charley looked down into the tank. "Like these two. Whole process takes couple two, three hours," he said as he reached in and pulled out a pair that he packed into bread crates layered with wet hay. "Soon as you pull 'em from the water, their shells stops growing. These'll last a week or more in the crates, plenty of time to git where they're a'going. Prices is real good now in the north country because all them crabs in the Chesapeake ain't ready yet."

Rusty looked around the room. Excluding the one full of oyster shells, he counted eight rectangular fiberglass tanks connected by a web of PVC pipes and full of crabs. "Guess it's a lot cheaper using plastic than copper," he said looking at the pipes.

"Yep, that and the water passing through copper can kill the crabs."

Charley sat down on one of the two tattered easy chairs over in a corner under a tin-shaded clip-on light. Between the chairs was a small, white plastic table with a pile of magazines and a half-filled ashtray. Charley picked up a magazine. "Take a load off, Rusty," he said.

"Nah. Think I'll just watch them for a while. Pretty fascinating."

"Suit yourself. Tell you one thing fer sure; few days from now, you won't find 'em so 'fascinating.'"

Rusty walked from tank to tank. Occasionally he'd hold up a crab. "This one ready to switch?" he'd ask, or, "What do you think about this one, Charley?" or, "Looks like this one's ready."

Charley sighed and put down his magazine.

"Glad to see you're taking this so serious," Charley said as he walked over to inspect the crab Rusty was holding. He nodded. "Yep, she goes over yonder. So do these," he said, looking down. Rusty lowered the three crabs into the last tank. "Believe you got the hang of it alright," Charley said as he walked back to the easy chair. He looked at the clock on the wall. "Reckon I'll hang out fer a little bit more, case you got any more questions, then I'm going to git some shut-eye." He picked up the magazine and resumed reading.

"Charley, what happens in the Gulf? I mean, if these she-crabs are so defenseless and all, how do they keep from getting eaten by everything?"

Without looking up from the magazine, Charley answered, "That's where the jimmy comes in. He latches on to 'em and covers 'em up when they start to shed. Sorta carries her around underneath him and nothing can git to her. And now she's also becoming a real lady, produces all sorts of orangish eggs. The jimmy gits turned on and fertilizes 'em, then keeps a hold o' her 'til her shell's hard enough and she kin protect herself." He looked up. "Old Mother Nature's got just about everything figured out... 'cept us, o' course." He went back to reading. Twenty minutes later, Rusty was alone.

He wandered from tank to tank, shuffling crabs. He didn't sit, didn't take a break. Like Charley said, he was taking his job seriously. But it had been a long day and the noise from the pump and the constant gurgling of the water lulled him. He began putting his hands on the edge of the tanks, leaning against them, as he inspected the crabs. A couple of times he nodded off, standing, only to jerk awake and quickly check the crabs again. The easy chairs beckoned, but he willed himself to keep moving. Finally, towards the end of his shift in the early morning hours, he couldn't resist any longer. He told himself that he would just, like Charley had encouraged him earlier, take a load off, but only for a couple minutes. He walked over and sat. The cushy chair engulfed his big frame. Less than a minute later, he was asleep.

Rusty was out on the water, crabbing. His boat was much bigger than Jimmy's, beamier and longer with lots more open space behind the wheel. The crab crates were stacked up high, and the gaff, bait buckets, lines, everything was in its place. His boat was shipshape. The stainless winch spool was shiny new and reflected the morning sun like a mirror. He eased off the throttle and the motor purred as he approached a line of buoys. The light chop sparkled like a million diamonds. He looked up. High overhead, a spearhead of white pelicans soared in the thermals. He was a happy man.

As he began pulling traps, he noticed a boat approaching from way off. It was the only boat he had seen all day. It made him curious. He pulled out his binoculars and took a long look. A crabber. Soon he could tell, no mistake, it was Jimmy's boat. Moments later he could see two men: Jimmy and Charley. Charley looked worried and Jimmy looked pissed. They were headed straight for hm. He emptied the trap balanced on the transom, and threw it overboard. He sponged off the trap's mess on the transom as he waited. It didn't take long; Jimmy and Charley were going flat out.

Jimmy throttled down only when his boat was close. The wake caught up with both boats, making them rock like bobbers. He saw that Jimmy's hand was still bandaged, and he had a pistol stuck in his belt. Charley lashed Jimmy's boat to his. The two boats rocked together. No one said anything. Charley wouldn't meet his eyes: he looked everywhere else. Jimmy, though, was staring hard at him.

Finally, he said, "Hey, Jimmy. How's the hand doing?"

Jimmy didn't say anything, just kept staring at him. The silence lasted until he asked, "Is something wrong?"

"Might say so," Jimmy answered. Jimmy looked away, spat in the water, then turned back to him. "You know what, Rusty? I liked you, I really did. Thought you was square, hell of a man. But all you are is a goddamn liar." He held up his bandaged hand. "I got this because of your lies and spying. But that's not what pisses me off," he said, pulling the pistol from his belt. "What pisses me off is that I thought you was a friend. You even fooled Crystal. She thought you was a good guy, too. Ain't nothing worse than having a friend stab you in the back. Nothing! So, motherfucker," Jimmy cocked the pistol and pointed it at his head, "I'm afraid your spic and span boat here's going to git a little dirty…"

Crash!

"Goddamn it all to hell!"

Rusty's eyes flew open. Jimmy was holding on to his bandaged hand, bending over a pipe wrench. He looked sheepishly at Rusty.

"Sorry to wake you," Jimmy said, looking down at his hand, "but the wrench slipped and banged into this damn hand."

Rusty blinked awake and stood up at the same time. He rushed over to Jimmy.

"Here, let me help you."

"Nah, I got it alright," Jimmy said as he put the pipe back on to a dripping pump fitting. He gave it a twist. "There, all set."

Rusty walked quickly around the tanks, peering down into each. "I fell asleep," he said, needlessly.

Jimmy laughed.

"Don't worry none, I checked when I came in a little while ago. Everything's fine; you musta just fallen asleep before I got here."

Jimmy walked over to the easy chairs. He lit a cigarette as he sat down. Rusty sat in the other chair.

"You suppose to be down here, Jimmy?"

"Crystal's asleep. I turned off her alarm so I could take her shift. I feel about as useless as a tit on a boar hog. But, I slept a lot since I seen you last and feel mighty better for it."

Jimmy didn't look as flushed.

"Yeah, you look better, Jimmy."

Jimmy smoked as Rusty relaxed in the chair.

"So, that mean you're spelling me?"

"Yep, until Crystal finds my side of the bed empty. Then she'll be down here in a heartbeat."

"You're a lucky man, Jimmy. She's a fine woman."

Jimmy ran his good hand over the bandage. Squinting as smoke curled up from the cigarette in his mouth, he asked, "How come you ain't married?"

Rusty laughed.

"Always seems like the good ones are taken. Like Crystal. I don't get out much to where I meet many women, and I never felt like I was going to meet the woman of my dreams in some bar. Most of the time I tend to be working or tinkering on engines and machinery someplace."

"You're a damn good mechanic, alright; I'll give you that." Jimmy stubbed out the cigarette. "Where did you say you worked doing roads and such?"

"Very tip of north Georgia, mostly. Had some state jobs that I milked pretty good, but, believe it or not, I really made most of my money putting in driveways up in the mountains for the rich people. Had a lot of work just cross the border in North Carolina—in Cashiers, Brevard, and Highlands. Lots of wealthy Florida people go up there in the summers, have second homes. Seems the higher up and the better the view, the more status you have, and those people love status.

"Anyway, they'd want to build on top of the mountains and I was the best at figuring how to get them up there. I charged them a shitload, but I didn't overcharge them. No one else could do the work as well as I could, or even wanted to, as steep as it was. I'd also do it right the first time, no washouts, the road would hang in there. But, they had to pay big bucks for it."

"What did you do with your business?"

"I had a guy who worked with me for over ten years. Real good operator, although not great with the clients. I sold the business to him and he's running it out of Dillard now. Gave him a hell of a deal."

"What's his name?"

"Sam Richter. Why all the questions, Jimmy?"

"No reason; just curious. So you know how to operate heavy equipment, crawlers and such."

"Yup."

"How about later tomorrow going out to the track with me? We got a D-8 coming in on lease to dress up the course. None of us kin operate it all that good and could use a good man. It'd make it go a whole lot faster and save us some money if we kin git her done quicker."

"What about all the crabs?"

"Crystal and Charley can handle that just fine. We can get Norm in a pinch, too."

Rusty stood up and stretched.

"Sure, why not? Been awhile since I been on a machine, though."

Jimmy didn't say anything for a couple of beats. Finally, he said, "I'll pick you up about ten in the morning tomorrow. Crawler should be there by then."

"Alright. Guess I'll go get some sleep."

Jimmy pulled out another cigarette as Rusty left. Walking towards the humpback bridge, Rusty wondered about all the questions. 'Just curious,' my ass! Most likely it was because of those two bumbling troopers! And this running the dozer out at the track. The more he thought about it, the more he'd bet it was a test to see if he really could operate machinery. That wouldn't be a problem, of course, but he sure as hell hoped the captain had re-briefed Richter like he said he was going to. If not, he was royally fucked: simple as that. He stopped in the middle of the humpback bridge and looked to the east. The sky was already beginning to lighten. He turned left on to Main Street and headed for his cabin.

CHAPTER TWENTY-FIVE

Hands on hips, Rusty stared at the Cat D8. He shook his head.

"I sure hope they're not charging you a pant load for this junk. Where'd you lease it, Jimmy? Rent-A-Wreck?" Rusty kicked at a chunk of limestone stuck in the track. There was limestone caked everywhere like cement. "Limestone's probably the only thing holding the tracks on. There's way too much slack in it."

"Their problem, Rusty. It's just a rental."

"Yeah, and that's the way it's been treated. Jimmy, I ain't runnin' this thing without some maintenance first. Looks to me like the track's been slipping plenty. Look at the shape of the shoes; couple of cracks, and worn way too thin. And probably won't go for more than a hundred feet without the tracks falling off. Hell of a lot easier to tighten tracks now than to put one on later."

"You saying it's in too rough of shape for you to operate, Rusty?" Making excuses already, Jimmy thought. Trying to git out of it.

"Nope, not at all. You must have some grease around here…" Jimmy nodded. " And a tape measure?"

Jimmy nodded again and walked over to the equipment shed. Rusty hopped up to start the dozer. He moved it forward and, without touching the brakes, let it coast to a stop. Jumping off, he waited for Jimmy to return. Jimmy handed the tape to Rusty who hooked it to the top grouser over the sprocket. He then stretched the tape to the other grouser over the front idler.

"Jimmy hold this, will you?" Jimmy hung on to the tape while Rusty searched for a stick. He found one and laid one end on the lowest grouser tip, and marked with his thumb where the stick passed the tape measure line. He measured the distance.

"Thought so. Should be four and a half inches of sag. It's more than double that. Nothing like sloppy track to wear out the bushings and sprockets. The maintenance people ought to be shot!"

After knocking off several more chunks of limestone around the track, Rusty picked up the grease gun and walked to the rear of the dozer. He took the caps off the hydraulic fill and relief valve, and started pumping grease. Jimmy could see the track tighten. Rusty checked the track sag a couple of times before putting down the grease gun. He measured the sag one last time then put the caps back on. He walked around the dozer and tightened the other track. Finally, after checking this and that, he climbed up and restarted it. As it idled, he asked, "Now what, just exactly, do you want done, Jimmy?"

"Smoothed up. Got some ruts in the straightaway here, there, and yonder, but not too bad. It's the woods section that's all dug up, especially on the S's and hairpins."

Rusty was looking out over the straightaway.

"Yeah, I can see the ruts. Won't take long." Rusty turned back to Jimmy. "You want the woods road crowned so it sheds water better?"

"Surely never been asked that before, but no need now; maybe after the practice sessions. Jest need 'em smoothed up so the drivers can git to know the course some in good condition. They'll be messing it up all week. We'll have to smooth it up again before the race."

Rusty nodded and put the dozer in gear. He drove out to the far side of the straightaway where there were several ruts. Keeping the dozer in high gear, it didn't take him long to grade out the bad spots. Jimmy sat in the grandstands and watched as Rusty hit every bad spot in the straightaway. When he had finished, Jimmy followed him to the woods road just as Charley pulled up to the grandstand in his Mustang. He whistled over to Jimmy who stopped at the woods' edge. Carrying a grease-stained, brown paper bag, Charley walked up to Jimmy.

"Crystal wanted me to bring you two some lunch. She's on crab duty right now," Charley said. He looked down the woods road, then over his shoulder towards the straightaway. "How's Rusty doing?'" he asked.

"Not bad; judge for yourself."

They entered the woods. Rusty had not geared down and was going clackety-clack back and forth down the road. Here and there was a pile of new material to be graded in. His blade was tilted, and his touch was light. He expertly feathered out the limestone, and Jimmy and Charley could see that he was putting a slight crown in the road. They watched him for a spell as he worked his way through the first S.

"Reckon I ain't never seen no one go so fast and have a lighter touch at the same time," Charley said in appreciation. "That boy sure does have hisself some talents."

Jimmy didn't say anything. When Rusty approached the quarry and hairpin, he stopped the machine and got off. He was stretching his back when Jimmy and Charley walked up.

"I told you it'd been awhile," Rusty said, straightening up. "My back's not used to it."

"You're fast, Rusty, tell you that," Charley said.

"Got us some lunch here, Rusty," Jimmy said. "Let's go over by the water and have us something to eat. Smells to me like it's some of Crystal's fried chicken."

They sat on small limestone boulders at the water's edge. Jimmy handed Rusty some chicken, a bag of chips, and poured him some sweet tea. When Jimmy picked up a piece for himself, Charley eyed him long enough that he tossed it over.

"You're worse than an old coon dog begging, Charley! And I'll wager you already had yourself at least a piece or two at the house."

Charley dragged a sleeve across his mouth.

"Mighta."

"Damn fine chicken, Jimmy," Rusty mumbled, mouth full.

It didn't take long for them to devour everything. Jimmy handed out toothpicks. Contentedly, they worked the picks, face to the sun, the quarry water bright turquoise.

"You're doing a nice job, Rusty," Jimmy said. "Didn't think you'd come close to finishing by the end of the day, but at the rate you're going, you'll be done in three hours max. Maybe you'd like to take the 'Cuda for a spin after you're done."

Rusty looked eager, but he said, "Nah, be just my luck to wrap it around one of the oaks right before your race." He looked at Jimmy's bandaged hand. "I've been meaning to ask, Jimmy, with the race only five days away, just how the hell you going to manage steering, let alone shift, with that hand?"

"Ain't going to need to because I won't be driving."

Rusty turned to Charley.

"You then, Charley?"

"Not me, no sirree bobby! I'm drinking beer and in the pit crew. Won't catch me out here, not by a long shot," he said, shaking his head.

"Then who's driving, Jimmy? Tiny?"

Charley laughed.

"Tiny drives like a little old lady; he hates to go fast. Anything over forty in that pick-up of his gits him all riled up," Charley said. Rusty recalled the ride with Tiny to Perry and had to agree.

"There's not nobody in town capable, Rusty, and besides that, no one who'd want to. Sure would be a shame, though, for Crescent Beach not to have a entry in its own race, especially after working so much to git the 'Cuda tuned up and that switch installed and everything," Jimmy said. He hesitated a couple of beats before adding as he continued to look at Rusty, "Was hoping you might consider." Rusty's mouth dropped in surprise. He looked at Charley who, like Jimmy, was watching him closely. It was obvious they had discussed it. "I realize your moonshining days are a thing of the past and all, but if you had the balls to do something like that once, then I figure you got the balls to do this old race. Have you done any fast driving since?"

Rusty recalled what the captain had said way back at the blimp station: 'I doubt if you'll need those skills here.' "A bit," Rusty answered. "Couple times a year, on weekends when there weren't any races on the Charlotte Motor Speedway, they'd let amateurs in for a fee if they signed waivers. A few of the boys from work and I'd trailer up a rig and run around some. No offense, Jimmy, but that's on a paved oval, nothing like this, and there weren't any other drivers, especially amateur wannabees coming at you in a high speed demolition derby!" At least, not a total lie; he had driven several times test-driving cruisers on the Daytona Speedway.

Jimmy laughed. "No offense, taken. But before you answer, what do you say you go around a couple of times and see how it feels?"

Rusty looked out over the water before answering. "Okay, Jimmy," he said, finally, "but no promises." He brushed off the crumbs from his pants and stood up. "I better get back on that crawler or we'll be running out of time."

A couple of hours later, Rusty, hands resting lightly on the wheel, was in the cab of the throaty 'Cuda. Jimmy stood next to the driver's window and Charley was in the top row of the grandstand, beer in hand and a cooler next to him.

"I'm going to go around a few times, Jimmy, before I try it at any speed."

"However you want, Rusty. But when you're ready to give it a real shot, line up even with the gate here. That's about where the starting line is. I'd like to time you."

"Fine."

Rusty slowly pulled away and shifted through the gears, picking up speed. He downshifted at the end of the straightaway and headed into the woods. He made four laps, varying the speed in different areas of the track. He thought it was good that he had spent the time on the dozer as he recognized individual trees that indicated what was just ahead. The fourth lap was a lot faster than the previous three. He pulled up in the middle of the track, parallel to the gate. Jimmy was sitting with Charley now, both had beers.

Rusty yelled up, "Anytime you're ready, Jimmy..."

Jimmy put his beer down and stood. He took off his watch and raised his hand as Rusty began to rev the engine. He looked from the watch to Rusty and let his hand drop. The Barracuda roared and flew off the line, limestone flying from the rear wheels. Rusty ran up high revs through the gears, then only instants later began downshifting as he approached the woods and the S curve just a little ways in. He disappeared into the woods. Charley and Jimmy listened to the 'Cuda's screaming, gauging where Rusty was on the track by his accelerating and downshifting. Jimmy looked at the watch when they heard him shift all the way down for the first hairpin. Then there was the acceleration through the longer S curve before the shifting down again for the second hairpin. When he entered the clearing and straightaway, he must have punched the nitrous oxide switch because the 'Cuda's scream was different, higher, and it almost left the ground with the surge. It was coming down the straightaway faster than any car Jimmy had ever seen on the track. Charley said, "Holy Shit!"

Jimmy agreed. "Yeah, holy shit!"

When he passed the gate, Rusty immediately began downshifting and applying the brakes; he had to or he could never have stopped before the woods. Jimmy looked at his watch. Rusty's lap beat his own best time by a full ten seconds. He shook his head in disbelief. When Rusty got turned around and pulled up to the gate, Jimmy and Charley were there to meet him. Rusty turned off the car and Jimmy handed him a beer through the window. Rusty cracked it and took a long swig. Smiling, he said, "Damn, that was alright! How was the time?"

Jimmy smiled back. "Not bad; you'll do," he said.

CHAPTER
TWENTY-SIX

The line of cars and pick-ups extended a quarter mile out the limestone road from the Black Hawk Hunting Club gate. Big John and his son, Johnny, each with a carpenter's nail pouch around his waist, were charging admission. They were also wearing brand new white tee shirts emblazoned with a crossed pair of checkered flags on the front, and

CRESCENT BEACH 250
1993

on the back. For one of the few times each year, Big John had shed his overalls in favor of a pair of jeans and, even with an extra large, Big John's shirt rode up on his considerable belly. A tall pile of the tee shirts was on a plastic table next to the gate; they were selling like hotcakes.

It was still early, a couple hours before the race that was slated to start at eleven, and a beautiful sunny morning with a low seventies forecast by early afternoon. People were festive, and some of the good ol' boys, wearing baseball caps and cowboy hats and sitting in growling, glass-pack mufflered pickups with enormous tires, already had coolers open and beers in hand. Beyond the gate, a steady stream of vehicles was passing through the live oak tunnel and entering the large clearing. They were met by a good percentage of Crescent Beach's youth who motioned them to the roped-off parking areas. Smoke from a myriad of cookers and grills in the barbeque area next to the lodge rose straight up; men and women were hustling around pulling pork from pigs cooked since before sunup that now lay on plastic covered picnic tables. Beans were bubbling in pots, there were bowls of coleslaw, and piles of hushpuppies and fish ready to be fried. Several carney-looking units were scattered around selling cotton candy, big pretzels, popcorn, and fried dough as well as several people manning tables with more of the race tee shirts and programs. Vendors in cowboy hats and pearly snap button shirts, their bellies hanging over western buckles, were selling NASCAR souvenirs. Church women in long skirts, their hair in a bun or single long braid, stood behind tables of homemade pies, cookies, and other pastries. There was plenty of noise from racecars getting their final tune-up and from the generators powering pneumatic tools. The compressor noise from a refrigerated truck, diplomatically parked away from the church people and armed with a choice of beer from three kegs, added to the din as did the occasional announcements over the loudspeakers from the judges' booth. The scent of petroleum products permeated the air and the grandstands were already more than half filled. People were randomly setting up chairs, tables, and coolers along the straightaway fence.

The Perry fast squad's emergency vehicle was parked next to the Crescent Beach fire truck near the racetrack entry gate, just to the side of the elevated judges' booth. Dressed in dark blue uniforms with red and yellow insignia patches, and each holding a can of Mountain Dew, two members of the fast squad were standing by the gate, talking and pointing out towards various race-cars in the paddock area on the far side of the track. A pair of Perry's uniformed finest stepped out of their cruiser to join them. Alongside the fire truck, Norm and Tammy sat in white plastic chairs. Norm wore sunglasses, light pants, and a navy blue nylon windbreaker. His floppy sunhat was held down by a thick pair of red and black earmuffs. Tammy, her hair in a ponytail, wore tight jeans, one of the race tee shirts, and a pink baseball hat that read Crescent Beach Club. A similar windbreaker hung on the back of her chair. Like the fast squad and policemen, they were looking across to the paddock area. Tammy turned to Norm.

"I'll bet you're the only one here wearing hearing protection."

"What's that, babe?"

Tammy laughed and motioned for him to take off the muffs.

"I said, I bet you're the only one wearing them things today."

"Yeah, and I'll probably be the only one whose ears aren't ringing tonight. Absolutely insane event." He looked across the track to Crescent Beach's pit in the paddock area. "Looks like a bunch of M&Ms tumbling around over there. Also seems like Jimmy's a bit hyper this morning."

"That's probably because he's not driving. He was always cool as a cucumber when he was racing."

Tammy could see Jimmy, Rusty, Tiny, Beau, Charley, and the pair of young mullet fishermen Jimmy had recruited, talking over by the Barracuda. Aside from Rusty, they were wearing bright blue worksuits. Their neighbors were in red to the left, and yellow to the right.

"Now, Rusty, just because you can fly around the track in record time don't mean nothing! This race is about survival, bumper cars with basically no rules. You

don't always have to be in the lead. In otherwords, bide
your time and make your moves when it makes sense.
It's a long ass race," Jimmy said.

"Sorta like survival of the fittest, Rusty," Charley added as Jimmy nervously pulled out a Camel and snapped
a match with his fingernail. Jimmy blew the smoke out
hard as he looked over to some of the other drivers. He
turned back to Rusty.

"And you know all about the judges' flags, right?"
Jimmy asked. "And if I wave a black flag, means we seen
something wrong with the 'Cuda and you bring her on
in lickety-split. Got it?"

"Jimmy, you've told me all this a hundred times. You
got to calm down; I swear you're more nervous than I
am. Got a question though…"

"Shoot."

Just then, their neighbor began to rev his engine.
Rusty had to shout.

"Who's watching all the crabs? Crystal's here cooking somewhere, and Charley's right here, and Norm's
over with the firemen."

Jimmy rolled his eyes in disbelief.

"Good Lord, man!" he shouted back. "Don't you
be worring about them crabs! I got that covered. You
got other things to worry about, like Butch's tricks, that
Mustang from Crystal River, and a couple other of them
crazy redneck bastards. They play it hard; believe me, I
know firsthand."

"You don't git carsick, do you, Rusty?" Tiny asked.

"No, I don't get goddamn carsick, Tiny. Would I be
here doing this if I got carsick!"

"You went shrimping with me, didn't you, and you
knew you got seasick. But I was just asking. No harm
meant."

Rusty put a hand on Tiny's massive shoulder.

"Sorry, Tiny, I shouldn't have snapped at you. Nerves, I guess."

"Don't blame you none. Wouldn't want to be in your boots about now."

The paddock area was a hive of activity. Split off from the straightaway by a series of anchored tractor tires, it was jam-packed with a collage of different colored cars. Thirty-four entries had set a new record for the CB 250. Mechanics under raised hoods were fiddling with car-buretors, pneumatic air wrenches were spitting out lug nuts, brakes were being checked, new wheels mounted. The drivers were drinking coffee, water, or Gatorade, and conversing with mechanics and race organizers. Tools and equipment that weren't being used were spread out under trees at the woods' edge. There were well-trod paths through the trees to blue and white porta-potties.

"Where's Number Twenty-two from?" Rusty asked, pointing four cars behind them.

Jimmy shrugged, saying, "He's new," and pulled out a program from his pants pocket. "Well, I'll be damned. Pensacola. Ain't never had nobody from Pensacola; that's a pretty fur piece. Word must be getting around." He looked towards the Pensacola team. "He's a damn fool, though, bringing that T-bird to a race like this. Must be a '87 or '88 and worth a bundle."

"That boy's the best of the lot: smooth and fast. I watched him during the practice runs. He's young, but I'll bet he's raced somewhere before, and not just on some back country roads," Rusty said.

"Maybe, but like I say, it's as much about strategy as speed. Gotta be smart and bide your time and protect the front end. Most are straight up, ok guys, but Butch and a few other of the tricksters kin force you into a tree, putting you out in a heartbeat. And like I say, that number 43 Mustang over yonder. That's Tommy Smith from Crystal River. He's won the race twice, and not by tricks, but by good driving and timing. He's a smart one and got balls to boot."

Rusty looked around at the different racing teams, then down to his new sweatshirt. "At least I'm sort of color coordinated with you guys."

"Not my fault you're taller than me and outweigh me by forty pounds so you don't fit into my suit. Just be happy we tapped the kitty for a new helmet." Jimmy said.

"But Jimmy, purple with glittery flecks! Looks like a damn bowling ball!"

"Was on sale." Jimmy smiled. "Guess they had a hard time selling it."

"I'm not putting it on until I get in the car; tell you that!"

"Nope," Jimmy said, shaking his head.

"What do you mean, 'nope?'" Rusty asked.

"Gotta wear it for the start. One of the few rules."

"Right, that's what I'm saying."

Jimmy continued to shake his head.

"Guess no one told you it's a Le Mens start," Charley said.

"Le Mans, Charley," Beau corrected.

"Whatever."

"Say what?" Rusty asked.

"Gotta go to the other side of the track and line up with everybody else and run over when the gun goes off," Charley said. "Just like they done with that sports car shindig down in Sebring."

"That's why I told you to wear them sneakers," Jimmy said.

"You could have told me why! You never told me anything about a damn footrace! Hell, Jimmy, except for a couple of bubbas, I'm older and slower than any driver here."

"Won't matter much in a race as long as this one, and, anyways, we got a pretty good spot here in the paddock when we picked our number out of the hat. Even if'n you're dead last running over here, you still should be in the middle of the pack."

"Can't believe Butch got the very first spot in the paddock," Rusty said, looking over.

"That's because he won last year," Charley said. "He gits the number one spot and don't gotta run neithers, just hop in his rig when the gun goes off. Gits the glory to be the first out; but it'll bunch up soon enough."

Jimmy looked at his watch. "About an hour to go if you want to practice running or something."

Rusty looked blankly at Jimmy, the others, and walked over to sit in the shade.

"Guess he don't want to do too much; save his energy some," Charley said.

Across from the paddock area, cars and trucks were still pulling in, bumper to bumper, among them Craig and Ralph in Ralph's little pickup. Ralph gave the young girl who led them to their parking spot a dollar bill. Her smile was ear to ear.

"Now keep an eye on my truck, will you Laurie?"

"You betcha, Mr. Ralph!"

Ralph and Craig walked around taking in the sights. They found Crystal in the BBQ area frying fish.

Ralph said, "See you're putting all the fish Jimmy and his clients caught to good use, Crystal. Proceeds going to the summer camp?"

Crystal looked up. Her hair was covered by a blue kerchief and a few beads of sweat were making the journey from forehead down to the tip of her nose. She reached for a handtowel and mopped her face."

"Some. We'll see what's left over from the fee to set up here. You'd think Jimmy and the Race Committee'd cut me a deal. But business is business, I guess, and they got plenty of bills to pay to put this thing on."

"How'd Jimmy sleep last night?" Craig asked.

Crystal laughed.

"Don't think he slept none, judging from all his tossing and turning. Didn't help my sleep neither, tell you that."

Long stainless fork in hand, she bent over her fish. Craig and Ralph let her tend to her job and continued on.

" About as many people here as for the scallop festival. Quite an event," Ralph said, looking around.

"Scallop Festival's no where near as noisy."

"No thanks to you, as I recall. You were always out drinking and carousing in that airboat of yours making all sorts of a racket. Heck, I'll bet you never even picked up a scallop."

"Hell yeah, I did. Buckets full. But you're right; I did hot-dog it and, yeah, I drank more than my share of beer. But," he said, smiling, "Reverend, I've seen the light. Am walking the straight and narrow, thanks to you...How about some popcorn?"

"If you're buying."

They walked up to one of the carney trailers and Craig bought two bags along with cokes. Tammy saw them on her way back from a porta-potty and motioned them over. She pointed to Norm and they nodded.

"I swear Craig's a different person now that he's not drinking," Norm said to Tammy as he watched them approach. "Looks better, too; lost some of that flab. And those two are inseparable these days..." He looked at Tammy. "Makes you wonder."

Tammy laughed.

"Craig? No way! He's just discovered that Ralph, homo or not, is a good egg. About time is what I say. Not to mention he's grateful to Ralph for most likely saving his life."

Ralph offered popcorn to Tammy when they walked up.

"You got that airboat sold yet, Craig?" Norm asked.

"How the hell can I with the motor in pieces and Jimmy taking up all of Rusty's time? Rusty's only got it stripped down to soak things in oil because of all the salt, but he did say it shouldn't be too bad of a job. Said that after the race he'd make it a priority. Hell of a nice guy, Rusty."

"Who's minding the Club, Tammy?" Ralph asked.

"Minnie and Maybelline, although they'll probably be polishing glasses all day. Everybody's here."

"They didn't mind pulling duty?" Craig asked.

"Not Minnie, but Maybelline wanted to come out to wish Rusty luck and cheer him on. Rusty wasn't too excited about that, so I helped him out and talked her into working."

"Where's the 'Cuda Crew?" Ralph asked.

"About straight across," Norm answered.

The paddock area had thinned out and they had a clear shot at the Crescent Beach team. A couple of officials crossed the track and climbed up to the judges' booth to their left. Norm looked at his watch. "About fifteen minutes before show time," he said. They saw Rusty get up out of a chair and begin stretching. Jimmy was pacing back and forth next to him. The rest of the crew sat in chairs at the edge of the woods. Everybody was nervous and trying hard not to show it. Charley and Tiny cracked their first beers of the day.

"Getting loose for your windsprint, Rusty?" Charley asked after taking a long pull of beer and extending his legs out in front of him.

"Nope. I'm stretching every muscle I can think of that's going to begin complaining in the next couple of hours; that is, unless you're planning on helping me out some."

"Don't even think it," Jimmy said.

"Not to worry, Jimmy. I'm plenty happy right here. You just stretch away, Rusty." Charley took another swig before adding, "Silence's pretty loud, ain't it?" Rusty looked right and left, suddenly realizing that not a single car was running and all the hoods were down. Charley was right, the silence was loud.

"Must be getting close. Drivers are putting on their helmets," Rusty said.

Jimmy looked at his watch.

"Better get ready. You taken a pee lately?"

Rusty shrugged.

"Little while ago. Why?"

Jimmy didn't answer. Instead he walked to the edge of the woods. When he returned, he handed Rusty an old Maxwell House coffee can.

"Here," Jimmy said, handing him the can.

"What's this for?" Rusty asked.

"Guess."

Rusty looked at him in disbelief.

"At a hundred miles an hour! You gotta be kidding, Jimmy!"

"Put it in the rig and use it during yellow flags, there'll be plenty of 'em. Don't need no extra pit stops."

The loudspeaker blared, "All drivers, except last year's champion Butch Spencer from Steinhatchee, prepare to take starting positions on the judges' side of the track. Race will begin in ten minutes."

Butch's name drew a mix of boos, cheers, and cat-calls. A few from the Crescent Beach contingents yelled, "Traitor!" and "Bad Boy Butch!"

Rusty went over to the Barracuda and traded the can for his helmet, a thousand butterflies instantly fluttering around his stomach. When he returned, Jimmy offered his left hand.

"Good luck," he said.

"Thanks, I'll need it."

Beau came up to shake too.

"Ditto, Rusty, and don't forget, you're a Scottish warrior."

Tiny yelled over, "Make that two Scottish warriors on this here team, and they ain't never been beat neithers!"

Rusty smiled and gave Tiny the thumbs up. "Don't you and Charley pound those beers too hard, Tiny. I might need you to change a wheel or three," he said.

"Don't you go worrying about us. Crew chief here," Charley said, jerking a thumb in Jimmy's direction, "won't allow it. Regular Moose-alini."

"Mussolini, Charley," Beau said.

"Whatever. Anyways, was lot easier to git along with Jimmy here when he was driving. But, we be professionals, right Tiny?"

"Right." Charley and Tiny tapped cans and took swigs.

"You just do the driving and we'll do the rest," Charley said. "I'll take care of the gas, Beau here's got your windshield covered, the fisher boys got your tires, and Tiny's jackman, though he probly don't need no jack."

"Now don't forget to put on your helmet," Tiny added.

Rusty looked at the helmet, then at Jimmy. He shook his head and slowly pulled it on, fastening the chinstrap before crossing the track with the other drivers. He took his position almost exactly in front of the big gate.

Craig, Ralph, Norm, and Tammy had a close-up view of Rusty's back, not ten feet away. Norm whistled a catcall and yelled, "Nice helmet, Rusty! Been to the lanes lately?" All four laughed when Rusty flipped a bird behind his back and held it there. "What's that, your IQ?" Norm couldn't help adding. Rusty flipped a bird with his other hand and kept both behind him.

"Bet he's nervous as a motherfucker," Craig muttered.

"Watch your language! We've got a lady present." Ralph said.

"I've heard worse, Ralph," Tammy said.

Norm wondered how Ralph would have reacted if Craig had said cocksucker. The loudspeakers blared again. "Two minutes until race time." The packed grandstands quieted to a buzz in anticipation. Tammy yelled out, "We're rooting for you, number 666. Go git 'em, Rusty!"

The loudspeaker came on again. "Ten, nine, eight," Rusty leaned forward, "seven, six, five, four, three, two, one, Bang!" The drivers sprinted across the track as Butch roared out of the paddock. One heavy-set driver looked like he had stepped on a banana peel when he slipped on a patch of oil. The crowd erupted in laughter, then applause when he gave them a quick bow, instantly becoming the darling of those without a town to root for. Dodging the fishtailing drivers accelerating out of the paddock, the driver ran up to number 44, a Chevy Super Sport. Rusty ended up in the middle of the pack after lumbering over to the 'Cuda. He flicked the Maxwell House can off the seat as he quickly climbed in and bits of limestone flew out from his rear tires as he floored it out of the paddock area. He hadn't reached fourth gear when he had to brake and downshift at the gridlock funneling into the woods. He was right on the bumper of number 22, the T-Bird from Pensacola.

CHAPTER
TWENTY-SEVEN

Butch looked in his rearview mirror. Everyone was watching him, the champion. With an arm upraised out the window, he had roared by the grandstand and, although impossible to hear the crowd, he knew they were cheering him, screaming his name. He was the Man, the King! There had never been a repeat champion, but he planned to be the first; whatever it took, he was going to win. As he downshifted for the woods, he checked his mirror again. The other cars were entering the track; come on, buttholes, we'll see who's got 'nads around here!

Butch hadn't won the year before on trickery alone; he was a more than adequate driver and way more than willing to take chances. He negotiated the short S turns, and downshifted for the hairpin in the quarry before accelerating out and attacking the long S. He hit eighty-five before downshifting again for the second hairpin where it opened up to the straightaway. He gunned his Charger and was doing over a hundred when he passed some guy just coming out of the pits in a Plymouth Roadrunner. Dumb slob got hisself lapped before he even started. Butch downshifted again and entered the woods. He soon caught up to a couple of cars at the hairpin. He tapped his fingers on the wheel as he slowed. Come on you damn faggot turtles; got a big fast rabbit here wants to git by! He was inches from the bumper of the car in front of him. As they came out of the sharp curve, he saw an opening and punched through, accelerating hard up into the long S. He could see more cars ahead of him negotiating the second hairpin.

Rusty, mired in a pack of ten cars, was a respectable distance from the bumper of the T-Bird as the pair negotiated the narrow woods track. They passed a couple of cars, but there were still four dead ahead of them. The best chance to pass safely, Rusty knew, was the wide straightaway, that is, if his car had enough muscle: he'd find out shortly. Both he and the T-Bird stomped on it coming out of the second hairpin, one pulling left, the other right. Rusty hit the nitrous oxide switch and the 'Cuda leaped forward. Rusty had no problem passing the other cars, but neither did the T-Bird. Rusty and the young T-Bird driver glanced at each other as they started downshifting for the woods again; they entered side by side. Up ahead was another cluster going into the short S with the Mustang from Crystal River trying to get by. They soon pulled up behind him. Rusty was content to wait for the straightaway, absolutely no need to take chances this early. They went in order through the hairpin, long S, and the second hairpin. But the Mustang, Rusty, and the T-Bird broke out after the hairpin and roared by the other cars in the straightaway, bringing Charley and Tiny out of their seats.

"Holy shit," Charley said. He pitched his beer can into the woods. "Was Rusty hauling ass or what!"

Jimmy was all smiles. "That's my boy," he said. "Only ninety-eight more laps to go," he added.

Two clusters ahead of Rusty, Butch was behind the Super Sport driven by the driver who had slipped on the track. Unlike Rusty, Butch liked the thrill of riding bumpers, relying more on reflex than strategy. When the five-car cluster entered the straightaway, the cars fanned out, but Butch's yellow Charger wasn't fast enough to pass. They were neck and neck with no one willing to give up his space as they approached the woods. The fans went wild, smelling an early collision. But at the last second, with frantic breaking and downshifting, the two outside drivers gave way. Butch was one of three inside, flying into the woods, only inches between him and the trees and the Super Sport. Shit, Butch thought, car ain't got muscle enough to pass on the straightaway; bet your ass them grease monkeys going to git an earful. Butch's Charger pulled ahead of the other two in his group and slid perfectly through the short S before he downshifted for the hairpin. Only way to win this dang thing, he knew, was out here in the woods.

The cars had thinned out some and the Mustang, T-Bird, and Rusty formed a tight line, slowing down for the hairpins but accelerating hard during the long S and the straightaway. They wowed the fans, but no one gained advantage. They kept that position for twelve laps, slowly working their way up past the others until they were seven, eight, and nine in the standings, with Butch still leading.

It was on their thirteenth lap when the first yellow flag came out. A Chevy Monte Carlo, trying to pass a Ford Torino in the short S turn, cut in too soon, slamming the front right side of the Ford that spun him around two hundred and seventy degrees. His right rear end slammed into a pine, his tire was shredded, and the car ended up broadside across a third of the track with the driver's door facing the oncoming cars. The Super Sport and a red Plymouth Belvedere barely veered to the right in time, their bodies kissing, but both drivers managed to stay in control and miss the Ford. The Ford's driver leaped out and ran into the safety of the woods while the Track Marshalls called the tower and yellow flags were waved around the track. The Pettibone operator waited until racecars, frozen in order, came by at the mandated speed of fifteen miles per hour before coming out to pick up the Ford. With its eight-foot forks, the loader carried the car off like a gigantic beetle with its hapless prey. Minutes later, the green flag came out and the race resumed.

On the twenty-fourth lap, the Mustang, T-Bird, and Rusty had caught up to Butch on the first hairpin. Butch recognized the Mustang and the 'Cuda, and knew that the Mustang was a serious challenge. Coming out of the turn, Butch cut off the Mustang as it tried to pass, but in swerving over, the T-Bird bolted past, taking the lead. Rusty, waiting for the straightaway, hung with the Mustang as Butch continued to block its path through the long S. The three cars hit ninety before braking for the final hairpin which was becoming badly torn up. Fine limestone was hanging in the air from the T-Bird, and Butch added to it when he fishtailed through. Across the track, the fans watched Butch come into the straightaway amidst a cloud of dust. Suddenly, bursting through the white cloud, came Rusty and the Mustang. They fanned out right and left, and Butch, hands clenched white on the wheel and eyes bulging in frustration, was passed.

His nerves as well as the heat from the engine had Rusty coated in sweat. He couldn't remember having to concentrate so intensely for so long. He was exhausted, his back and neck were stiff, and he knew he must be dehydrated to boot. And, according to Crew 'Cuda who'd been holding up signs, this was only the twenty-fifth lap, a quarter of the way. Eight more before the first of two pit stops. Why the hell had he agreed to do this? But, too late now, he thought shifting down for the short S. At least Jimmy had been right: he had been able to piss in the can and throw the contents out during the yellow flag.

Along the fence as well as in the stands, some of the fans were well on their way to inebriation. A fight broke out between a crab fisherman from Steinhatchee and a lineman from the University of Florida football team who had come with a small contingent to cheer on Gainesville's entry, Number 44—the Super Sport whose driver had slipped during the start. Butch, being last year's winner and awarded the easy head start, was the subject of early race conversation in the stands. The football player's group, surrounded by knowledgeable locals, heard all about Butch's dirty tactics the preceding year. By the time the football player was into his second six-pack, he began to bellow out uncomplimentary epithets every time Butch hit the straightaway. The Steinhatchee fisherman took offense, but didn't do or say anything until the college boy began to scream his head off and pump his fist when Butch was passed on the straightaway. The fisherman couldn't hold back and gave him a hard shove, telling the two hundred and eighty pounder to shut the fuck up. The obligatory fuck yous were traded back and forth until they began swinging at each other. Unfortunately, they were near the top, six rows up, and when they muckled on to each other, they fell into the row below. The fans tried to break them apart without success, so they pushed them down to the next row. This was repeated until they ended up like two tangled polecats on the ground between the stands and high fence.

The fracas did not go unnoticed and Perry's finest rushed over to separate the pair. The football player, accustomed to repeated head dingers on the gridiron, was unfazed by all the thumping and bumping of the hard bleacher planks on the way down. The fisherman had a pretty good gash on his cheek caused by the protruding head of a galvanized nail. He pulled up his tee shirt to staunch the bleeding. A furious woman the pair had landed on in the third row carefully stepped down, cradling her right forearm and yelling at the pair, saying the big louts had broken her wrist. One of the deputies went off to fetch Norm, the other brought out a notebook and pencil, saying that it looked like he'd have to take them to Perry. However, no one, including the deputy, wanted to miss the race, and the questions and answers paused as the trio turned to watch when the cars thundered by. The deputy finally lowered his notebook and offered a deal: if the two men would shake hands and behave themselves, he'd give them a second chance; but if they blew it, there'd be a big fine and a couple weeks' lodging in the Perry city jail. The two men were suddenly all smiles and shook immediately. No hard feelings, they said, just got caught up in the moment. The deputy told the fisherman and the lady to wait for Norm to have a look. The deputy, fisherman, and woman stepped off to the side of the stands while the football player climbed back up to row six. He cracked a beer and yelled down to the fisherman. "When you get patched up, one of these got your name on it!" he said, waving a can. The fisherman smiled and gave him a thumbs-up.

The other deputy found Norm and explained the situation. Norm stood up and handed Tammy his ear protectors.

"Duty calls," he said, grimacing when two cars roared by. He picked up his emergency doctor bag, and Tammy watched him follow the deputy along the fence. She looked at the earphones in her lap; why Norm remained in Crescent Beach was a mystery to her. So many things bugged him: the airboats, this race, the litter, and a dozen other things. And they were definitely the odd couple. The sex was good, very good, no problems there.

But there were rough edges. She never felt comfortable with all his education and rich upbringing. He never flaunted it, but when he talked with educated people, like Beau and Virginia, he talked different. And there were the times when he couldn't help himself and corrected her grammar, or when she bluffed knowing what the hell he was talking about—some national or world event—because she was too embarrassed to let him know how ignorant she was. Or like now when she was enjoying the hell out of this race while he wore earphones, resenting having to attend. The deafening noise, the large crowd, even the smells of exhaust, oil, and tires, all of it excited her. You could feel the raw power of the throbbing engines as the cars flew by. Races turned her on, plain and simple.

But maybe that had something to do with the old mud bogging days with Bobby. No racing, nothing like the CB 250, just take turns with the others driving down and around flooded boggy areas, not going fast, just ripping it up and throwing mud everywheres. They drank Dr. Peppers laced with Southern Comfort from noon on, and went to burger joints afterwards with her his road queen sitting up in that high cab, riding almost in his lap, her hand on his thigh. After something to eat, they'd cruise the back roads. Bobby said there wasn't a ditch he couldn't ride no matter how much water was in it, and mostly that was true. He prided himself on having the muddiest and loudest truck in town. You could always hear him coming from the mill a long ways off and most of his paychecks went towards something on the truck.

It was in the back of that truck where he first did her. She was sixteen. She remembered it clearly; heck, what girl didn't remember the first time? Bobby had thrown a blanket down and she helped him take off her bra. They were in a hurry. They had been touching here and there all day long so they were all jazzed up, half drunk, and ready. It didn't last long, probably because of all the anticipation, but she remembered a couple things real clear. Bobby's white buttocks had stood out like a brand new half volleyball in the dark night. His butt also got bad bug bit. Must of been skeeters, she had thought, but when he showed her the little red dots in the light of the cab, they looked more like chigger bites. She also remembered the red streaks from where he had madly scratched, and from where she had held him hard.

"Did Rusty pull in yet?"

Startled, Tammy looked up from the earphones in her lap.

"What, honey?" she asked, a little guilty because of memory lane with Bobby.

"Did Rusty come in for a pit stop? The T-Bird's in."

Tammy looked over to the paddock, but couldn't see the T-Bird until she stood up and saw the T-Bird's team frantically gassing up the car, wiping the windshield, checking the tires, and talking to the driver who was drinking water. Tammy turned back to Norm.

"Why, Norm, you're actually paying attention to what's going on out there," Tammy chided, as she handed him the earmuffs.

"Rusty's representing the town...and I also don't want to see him get hurt," he said, not meeting her eyes.

They watched the T-Bird accelerate out of the paddock. As it exited, Rusty entered from the other end.

"Here he comes now," Norm added, needlessly.

Rusty pulled up to Crew 'Cuda. Charley began fueling the car while Beau cleaned the windshield. The two young fishermen inspected the tires before cleaning the rear window. Jimmy leaned down. "How you doing?" he asked.

"Damn hands are cramping some and my back's felt better. I could use some water bigtime," Rusty croaked.

Jimmy slapped his forehead. "Damn! " he said, rushing over to get a gallon of spring water and quickly filling both a large glass and one of those heavy-duty plastic water bottles with a retractable nipple. "Here, keep this one with you."

Rusty put the nippled bottle next to the Maxwell House can, then chugged the glass of water. He pulled off his sweatshirt. "Man, it gets hot in here! This sweatshirt's soaked! Any advice, coach?"

"Nope, you're doing real good, real good. Still got two thirds of the race to go, so bide your time, don't go crazy. You were riding at number three afore you pulled in here which is about perfect. But, be careful. As guys git tired or when it gits closer to the end, going to be more wrecks and things going wrong. So, be real careful. We'll flag you again for your next stop." There was a pounding on the rear fender from Charley. "You're all set. Go git 'em, Junior." Rusty smiled and jammed it in gear. He looked back towards the entrance of the pit. The Mustang was coming in. Rusty took off like a shot and pulled out to clear track. In seconds he entered the woods.

Butch did not come in on his scheduled pit stop and his crew looked pissed off. Jimmy wondered what was up. Butch, his car running on fumes, finally pulled in on the forty-seventh lap, a good dozen laps later than any other driver.

"What the hell you doing, Butch!" his pit crew chief screamed at him.

Butch ignored him and yelled to the crew, "Change them fucking tires as well as gas 'er up! And fill her to the brim, and I mean fucking brim!" Butch turned to the pit crew chief. "You got me a dog here! Ain't you noticed I get passed out there on the straightaway! Think that's my fault! Goddamn thing's slower 'n molasses, ain't got no goddamn balls! Oniest chance I got to win is make this one goddamn stop. Everybody else's scheduled for two. Might give me a fucking chance to make up what I'm behind and git the lead back. Then if'n I kin hold 'em off, maybe I kin win this goddamn thing!" To the fuel man, again, "I mean to the tippy top!" With new tires and gas up to the brim, Butch took off.

Once things got settled after the pit stops, Rusty had dropped to number five, although not more than a couple hundred feet separated the first seven drivers. The order held for a good twenty laps with the T-Bird in the lead, Butch at number two and the Super Sport from Gainesville at number 6, right behind Rusty. The Mustang had some problems during its pit stop and had dropped to tenth place, but had worked his way back up to seven where he was held back by the congested pack of frontrunners. Aside from the Ford Torino, four other cars had dropped out because of mechanical problems. On lap fifty-two, there was a red flag stopping the race. A tire blew on a Plymouth Roadrunner accelerating into the long S curves, causing it to swerve and broadside a Mercury Cyclone that flipped and skidded on its roof for a hundred and fifty feet before it ended up lengthwise across the track with, luckily, no one right behind them. The Plymouth spun into the woods, its rear end destroyed by a fourteen-inch diameter pine tree. Miraculously, no one was hurt, but both drivers needed assistance to get out of their cars.

Twenty minutes later, the track was cleared and the race restarted with the green flag. Around and around they went. Rusty, the Super Sport, and the Mustang worked up to three, four, and five positions, with the T-Bird and Butch remaining at one and two. It was grueling. Rusty's whole body ached, he kept flexing his fingers to relieve the cramping. He had finished the bottle of water five laps earlier, and he eagerly awaited Jimmy's black flag. He didn't care if it would set them back, but he had to get out of the car to stand up straight, even if only for a couple of moments. Around the track he went again, but still no flag. He knew he was due from the lap signs, but looked like Jimmy was waiting on the other drivers. All Rusty cared about was taking a break and water. The limestone around both hairpins had been worked loose, with the second hairpin the worse. The drivers had accelerated and spun their wheels so hard coming out of the hairpin into the straightaway that it had dug a hole right across the width of the track. It was getting worse each time because the drivers were losing traction as their tires wore down which in turn led to more spinning which dug the hole deeper. There was no getting around it either as it was framed by pine trees. Rusty's car dropped in, jolting his back; he could feel it from his neck to his toes. He glanced in his rear-view mirror. The Mustang had passed the Super Sport and was now on his bumper. When they came out to the straightaway, Rusty saw Jimmy waving the black flag and pulled in. The T-Bird was already in, being serviced by its crew. The Mustang stayed on the track and was a blur speeding past, trying to catch up with Butch.

Rusty was already opening his door before the car came to a complete stop. He climbed out as Jimmy came running up with a bottle of water. Rusty traded the empty for Jimmy's. The two young fishermen and Tiny began changing tires while Charley had gas pouring into the tank. Tiny and Charley had surprised Jimmy when they had stopped drinking after the first beer; they were dead on serious. Pumping the jack, Tiny asked Rusty how he was feeling.

"In a word, Tiny, shit! I feel like shit," Rusty said as he reached for the sky then tried to touch his toes. He made it about halfway. The high speed rat-a-tat-tat and whirring of the pneumatic air wrenches filled the air. Rusty bent over again, this time extending his

fingers hard as if that might help to touch his toes. Tiny
pulled the jack out from the car, and Charley thumped
the fender again. Rusty creaked back into the cockpit.
Beau was looking out to the track as Butch roared by.
The Mustang was heading to the paddock. Beau yelled
to Jimmy, "Butch's over a lap ahead and adding!"

"Rusty, Butch took his pit stop at lap forty-seven and
my guess is he ain't gonna take another," Jimmy said.
"He's trying to gain enough laps while everyone else is
making stops. It's a ballsy move with a good chance he's
going to run outta gas; you never know for sure. But he's
ahead right now so he's the one to beat." The T-Bird
passed them and pulled on to the track. "And that guy,
too. So, this is it, Rusty, when men are men. Crescent
Beach is counting on you. " Tired, hurting, not smiling,
Rusty nodded and put the 'Cuda in gear.

Two yellow flags, one red flag, no serious injuries, various mechanical issues, and some twenty laps later, only
eighteen cars remained out of the thirty-four entries.
Butch was still leading.   Number 43, the Crystal River
Mustang, was in second, number 22, the T-Bird from
Pensacola in third, number 666 with Rusty in fourth,
and number 44, the Super Sport from Gainesville in
fifth. They were all bunched up coming out of the first
hairpin, Butch doing his best not to let anybody by. As
they accelerated into the long S, an official began waving yet another yellow flag. The group slowed down,
although Butch took his time. When they entered the S
and the official disappeared from view, Butch eased up
to twenty-five mph, ten over the fifteen prescribed during a caution flag, allowing Butch to pick up a little real
estate. A few minutes later the green flag came out.

Fuckin' brainstorm that one pit stop, Butch thought
as he glanced in his mirror. Ten laps to go with a lap and
a half lead. He went into the second hairpin at a crazy
speed with front wheels pre-turned when he entered the

soft limestone of the hole.   When the front wheels hit
the far edge, the whole car as well as Butch's body shuddered with the blow, but somehow the tires held and the
impact succeeded in turning the car sharply and bouncing him out of the hole without spinning. He gained a
whisker of time that, combined with what he had picked
up violating the yellow flag, enabled him to stay in the
lead. But, when he reached the woods, he saw that the
Mustang was on his bumper again with the T-Bird and
Rusty just behind the Mustang. The Mustang continued
to ride Butch's ass. Butch held his own through the two
S curves and first hairpin, but when he played it safe
on the final hairpin, all three cars caught up and then
passed him on the straightaway. Still, Butch thought,
the others are a lap behind. The Super Sport from
Gainesville was just back of Butch, two laps behind him
in the standings.

The crowd was revved up. The race had the makings of a doozey finish and everyone, drunk or sober,
was fixated with most screaming their heads off. Craig,
Ralph, Tammy, and even Norm were standing up, fingers
laced through the tall fence, cheering Rusty every time
he went by. Crew 'Cuda was on their feet, with Jimmy
chain smoking and pacing back and forth. Tiny wanted
to cover his eyes he was so nervous. All the cars looked
beat up and pallid from the limestone. But around and
around they went.

With just two laps remaining, the three cars had
caught up with Butch again who was doing everything
he could to keep them from passing. Jimmy had been
right, Rusty thought: Tommy Smith from Crystal River
in the Mustang was one hell of a driver. He was giving
it his all trying to get by Butch who kept swerving to
block his every move. If the three of them could get
by Butch, then the straightaway would decide the race,
and it would be close. The four cars power slid through

the short S and, as they approached the hairpin, Butch's Charger seemed to jerk and stutter as if it were out of gas. All of the drivers were aware of Butch making a single pit stop and they thought that his luck must have finally run out. Butch moved over on the track, giving the Mustang room before the hairpin. Butch knew he was licked and was letting them by, Rusty thought. Maybe the kid's not as bad as everybody says.

But it was a sham. When the Mustang started to pass, Butch gunned his Charger and slammed into the Mustang, forcing it into the quarry pond. A shower of water and steam enveloped the car before it settled in five feet of water. With Butch way over to the right, the T-Bird tried to sneak into the hairpin ahead of him, but he had to slam on the brakes as Butch swerved back. Rusty just missed going into the water too as he jerked the wheel to avoid the T-Bird. Coming out of the hairpin, Rusty glanced at the Mustang. The driver was already climbing out of the window. Must be pissed as hell, Rusty thought. He wondered if the Mustang had been doing a hundred instead of thirty, if it would have made it across.

The T-Bird began pressing again, feinting and thrusting, close on Butch's bumper. Butch stomped hard on the brakes every now and then, hoping, no doubt, to damage the T-Bird's radiator; but the driver had the reflexes of a mongoose fighting a snake. He continued to shadow Butch. Rusty held back, not wanting to get caught up in the cat and mouse. Close behind Rusty was number 44, but he had a full lap to make up. With two laps to go, no way, Rusty thought, they couldn't get by Butch in the straightaway. It was going to be between the 'Cuda and the T-Bird. Suddenly Butch goosed it right before the second hairpin and turned his wheels ninety degrees like he had done earlier. He hoped he could one-bounce around the corner and gain enough

again so he could make it through the straightaway to
the woods without being passed.

When the front wheels struck ninety degrees to the
edge of the hole, this time both sidewalls burst and Butch
lost control and started spinning. The T-Bird ran directly into the front of the Charger, tearing off the bumper
which in turn sliced one of the 'Cuda's front tires. The
bumper wedged between the 'Cuda's engine and chas-
sis with one jagged end in the tire and the other angling
down into the ground. The T-Bird's radiator had a hole
in it the size of a grapefruit, and water streamed out, instantly steaming on contact with the engine. The cloud
of steam covered the windshield like a London fog and
the driver knew he had to get into the pit immediately
before the engine overheated and seized.

The trees prevented the Super Sport from pulling
around the three cars. It stopped and waited for everyone to get out of the way. The red flag came out
but was immediately replaced by the green because the
T-Bird quickly backed off Butch's Charger and followed
the 'Cuda thumping in with the flat tire and plowing a
furrow with the wedged bumper. The Charger was also
able to crawl in with the two flats, but unlike the 'Cuda,
the tie rods were bent and cracked. Butch could barely
steer it into the paddock. No way could he continue.
To make matters worse, he ran out of gas and his crew
had to push the car with two flat tires all the way up
to their pit area. Tiny and the fishermen were waiting
for Rusty with a new wheel. But the bumper posed a
big problem: even when they took the wheel off, they
couldn't dislodge it. As the fishermen tugged, Jimmy
asked what had happened.

"Frigging Butch! He cobbled all three of us at the
hairpin! Fucked over the Mustang back at the other,"
Rusty spat. Rusty glanced at the T-Bird. Its hood was
up and its crew furiously trying to patch the radiator

both inside and out, pouring some sort of goop down its throat and smearing some sort of silver paste all over the front. A mechanic began filling the radiator, but then they couldn't get the car started. The team started to push it towards the track. Rusty's fingers danced on the steering wheel. He looked at his crew. C'mon, C'mon! Tiny wedged himself under the 'Cuda and, bracing body and legs against the frame, gave a mighty yank on the bumper. It popped out. Tiny rolled out of the way, the fisherman had the new wheel on in seconds, and Charley yanked out the jack. "Go, man, go!" yelled Jimmy. Rusty took off. Only seconds later, the T-Bird popped off and was after Rusty. The Super Sport, now the new leader, had just entered the woods.

The driver of the Super Sport couldn't believe his luck when the others went into the paddock; the track was wide open and the race was there for the taking. He quickly made up the lap he needed while the others remained in the paddock. Before most of the fans realized what had happened, he was the frontrunner with a single lap to go. But as his mirror testified, the Barracuda and T-Bird had re-entered the track. He had to go all out; if they caught up before coming into the straightaway, they would take him. This had to be the lap of his life.

And it was. The only time he slowed down was for the hairpins; he hit an incredible ninety-eight in the long S. The final hairpin he took conservatively, then shot straight ahead for the checkered flag. Rusty and the T-Bird did not gain on him in the woods. They too were going flat out, but they didn't make up any ground. There was no chance to catch him, but second was up for grabs. The T-Bird and 'Cuda raced the last lap as if joined in the middle. They squeezed through the final hairpin together, exiting in a thick limestone cloud, their engines redlining all the way to the flag.

Rusty'd bet they'd hit one-fifty. The fans were in awe, their screams primeval. It was a photo finish.

Both drivers furiously downshifted and applied the brakes before entering the woods one last time where, braking further, they followed the leader in a luxuriously slow lap before pulling up to the judges at the finish line. It was determined that the Barracuda and T-Bird had tied, and the fourth place car was brought out of the paddock for third place. The area closest to the finish line was mobbed with fans trying to take pictures of the winners. Many of the fans were exiting the stands, but in the sixth row the football player and fisherman, best friends, were in deep conversation. They had stopped paying attention to the race long ago and now the football player, arm around the shoulder of the fisherman, was explaining the finer nuances of blocking off the line of scrimmage. Both were too drunk to stand. They had missed the fracas at the hairpin and had no idea the race was over until a buddy of the football player high-fived him. When the clueless football player realized what was going on, he jumped to his feet and pumped his fist in the air. Losing his balance, he pitched forward to the row below, starting a mini domino effect of flattened spectators extending three rows down. Fortunately no one was hurt, and when the football player was helped back to his seat, he began to commiserate with the fisherman about Butch.

"No need to feel bad; Butch is a flaming asshole," the fisherman slurred, patting the football player on the back. "I was just rooting for Steinhatchee. Everybody knows Butch is a real jerk; always has been and always will be, and I'm proud to say he's from Crescent Beach here, not my town. And I'll tell you what," he said, standing up unsteadily. "Never thought I'd drink to Gainesville, but here's to your driver and team!" The fisherman raised his beer can that had been empty for an eternity. He brought it to his lips, shook it, then dropped it to a considerable pile below. "That is," he said eyeing the cooler between them, "if I had anything to toast 'em with..." The football player, weaving and all smiles, studiously cracked his last two beers.

Crew 'Cuda had rushed over to the winners' area where Rusty was slowly extricating himself from the car. It looked painful; he was all bent over. When he finally was able to straighten up, Jimmy, smiling ear to ear, gave him a big hug. "Not bad for a rookie!" he exclaimed. "Hell of a race, Rusty, hell of a race!" Rusty shook hands with his crew, then walked over and extended a hand to the winner.

"Congratulations. Fine job."

The T-Bird driver came up to shake the winner's hand, too. "Ditto," he said.

The Gainesville driver was euphoric, red blush on his fleshy face. "Just can't believe it, can't believe how it opened up. I was hoping for fourth at best. Was a race between me the tortoise, you two hares and the Mustang, and one snake. Thanks to the snake, the tortoise won."

There was a sudden commotion in the crowd with people pointing and looking over to the paddock area. The water soaked Mustang driver, tire iron in hand, was being restrained by his pit crew. He broke away and started running towards the end of the paddock area where Butch and his crew were examining the front end of the Dodge Charger. Butch heard the shouts from the Mustang's crew and looked up. When he saw the driver and tire iron, he took off for the woods. The Mustang driver sprinted after him with Butch's crew stepping aside.

"Never ketch him, not in a hundred years," Charley said, looking over. "Butch was always the fastest kid in town, especially after he shot out a streetlight or something." He turned back to Rusty and the others. "And he knows these woods better than most."

"Too bad; he deserves a good thrashing," the T-Bird driver said. "Enjoyed your company out there, Brer Hare," he said to Rusty.

"Thanks. Rusty's the name," Rusty said. He took took off his helmet. "Not my choice of colors," he said, looking at it sheepishly.

The T-Bird driver laughed. "I'm John." He looked at Rusty for a second. "Damn, you look familiar."

"Don't know how that could be. You're from Pensacola, right?" John nodded. "I'm from north Georgia." Rusty glanced at the low sun; must be pushing six, he thought. "You going all the way back tonight?" John shook his head and unhooked the strap of his helmet and pulled it off. He ran his fingers through his thick black hair. Rusty recognized the young man and the mannerism immediately. He had ticketed John on U.S. 95 outside Daytona last year, around midnight following the Daytona 500. He usually remembered the ones going over a hundred, but especially this one because John had pulled over immediately when he spotted the cruiser coming up from behind; Rusty hadn't even turned on his light and siren. Never knowing what to expect, especially that time of night, Rusty had approached the car carefully. He was relieved to find a polite young man with no issues.

"Driver's license and registration, please. Know how fast you were going, son?" Rusty asked.

"Yes, sir, around a hundred and ten."

Rusty looked at the license and registration using a penlight, then shined the light on the kid's face.

"A hundred and sixteen to be exact," Rusty said. "Been to the races today by any chance?"

The kid ran his fingers through his hair.

"Yes, sir. I'm a substitute driver for one of the teams."

"That a fact?" Rusty said, writing out the ticket.

"Yes, sir, but I wasn't needed."

"So maybe you were taking some of that energy out here, huh?"

"Yes, sir, something like that."

"You must be a pretty good driver."

"Do all right...except for maybe right now."

Rusty laughed. He handed back the license and registration.

"Have to give you a ticket, son, but I wrote it out for eighty, not a hundred and sixteen. Keep your speeding for the track."

"Yes, sir, and thank you sir."

Rusty thought, shit, that's all I need, for John here to remember where he saw me. At least I was wearing my Stetson and it was dark. He looked at the helmet in his hands, wishing he had kept it on. John said something. "What's that, John? Was spacing out, probably all those fumes I've been breathing for the last six hours."

"I said, my Crew and I are staying over in a cabin at Crescent Beach. Made reservations with a lady named Tammy."

Rusty laughed.

"Then we're neighbors; I'm staying in one of hers, too. She runs the local bar and restaurant there. Maybe buy you a beer when all this," Rusty said nodding towards the judges heading their way with trophies, "is over."

"Sounds good to me."

An hour later, with the four foot second place trophy strapped to the top of Jimmy's pickup, Jimmy and Rusty were escorted by Charley and Tiny in the Mustang convertible. Rusty watched them drinking beers and laughing. The beers looked damn good. "They didn't leave you any of those beers did they, Jimmy?" Rusty asked. Jimmy shook his head. When they crossed the cattle gap, Charley slowed to a crawl and began honking his horn. "Shit!" Rusty said. Fishermen looked up from mending nets and cleaning boats, their wives came out of houses drying hands on aprons, and children climbed on their bicycles to ride along side Jimmy. Rusty was mortified. He hadn't even wanted to take the trophy, saying John should take it to Pensacola and Crescent Beach could have another one made. The judges, at Jimmy's urging, disagreed and said the two drivers should flip a coin. Now the trophy was on its way to the Club for the rest of the weekend and would be delivered to City Hall on Monday.

Jimmy dropped Rusty off and continued on to the Club, but not before he made Rusty promise to meet him there later. Rusty entered the cabin like a zombie and threw himself down on the bed. Eyes closed, sleep tugged hard and he was soon halfway between consciousness and dreamland. He tried to play the race over in his mind, searching for the glory parts, but he couldn't stick with a single thought. Different images drifted in and out: he was in the race nervously hitting the short S section for the first time, then came the hairpin, Jimmy was suddenly hugging him after the race, then he was trying to piss in the can during the yellow flag, Crystal feeling so comfortable in his arms as they danced, now in Jimmy's boat catching his first red, crabbing with Charley, shrimping with Tiny, watching Butch force the Mustang into the pond, coming through the final hairpin bumper to bumper with the T-Bird, finally John running his fingers through his hair while nervously watching him write a ticket. He opened his eyes and looked at the cheap wall clock. He was amazed that only fifteen minutes had passed; it had seemed like hours of memories. He stood and undressed, still half asleep. The cabin's shower wasn't much more than a tin cubicle with no place to put the soap and shampoo except on the bottom, but the water was hot and there was lots of it. Such a luxury. He didn't move or lather up, just stood there, water pouring over his bowed head.

How could something so simple be so wonderful! His muscles absorbed the heat, his legs suddenly tired. He redirected the stream, then got down to sit with knees propped up, leaning against the back wall, water hitting his head and chest full force. He fell asleep and stayed there until the water turned cold.

When he dressed, he debated whether to take the bug out of the life vest and tape it on. He took it out and looked at it, tiny in his meaty hand. Why? The smuggling seemed so remote and irrelevant now. Insignificant. To turn Jimmy in seemed immoral at this point. He shook his head. What a shitty situation. It was time to leave Crescent Beach; he was just too much a part of everything here. But not just yet, in a few days. Definitely, in a few days. He looked at the bug again and sighed. Until then, he still had a job that he said he'd do. Hardly a chance anything would come up in a couple days anyway. Slowly, he taped the bug to his chest.

The Crescent Club was bonkers. Saturday night, first week of March with the warming waters prime for trout fishing, the CB 250, plus the usual crowd of pool players and barflies. Every table was taken, people elbow to elbow at the bar, it was standing room only. Tammy was tending bar, her hands a blur grabbing this and that while pitchers stood filling under all three taps. Norm was back there, too, helping out. Minnie and another girl Tammy had hired forced their way through the crowd to the tables, holding trays up high. When Rusty entered, the first thing he saw was the trophy hanging from a rafter up above the bar. He saw that the rope had been tied in a bowline around the gold car on the trophy's top. Must have been Jimmy, Rusty thought; Jimmy always tied bowlines, and loved showing his fishing customers how he could tie one left handed behind his back. He spied Crew 'Cuda seated around two tables pulled together with a big RESERVED sign on it. They saw him at the same time and waved and cheered. People looked over to the table, then towards Rusty. The locals among them picked up the cheer and Rusty, redhead that he was, blushed furiously. He threaded his way over; there was already a good number of empty beer bottles in the middle of the table. His stomach turned over when he saw that John and his T-Bird crew were there too.

Jimmy pulled out the single unoccupied chair. "Reserved for you, my man, as well as this," he said, handing him a bottle. "Tammy has agreed that everything, dinner plus all the beer you can drink, is on the house." Rusty accepted the beer and sat down. Tired as he was, he was overwhelmed. He couldn't help wondering what the Captain would think if he ever heard this tape: some job, drinking unlimited Budweisers all night! Everyone at the table, including the T-Bird team, congratulated him. He continued to blush with the attention. He quaffed the first beer, and he had no more than set it down when another was handed to him.

"Couldn't have done better myself," Jimmy crowed, "although I don't know if I could have kept up with John here like you did, Rusty. Did you know that he's a substitute driver for the Busch team in Daytona?"

"That really true, John?" Rusty asked.

"Yup. The timing with your race being just a bit later than Daytona was good. The T-Bird's my own car, and the guys brought it over while I was on the east coast. We heard about this race last year and asked around. It sounded like fun, so we decided to try it. Glad we did, even though we got gipped out of a trophy."

Rusty laughed. "Jimmy and I'll make sure the new one gets sent to you right off...Trophy's in the mail, so to speak. But, you can count on it."

"Think you'll do this race agin?" Jimmy asked.

John was somewhere else. "What?" he asked. Jimmy repeated himself. "Oh, yeah, for sure. Really enjoyed today except for that maniac in the Dodge Charger. Sorry, I was just trying to remember where I've seen Rusty before. I swear, Rusty, I know you from some place. Even your laugh is familiar." John picked up his beer and took a long pull with a far off look. Rusty abruptly changed the subject.

"Tiny, imagine you've about taken enough time off from shrimping," Rusty said.

"Got that right. Heading out tomorrow afternoon with the tide. Shrimps is really out there right now, spring crop. Sure hate to miss any more of 'em. Wanna come out? I need the help, and now that you're an old hand and all."

"Are you kidding!" Rusty laughed. "I'm going to sleep for two days. I'm not a young buck like John here; that race about killed me."

"Then how about mid week. I'm going to fish my way to Apalach, then take a night off with some of them shrimpers up thataways. Couple good bars there that'd put Tammy's to shame." Tiny winked. "Some pretty women, too."

The idea was appealing. Spend the last few days, out on the water, all innocent enough. No chance of getting anything on Jimmy. Leave Crescent on the return. Why not? Good ending. "I'd like that, Tiny. You got yourself crew." Tiny smiled as they shook.

"Hey, there's the Mustang driver," John said, standing to get his attention.

"That be Tommy Smith from Crystal River," Jimmy said, also standing and waving him over.

Tommy Smith came to the table, sitting down when Tiny magically produced an empty chair. He shook hands with Jimmy who introduced him to everybody. Soon John, Tommy, and Rusty were animatedly rehashing the race in detail. When Tommy described being run into the drink by Butch, Charley said, "That don't surprise me none, dirty trick like that. Did you ever ketch up with him?" Charley asked.

"Not even close. He disappeared in the woods like magic. That's why I'm here and not back in Crystal River," Tommy said, looking around. "I was hoping he might show up so I could take care of unfinished business. Any of you seen him around?"

"Nope," Charley said. "And doubt if we will for a spell, considering he probably knows you're here. How much you charge us, Tommy, to stick around for a couple o' years?"

Non-stop beers and eventual grouper and trout dinners made the way to their table. Around eleven, the crowd began to thin. Rusty was exhausted. He started to beg off, saying it was time to get some shuteye, but Jimmy insisted on one last beer together.

"Out on the deck then, Jimmy. If I don't get some fresh air, I'll fall asleep right here."

Jimmy went off to get the beers as Rusty stood up stiffly and said goodnight to everyone. John, a little toasted, said, "Right on the tip of my tongue, Rusty. I'll remember before the night's out."

"Don't bother, John; not important. Just want to say that I'm very glad to have driven with both you and Tommy here," Rusty said, shaking their hands. "And if I have anything to say about it, it'll never happen again." Everyone laughed.

The breeze was cool and the night, like the day, was clear. There was no moon and the stars sparkled. The stars, like the sunsets, were special in Crescent Beach. Jimmy came out with two beers, and they leaned against the railing. They tapped bottles and took a swig.

"Long fucking day," Rusty said.

"You got that right," Jimmy answered. They looked out over the water, a comfortable silence between them. Finally, Jimmy said, "I owe you an apology."

"What for?" Rusty asked. He noticed Jimmy was slurring a little.

"For doubting you."

Rusty laughed.

"Hell, Jimmy, I've never raced formal-like; I doubted myself plenty. No need to apologize."

"That's not what I meant."

Rusty looked at him curiously.

"I've been involved with a little side business which I'm sure you know something about, seeing as you've been around here a spell, been in a similar business yourself, and you ain't stupid. " Rusty didn't say anything. "You heard about that drug bust a while back?"

Rusty was suddenly wide awake. Shut up, Jimmy! he thought. "Yeah?"

"Those Stateys you got in trouble with when you stuck up for Crystal seemed to know exactly when Charley and I left here to…well, to help off-load a shrimper with some bales on it. Only way they coulda known was for someone here to tell 'em." Jimmy looked apologetically to Rusty. "And because you were the only stranger around, made sense to me that maybe it was you. Crystal thought I was plum loco, and she's one mighty good judge of character and all, but I still doubted you. I even made a couple of calls to check up on you in north Georgia, and that was why I asked you to do that dozing for us. I had our usual operator all lined up, but I wanted to see if you was speaking the truth about all your experience. Shit," Jimmy said sheepishly, "that sure showed me—ain't never seen none better. Anyway, I just wanted to tell you, that's all. No hard feelings?"

Rusty smiled; it hurt. "None at all, except maybe you should listen to Crystal more often."

Jimmy nodded. "Got that right," he said.

"One question, though," Rusty said.

"Shoot."

Rusty nodded towards the bandaged hand.

"That have something to do with the bust?"

Jimmy looked at his hand. His expression soured.

"Sure did." He looked at his beer, then at Rusty's. "How about one last round and I'll tell you all about it?"

Rusty handed him his empty. Jimmy no sooner went in to get beers when John the T-bird driver came out. He was unsteady. When he saw Rusty, he blurted, "I figured it out! State cop gave me a ticket over in Daytona last year. You're the spitting image, I swear. You got a twin brother or something?"

Rusty forced a tight smile. "Not that I know of, John."

"Trooper was a nice enough guy, really; only gave me a ticket for eighty when I was doing over a hundred and ten."

Rusty looked over to the door, praying Jimmy would take his time.

"You were lucky; most State Cops never even blink giving me tickets; act like they love their job to death. But, shit, you got to excuse me. I've been out here talking to Jimmy and been holding it in. I got to pee real bad," Rusty said.

"No prob, man. I was just heading to my cabin. Been a pleasure."

"Ditto, Brer Hare. You take it easy, now." Rusty said, shaking his hand again.

Rusty entered the bar and saw Tammy handing Jimmy two beers. Rusty got his attention and motioned he was going to the bathroom. Jimmy nodded. Rusty went in to the men's room to check that his bug was in position.

Outside, Jimmy began, "I've been in this smuggling business a long time. Probably brought in over a hundred loads of marijuana bales. Know about every-body that's in the business, or was in the business, in these parts. Even some down south around Everglades City. Been doing it since the late seventies, if you can believe it, and man, I could tell you stories that would raise the hair on your balls. But, mostly it was pretty low key. Just use the weather to your advantage and there weren't no problems. The people I dealt with were okay-Joes, mix of family men and youngsters. Probably the same when you were running the 'shine. The fam-ily men were just trying to add to their shitty income, and the youngsters were pretty wild with most of 'em spending their earnin's all at once like. But everybody knew each other and there was hardly no trouble. But a few years ago it begun to change. Cocaine entered the picture and, as far as I'm concerned, screwed everything up. Changed the kind of people running the show. The youngsters started gitting into that shit and they started doing crazy bad things.

"What happened to my hand, there was this guy goes by the name of *El Espantoso* which, I hear, means 'the ghost,' but I think his real name is Arias; at least that's what's inscribed on the handle of his fancy ass Beretta. He's a big player from Miami and he don't fuck around none. Guess he was plenty upset about the bust that went down, cost him a lot of dough. That, plus he had some old business that concerned me, and he was in a bad mood. Took it out on me and a couple other fellas. Called us in to the Old Town hammock where he's got a cabin he uses when he's in the area. He and a couple of his goons was all coked up, and *El Espantoso* had them hold my hand down and the s.o.b. shot it. End of story."

"Why don't you get him busted, Jimmy? Make a deal and tell the authorities about the son of a bitch."

Jimmy shook his head.

"Not a chance. I got family, Rusty, and that mafia fucker or whatever he is threatened them. Knows where my family lives, even mentioned the twins. Done his homework, that's for sure." Jimmy's expression hardened. A vein stood out on his forehead as he looked at his hand. He looked back up at Rusty and smiled. Rusty involuntarily shuddered when he saw that smile. "That was his mistake, Rusty. A big mistake, threatening my family. Ain't no one going to threaten my family and git away with it. Things around here have a way of taking care of themselves."

Jimmy stopped speaking and stared out to the Gulf. Rusty didn't say a word. A minute or two later, Jimmy finished his beer and held it up. "One more?"

"Nope. I'm bushed."

"I imagine. Me, I'm celebrating into the wee hours, and I'll do it for the two of us. Tomorrow it's back to crab sitting. Good news is that Crystal and I got the grandyoung'uns coming in this next Friday. Can't wait to see them little guys! My daughter and her husband are going to take a cruise to Nassau to git away for a few days; a little present of mine thanks to my other occupation. Anyway, I just want to say again, hell of a good race, Rusty, and you're a damn good man."

Jimmy came up and hugged him hard before heading back to the bar.

CHAPTER
TWENTY-EIGHT

Hero, tethered to a one inch steel rod driven deep into the sandy soil, had worn a circular path through the sparse grass and thick leaf litter of the cabin's side yard. He lay in the shade of a big magnolia tree, licking himself in a scratched-together bed of leaves. Butch was sitting in an old ladder back chair on the porch of the cabin, leaning back against the rough siding. The sky was blue with only a few wisps of clouds although a pair of white lines painted by jets also streaked the sky. Butch didn't have a watch but knew it had to be pushing four because the sun had dropped below the edge of the roof. He reached for the jug of corn whisky on the deck and took a sip, shuddering a little before putting it down. A cloud of limestone dust appeared in the distance, slowly approaching. Could use some rain, Butch thought, watching the cloud of dust grow and taking another sip of whisky. It wasn't long before he could make out his brother's old Ford Fiesta. 'Bout time.

Tommy climbed out of the car and up on to the porch. He pulled a chair over and sat down. The jug was between them, but Tommy didn't touch it, and Butch didn't offer.

"Doncha think you should leave that stuff alone?" his brother asked. "You got into it pretty good last night."

"Hair of the dog."

"Where's Maw?"

"Out back, hanging up clothes."

Tommy looked at his brother.

"Damn, Butch; she's over seventy and all bent. Ever occur to help her some?"

"Believe she kin handle it." Tommy shook his head. Butch asked, "What did you find out?"

"Ain't nobody there," Tommy said, standing up.

"You sure?"

"Yeah. Tommy Smith and his crew all left Crescent about midnight Saturday. Ain't nobody seen 'em since."

"Where you going?"

"To help Maw."

"Don't suppose you got any beer in the car, do you?"

Tommy didn't bother to answer; he disappeared around the corner of the cabin. Butch folded his hands in his lap and went back to staring down the road. The sun continued to drop and he pulled the brim of his baseball cap down low. After awhile, he stood and looked over to his dog. "Hey, Hero, want to go for a ride?" Hero's eyes flew open and he was on his feet, panting and tugging at the chain. "Thought you might." Butch walked over and unhooked the dog. Hero ran over to the pickup and jumped on to the bed and then up on top of the extended toolbox. Butch closed the tailgate and hooked Hero's spiked collar. He returned to the porch for a final swig before climbing into the cab.

Butch drove straight to the Crescent Club, but nothing was happening down below; it was still too early for pool. Might as well kill time and drive around some, he thought. He went out to the point, but no one was there yet to take in the sunset. He drove by the big fishhouse, but it was afterhours and deserted. He turned around and headed towards the bridge over the canal. Wonder whats the fancy folk is doing? he thought. He stopped in front of the bridge. Maybe let Hero have a little fun today. He got out of the cab and walked up to Hero who was perched on the toolbox like the bulldog ornament of a Mack truck. He unhooked him and gave him a pat. "Have yourself a good old time, Hero. Maybe you kin liven up this ghost town some."

A few blocks away, Beau had his arm around Virginia's waist and was leaning over to pat Skillet. Virginia had a garden trowel in her hand. "Be alright to put off dinner 'til dark, Sugah?" he asked, straightening up and pushing a wisp of gray hair back from her face. "More water plant stuff. I swear it is one of the seven Herculean tasks—it's not only building the darn thing, it's replacing all the town's asbestos water pipes, installing new fire hydrants, processing all the bids and the state and federal grants. The list is endless. Plus, I'm not an engineer; most of it's Greek to me."

Virginia escorted Beau to his golf cart. Skillet had already jumped into the passenger seat and was looking straight ahead.

"Can't you get one of the other councilmen to help you?" Virginia asked. Beau just looked at her. "Guess not, huh? But just think, dear, once it's done, we'll actually be able to drink the water and not take a bath in a mud puddle."

"And I won't have to change clogged filters and put salt in the Culligan every other week for the hot tub. That alone, I guess, makes it worth it." Beau turned to Skillet. "Sorry, Skillet, out." Skillet stared straight ahead like he hadn't heard. "C'mon, you've been inside City Hall all day. You need to be outside and help Sugah here with her gardening. C'mon now, OUT!" Skillet indignantly climbed down and walked over to Virginia.

"Good boy," Beau said, and gave Virginia a peck on the cheek. "Around eight, then?" Virginia nodded, and Beau scooted off to City Hall.

Virginia smiled at Skillet watching Beau go down the street. "C'mon, Skillet. He'll be back before you know it. Help me transplant some hibiscus." Skillet, tail wagging and Beau seemingly forgotten, followed Virginia at a trot over to the greenhouse where she loaded a wheelbarrow with small potted hibiscus that she brought over to the brick walkway leading from the house to the street. On hands and knees, she began to plant, and Skillet lay down nearby.

Virginia and Skillet heard the truck coming at the same time, but it was Skillet who knew who it was. As soon as it was in sight, his hackles were up and he began barking. The truck was still a couple of houses away when Hero leaped from the back. Skillet stood his ground protecting his mistress, but the pit bull was a seventy-five pound cannonball. He hit Skillet at full speed, bowling him over, and sunk his teeth in Skillet's neck in a heartbeat. Skillet had gotten in only one bite, a mouth full of spiked collar, before the pit bull had him on his back. He tried to put up a fight, but Hero's hold was relentless and gave Skillet no quarter. Skillet outweighed the pit bull by at least fifteen or twenty pounds, yet Hero picked him up three-quarters the way off the ground, shaking him from side to side, trying to snap his neck. Virginia ran over to pull Hero off. Not a chance. She jabbed at him with her trowel; Hero paid no attention. Skillet's neck ripped open causing Hero to lose his grip momentarily; Virginia screamed when she saw the exposed flap of skin. Blood was everywhere. Skillet got in another couple mouthfuls of spiked color while the dogs briefly thrashed until Hero had Skillet's throat again. Virginia circled the dogs helplessly, trying to break them apart. She saw Butch pull up in his truck, a smile on his face.

"Do something!" Virginia shrieked at him. He took his time getting out.

"Looks to me to be a fair fight, Ma'am. Your fancy-ass dog's been asking for it for a long time now, and Hero there's just a'letting him know who's boss."

"He's killing my dog! Get him off!" Butch leaned back against his truck and folded his arms. Virginia ran to the backside of the greenhouse where there was a stack of 2x4's. She grabbed one and ran back. She started hitting Hero on the head as hard as she could. That got Butch moving.

"Now you jest hold on there!" Butch said, reaching for the 2x4. Virginia swung it at him; he blocked it with his forearm and yanked it away. Virginia, tears streaming down her face, began screaming in rage and frustration. Butch saw neighbors running up the street. He turned back to the dogs. Skillet was hardly putting up a fight, Hero was still shaking him, and Virginia, sobbing and helpless, was ineffectually trying to reach in. "C'mon, Hero, that's enough; you beat him bad," Butch said, brusquely pushing Virginia out of the way and grabbing on to Hero's collar. Hero paid no attention. Butch cuffed the dog. "I said, that's enough!" Hero kept at it. "That's enough now, goddamn it!" Butch slugged the dog a couple of times, still the dog hung on as Butch shook his stinging right hand. "Why you son-of-a-bitch!" Butch grabbed Hero's collar with both hands and pulled it against Hero's throat as hard as he could, choking the dog. Finally, what seemed like forever to Virginia, Hero let go. Several people ran up as Butch dragged Hero back to the truck and chained him. Butch drove off as a circle formed around Skillet.

Skillet lay motionless on the ground, blood oozing out of his mouth and neck. Virginia kneeled by him. "Oh God! Oh Skillet!" She stroked his head, blood covering her hands. She looked up at the circle of faces.

"Please," she said, tears continuing to stream down her face, "Someone go get Dr. Norm."

Big John's boy said, "I'll git him, Miss Virginia. Doncha worry none." The boy was off like a shot. Virginia put Skillet's head in her lap and continued to stroke his head. "Oh, my poor Skillet."

"Dr. Norm! Dr. Norm!" Johnny yelled running up to the house. Norm came out to the deck. Johnny stopped at the foot of the steps.

"What is it, Johnny?" Norm asked. Johnny was desperately trying to catch his breath.

"Miss Virginia sent me; it's bad, real bad," Johnny managed between gasps.

Beau! Norm thought, rushing down the steps and into the clinic for his bag. Johnny followed him.

"Butch's dog done bit Skillet almost to death! Bleeding all over and he weren't moving none!"

"Come on, Johnny, jump into the car!" The tires spun in the limestone as Norm floored the Subaru. Less than a minute later, they were at Beau's house. Norm rushed up to Virginia who was still stroking Skillet's head. He kneeled down and gently took Skillet's head in his hand, turning it so the dog didn't choke on the blood. Skillet's breathing was irregular and raspy. Norm pulled the flap of fur and skin away and closely inspected his neck. The punctures were very deep. It was bad. Virginia didn't say a word. Norm turned to her.

"Do you have a blanket we can use to lift him into the back of the Subaru?" Virginia nodded and hurried off to get it. Skillet tried but failed to get up. Norm wanted the dog as still as possible. He lightly stroked his head, telling him over and over, "You're a good boy, Skillet, you're a good boy." Virginia returned with the blanket. The neighbors helped Norm slide the dog on to it and lift Skillet into the back of the Subaru. Virginia jumped in with Norm while the others followed on foot to help unload Skillet at the clinic. Norm asked Virginia if she knew how much Skillet weighed. She shook her head. When they entered the clinic, Norm brought over a scale, and requested that Skillet be put in his arms. He stepped on the scale: Skillet was no lightweight. He weighed himself with and without Skillet: the dog weighed just over ninety pounds. Norm rolled up his sleeves and washed: he was all business. He cleared everybody but Virginia out.

"The first thing we have to do is anesthestize him so I can clean him up and see how bad it really is," Norm said, as he shaved Skillet's foreleg. Virginia looked frightened. Norm sighed. "Yes, Virginia, no mistake: it's bad. And I'm going to need your help." Norm inserted the needle of a syringe, then taped both needle and syringe to Skillet's leg. Once the dog was under, he said, "If he starts to move around, I need you to give him a little more of this. Can you do that?"

Virginia nodded. "Just show me what to do."

Norm demonstrated at what rate to depress the syringe, then began his inspection. Surprisingly, he found wounds all over his body, not just his neck. Norm began shaving the areas and, by the time he finished, Skillet looked like he had a bad case of mange. Virginia told him about Butch and Hero while he cleaned the wounds.

"A pit bull's teeth are two inches long, Virginia, consequently these punctures are very deep," Norm said, as he flipped a bloody cotton ball from his tweezers into a dispensary. "Infection is what we have to worry about."

Norm began to suture some of the wounds when the clinic door flew open. Beau stood there, tall in the doorway, totally distraught. He didn't or couldn't say a word; he just stared at Skillet. Norm kept sewing. Virginia calmly said, "I think you should shut the door, dear. Skillet doesn't need any germs from outside."

Beau reacted like he had touched an electric wire. He quickly shut the door, and leaned against it, eyes locked on Skillet. No one said anything. Norm continued to work in silence, Virginia kept at the IV. The only sound was the click of Norm's scissors cutting thread. This went on for a long time until Beau croaked, "Tell me what happened, Virginia." Virginia, without taking her eyes off Skillet, repeated what she had told Norm. When she had finished, Norm said to no one in particular, "The mouth looks bad, but you'd be surprised at how quickly a dog's mouth heals on its own, so no sutures here. Be awful sore, though." Norm kept dabbing at two particularly ugly wounds dangerously close to the jugular vein. He pointed at the two wounds as if he were teaching a class in med school. "These two are the worst and, because they're so deep, they're hard to clean which means there's a greater chance for infection. I'll have to open them up some so I can better examine and clean them. But, they're close to the jugular right here, so it's kind of tricky…"

Skillet began to squirm, and Norm looked at Virginia. "A little more, Virginia." The last thing he needed, Norm thought, was for Skillet to move now. Virginia depressed the syringe and Norm began to cut again. Beau couldn't watch, he eased out of the door while Virginia marveled at Norm's steady hand. Norm, for his part, was impressed with Virginia who had been rock solid throughout. When he finished, he calculated that he had tied off close to a hundred stitches. He did not sew the two punctures by the jugular vein so he'd be better able to monitor for infection the next couple of days; that is, if Skillet made it that long. He lay his tools down on the table and walked over to wash up.

"Well done, Virginia, you were terrific," he said, wiping his hands with a towel. "You've been on your feet close to three hours. Please sit down." He pulled up a chair for her.

"Will he make it, Norm?"

Norm walked over to a bookshelf and pulled down the Merck Veternarian Manual before answering.

"You'll have your answer in the next twenty-four to forty eight hours. Again, it's all about infection." He pointed to the book. "I'm still kinda new at this veterinarian stuff; just want to see how much penicillin to minister." He began reading. "Good," he said, putting the book back. "I should have plenty. Now if I can just find the makings for an Elizabethan collar." He started rummaging around the clinic.

"A who?" Virginia asked.

"A lampshade-type thing to go around his neck so he can't bother the wounds when he comes out of it."

Outside, Beau was in his golf cart, leaning forward with hands on the steering wheel, staring straight ahead. He should be in there with Skillet, but he couldn't—he just couldn't watch him get cut like that, couldn't stand seeing him lie there inert with all those shaved and ugly sewn-up patches everywhere. God, how that must hurt. And poor Virginia! Fucking pit bull; fucking breed should be eliminated! Evil dogs! How many times did they make the news, mauling someone's pet, even killing a child. But who's worse, dog or owner? Says a lot about a man who has a dog like that and, breed or no breed, that dog was raised mean.

The longer Beau sat there, the more worked up he got. He kept picturing the savage dog and its smug redneck owner. Beau's knuckles were white from gripping the steering wheel so hard. Skillet was on his own damn turf, protecting *his* mistress! It was the pit-bull that had invaded! And Butch just stood there and watched his dog rip Skillet apart. Fucking lowlife shoved my wife! Couldn't even control his own dog at the end. That dog should be eliminated! These thoughts played over and over in his mind until Beau couldn't stand it any longer. He drove full speed to his house and left the cart out on the street instead of in the carport: he wouldn't be there long. He went up the brick walk, but stopped halfway and looked around. On either side of the walkway were the new flowerbeds where Virginia had been working, although most of the hibiscus was still in the wheelbarrow. On the lawn not far from the edge of the street he saw the 2x4 Virginia used to hit the dog, and near it, her trowel. He saw a dark puddle of Skillet's blood. He turned and, strides lengthening, almost ran up the stairs. The motion sensor light clicked on as he took the steps two at a time. When he reached the top, he stopped; he could feel his heart thudding in his chest. Whoa, won't do a bit of good if you have a heart attack! He rested for a few moments before continuing inside.

He went straight to the living room closet where he removed the false panel and opened the gun safe. He pulled out an oily cloth bundle that contained his Colt Woodsman pistol. He unwrapped it and disengaged the magazine which he loaded with High Velocity 22 long hollow points. He quickly snapped the full magazine back into the semi-automatic, and turned on his heels. He didn't bother putting the panel back or closing the closet door. The motion sensor light clicked on again as he came down. Beau jammed the pistol into his belt and hopped into the golf cart. If Butch were still in town, he'd be at Tammy's, playing pool. He floored the golf cart.

He slowed down as he approached Tammy's. Several players were standing around the pool table while someone lined up a shot. Beau saw Butch laughing, holding a cue in one hand, a beer and cigarette in another. Butch's truck was parked near the Club steps with Hero lying down on the toolbox, asleep. Beau got out of the cart. The pool players were intent on the game and paid no attention. He pulled the gun from his belt, putting the six-inch barrel up to Hero's head. He squeezed the trigger. The sound of the shot wasn't so much loud as it was sharp. It got everybody's attention; so did Hero's flopping around on the top of the toolbox until he fell into the back of the truck. Butch and the others were too stunned to move. Not Beau. Pistol in hand, he walked around the truck, shooting each tire. Butch rushed up to the truck, all four tires whistling with Hero dead in the back.

"What the fuck you done, old man!" Butch screamed furiously, spittle flying from his mouth as he rushed Beau, cue stick raised, but stopped when he stared into the barrel of the pistol. The pistol didn't waver as Beau pointed it between Butch's eyes.

"You sorry son-of-a-bitch redneck. I'll shoot you between the eyes if you move an inch! You got that, Butch?"

Butch nodded.

"Put that cue down."

Tammy and Minnie, plus a handful of customers, had run out with the shots and crowded the head of the stairs. Butch knew they were watching him. He began to wave the pool cue slowly back and forth. "You're a pretty good shot with a sleeping dog and tires that ain't moving. Kin you hit a moving target with that puny plinking pistol?"

"Count on it, Butch! You just come on and make my day!"

Jimmy's pickup screeched to a stop. Jimmy jumped out, taking in the situation. Butch looked over at him; Beau didn't take his eyes off Butch.

"Look what he done, Jimmy!" Butch yelled. "Fucker's crazy!"

Jimmy walked over, stopping between Beau and Butch with his back to Beau.

"Beau," Jimmy said, looking at Butch, "this piece of shit white trash ain't worth the trouble you'll git into if you kill him. Better go on to Norm's. They're getting ready to move Skillet back home and Skillet'll be needing your help."

Beau didn't say anything. He walked around Jimmy so he could see Butch. He kept the gun leveled at him.

"Butch, if you ever, and I mean ever, step foot on my property again, I'll blow your fucking head off. And if I'm not there, my wife will. Is that understood?"

Butch laughed in bravado, thinking Beau wouldn't dare shoot with Jimmy right there, but Jimmy shrugged and stepped back out of the way. "I said my piece."

Beau quickly stepped forward and, eyes wide in the fury piqued by Butch's laughter, put the barrel up to Butch's forehead. It was obvious to everyone that Beau was on the brink of blowing Butch away. It was dead silent.

"I SAID, IS THAT UNDERSTOOD, YOU ABSOLUTE PIECE OF SHIT!"

Butch started to shake; he also pissed in his pants. "Yes, sir, yes, Mr. Beau!" Beau kept the gun at Butch's forehead, his hand now shaking crazily. Butch hoped the pistol didn't have a hair trigger. So did Jimmy. Finally, Beau lowered the pistol. His whole body was shaking from the adrenaline. He looked at Jimmy.

"I think I'll go see to Skillet," Beau said. He turned his back on Butch who almost collapsed with relief. Putting the gun down on the seat of the golf cart, Beau slowly drove off. He passed Charley who roared up in the Mustang and parked directly behind Butch's pickup. Charley jumped out and walked purposefully up to Butch, stopping only a foot away.

"Now what!" Butch said. "What the fuck do you want, Charley?"

"Beat your ass."

Butch laughed and looked at the other pool players and the group up on the deck. "Coon-eye Charley wants to beat my ass. Don't that beat all!" He turned back to Charley. "You ain't won a fight in ten years, Coon-eye. Why doncha jest run along afore you git hurt." Butch began shifting the cue stick from hand to hand.

"That's because I been drunk most of them ten years. I ain't drunk now, Butch, and you ain't got Tommy to hold me none neithers."

Butch smiled thinly and shifted the cue so he was holding it like a baseball bat. "Come and git it then, Coon-eye." Charley began to circle Butch; Butch made a couple of feints with the cue.

"Put down the pool cue, Butch. Let's make this here a fair fight," Jimmy said.

"Like hell I will!" Butch spat, glancing at Jimmy. Charley leaped at Butch who caught the movement out of the corner of his eye. He swung the cue, hitting Charley on the shoulder as he was being tackled. Butch went down hard with Charley on top of him. Butch still had the pool cue in his hands, but couldn't do much in such close quarters. He let go of it and grabbed hold of Charley's hair, yanking backward as hard as he could. Charley put a bite on Butch's forearm that would have made Hero proud. Butch screamed and let go of the hair allowing Charley to quickly head-butt him twice, smashing his nose with the first. Butch was dazed and Charley took advantage. He quickly sat on top of Butch and began pummeling him with his fists.

Tears started running down Charley's face as he hit Butch. "This one's fer Skillet! And this one! And this one!" Charley kept hitting Butch, beating him to a bloody pulp. Finally, when he was so tired that he could hardly lift his arms, Jimmy pulled him off. Charley, unconsciously holding his left shoulder, looked down at Butch. "And this one's fer me!" he said, viciously kicking him in the ribs. Charley staggered back to his car and drove off.

CHAPTER
TWENTY-NINE

The Coast Guard Ensign looked over the shoulder of the AB monitoring the WSR-57 Radar screen.

"Sure looks like we better bring her down, sir," the AB said, pointing. "My guess is it's going to get pretty nasty around here within forty-eight hours, whole lot of activity: polar jet from Canada, and a Pacific jet from the west, and a major subtropical from Mexico have merged. You can also bet the barometric pressure's going to tank." He turned to look at the Ensign. "In the year and a half I've been here, I've never seen anything like it."

"That's what the National Weather Service has been saying for days up in the northeast," the other AB put in. "Real low barometric pressure and going to snow like hell. They're saying the snow's going to hit the fan come Saturday. Been predicting a blizzard for the entire east coast."

"How can they do that so far in advance?" the Ensign asked.

"Basing it on the newest thing—computer-forecast models," the first AB said.

"What do they say for around here?"

"Warnings for some coastal flooding, but mostly they believe it will swing up north of us. Coastal flooding's not unusual this time of year anyway, what with spring tides and especially now with the full moon just a couple days behind us. But I'm betting we get some pretty high winds to go with it; that's why I think we should bring the blimp down."

While the Ensign and ABs were discussing the weather, Tiny and Rusty were approaching the island of St. George, a little less than ten miles from Apalachicola. Four porpoises were rolling off the bow. Rusty was transfixed.

"God, I could watch them all day," Rusty said.

Tiny smiled. "Then I got a treat fer you," he said, and throttled up to just over twenty-one hundred RPMs. The porpoises dived and disappeared. Rusty looked all around, but didn't see a single one. He looked questioningly at Tiny who was still smiling. "Might wanta check out the stern," he said.

Rusty left the wheelhouse and went aft. As he walked back to the transom, he looked at the thick wake. No sign of any porpoises. No sign of anything. He wondered why Tiny had sent him here. He was just about to turn around when two fleet dark shadows in the water just outside the wake caught his eye. Suddenly two large porpoises broke the surface, leaping high in the air. They splashed down not more than six or seven feet from the boat. Then another farther back on the edge of the wake, followed by a very small porpoise, maybe a baby, surfing the wake not fifteen feet away with a much larger porpoise streaming close at its side. Soon maybe a half dozen were cavorting, although it was hard to tell how many because they seemed to be taking turns and all were glistening gray with that wonderful smile. Rusty leaned out over the transom, trying to get a better look when one popped out of the center of the wake, almost close enough to touch. It had misjudged its speed and distance because Rusty knew there was no way it wasn't going to land in the boat. He took a step back, putting his hands up in defense, but a split second later, the porpoise turned ninety degrees and splashed sideways in the water just behind the boat, soaking Rusty in the process. Rusty believed he was splashed intentionally and laughed out loud. Even more joined in; it was as if they were putting on a show. They must see me, he thought, just as I can see them. They were tireless, and Rusty would have been hard pressed to say how long he watched them; time stood still, he was enthralled. They frolicked until Tiny cut back on the throttle and the performance was over. Rusty was sad to see the porpoises veer off, but he was left with a warm glow: tarry delight so seldom met.

He returned to the pilot-house, all smiles. Tiny looked him up and down.

"How'd you manage to git your britches wet?" he asked.

"Tiny, that was amazing! Frigging marine-land back there! How'd you know they'd do that?"

"My daddy showed me way back. Not quite sure why they does it—pitch of the engine about maxed out, size of the wake, little a both most likely. And who knows, maybe they's just in a good mood too because the weather's so doggone nice. But almost never fails if they're around." Tiny pointed off the bow towards a perfectly straight pass bisecting St. George. "That there's the New Cut. Some call it the Government Cut because it was built by the Army Corps of Engineers. Got lotta rich people on the big island; that's Little St. George off to port."

"When was the cut built?"

"Fifty-four." Tiny pushed the throttle forward. "Bit of a current here," he explained.

They passed through.

"Lots of money around alright," Rusty said, looking back at the impeccably landscaped properties sloping up to well fenestrated mansions.

"Yep. Don't think too many of them is shrimpers by trade." Tiny pointed off the bow again. "Heading to Turn Corner now, about three miles ahead, and that's where we pick up the ICW we'll be taking in to Apalach."

"IntraCoastal Waterway, right?" Rusty said. Tiny nodded. "I thought that ended down near Tampa somewhere."

"Does, at Tarpon Springs. Stops there and ain't nothing but pure Gulf until Alligator Point a bit to the east of us in the big bend where Florida begins to curve around and head south. From Alligator you kin cruise west on the ICW, protected like, to Texas if you want with water calm enough even you might make it the whole way without a'dropping your cookies."

"Not me. Shrimping last couple nights and," Rusty looked at his watch, "five hours cruising so far today is plenty. I'll be glad to step ashore. At least I seem to be getting better," Rusty said, tapping wood.

"Make a shrimper outta you, yet…But no shrimping tonight. Tonight we's going to play. Gotcha a hot date, friend of the girl I sees. She's a real sweetheart although she ain't made the best decisions about the men she's hung out with. But I can absolutely guarantee there's a couple of things you'll love about her."

"Like what?"

Tiny smiled. "Reckon you'll see soon enough," he said, cryptically.

"If she's such a sweetheart, how come she's my date and not yours?"

"Because I like living. Sally'd cut my balls off if'n I tried to mess around with Annie."

Approaching Turn Corner they passed a shrimper dragging. Tiny gave him a couple blasts from an air horn and waved.

"Why's he dragging now during daylight?" Rusty asked.

"He's gitting white shrimp; they's the twenty-four hour variety—catch 'em anytime. Like I told you, we only got the hoppers that come out at night down our way. The smaller boats like that one there kin fish fine in the bay, but the bigger boats, fifty to a hundred feet, they goes out past the Cut to the Gulf."

Apalachicola and a long bridge over the river were dead ahead.

"That's some bridge. How long is it?" Rusty asked.

"About five miles bridge and causeway all together, and the bridge's only about five years old. Used to be a swing bridge. Big improvement for us fisher folk with no blasting on the horn and waiting for it to swing open slow as molasses. We just go right on under the High Hump here like we be doing, and now we's officially on the Apalach river. That there," Tiny said, pointing to the left, "is Miller Marine. Then you got Rainbow Marina and Boss Oyster coming up. We'll tie up for the night at City Dock yonder, but first we gotta unload at Buddy Ward's just to the far side of City Dock." The river soon split and Tiny steered left. "We're on Scipio Creek now. Dead ends a ways up at a mill pond."

Water Street running along the creek had seen better days. As they passed City Dock, Rusty looked over at what had been a handsome Victorian two-story brick building. Arched brick over the windows and varied corbelling details were a testament to different times. The roof had fallen in, plywood was tacked over the windows and doors, and ivy had run amok and covered over a third of the facade. On the wharf side of the street, most likely undermined by Scipio Creek,

cement slabs had settled at odd angles. A good portion of the dock was nothing more than a pile of timbers, with the remainder serviceable, but scary looking. The simple one-story wooden buildings farther
down the street looked like they had been painted in
a different century. The waterfront and channel were
busy enough with the comings and goings of all sorts
of boats, but, looking up the streets leading away from
the creek to the center of town, there was little activity. There were no glitzy cafes on the water, only tin-
roofed fish houses with stacks of pallets, compressors
for refrigeration under the eaves, rusty hoppers for
sorting, and shelf units on casters. A workingman's
town, Rusty thought.

"Looks like we got three ahead of us," Tiny said, as
they approached the fish house with a small sign that
read:

Buddy Ward & Sons Seafood
Since 1957

One of the shrimp boats pulled away from the dock
as Tiny eased up. A tall, well-built man caught the bow
line and lashed it to a piling.

"How'd you do, Tiny?" the man asked as Tiny slipped
the stern line over a post.

"Real good for a change, Buddy, real good. If'n
you're feeling rich these days, won't last long with what
you're going to pay me. Lotsa jumbos."

"Don't suppose you want to tell me where you been
fishing?" Buddy asked.

"Nope; but I expect you know already."

"How's the weather over Keaton Beach anyway?"

Tiny laughed. "I ain't even going to ask...Buddy, this
here's a good friend of mine. Trying to turn him into a
shrimper."

"Thought you said he was a good friend." Buddy turned and extended a hand. "Buddy Ward, glad to meet you."

"Rusty McMillan. Likewise." Buddy's grip was every bit as strong as Rusty's.

"Probably be a good twenty minutes or so, Tiny."

"Buddy, we ain't in no hurry. As of right now we're justa idling along. Take your time."

Several hours later, after cleaning the boat at City Dock, Rusty and Tiny cracked their first beers from a six-pack Tiny had bought from a Piggly Wiggly a few blocks away.

"Only time alcohol comes aboard the *Never Been Beat* is when the work's done and we's a'staying put." Tiny took a long pull. "Don't mix with boating none; kin git you in a heap of trouble lickety-split if your mind ain't clear. My daddy drank his fair share, but he never, ever drank before he went out, and no alcohol was ever allowed on his boat."

The trawlers at City Dock were lashed three deep with the *Never Been Beat* in the middle. Tiny put his beer down and got up off the transom. He pulled a wad of bills from his front pants pocket and started peeling off twenties.

"Here's your pay, sailor, in cash, with no worries from Uncle Sam." Rusty took the bills and, without looking at them, put them in a pocket. "Ain't you going to count it?"

"Nope. I trust you, Tiny."

"Well shucks, I done give you a twenty-dollar bonus. How I'm to git credit for being a nice guy employer if you don't count it?"

Rusty pulled the money back out and counted it. "Thanks, Tiny," and put the money away again.

"You're welcome. Figure me being so generous and all, should be good for a couple beers."

"Next six-pack's on me," said Rusty. The evening sun, just above the two story buildings of Water Street, painted the marsh grass of Scipio Creek in amber tones. It looked to Rusty like a long field of wheat interrupted here and there with the dark green of a clump of cedars; quite a contrast to the tangle of crumbling bricks, cracked cement, and rotten docks street side. Rusty swigged his beer. He turned to Tiny. "Damn shame that building's gone to seed. Must have been pretty nice once."

"You got that right. Bunch of buildings around here was real nice. Used to be quite a place, old Apalach. They was shipping cotton and sawing lumber even afore the Civil War. Was paddle wheelers on the river, and big ships all the way from across the ocean came in to port. Then they got a railroad and billions of feet of lumber got shipped out. But they finally run out of virgin timber in the twenties and that was that. Last thing done in that old building," Tiny said, pointing across the street, "was making tents during World War Two. There's a big loom on the ground floor with weeds growing all around it. Must be all of sixteen feet wide!"

Rusty looked at his watch. "Shouldn't we get cleaned up, or does Sally like you smelling fishy."

"She likes me any way she can git me, but ain't no hurry because she's a waitress at the local diner. Don't git off work 'til nine. She and Annie going to meet us at the Oasis, about a two minute walk from City Dock here...You got a coin?"

Rusty reached into a pocket. "Yeah, why?"

"Flip to see who showers first. Heads."

Rusty flipped. Heads it was. Tiny was in no hurry; he reached for another beer. So did Rusty.

"So, what's the plan?" Rusty asked. "With the girls, I mean."

Tiny smiled.

"You mean if'n you hit it off with Annie?"

"Yeah, something like that."

"You got the boat to yourselves. I'll be staying over at Sally's."

"But what if one of these," Rusty said, looking around at the shrimp boats, "has to leave?"

"Most everybody going out will be gone by the time we head to the bar. If not, key's in the ignition."

"Tiny, I don't dare…"

"Not you, them. They'll move it, if'n they have to. But, I'll talk around and make sure we're covered, don-cha worry none. Now," he said, after draining his beer, "reckon I'll go git wet."

By the time they were showered and shaved, talked with their neighbors, and finished the six-pack, they headed out to the Oasis for a quick dinner before their dates arrived. Tiny was wearing a clean lightweight sweatshirt and jeans, and had traded his white rubber boots for a pair of sneakers. His hair was plastered down. Rusty was also in jeans and wore a green wind-breaker that contrasted sharply with his wiry red hair. Tiny hadn't exaggerated: it was a two-minute walk. They passed a few more Victorian two-story brick buildings in better shape than the one with the loom, but still boarded up. The Oasis was thriving just fine. The long bar was crowded, mostly with fishermen in their white boots, and the Oasis also had a package store accessed from a separate door outside, and through a door for the bartender behind the bar. Two pool tables were at the far end. Tiny and Rusty sat down at one of the tables near the front door. When the waitress came over, they ordered hamburger baskets and beers.

Tiny had just finished his last French fry when he looked up and said, "Here they come." He stood. Rusty followed suit. It was obvious who was who: Sally, the shorter of the two, was still dressed in her diner uniform. The taller girl wore a white sweater that was stretched out so thin at the chest that the buttons were threatened and Rusty could see hints of a black bra underneath. So, that's what Tiny was talking about, he thought. Tiny, his arm already around Sally's waist, introduced Annie who had big brown eyes and wore her brown hair straight and long. Rusty tore his eyes from Annie's conical breasts and held a chair out for her. She flashed a bright smile.

"Why thank you, Rusty. Don't believe anyone's done that since prom night of high school, and that was a long time ago!" She had the biggest boobs in her high school class and the boys had tripped over themselves paying attention to her.

"You must not be a shrimper," Sally said, sitting down after giving up on Tiny to hold her chair out.

"Nope, retired dirt-mover; used to put in roads and driveways." The waitress came over. "What would you ladies like to drink?" Rusty asked.

"Seven and seven," Sally said.

"Make mine one of those fruity things with a little umbrella and lots of vodka."

"And a couple more beers," Tiny added.

"What do you do, Annie?" Rusty asked, trying to keep his eyes up. Her boobs jutted out over the table; it'd be a short reach. Maybe he should sit on his hands.

"Work in a fish house. Been doing it forever—since high school anyways."

The waitress soon brought them their drinks. Tiny told her they'd need a refill in ten minutes. Two drinks later, Tiny got up to dance with Sally to a slow jukebox Willie Nelson. Rusty looked at Annie who smiled and nodded. They joined Tiny and Sally out on the floor. Rusty forgot to hold the chair out for Annie when they came back, and she quipped, "There goes the honeymoon." Everyone laughed. Annie looked beyond Rusty.

"Oh shit," she muttered. Rusty turned. A short, stocky fisherman in white boots and work-stained pants and sweatshirt was walking towards them from the bar. His beard was blond as well as his buzzed crew cut, and he looked about as tall as he was wide. The sweatshirt's sleeves were cut off at the shoulders, accentuating heavily muscled arms.

"If it ain't Captain Never Been Beat. How ya doing, Tiny? Just get in today?"

"Yep, we're down at City Dock. Imagine you know the ladies here, Billy." Billy was looking at Annie who was looking anywhere but at him. "Billy, this here's Rusty."

"Howdy," Billy said, but he was still looking at Annie. "How ya been, Annie? Ain't seen ya fer a spell." Annie shrugged indifferently. "This here Rusty your date?"

"That's right," Rusty said.

Annie smiled at Rusty. Billy put his hands on his hips and turned to Rusty, flexing those big arms. "Mind if I join you?" he asked, pulling up a chair and sitting down next to Annie without an answer. Annie moved her chair towards Sally. Rusty looked over at Billy, then slowly turned to Tiny. Tiny quickly spoke up.

"Billy here's a pretty good arm wrestler, Rusty."

"That a fact," Rusty said.

"Yeah," Billy said, still flexing and glaring belligerently at Rusty. "Only person to ever beat me is Tiny, but everyone knows he ain't human."

"So that makes you human? Could have fooled me," Rusty said.

"Just what do you mean by that, Red?"

"Rusty's the name, bub."

"Now just a minute here," Tiny said. "Billy, this is what you might call a private party and if'n I'm not mistaken, you wasn't invited. But seeing's as you're here, how about a little arm-wrestling contest—you and Rusty.

If you win, we buys you a couple of beers and Rusty here rides off into the sunset. If'n he wins, you buy us the beers, and you skedaddle."

Billy smiled; he was missing a couple of molars. "Fair enough, huh Annie? You're on!" Annie gave Tiny a scathing look. Tiny smiled innocently at her as Billy moved his chair closer to the table and put his elbow down. "Come on, Red, any time," he said, loudly enough so everyone at the bar heard. Rusty looked at him.

"Billy, I'm not usually a betting man, but in this case..." Rusty peeled off two twenties and laid them on the table.

Digging into his front pocket, Billy said, "I only got a little over twenty."

"High roller, huh? Then make it twenty," Rusty said, putting one of the bills away. "Just make sure you have enough to cover this and buy those beers too."

Billy snorted. Tiny addressed the bar, "Anyone else want to take part in this? I'm putting my money on Rusty here." Soon the bar was abuzz, and bets made. Tiny had sixty bucks rolling on Rusty. Rusty stood up to take off his windbreaker. He was wearing one of those knit short sleeve shirts with a collar and a little alligator on it. His muscles strained at the shirt like Annie's boobs with her sweater. He looked very fit and she looked at him with renewed interest. He sat down and clasped hands with Billy. They both looked at Tiny for the signal to start.

"One, two, three, GO!"

It didn't take long. In fact, it was over in a second. Rusty slammed Billy's arm down so hard that the bottles of beer tipped over.

"You cheated, jumped the gun!" Billy screamed, holding his arm.

"Let's do it again, then," Rusty said, calmly.

Billy shook his arm for a second, then they re-clasped, looking at Tiny.

"One, two, three, GO!"

This time they stayed locked in a vertical position. Rusty waited a little before he asked, "This time's fair, isn'it Billy?"

"Yeah," he said, straining.

"Didn't hear you good, Billy."

"I said, yeah, it's fair!"

"That's what I thought you said," and Rusty slammed Billy's arm back down on the table. The beer bottles turned over again. Billy, beet red, grabbed hold of his arm and looked at Annie who was watching Rusty with adoring eyes. Billy turned even redder.

"Let's have your twenty, Billy-boy," Rusty said.

"I'll let you have it alright!" Billy screamed, grabbing one of the beer bottles and jumping up. For a big man, Tiny moved very quickly to get between them.

"Billy, don't try nothing! Rusty here was a MP in 'Nam for three tours o' duty. Believe me, he'll hurt you bad and you won't be able to fish for a long time, maybe never if'n you git him riled." Rusty remained sitting, both hands on the table, looking calmly at Billy. "If I was you, I'd just leave peaceably; don't worry none about whatcha owe us. I'll git it from you some other time."

Billy continued to stare around Tiny's wide frame at Rusty. Finally, he turned and flung the bottle the length of the room where it crashed against the wall beyond the pool players. Abruptly, he turned on his heels and strode off. The bar was silent for a few seconds before the chatter began and things were back to normal. Annie moved her chair close to Rusty and put a hand on his forearm.

"Thank you, Rusty." She looked embarrassed. "Billy and I have a little bit of history between us, and..."

"No need to explain, Annie. Let's just start enjoying ourselves again. Another umbrella?" She nodded and smiled up at him as she thrust one of her bosoms against his arm. Rusty was rock hard before he could get the waitress's attention.

By the time they left the Oasis, none of them were feeling any pain. Tiny and Sally left in her car while Rusty and Annie walked to the boat. When they arrived at City Dock, Rusty took Annie's arm. The three inch thick creosote timbers were rough and spiked down like a puzzle without a pattern.

"Careful, don't want to twist an ankle...or get any slivers either," Rusty said. "These planks are nasty."

The *Never Been Beat* had been moved and was tied directly to the dock. The tide was low and Rusty jumped down in. He put his arms around Annie's waist and lowered her effortlessly. On deck, she kept her hands on his arms, his hands remained around her waist. There was plenty of light in the dock area and Rusty could see she was starry-eyed. He drew her to him and they kissed long and deep. It had been months since Rusty had a woman; he was very much aroused. He believed she was, too. He led her into the pilothouse cabin. They kissed again while he willed himself to keep his hands off those breasts for at least a couple more heartbeats. When they surfaced, he said, "Not much room, and I can assure you those bunks aren't soft."

" But I am," Annie said, as she began to unbutton her sweater. "Would you help me with my bra?" She looked questioningly at him as she folded her sweater.

"Are you kidding! Did the sun come up this morning!" She smiled and turned her back to him. Rusty quickly helped her. It was a damn harness. They swung free, and seconds later he thought he had died and gone to heaven.

The next morning, Tiny didn't arrive until ten. He had two large coffees and a bag of donuts from the local bakery. He found Rusty in the lower bunk.

"Hope you found my bed comfy, Romeo. Here, got a cup of java for you." Rusty wrapped the sheet around him and sat up. He gratefully accepted the coffee. "When did Annie leave?"

"Six. Don't know how she's going to make it through the day on an hour's sleep, if she even got that much." Rusty blew on the coffee and took a sip. "Nice girl," he added. "Wouldn't mind seeing her again." He took another sip. "So, what's the plan for today, Captain?"

"Take on fuel and head straight for home."

"Thought we were going to drag some on the way back."

"No time to scratch the bottom, now," Tiny said, turning the radio dial to the weather frequency. "Was watching the weather on Sally's TV; there's a low pressure with pretty good winds heading our way and it's coming fast. I want to git home and the *Never Been Beat* squared away and snug in her berth." He looked into the bag. "You want plain or glazed."

"Glazed."

Two hours later, after passing through the Government Cut, Tiny set the automatic pilot due east and joined Rusty in the stern who was scrubbing the deck.

"Looking good, mate," Tiny said, pulling a heavy coil of line over to a plastic chair. He began to braid several strands of hemp that had separated. Rusty put brush and bucket away, and brought out a plastic chair to sit near Tiny.

"Hard to believe bad weather's brewing out there," Rusty said. Tiny put the braided section down in his lap and looked out at the Gulf.

"That there's what's called a slick calm. Ain't even a ripple." He looked overhead. "Not a cloud in the sky neithers, and it be unnatural warm. Something's brewing alright," Tiny said, shaking his head.

"Calm before the storm?" Rusty asked.

" Appears so," Tiny said, picking up the line again.

Rusty kept an eye out for porpoises until the steady throb of the diesel lulled him to sleep. When he woke, his neck was stiff and the sun much lower. He put away the chair, and went up to the pilothouse where Tiny was fiddling with the radio. Rusty was surprised to see land off in the distance.

"Guess I conked out," Rusty said.

"Had good reason, Romeo. So, you going to look Annie up agin?"

"Like to, but going to be hard. I'll be leaving Crescent tomorrow or the next day."

Tiny abruptly turned the radio off. "What fer?" he asked.

Rusty shrugged. "Time to move on," he said.

Tiny just looked at him. "Thought maybe you'd stick around. You fits in awful good."

"That's the problem—too good; it gets harder to leave every day, and I gotta leave. Simple as that." Wonder how much you'd think I fit in if you knew what I'm going to report in a couple of days, Rusty thought. Your buddy Jimmy's chopped liver thanks to yours truly.

"Maybelline's going to be heartbroke."

Rusty laughed. "Can't help that," he said.

Tiny turned back to the radio; he didn't look happy as he flipped on the weather channel. He kept fiddling with the knob before sticking his head out the side window and looked behind them.

"Beginning to cloud up," he said, finally.

They continued to motor east until they could see Crescent Beach. Rusty picked up the binoculars and scanned the town. "Blimp's down."

Tiny nodded. "Bet your boots with the winds that be coming."

Rusty swung the binoculars over to his cabin, the Club, the crescent-shaped beach, then finally to Snowy Key. Something splashing caught his eye. Porpoises? He focused. Someone was in the water on the Gulf side of the island. Rusty steadied the binoculars against the corner of the pilothouse. It was Ralph. Suddenly he saw Craig run bare ass straight at Ralph. He dived at Ralph who was madly trying to run away in the waist deep water. Craig got him in a bear hug. They thrashed around and Rusty could see that Ralph was naked, too. When they stopped horsing around, they stood there for a moment before embracing. Suddenly, Ralph pointed out in their direction, and, hand in hand, they quickly left the water.

Rusty was flabbergasted. Ralph and Craig, lovers! With mouth open, the words on the tip of his tongue, he turned to tell Tiny what he had seen. Tiny was looking back again at the clouds. Rusty shut his mouth. If he told Tiny, it would be all over town before dark, and Craig would be out of the closet into the frying pan. Fine payback for turning into, by all accounts, a good egg. Everybody said that he was a different person since flipping his airboat, giving up drinking, and hanging out with Ralph; said the accident had finally knocked some sense into him. Damn! He remembered that he still had Craig's engine apart. At least all the parts were clean and ready to go. Got to tell him I'm leaving and that he'll have to get someone else to reassemble it. Going to be funny talking to him, knowing. Whatever. It's their business, not mine, or the town's. Rusty put the binoculars down. Fifteen minutes later, the *Never Been Beat* entered the main channel.

CHAPTER THIRTY

"Do you think he saw us?" Craig asked, as he pulled the shower door shut behind them.

"No way. We were out in the water no more than a few minutes, if that. Even if Tiny happened to be looking in our direction, he would have needed a telescope trained on us right then…The Gulf's still pretty chilly, isn't it? Shower feels like heaven!" Ralph said.

"But if he did…"

"Craig, don't worry about it," Ralph said, reaching for the soap. "Turn around." Craig turned and Ralph started to soap his back.

"It's just, well, just that…"

"That no one knows and you want to keep it that way."

"That's right. I'm not brave like you. And I got an image."

Ralph sighed. Craig couldn't hear him because of the shower. "What, macho ladies man?" Ralph asked.

"Yeah, something like that. And I'm not like you. I go for the ladies, too. Bisexual, they call it."

"Got another name for it: AC-DC. Lots of names out there. Let's see; if people find out about you and me, and they are polite, they'll call you a homosexual. Or, horrors, behind your back, a fairy or homo or queer, a cocksucker or maybe fag or faggot, or like in England, a poof. If you go to Miami or south of the border, you'll be a *maricon,* or a *mariposa,* or maybe *café con leche.* Yeah, you better stay in your closet, lots safer there!" Ralph slammed the bar of soap back into its holder and turned his face up to the shower.

"No need to get sore, Ralph." Ralph ignored him. Craig reached for the soap and started to wash Ralph's back. Ralph continued to ignore him. "Some day I'll probably come out, but not yet. I just can't; it's like going back on thirty-five years of, of, I don't know what, life, I guess. At least my father's not alive. If he were living, no way, I just couldn't; he thought I was the coolest stud. What'd your parents do when they found out?"

Ralph turned and took the soap out of Craig's hand. "My father was disappointed, of course, but got used to it. Hardest part for him wasn't so much my being gay, but his having to acknowledge it with the neighbors and friends. As for my mother, she said she'd guessed all along. Said I was such a sensitive, gentle boy, too genteel to be a ladies man. Effeminate, in other words." Ralph laughed. "That was about when I started working out." Ralph began to wash Craig's sizeable hairy chest. "Guess no one ever accused you of being effeminate."

"And certainly not genteel, " Craig said, closing his eyes as Ralph worked up a lather. Ralph slowly ran the bar of soap down Craig's body.

"Well, well...what have we here?" Ralph asked. "Do we perhaps have a macho ladies man aroused? Didn't think that could possibly happen to a real ladies man," Ralph teased, as he gently stroked Craig's erection.

"Very funny, Ralph. You're a real stitch." Craig reached up and turned the shower off.

"Party pooper," Ralph said, with mock disappointment.

As they toweled off, Craig asked, "How much time do you need for the vegetables?"

"Not long, but you should probably get the charcoal going," Ralph said, toweling his hair. Craig watched the muscles work in Ralph's shoulders, back, all the way down to his perfectly formed buttocks. He started drying Ralph's back, his erection just nudging the cleft of Ralph's cheeks. Ralph leaned backwards against Craig's chest. Chin on Ralph's shoulder, Craig asked, "How about we play around a little before I start the fire?"

"Are you sure, Mr. ladies' man?" Ralph asked softly as he turned to face Craig.

Craig looked down. "I'm sure," he said, smiling.

* * *

"There's one," Luke exclaimed, running around the crab tank.

"Over there," Matthew added, while racing on his brother's heels.

Jimmy watched the twins excitedly circle the tanks as they kept a close eye on all the crabs. If only their energy could be bottled. They'd been at it for a couple hours and still hadn't lost interest. The only danger was maybe them crabs would die of too much handling, he thought. He shook a Camel out of the pack to his mouth. Wind was picking up pretty good; he could hear the cabbage palm brushing the side of the house. Got to remember to prune that tree. He stood up to check the barometer. Must be a little whacky, he thought, fallen almost two millibars in the past hour.

Crystal came through the door. "Boys, I'm in hot water. Your mama's on the phone, expecting you'd already be in bed. Wants to say goodnight. Scoot now and go on up to talk to her!" Matthew and Luke took off. To Jimmy, she said, "She's calling from the ship in Ft. Lauderdale. Still at the dock. Said it was just their luck that the weather's turning bad and there's a good chance the trip will be cancelled." She looked at the clock on the wall. "Want me back down in a couple of hours?" Jimmy nodded, as he heaved himself out of the tattered armchair. Cigarette in mouth, he walked around the tanks. The boys had done good, not one peeler out of place.

He sat back down and thumbed through a magazine. Tiny and Rusty had returned earlier in the evening, and Tiny had told Charley that Rusty would be leaving town tomorrow. Damn shame. And damn sudden. Wonder why? He's retired, in the middle of fixing Craig's airboat, gave no hint that he had anything else going on. I should ask him tomorrow when he comes by. The twins startled Jimmy when they burst into the room dressed in their pajamas.

"Hey, I thought you two rug rats was going to bed."

"We are, but Grandma…"

"Said to say goodnight first."

"Long as you're here, then how about helping your old granddaddy a little longer with them crabs. My legs is awful tired." Jimmy smiled as the boys immediately and very seriously began patrolling the tanks. As he watched them, he thought about what *Espantoso* had said. He was viciously stubbing out his cigarette when Crystal entered.

"Matthew, Luke, you were just supposed to say goodnight; your mama would skin me alive if she knew you was still up! Now you kiss your gran'daddy goodnight and skedaddle upstairs this minute! I'll be right up behind you, and you better be in bed when I get there!"

"Yes…"

"Ma'am."

The boys were gone in a flash. "Jimmy, wind's holding the tide in. Might want to check the lines before bed."

"Plan to." Crystal followed the boys upstairs while Jimmy checked the barometer again. Still falling fast.

When Crystal spelled him, Jimmy took one last look at the barometer before going out with flashlight to check on the boat. Tide still coming in, though it was hard to tell because the water was so high: it was already lapping on the grass at the edge of the dock. He made sure the lines were secured. No rain, but he estimated the gusts at forty miles an hour. He hoped no one was out at sea; hell of a night to be on the water.

* * *

Beau and Virginia were watching the eleven o'clock news. Virginia was on the couch knitting, two needles clicking away with navy blue yarn coming up out of her knitting bag. Beau was laying on the floor next to Skillet who was on his beanbag bed. Beau had a highball glass with Laphroaig single malt in one hand while the other was wedged up under Skillet's Elizabethan collar, awkwardly stroking the top of Skillet's head. Skillet whimpered in his sleep.

"I don't know how much more of this I can stand," Beau said, looking at Skillet. "If only he'd eat something. Norm said that would be a good sign."

"Norm also said if he made it through the first few days, he'd have a real good chance, so just be thankful he's still alive. I don't think there's a vet in the world could have done more for Skillet than Norm. He was over again today to give him another penicillin injection." Beau didn't say anything; he just kept stroking Skillet. "And can you believe the community's response! Did you have any idea how much Skillet's loved in this town? I can't go anywhere without being asked how he's doing, and I had at least five telephone calls today. There were two more cans of Alpo on the steps along with a handmade leather collar, two bottles of flea spray, a box of doggy biscuits, and a rubber duck." Virginia smiled. "Two guesses where the rubber duck came from."

"Flea spray was probably left overs from the post office epidemic," Beau said, but tears had welled up in his eyes. "Who wouldn't love Skillet? Except that profligate!"

Virginia stopped knitting and turned to Beau. "Beau, would you really have shot him?"

"Sugah, I don't know. It was close, I'll tell you that. If he had wised off one more time…" Beau didn't finish the sentence.

"Thank the Lord he didn't…and you didn't. Just think where you'd be, where we'd be!"

"With the good guy in jail for the rest of his life and that shithead, pardon my French, killing cabbage palms and feeding cats for breakfast to some new pit bull. At least, thanks to Charley, that son-of-a-bitch got his. He's still in the hospital. Of course we, the taxpayers, will pay for that. Beau paused to take another sip of single malt. "And I'll tell you what…"

"Sshh, dear, the weather's on." Virginia turned up the volume. A meticulously coiffed blond in a tight skirt and blouse pointed at a weather map of the entire east coast.

"…already begun in the Southeast. Asheville, North Carolina, reports five inches of snow, Knoxville, Tennessee, reports four inches as does Birmingham, Alabama. Meridian, Mississippi, reports five inches. Thunder in Alabama has been reported along with the snow which indicates the severity of this storm. Barometric readings are predicted to be record low in many areas of the eastern seaboard, and due to these very low readings, perhaps one of the great storms of the century is underway. For the storm roaring up the east coast on Saturday, there are coastal flood warnings from Rhode Island to Virginia Beach, and blizzard warnings are in effect from Washington to Boston, with the entire north country to receive a major snowfall Saturday through early Sunday when the storm will then begin to head out into the Atlantic.

"All of this is being caused by the mergence of this cold system here from the north," she said pointing with her stick, "with the intense energy system from the west here, and this low pressure along the north coast of the Gulf of Mexico. Here in Florida, there is a coastal flood watch for the entire west coast, and there will be severe thunderstorms which could generate tornados. Tornados have already been reported just north of the Tampa/St. Pete area. Once the storm clears out Saturday morning, arctic-like weather will take its place..."

"Good thing you don't have the gardens in Charleston anymore. Can't remember the last time they got snow," Beau said. "You should call your sister."

"Maybe tomorrow."

"At least we lucked out," Beau said, standing up, empty glass in hand.

"What do you mean?"

"Looks like the storm's swinging north. Forecast is the same-old: heavy thunderstorms accompanied by a coastal flood watch. We get that twenty times a year easy." Beau walked over to a window as Virginia turned off the TV. The cabbage palm fronds were waving wildly. "Pretty good gusts out there. Good night for a hot tub and a single malt," he added.

"At this hour! And more whisky? You'll fall asleep and come out looking like a prune. Dehydration is not good for you, dear."

Beau ignored her and walked back to their bedroom. He soon returned in a bathrobe and flip-flops, carrying a towel. "Sugah, I need a break from Skillet; his continual whimpering tears me up and taking a hot tub in the middle of a storm fits the bill. And so does this fine peaty single malt," he added, filling the glass over halfway.

"Suit yourself, dear; but, you'll regret it in the morning. I'll leave the porch light on for you."

Beau went down to the hot tub. The wind caught the cover and almost took it out of his hands. He wedged it between the tub and fence before climbing in. He took a good sip of whisky, the wind gusting in his face. He could hear the waves lapping at the seawall and the palm fronds' mad rustling. A dead frond flew by. Beau took another sip and scooched down lower into the tub, only his head and the hand holding his drink out of the water. It was exciting, he felt like he was braving the elements. The best part, though, was the sound of Mother Nature's fury rather than Skillet's whimpering. Within an hour, Beau was passed out in the hot tub.

* * *

Charley could feel the *Stingray* sway slightly. He looked over to his travel alarm clock on the table—little past midnight. Minnie must have gotten out early. Momentarily he heard her walking above deck. She soon ducked down through the cabin door and entered the galley.

"Hey there. Whatcha doing?" she asked, seeing Charley poised with a tiny paintbrush in one hand and a lampshade in the other.

"Putting the finishing touches on Skillet's new fancy-ass collar so he don't go pulling out his stitches." Charley began to clean the brush in a glass of water as Minnie picked up the lampshade.

"Figure I kin cut out them metal support doohickeys and it should slip over his head just fine," Charley said, drying the brush and putting it back into a children's tin watercolor paint set he bought at the Dollar Store. "Hell of a lot better looking than Norm's."

"Charley!" she said, in surprise. "This is good, real cute! I didn't know you could paint."

"Lots of things you don't knows about me, sweet-heart," Charley said, nonchalantly, although proud as punch. "Always liked to doodle some. But this weren't easy, being as it's drawing on something curved. Took me a bunch of sketching, but," as he took the shade from her to inspect it, "didn't turn out too shabby." He turned the shade. There was a lab chasing a mailman, a lab peeing on a fire hydrant, a lab chasing a cat, and a little yellow rubber duck floating in a bathtub. The labs had an uncanny likeness to Skillet.

"Can't tell you, Minnie, how bad I done felt when I see Skillet on Norm's table. It hit me in the gut hard. My stomach felt sorta like when you come speeding over a hill and there's a state trooper a'setting at the bottom with a radar gun."

Minnie took the lampshade back out of his hands and carefully set it down. She drew his head to her and kissed him hard on the lips.

"What's that fer?"

"Being so sweet about Skillet and all." She picked up the lampshade again and looked at it closely. "You really do have talent, Charley."

"Maybe you'd like me to paint you in the buff sometime?"

"Charley!"

"Well, wouldcha?"

"Of course not! I could just imagine if that got around!" But Charley could see she was thinking about it.

"You got off early tonight. The weather?"

Minnie nodded. "No one out much—just a hand-ful of sports fishermen that picked the wrong weekend.

Norm said he'd help Tammy close up. Probably all done by now."

"They's quite an item, them two." Minnie didn't say anything. "Anyway, I got a favor to ask."

"Sure, hon, what?"

"Much as I want to, I can't stay with you tonight. And I knows it's late, but I wonder if I kin follow you out to your place, then you give me a ride back. I want to git the Mustang outta here."

"You don't think the weather's going to turn that bad, do you?"

"Don't know fer sure, but one thing I does know is about every critter in town been hightailing it to safer ground. This afternoon I seen coons and armadillas a'heading out, rat snakes climbing trees, and the marsh side of town been ungodly still. Believe something's up and I want to be here with the *Ray* case she needs me."

Minnie looked at Charley. He wasn't wrong often. "I guess we should get a move on, then. If you're right, Charley, guess I'll have to add weatherman to your many talents."

Charley put on a windbreaker and baseball cap, and grabbed a flashlight. He led the way out; they were met by a blast of wind that almost took his hat off—he just got a hand on it.

"That one be forty mile an hour, at least," he said. He shined the light over the deck to the ladder; there were white splotches everywhere. Minnie tried to skirt them.

"Yuk!"

"Had a Osprey camping out in them pines there the last couple o' days," Charley said, pointing with the flashlight. The pines were swaying side to side. "Had him a big old mullet this afternoon."

"Well, it's disgusting. You should clean it up," Minnie said as she disappeared down the ladder.

"Already cleaned up them fish parts he dropped," Charley said, following her over the side. "Was hoping the rain that be coming might take care of the rest."

* * *

"Don't complain, it's way past your bedtime, Huey," Tammy said, covering the parakeet's cage. The other cages already had towels draped over them. "Goodnight everybody," she said, turning out the light and entering her bedroom. Finally, the last chore was done, she thought; but, tomorrow was Saturday and it would be an even longer day. She began to undress. Norm was already in bed, hands behind his head, watching her. She was exhausted and not in the best of moods.

"Why do you stay here, Norm?" she asked, hanging up her blouse, a bite in her tone.

"What? With you, here? Now?"

"No, you're here now for the sex; that's simple enough. I mean here as in Crescent Beach."

"Here for the sex! What kind of comment is that?"

"You're not answering my question."

"That's a hell of a question!"

Tammy climbed into bed and pulled the covers up. "Let's see. You don't like airboats, the stock car race, the litter everywhere, you complain about rednecks and their noisy pickup trucks, people beating on each other, poaching, and bad English. All that's Crescent Beach. So, what do you like about it?"

He took his hands away from his head and looked at her. She was up and down with him lately. He didn't have a clue why.

"I don't know what your problem is, but seems like I'm bugging you." She didn't say anything. He shrugged. "Alright, here are some, just some of the things I like about Crescent Beach." He started counting them off on his fingers. "The no nonsense community with their live-and-let-live attitude—sort of like living on an island where most everybody pulls their own weight. I like people never too busy to take the time to stop and talk. I like the strong family ethic. I like the respect shown by the children and young adults who are polite and call me sir and call you ma'am. I like the empty roads. I like what I feel when I see Tiny come into town in the morning with the sun on his outriggers, or going out in the setting sun as a silhouette. I like watching the snowy egrets fish in tandem with the mergansers up and down the canals, and the great egrets fishing in the marsh during the high spring tides. I love listening to the whip-poor-wills and the hoot owls at night, the chattering Clapper and Virginia rails out in the marsh during the days, and watching the white pelicans riding the thermals. Then there are the sunsets off the point and the sunrises coming up over the marsh. And don't forget the fishing...I'm running out of fingers and toes. Do you want me to go on?"

Tammy remained silent. She was picking at the ends of her fingers. Norm sighed.

"I admit I probably complain too much about those things you mentioned; but they are in the minority." Norm thought about them, and finally couldn't resist. "I'll always hate those airboats, though. Most of them are out-of-towners, come here for the day, or night for that matter, to raise hell. It's one thing to go straight to a fishing site, but most hot rod around like Craig used to, and we all have to listen to THEIR noise so loud you can't think. One moment it's blissfully quiet and serene, the next you're in the middle of an airport! You know what it's like fishing out on the Gulf when one comes around. Then they go home and park them in the side yard; no noise for them in their homes, just ours. It's the absolute epitome of inconsideration and selfishness.

As for the other things, I guess part of it is that we live in such a small town. We've got less bad things going on here than most places, but because we're so small, they stick out—like Butch, or even when someone just backs their pickup by the ballfield when no one's around and dumps his garbage, even though the dump takes everything on this God's earth and is located not more than a half mile away. Stuff like that just brings me down.

"Now, I don't know what you were referring to when you said I complained of the bad English. Where'd that come from?"

"You don't find nothing wrong with my English?"

"Double negative."

Tammy looked up from her fingertips. "Double negative? What do you mean?"

"You just used two negatives—don't and nothing—together. Not supposed to do that…bad grammar."

"Well, excuse me! Sorry my grammar's not perfect! Maybe you should go to Sarasota and get your pretty little ex back from the tennis pro!" Tammy turned away from him, pulling the sheets up over her. She reached out and turned off the bedside light. Norm didn't say a word. He looked from her silhouetted curves to the two windows lit up from the outside streetlamp. Palm frond shadows danced on the window shades.

"Do you want me to leave, Tammy?" Norm asked softly.

She didn't answer right away. Finally, she asked, "Do you realize how many times you've corrected me when I'm saying something?"

He thought about that. "No, no I don't."

She rolled over and sat up. "About every day. Every damn day!"

Norm was beginning to get an inkling what this was all about. "If I did, I did it unconsciously. And I certainly never meant to insult you."

"It just makes me wonder how long we're going to last, what with you being so educated and all. I'm sure your wife spoke perfect English. Norm, I never will."

"Tammy, come here." Norm laid out his arm. Tammy hesitated, then moved over. He drew her to him. "I apologize, I really do. I swear I had no idea, and it's so trivial in the scheme of things. We've got good jiu-jiu, you and I, and how we talk doesn't have anything to do with anything, just as long as we do talk and do communicate." He tilted her chin up. "I love you, Miss Tammy, and I ain't here jest fer the sex! Got that?" Tammy smiled and nodded. He kissed her lightly on the lips. "There! Now that we've gotten that settled, let's screw our brains out!" She laughed and pretended to push him away; but she was still in his arms, and stayed there.

They watched the shadows on the window shades for awhile before Tammy asked, "How's Skillet?"

"About the same; the good part is that he was a healthy dog to begin with and, so far, infection hasn't reared its ugly head. A day or so should tell all. Beau, though, is a basket case; Virginia's keeping that household together right now. We've just got to keep our fingers crossed."

Tammy nodded, and they turned back to watch the dancing shadows. A gust of wind shook the house. It wasn't long before they fell asleep in each other's arms.

CHAPTER THIRTY-ONE

Although meteorologists had issued timely warnings for the country's entire eastern seaboard, no evacuation notice came out of Tallahassee for Florida's Gulf Coast. When the upper level arctic trough from the mid west met up with the strong surface low pressure in the northern Gulf of Mexico, a huge cyclonic storm formed that extended from Central America to Canada. Southerly winds preceding the storm as it headed east toward Florida had the effect of holding in the spring tides in the Big Bend area of Florida's northwest gulf coast, keeping the water stacked up as an extensive squall line several hundred miles long began to move in to the area early Saturday. The bands of rapidly moving showers were accompanied by non-stop cloud to ground lightning strikes and produced at least eleven tornados. The cool temperatures that chilled the air aloft, making it denser and sink, resulted in prodigious gusts of wind from the convective downdrafts called downburst clusters. These gusts blew in from the west, whipping up and pushing the incoming tide in front of it. It was one of these gusts that almost blew Tiny and his truck into the creek.

Most every morning it was Tiny's custom to take an
early morning drive to check on the *Never Been Beat* and
the Gulf. The weather reports and the rising winds the
night before definitely had his attention and, consequently, he started his rounds a little after three a.m.,
an hour earlier than usual. As he exited his little house
and pulled the key from his jeans, he could see that
his pickup was dripping with Gulf spray and that Main
Street glistened in the streetlights' amber tones. And
people wonder why us fishermen drive rusty pick-ups, he
thought, shaking his head. Driving down Main Street,
he had to turn on his wipers to see anything. When
he passed the next to last house before the point, his
mouth dropped in surprise. The Gulf was wild, really
wild—he had never, ever, seen waves so big, not even
during the storm when his father had drowned. They
looked at least fifteen feet tall, their spray like rain, and
the tide was so high that the waves rolled right across the
road, slamming into the foundation of the large house
on the point.

He didn't dare drive any farther, nor did he need to
see any more; he knew that he had to get to his boat.
The water was up another foot in the blink of an eye
and was coursing down the road towards his truck. Tiny
jammed the truck in reverse and turned around when
a powerful combination of wind and wave ripped up a
twelve foot slab of road pavement. The slab flipped into
a streetlight, knocking it over in an arc of sparks. Tiny
could see the sparks in the rearview mirror as he sped
towards his boat. While leaning on the horn to wake the
town, the streetlights suddenly blinked out.

When he arrived at the dock, or at least where the
dock should have been, another violent gust of wind seriously rocked the truck. The dock was a foot-and-a-half
underwater, and gaining. The nylon lines of the *Never
Been Beat* looked like they'd snap at any moment; they

were stretched thin as wire as the onrushing wind and waves pushed the boat back up the creek. With boots full of water and praying that the lines would hold a little longer, Tiny awkwardly climbed aboard and slushed his way to the pilothouse where he grabbed the ignition key from under a cushion. Once the engine was going, he turned on the shrimping lights; he almost wished he hadn't. The creek was full of all sorts of flotsam wrapped in a thick blanket of marsh grass and seaweed: jagged boards, nets, timbers, buoys, pvc plumbing, crab baskets and traps. He quickly put the motor in gear and eased forward to take the pressure off the lines. Even with the lights on, he could barely see in front of him because of the waves crashing into the bow, sending sheets of spray into his windshield. *The Never Been Beat* bobbed like a toy boat in a stirred up bathtub. At least he could still see the dock pilings through the side windows; that was good because he had to keep away from them at all costs. He needed to slack off the lines and get more into the center of the creek. He glanced over to his truck, water up to the door and rising; a gut wrenching sight after all the miles they had spent together, but the *Never Been Beat* came first. He quickly turned back to the controls.

Getting the throttle right was tricky; he had to speed up with the gusts, but not too fast or he'd go too far forward and rend the lines. The same went for not going fast enough. But he had to slack off those lines, both to get away from the dock and, he realized, to allow for the rising sea. He needed a mate, damn it! He started to get a feel for the gaps between the battering waves, but he still had to contend with the violent gusts. The boat kept rising with the incoming water. He experimented with the automatic pilot until he felt he had the RPMs right to give him enough time to adjust one of the lines. He went for the aft line first. He never unlashed and lashed a line so quickly in his life, giving it over twice as much length. He was back in the pilothouse in a flash, sweating heavily although he was soaked to the skin with cold seawater. He disengaged the automatic pilot so he could trim her bow. He waited impatiently until he thought the time was right again. Now! He put her on automatic pilot, streaked out and around the pilothouse to the bow line. Just as he had the line free from the cleat, a rogue wave smashed into the boat, knocking Tiny on his ass, the rope slipping through his hands and causing the boat to turn dangerously to port. Abandoning the line, Tiny ran back to the pilothouse to take the controls. Frantically spinning the wheel and jamming her into reverse, he got her headed into the wind again; he shuddered to think of the *Never Been Beat* broadside to these incoming waves. But the boat had slipped too far back and the aft line was taut as wire again. He spun the wheel the other way, gunned her forward, and eventually gained his original position. He didn't dare put her on automatic pilot; it was just too goddamned iffy! The loose line remained tantalizing close, he could see it, not ten feet away. He could also see that a birddog boat had broken loose and was being blown down the creek towards him. Ain't much I kin do about that, he thought, especially without that front line secure. Got a pole on board, but can't chance leaving the controls to push it away, not that I could in this damn wind anyway!

Just before the birddog boat hit, he throttled down so that the *Never Been Beat* faded back with the wind almost as fast as the smaller boat was coming onto it. The result was that the collision was relatively minor. Once the two boats were coupled, Tiny jammed down hard on the throttle to regain his position, which also resulted in pushing the other boat's nose out into the middle of the creek. The wind and waves caught it, turning it 180 degrees in the middle of the creek so that it skipped on by backwards, missing the *Never Been Beat* in the process. Tiny wiped his brow. Now if he could only get that bow line.

* * *

Out on Snowy Key, Craig and Ralph were abruptly awakened when a wave crashed through the bedroom window. It was pitch black with the power out, consequently a bad surprise when they jumped out of bed into a foot of cold, inky water.

"Holy shit!" exclaimed Craig. He felt his way into the kitchen where he took a large flashlight out of a drawer. He shined the light through a window; the dock wasn't there, and he could just see his Boston Whaler fifty feet off shore with its stern line dragging a broken post. It was upside down with the waves ushering it towards the mainland. The height and thickness of the waves were unbelievable! He frantically hit the backup generator switch near the front door. With the waves and wind so loud, he wasn't sure the generator was running until the lights came on. Ralph came out of the bedroom. They were both naked. They heard another wave crash through the bedroom window, the sound of wind and sea getting louder by the second.

"Get dressed!" Craig yelled.

"Clothes are soaked!"

Craig rushed to his bedroom bureau. He threw open the second drawer which was now only a few inches above the water. He yanked out sweaters and sweatpants.

"Throw these on! At least the sweaters are wool." They both dressed quickly, the sweatpants getting soaked immediately. Craig tucked the flashlight under the sweatpants' drawstring and waded to the louvered door of the hallway closet. He tugged the door open and grabbed two life jackets off the top shelf, tossing one to

Ralph. Craig looked around, not sure what to do next. "Dock's gone, and so's the boat...not that we'd stand a chance in the boat anyway!" Craig yelled. The water was up to their waists now, the waves slamming into the house, the rear wall bulging. Suddenly the lights went out. "Shit, there goes the generator." They could feel the house shift. Part of a wall splintered apart. "What the fuck!" Craig screamed. As if in shock, Ralph, hands down at his sides, stood motionless in the middle of the room. Craig tried to open the front door; it wouldn't budge. He pulled the flashlight from his pants and shined it around the room. He grabbed a floating chair to smash one of the windows on the leeward side of the house. He cleaned the jagged edges around the bottom as best he could with one of the chair legs. "C'mon, Ralph!"

Ralph finally focused. "Out to the water, are you crazy!"

"The oak tree on the deck! It's our only chance!" Craig sliced the side of his foot as he climbed through. "Hurry! Careful of the glass!" Craig hung on to the frame as best he could while Ralph climbed through. "Here, give me your hand." The water was almost up to Ralph's chest. Craig's grip on Ralph was like steel, his other hand shined the flashlight towards the oak only twenty feet away. The house shifted again and water began running out the windows. The windward wall gave way just as they reached the oak. They could feel the deck begin to move. Craig dropped the flashlight so he could awkwardly hug the tree with one arm while pulling Ralph with the other. "Climb up!" he yelled, getting a hand under Ralph's bottom and giving him a push. Ralph grabbed one of the thick branches and began climbing. Waiting for Ralph to get up higher, Craig hugged the oak. Suddenly a massive wall of water broke over them, pushing Craig underwater. He had bodysurfed on the east coast a lot as a kid, but this gave getting slammed by a wave a whole new meaning. Luckily, the tree shielded him from a direct hit. Still, he struggled to hang on even as he was forced downward and felt the deck ripped away under his feet. He held his breath for the rest of his life, gasping mightily when he finally surfaced. He was floating horizontally, still hanging on to the oak. He tried to touch bottom, but without success; it had to be ten feet deep now at least, he thought. He could just see the faint silhouette of what was left of the lodge. The monster wave had carried most of it away: the roof, front and back walls, all gone. Only part of the sidewalls remained. He looked up, but couldn't see Ralph. He began to climb.

It was slow going, making maybe a foot at a time before being hit by a wave again. He tucked his head each time, willing himself to be part of the tree. God damn these waves! he thought. He yelled up, "How you doing, Ralph! Okay?" No answer. Hell, he could hardly hear himself over the wind and waves. He kept climbing. Finally, he began to ease above the waves. They began to strike him in the gut, then the knees, feet, and finally he was clear. But he was also beginning to run out of branches, their diameter thinner and bending under his weight. He didn't dare go much higher. He blinked his eyes free from the salt water and looked up. He could see the silhouette of the branches at the top of the tree. He looked to both sides. Ralph was nowhere to be seen.

CHAPTER THIRTY-TWO

What the hell? Norm maneuvered his arm from around Tammy and looked at his watch. Why is some redneck blowing the horn at 3:30 in the goddamn morning! The house rocked with the wind. Man it's blowing. He lay in bed, listening to the wind. The house shuddered again; Tammy turned over in her sleep. She's out for the count, he thought, fondly looking at the outline of her back. He softly traced her spine with a finger, thinking no one in Crescent Beach worked harder; don't know where she gets the energy. He looked towards the window. Something wasn't right, and it took him a couple of minutes to realize that there was no streetlight coming through the shade. No numerals on Tammy's clock either: power's out. The wind shook the house again. He got out of bed.

He raised the shade, but couldn't see much other than the live oak branches were wild. He went into the living room, passing Tammy's birds on his way to the front door. The birds were antsy, shuffling around in their covered cages. He pulled a large powerful flashlight from the bureau by the door and stepped outside. The wind pushed so hard that he was thrown backwards. Water was coming over the street and was an inch or two up the tires of the Outback. Tremendous breakers crashed at the edge of the Crescent Club with the water pouring through underneath. The pool table had shifted several feet. He shined the light back to the Subaru. In just seconds, the water had risen up another couple of inches. He bolted back inside, leaning hard against the door to shut it, and ran back into the bedroom. Madly pulling on clothes, he yelled for Tammy to wake up. Tammy jacknifed, the sheet falling away from her.

"What's wrong!" Another blast of wind hit the house.

"Water's coming up fast! Got to get out of here! I'll start the Subaru. Hurry!"

Tammy leaped naked out of the bed, alert and moving fast.

"The birds. Put the birds in the car," she said, dashing to the closet. Norm grabbed Huey on the way out. Water was up at least three more inches. He put Huey in the rear passenger seat, and went back for Henrietta. Tammy followed with the finches and lovebirds. Norm put the cockatiel next to Huey before opening the tailgate for Tammy. The wind tore the tailgate out of his hands, springing it on the hinges; it didn't shut right, but at least it hooked. The water was three-quarters up the tires. They hopped in and Norm carefully backed out to Main Street; even over the wind, he heard the exhaust pipe gurgle. He didn't dare drive fast, but still, a wake formed behind them.

They were just beyond the Club when the car stalled; no way would it start. "We've got to get up into the Club!" Tammy yelled, looking at the pool table heading inland. They struggled out of the car, the water above their knees. With a cage in each hand, they fought their way to the steps. Norm watched as the sea blasted against the thousand-gallon LP gas tank off to the side of the building. It was wiggling back and forth like a gigantic loose tooth. The stairs were loose, too. Norm led the way. When he reached the first landing, a tremendous wave broke just below him. It caught Tammy dead on, blowing her off the steps, and taking the two cages with it. When she surfaced, she screamed, "My birds!"

Tammy was hanging on to one of the lower balustrades, her back to Norm. She was poised to leap into the water after the cages, but she couldn't see them anywhere. The steps were undulating with the waves, noticeably much looser. "Tammy!" Norm yelled, "C'mon! You can't do anything about them now! C'mon! These steps are going to give way!" On cue, another, higher wave broke over the steps, and the stringers were torn away below at the slab; the bottom section began to float. Luckily, Tammy had been hanging on tightly. She hustled up to Norm.

When they reached the main entrance, Tammy said, "Shit! No keys; they're back in the house!" Seawater spumed over the deck. Norm wanted to let go of the birds so he could cover his ears from the incessant howling of the wind. "Kitchen window!" she yelled, and ran along the side the building. She took off a shoe and broke a corner of the window as Norm arrived with the two, unbelievably, still covered cages. She reached in and unlocked the window. Throwing it open, she quickly climbed through. Norm handed her the cages, then followed. Tammy shut the window.

Getting out of the wind was like stepping into a church after a SEC football game, the relative silence a tonic; but Tammy didn't stay still for long. She took the two cages out and placed them on the middle of the bar, immediately pulling off the beach towels covers. She hurried off to get a flashlight, matches and candles. Shaking her head, she handed Norm the candles, saying, "Damn generator's down; was on the list to get fixed. Who'd think we'd need it in March!" Norm lit candles while she examined the birds. They didn't look the worse for wear, and when there was enough light for the birds to see each other, they immediately began to squabble. Tammy smiled in relief. "They're all right," she said. Her smile disappeared, and Norm knew she was thinking about the other birds. He put a hand on her shoulder.

"You couldn't help it, honey: no one could have held on to them in that wave. You did your best." When the tears began to flow, Norm drew her into him. She put her arms on his chest and sobbed. It was the first time he had ever heard this tough little nut of a woman cry.

* * *

Rusty was all set. It had only taken about five minutes to pack the suitcase that he put on the cabin floor next to an empty cooler with his bright orange life jacket on top. Jimmy had insisted that he come by in the morning to fill the cooler with fish that they had caught, saying Rusty could get some dry ice in Perry to keep it frozen. Saying goodbye to Jimmy and Crystal was the last thing he wanted to do. How was he going to be able to shake Jimmy's hand and look him in the eye? And Crystal? Maybe he should say something to her like, 'Hey babe, see you in a bit with some of my trooper friends. Your old man's going to be gone for twenty years; so, what say you and I kick up our heels while he's in the slammer!' Or, 'Sorry you're going to have to leave Crescent Beach, but don't worry, the witness protection program will find you a safe spot. How about upstate New York? Oh, and sorry, no room for the grandkids and the rest of your family.'

He had gone to bed early, right after dining with Norm at the Club, but sleep was impossible. As he lay in bed, the wind kept picking up until the little cabin shuddered with the blasts. Good move, Tiny's, in

coming home.   Man, it's going to be awkward tomorrow at Jimmy's! Maybe he should get up and leave right
now. But, he stayed where he was, switching the channels of his mind, trying to conjure up something else
than ratting on Jimmy—like his night with Annie or
shrimping with Tiny. He switched over to crabbing with
Charley, and of course to the CB 250; but Jimmy kept
popping back up uninvited. All the repercussions for
Jimmy's family bounced around his head like pinballs.
Jimmy knew the game, damn it! He knew he could get
busted! But, like this? On and on it went until, thor-
oughly exhausted, Rusty drifted off to a fitful sleep.

He was dreaming that he was in rough sea aboard
the *Never Been Beat* when the cabin suddenly shifted off
its concrete blocks, jostling him half way out of bed into
two feet of cold water.   His eyes flew open; it was completely dark and, momentarily, he had no idea where
he was. Had he fallen overboard! Then he remembered: Tammy's cabin, the wind, the incoming storm
that Tiny had worried about.   He quickly untangled
himself from the sheets when a terrific gust tipped the
cabin further, causing Rusty to slide completely into the
water. Pushing himself up, his hand hit something soft:
the life preserver. Thank God! He strapped it on as
best he could in the dark, thinking how ironic to finally
need it on land.

He found the door of the cabin, but it wouldn't open;
the handle came off in his hands when he yanked. He
told himself not to panic; he'd be okay, he was wearing
a life preserver. But he had to get out of here! The two
windows were barely above the waterline, but swollen
shut and hard to get a purchase; even with his strength,
they wouldn't budge. Maybe they were nailed shut; he
had never tried to open them before. The cabin's single
chair bumped into him; he grabbed it and smashed one

of the windows clear. He thought he was hallucinating when he saw a tree move by, then realized the cabin was being pushed along by the waves and wind. The water kept rising, and began to pour in through the window; time to blow this popcorn stand! Outside the icy water was waist deep; he braced himself as the waves smacked into him. But the wind! It was horrific; branches and boards, all sorts of stuff, were flying by, and him with only his striped pajamas and the life preserver for protection. At least the preserver won't let me sink, he hoped.

What now? The fire station! That was the highest ground in town; certainly the water wouldn't reach there, would it? The wind tore at the tin roof of the cabin, working a section loose. Rusty could hear it flapping, but not for long; the wind tore it off, shooting it away in the darkness, an airborne scythe. The wind started working on the next piece; Rusty lowered himself in the water, making himself a smaller target. His eyes were adjusted to the dark now, and he got his bearings. He began pushing his way towards higher ground. Marsh grass stuck to his arms and upper torso. Suddenly he realized there wasn't a light on anywhere. Power was out, obviously. Gas. Strong gas smell; tanks must be tearing loose all over town. If this wind dies down, the town could blow sky high! The water was steadily rising, almost up to his chest. His heart was in his throat when he bumped into things under the water. Would sharks come in to shore with weather like this? Soon his feet were barely touching the ground; he was lightly dancing over whatever was below. Maybe a good thing, what with bare feet. A minute later he was floating. He wished he knew how to swim, but at least his head was above water and the waves were taking him inland.

* * *

"Jimmy! Jimmy, wake up!" Crystal yelled over the wind, shaking his shoulder.

"What? Can't be five o'clock already?" He tried to roll back over, but she wouldn't let him.

"Water's up high! Came in real fast!"

"Crystal, tide comes in twice a day! Goes out twice a day! It'll go out again."

"Jimmy, water's flooding and taking the crabs with it. Boat's busted free and it's up against the house. Going to get trapped between the deck and the water if we don't get it outta there. I tried to move it, but it won't budge."

That got Jimmy's attention. He jumped out of bed and ran into the living room in his skivvies. He flipped the switch for the deck lights. Nothing. He peered out the window. Hard to make things out, but no dock, no land in sight. He thought he caught quick glimpses of the very tops of the pilings between waves. At least that's where they should have been. Water had to be six feet up anyways. He looked at Crystal; her hair was plastered down, and her wet clothes clinging to her body. "Get the twins dressed!" Jimmy yelled. He rushed back to the bedroom to throw on his clothes. He ran to the twins' bedroom door. Crystal was trying to get two very sleepy boys dressed. "I'll see what I can do with the boat. Keep the twins here, but check on me when you can," Jimmy said. He bolted out of the house and was only halfway down the stairs before he was in the water. He shuddered: cold as a witch's tit! He jumped in and swam around the stairs. The boat was thudding against the lower section of the house. He climbed in and started her up. The boat had a lot of water in it and taking more. There was only a foot of space between the winch and the deck; probably a good thing she was sitting so low in the water. He put it into gear, easing it out from under, scraping hard against the house as the wave action kept the boat pressed in.

When the boat was out, he was met by the wind's full force that blew him a hundred feet past the house. All the water in the boat made it sluggish and unresponsive; he had to use all his skills to keep from being swamped as he fought to turn it around. He worked his way back, fighting wind and waves as well as dodging floating debris. He approached the rear, leeward side where there was an eddy of sorts; the house was like a big boulder in the middle of a raging river, a shield against the turbulence of wind and waves. But, a hard current pushed against the boat as the water poured in from the Gulf, passing under the house. He looked at the water level on the stilts, thinking that he had gotten the boat out in the nick of time. Now if he could only tie up and bail her out. He ran the boat right up against the house, pushing against it with the throttle engaged. Two partial lines of twenty feet or so remained secured to the boat's cleats, but there was nothing to tie to except the stilts which would be underwater soon. He yelled for Crystal. No answer; can't hear me with all the noise, he thought. He banged on the side of the house with the gaff. Crystal soon appeared in the nearest window. She threw it open.

"Going to throw you the line to tie up somewhere's." Crystal nodded and Jimmy threw. Crystal missed it and they tried again. She snagged it on the third throw and Jimmy put the motor in neutral as she struggled to pull him over. She tied the line to a closet door handle.

"Need a big pail! Got to bail her out!" Crystal quickly left the window, soon reappearing with a mop bucket. Jimmy began to bail. As he dumped water, he said, "If'n it gits over the stilts here, then you and the kids going to git in the boat and we'll head out. Going to need warm clothes and blankets ready to go." He looked at her, still in wet clothes. "Ain't going to do no good if'n you catch pneumonia—you gotta git them clothes off!" He pulled three life preservers out from under the seat, and handed them to Crystal. "Just in case. And I could use a blanket and maybe a jacket and hat when you got the time. How are the boys doing?"

"Fine. They're glued to the front window. Think it's awful exciting.'"

Jimmy laughed. "Can't argue that." He stood and leaned over, extending a hand out to her. She reached out and took it. He gave her a squeeze. "You always been my dreamboat, know that?'" She nodded and smiled. After another squeeze, she turned to go get Jimmy his blanket.

CHAPTER THIRTY-THREE

It took three direct hits of seawater before a sputtering, spitting, totally disoriented Beau woke up. The fourth wave got him moving, but it was more reaction to the cold water than anything else; he was still drunk and had no idea what was going on or where he was. There were no lights anywhere, the darkness a shade lighter towards the Gulf. Only standing up did he realize that he was in the hot tub, then remembered coming down after watching the weather. Out of habit, he reached for his bathrobe behind him where, soaked, it was on a hook, plastered against the latticework by the wind. He grimaced into the wind as he put it on and stepped down out of the tub into four feet of water. Shocked, he quickly climbed back up, only to have the next wave knock him backward, causing him to bang his knee on the hot tub and smash into the latticework. The pain in his knee made him nauseous.

He slowly pulled himself up by hanging onto the edge of the hot tub, this time ducking into the next wave when it hit. He climbed back down into the water, almost falling when his knee buckled. The water was up another six inches. He struggled towards the house, making little progress, the waves and rising tide carried him off to the side three steps for every one forward; he lost more and more ground, with the outline of the house receding from sight. Beau was weakening quickly, the water up to his chin. He began to tread water as best he could with the bum knee and his arms heavy. The water toyed with him. He kept bumping into things: boards, plastic pipe, rope, all the items from outdoor catchalls, carports, and pickup beds that could float. Thick marsh grass and seaweed stuck to his neck. There was lightning in the sky. He was beginning to lose feeling in his extremities.

He couldn't touch bottom anymore when a log, carried by a wave, rammed him in the shoulder, knocking him underwater. When he surfaced and realized what had hit him, he swam clumsily after it, using the last of his strength. Wheezing from the exertion, he grabbed hold of the end and held on for dear life as the log bobbed and surfed its way inland until it finally lodged between three cabbage palms. Beau continued to hang on to the log as the water continued to rise. With eyes closed and wondering how much longer he could survive in the cold water, something brushed against his cheek. More flotsam, he thought, without bothering to look. It kept brushing his cheek until he finally opened his eyes. Dead palm frond, but still attached to the tree! There had to be twelve feet of water under him, maybe more! The log became wedged so tightly between the trees that the water began to cover it. Beau's only option was to use it for a step up into the top of one of the trees.

He slipped on his first attempt, slicing a water-softened forearm on the sharp edge of a frond. He hardly felt it. He tried again. His fingers were dumb with cold and they worked only in ultra slow motion, but he managed to pull himself into the tree's crown. He tried to sit in the middle, but the fronds stuck straight up, making it impossible to get comfortable. He moved a little to the side, spreading the green fronds as best he could. He had zero strength and his knee throbbed. A faint light to the east enabled him to identify most of the debris hung up below; it was growing into quite a collection. For some reason there must be a current channeled right through the trees: palm tree junction, he thought. There was a rustling in the fronds to his right and a big rat scurried out and ran across his lap before disappearing into the fronds; Beau almost fell out of the tree. He nervously looked around, wondering what other creatures had sought refuge here.

The wind died down some, but it also turned colder. Beau's shivering was non-stop. When a good-sized blue plastic tarp wrapped itself around the tree, he slowly pulled it up, allowing most of the water to run off before wrapping it around his body as best he could. He snapped off dead fronds and stuffed them inside the tarp. He didn't warm up much, but at least it kept that biting wind off him. He closed his eyes, hoping daybreak was not far off.

Virginia's going to think I've drowned. Hell of a bad decision that hot tub, but nothing I can do about it now; just hope she and Skillet are okay. Should be; house is solid and the tallest in Crescent Beach. But still, that wind had to be hurricane level. How many years have we been together? Most of our lives, easy. High school sweethearts when I was what? Sixteen? Had to borrow father's Lincoln for our first date. She was so pretty and I was so damn nervous! Got serious pretty quick, he remembered, smiling; wasn't long before we were fogging up the windshield at the drive-in on Saturday nights. Talked me into escorting her to the debutante ball the following summer. What a crock that was, all that pretense. Still, it was fun and we turned a lot of heads out on the dance floor. Felt so natural to have her in my arms even back then. And her coming down all the way from Pennsylvania for those big college weekends, putting up with my fraternity's shenanigans! Was on one of those visits that we snuck over to father's summer house in Beaufort when I proposed by the swing under the big live oak: I swear her smile about lit up the horizon. She dropped out of the pre-med program at Bryn Mawr next semester, sacrificing her career for mine and so we could be married my senior year. Always so supportive—how did I ever rate a woman like that? There are givers and takers in this world, and she's a giver all the way. On to grad school, my teaching career, and finally retiring here. So how many years does that make? Come on, can't you do a little arithmetic! Damn mind's foggy. Fifty, that's it—a half century! He briefly opened his eyes and took stock: no new treasures in the swirling water. He returned to his reverie. Fifty years! We've got to do something to celebrate this summer. Maybe take a cruise. Wonder if you can take a dog on a cruise. Oh, Skillet, my poor Skillet. Who knows; maybe he'll outlive me if this water gets any higher.

The time slowly passed with memories. When Beau next opened his eyes, the sky had lightened and he began to look around. He couldn't believe what he saw.

* * *

Ralph bobbed like a cork. He also had swallowed a lot of seawater and the cold water was sapping his strength. High on the crest of a wave and through eyes stinging with salt, he could see a single bright light towards shore. It was his beacon of hope and it seemed that the water was taking him towards it. I just have to keep calm, keep my head up and I'll be all right, he kept telling himself. The wave took him for a little ride before letting him go and he settled back down into another trough. The cycle was repeated, over and over again.

Was Craig able to climb that tree, or did he get knocked off like me? At least he's wearing a life jacket, too, and he's a strong swimmer. Got as good a chance as I do. Golly, the last couple of weeks were great—he really is such a sweet, good man under all that bluster of his. Another wave took Ralph up again, and again he could see the light, closer, always a bit closer. Got to get out of this water! If hypothermia gets me, won't matter a hoot if I'm blown on to someone's doorstep. When the wave released him, Ralph saw a dark object off to his right. At least sixteen feet long, he estimated. Was that a tail fin! His bowels tightened. Bull Shark? No, too big. Great White blown in from God knows where! His bowels tightened further as he lay frozen in the water, not daring to move and making like the buoy he was. He watched the shape; its movements weren't natural. It was more like something foundering.

Cautiously, he breaststroked towards it. Twenty feet away, he saw that it was a boat, upside down with the motor's shaft sticking up—the tail fin! He suddenly recognized the distinctive shape of the hull. Craig's Whaler! He began to swim towards it as hard as he could, but when he was only a few feet away, he was picked up by a large wave that carried him right on by. He tried to swim back, but being in the cold water for so long had made him clumsy and he barely escaped the trough when another wave caught him and sent him forward again. He looked over his shoulder and just caught a glimpse of the boat. He knew he'd never get back to it wearing the life jacket.

Could he swim long enough in this sea without one? Was he strong enough still? Or was it suicide? But shore was a good ways off, and he had been in the water a long time. He HAD to get out of the water. He had learned about hypothermia when his scull had flipped a mile off shore in February water a few years back. Even though he had been mostly out of the water as he lay on the hull waiting to be rescued, he was chilled to the bone by the Gulf's spray, disoriented, his core temperature dropping to the low 80's; all signs of hypothermia. The crabber who picked him up said that cold water robs the body's heat twenty-five to thirty times more than cold air. He had no idea how long he had been in the water this time, but it was too long! He couldn't make up his mind. Concentrate, Ralph! Decide! Finally, he began to fumble with the straps. C'mon now fingers, do your job! He slipped out of the harness just before the next big wave arrived, and dove down. Surfacing, he struggled to swim into the wind, looking in all directions. No sign of the boat. Another wave, another dive. Up again in the trough. The boat should be here, damn it! Still nothing. Another wave; he dove again. Up. No boat. He began to panic and his blood pressure was off the charts. Another dive; still nothing! Lord, I'm tired. He could barely keep his head up. He stopped swimming. What's the use? Another large wave came towards him, but he didn't have the strength to dive again. Instead, he turned away from it, resigned. But there it was, the boat—behind him, not ten feet away! I must have dived right under it! Adrenaline coursed his body and, with arms and legs flailing like a gecko in slow motion, he crawled onto the hull. When he finally clasped the shaft of the motor, he began to sob.

Some time later when the boat approached the mouth of the creek, a new pattern of breaking waves began shoving it forward fifteen feet at a time. The beacon wasn't one light, Ralph realized squinting, but several, up high in the outriggers of a shrimp boat. Lord, what a beautiful sight! The Whaler tipped precariously as it was carried through the topsy-turvy chop where the wind and waves met the creek's current. Once through the chop, Ralph could see someone in the pilot house. Ralph lifted his arm—it weighed a thousand pounds. Slowly, he waved back and forth.

The horrific wind gusts had died down and the water had stopped rising, allowing Tiny to put The *Never Been Beat* into neutral and square away the lines. A steady, heavy wind out of the west continued to hold the water in and the temperature was dropping noticeably. Tiny had seen the hull even before it came through the creek's chop and went aft to get his long pole to fend it off. When he positioned himself in the front of the bow, he saw a man waving in slow motion. The man tried to yell, but not much came out. As the Whaler slowly approached, the man dropped his arm and his head sagged; he looked in bad shape. Tiny picked up a coil of line.

"Son, grab on hold of this here line and I'll pull you in." Tiny threw the line; it landed across the bow. Ralph couldn't reach it, and wasn't about to let go of the shaft. Tiny brought in the line and tried again. It hit Ralph. In slow motion, Ralph reached for it, but his hands wouldn't obey and he couldn't grip it tightly.

"Can't hold it," Ralph mumbled. "Hands don't work."

"Wrap her around that shaft." Ralph did as he said. Tiny exclaimed, "Ralph! Is that you!" Hugging the shaft, Ralph nodded as Tiny quickly reeled him in.

CHAPTER
THIRTY-FOUR

It was quarter to four in the morning when the sirens woke Charley: the fire truck!

He bolted out of his berth, quickly discovering that there was no power and that the *Ray* was seaborne. He lit two kerosene lamps and hung them from the galley ceiling: they swayed with the boat. Bundling up, he went topside for a look, shining a flashlight all around his lot. Water everywhere; it looked like a Tupelo and Cypress pond except the trees were pine and oak, and had no business being in a pond. I'll be a son-of-a-gun, he thought. The treetops bent in the steady westerly gale as he looked towards his nearest neighbor. The shack wasn't there, or at least, not above water. Dang! He shone the light off the bow. The *Ray* was slowly floating toward some trees. The water was full of odds and ends, and the bottom of the *Stingray* scraped against something. He wondered if it was his neighbor's house. He looked at the trees again. He'd need a pole to fend off. Now don't that beat all! Who'd think I'd be needing something like that? He looked around, wondering what he could use. He unlashed the aluminum ladder and took it up into the bow. As he pushed the boat away, he thought that it might not be the smartest thing to be waving a metal ladder around: sure hope all the thundering and lightning's done with!

He sat at the helm, continuing to shine his light back and forth. Ain't no one else here lives on a boat and, judging by the trees, that water's way up high! Sure hope everyone's got hisself to higher ground. He kept looking around. Dang spooky: ain't nobody nowheres! The wind was biting; he pulled his hat tighter and stuck his free hand into a pocket. The weird thing was he felt calm, not scared at all. Just like them snakes and rats, ain't a dang thing I kin do about it except hunker down for the ride. The *Ray* continued to float with the surge. Charley wondered what would come next. Off to port he saw some furniture and a refrigerator floating on its back. At eleven o'clock was a foundering crab boat hung up in some cabbage palm tops, although the water was so high, they looked more like palmettos than palms. Starboard there were buoyed fishnets wrapped around a power pole. Several red cedars were missing their tops, and the water was clogged with seaweed. A corner of a roof was sticking out of the water. Whose place was that? No creek, canals, or streets for reference. Everything was so different! His light reflected off something small and silver. There were a bunch of them bobbing around. The more he looked, the more he saw; they were everywhere. I swear if them don't looks like beer cans! They were floating in the same direction as the *Ray*, and he went to the side for a closer look. They is! I'll be a son-of-a-whore! Must be some of Tammy's delivery—that big beer truck in front of the Club yesterday.

A couple cans were real close. He leaned over the railing, but the *Ray* was too high. Last thing I need is to fall overboard! Need me a net, but don't...now wait jest a minute! He rushed down to the forward berth where he pawed through a cardboard box until he pulled out a cast net in triumph. He ducked into the head on the way back up to the deck. The toilet water was no longer clear and had seaweed in it. He pulled up a floorboard section by its recessed stainless rings to see how much water the Ray was taking. His old patch was holding okay, and luckily the plumbing pipes had busted outside the hull: there was only a little water seeping where he had stuffed oakum around them. On deck, he unwrapped and shook the net free. He adjusted the slip ring, and put a corner of the net in his mouth. There was a good group of cans six feet away. He threw, and slowly drew in the net. Four cans first throw! Hot diggety!

The *Ray* continued to ease along as Charley caught beer. He caught a lot of other things, too—marsh grass, a doll, sneaker, white boot, Yamaha hat, and all sorts of plastic items. Except for the doll, he threw everything back. The deck was a mess, but there was also an impressive pile of assorted beverages, not just beer. The sky was beginning to lighten when the boat ran into what remained of a metal roof; only a few rusty, jagged pieces were attached to the 2x4 skeleton. Charley put the net down, and grabbed the ladder. Mobile home, he thought, pushing against it. The water caught the side of the boat, pivoting it away from the roof, but turning it around in the process so that the stern became the bow.

Sunrise wasn't far off. Trees and water and junk were everywhere. A line of power pole tops. Main Street? Charley couldn't believe his eyes. But where's the houses; nothing but them waves! He saw a shrimp boat with all its lights on; looks like Tiny's, he thought. Must be under power to head into the wind like that; whoever it is knows what he's about. But there was another shrimper in port yesterday, and a dozen crab and bird-dog boats. Where'd they went? There's the Club plain enough way off yonder, but then where's Big John's and Tammy's cabins! No humpback bridge neither; shoulda been behind that shrimper. He looked to the south; the stilted houses were still standing. Beau's didn't look the worse for wear, but he could see that Norm's was missing some roofing in one corner.

The *Ray* floated into a triangle of cabbage palms where the stern became lodged in a mass of trapped flotsam. Charley grabbed the ladder again, but no matter how hard he pushed, he couldn't budge her; the wind and waves kept her hard on the trees. He sat on the transom, blowing on his hands and assessing the situation when he heard, "Charley! Help me out of here!" Charley ducked like he had been shot at and spun around to look behind him. There was nothing there but a palm tree with a blue tarp washed up into the top. The tarp moved. "Charley, hurry man! I'm frozen half to death! Can't hardly move my legs." Charley squinted up into the tree; sounded like Beau, but all he saw was the tarp and a bunch of dead fronds. "Can't make my hands work to get this blasted thing off me!" Charley climbed up onto the transom and tentatively reached up to peel away the tarp and fronds. Plastered with bits of fronds, Beau's face appeared.

"Beau! Whacha doing up there, for Pete's sake!" Charley exclaimed, pulling the tarp away in earnest. When he cleared the frond debris, he discovered Beau was in his bathrobe. "Lord have mercy! I ain'ta even going to ask!" Beau's legs were tucked under him.

"Legs asleep, Charley; at least, I hope that's all. You're going to have to untangle them."

Charley carefully worked Beau's legs out; they were freezing cold, and he started rubbing them hard. "Kin you feel that?" Beau nodded. "Now we's got to be careful-like. I want you to lean over my shoulder like a fireman's deadman carry and I'll do my best to git you down without crackin' your noggin." Beau nodded again. "Now, careful-like!"

Beau outweighed Charley by a good forty pounds, but Charley was wiry strong. He got him safely down as far as the transom, but they tumbled into the stern as Charley tried to step down from there. Charley twisted as they fell so that he'd take the brunt of Beau's body coming down; it knocked the wind out of him.

"You okay, Charley?"

Charley caught his breath. "Yep, goin' to take a mite more than that to keep this ol' polecat down," he said, getting them both to their feet. "Now we just gotta git you to the cabin where I'm goin' to git you outta that there skimpy thing and dress you up like a Es-kee-mo. Goin' to start that gas stove and git that cabin toasty warm and see if'n we can't git them legs of yours moving agin."

As they struggled through the cabin door and down to the galley, Beau said solemnly, "Charley, I am making you a promise."

"And just what might that be?" Charley asked, breathing hard.

"I promise on all I hold sacred that I'll never make fun of you living on this old boat again; it's the prettiest damn boat I've ever seen!"

* * *

"Blankets, bedspreads, clothes, hats, and anything else you can think of. Believe there's a small tarp in the living room closet." Jimmy finished bailing and sponging a dry area while Crystal rummaged through drawers and closets. She returned with an armful that Jimmy piled onto the tarp. She went for another load. The sun was up, but it was gray and windy, waves still running by the house. He looked again at the watermarks on the cypress siding: holding steady for well over an hour now. Must be up around thirteen foot, he thought.

"This about does it, Jimmy."

"The boys still asleep?" She nodded. "Make sure they don't go out to splash around on the deck. This ol' water's liable to go out as fast as she come in, and it don't matter to her what she takes out." Crystal nodded. Jimmy started the motor. "Wish me luck," he said, casting off.

Jimmy maneuvered around the house and was immediately blown sideways by the wind. Compensating, he carefully motored past trees and floating objects as he headed towards the humpback bridge, or at least where the humpback bridge was: all he could see were a few jagged timbers sticking out of the water. Water everywhere; the fish houses were gone, although the tops of power poles were visible. Tiny's boat, all lit up with the diesel running, was the only other hint of what was. Its starboard lines disappeared under the water where it was most likely tied to the pilings. Jimmy eased up to the *Never Been Beat.*

"Tiny! Hey, Tiny! You in there!" Tiny's grim face appeared in the pilothouse window. He was out on deck in a flash. "You okay?" Jimmy asked.

"Yeah, fine. But got Ralph in there," he said, glancing behind him, "and he's in bad shape. Pulse is slower than molasses. Needs doctoring bad!"

"Seen anybody else?" Tiny shook his head. "I'll try to git help. I just left the house; ain't seen nobody neither."

"Crystal and the boys okay?"

"They're good, but it was close. Another six inches of water, and they'd be with me. I'm heading to the firehouse."

"Ten-four," Tiny said, ducking back into the pilothouse.

Jimmy carefully went around the humpback bridge area. The way the waves were breaking, he suspected a rat's nest underneath. A movement off to port caught his eye; there was a low-riding johnboat slowly heading in the same direction. The man steering a small outboard waved; Jimmy waved back and altered course. Looked like Donny Cherry's boat. A boy was in the bow, bailing fast, and two heads huddled close under a blanket were in the middle. Jimmy pulled up alongside.

"Jimmy, can you take the Mrs. and Angie here? We're riding awful low, and them waves ain't helping none?"

"Don't gotta ask, Donny," Jimmy said, as he threw the boy a line. "Careful now," he said to Donny's wife and daughter, "don't wanna git any wetter than you already are." Jimmy helped them into the boat. "You two okay?" he asked.

"Just glad to be alive," Donny's wife said.

"Seen anybody else?" Jimmy asked Donny, as he handed dry blankets to the woman and her daughter.

"Nope, but we was late leaving; thought we'd ride her out, but..." Donny didn't finish, he just shook his head. "Never seen nothing like it. Must be," he pointed to the sky, "someone upstairs had a hand on us."

Jimmy nodded. "Heading to the firehouse?"

"Trying to," Donny said, as he motioned to the boy to throw back the line. The two boats began to motor in tandem with Jimmy in the rear. They passed a clump of tall pines that Jimmy reckoned was Charley's land, but the *Ray* wasn't there. Jimmy couldn't believe the amount of water and the amount of crap floating everywhere. It was worse than the worst flooding he'd ever seen on the weather channel. Who knows, he thought, maybe the weather channel would send someone down here and Crescent Beach would be on national TV. The two boats passed a bobbing trussed roof section, dodged another few trees, and there was the *Stingray*, bow facing them with its stern lodged in a triangle of palms. No one was on deck. Jimmy motioned Donny to keep going;

he wanted to see if Charley was aboard. A wave caught Jimmy's boat on the approach, causing it to bump hard into the Ray, at least hard enough to have Charley scurry out of the cabin.

"Jimmy! Well, I'll be; thought I heard someones knock. Morning ladies," Charley said, doffing his baseball cap. "Fine weather we be having." Charley noticed all the clothes and blankets in the boat. He turned serious. "How bad's things, Jimmy?"

"Don't know yet. Heading to higher ground to see what needs doing. The *Ray* okay?"

"Yep, holding up just fine. Got me a passenger." Jimmy looked questioningly at Charley. "Found Beau up in one of them trees," he said, pointing behind him. "Was about naked and frozed to death; but, he's a'hanging in there. If you see Miss Virginia, you might tell her Beau's here. Probably worried to death about him."

"Will do." Jimmy shoved off. Evidence of buildings began to appear: a chimney, a couple peaks, a dormer. He soon saw that Donny had veered off course to pick up a couple stranded on a rooftop. Beyond them was a family of five, huddled on the leeward side of their chimney. Jimmy picked them up, and the two boats continued on to the firehouse. Judging by the houses, the water was getting shallower quickly. By the time they reached the firehouse, Jimmy had to tilt his motor up. The fire truck, with at least twenty people sitting on top, was outside the building. More were standing in line or wading around in the building. Jimmy could see a few women and girls crying, but mostly everyone looked stunned. Rusty, knee deep in water and still wearing his life jacket and pajamas, was pouring gas into the truck from a Gerry can. When he saw Jimmy, he shook his head.

"You'd think they'd keep her gassed up," Rusty said, continuing to shake his head in disgust.

"Nearest gas station is twenty miles; people been known to siphon some when they're in a pinch. Usually replace it sooner or later," Jimmy said, as he helped his passengers down out of the boat. "Bad timing." He took a better look at Rusty; his hair was plastered down and he was completely soaked. "Looks like you finally got some mileage out of that life preserver of yours."

"Saved my life." Rusty put the cap on the truck and gave the thumbs up to the driver who was watching him in the mirror. Jimmy gauged the height of the truck's engine with the water.

"Think she'll stall out?"

"No telling," Rusty answered, wading up to the cab. He motioned the driver to roll down his window. "Take her real slow; that wind is still kicking up waves." The driver nodded and put it into gear. Rusty turned back to Jimmy. "Just hope he can make it to dry ground, drop everybody off, then come back for others. Could use Norm big time; seen him in your travels?"

"Nope, but I pretty much came straight here. Take some of these clothes and such and pass 'em around inside. Then hop in and we'll go find him. Sure hope he and Tammy was at his place last night."

Jimmy had Rusty change into ill-fitting dry clothes and wrap a blanket around him as they made their way to Norm's house. The first person they saw was Virginia, out on the deck. She came down a few steps to the water's edge as they approached. Her face was tight, fingers pressed white as she squeezed the railing. "Beau," she began, but couldn't continue.

"He's okay! " Jimmy said immediately. "Don't know how he got there, but he's with Charley, safe and sound in Charley's boat."

Virginia's eyes closed and she collapsed onto a porch step, burying her face in her hands. She whispered, "Oh, God, thank you, thank you!" a few times between hard sobs. Finally, wiping her eyes and composing herself, she pulled herself back up by the railing.   She looked around. "What can I do to help?"

"Nothing now; not until we figure what's what. You're better off here until the water goes out; but I know we kin use more blankets and jackets and such." On cue, it began to spit snow. The three were dumbfounded. "Well, I never…Florida?" was all Jimmy could say before Virginia rushed off to get warm gear. Rusty followed to help. When they returned, they dumped a heap into the center of the boat.

Virginia asked, smiling, "When you see Beau, would you tell him that Skillet ate some breakfast, and even got up to take a tiny poop by the front door?"

"I can vouch for that," Rusty said. "I almost stepped in it. Pretty small, alright: didn't look much bigger than a cat's."

Jimmy smiled and nodded to Virginia. "I'll tell Beau soon as I see him," he said, as Rusty hopped aboard and shoved off.

There was no one at Norm's. "Was afraid of that," Jimmy said. He handed Rusty binoculars. "See anyone at the Club? Nothing much else above water over there."

Rusty shook his head. "Nobody, but who'd be standing outside in this weather?" Rusty said, putting down the binoculars. The wind and snow flurries continued.

Norm and Tammy saw the boat heading towards them. Norm could also see the damage to his roof and that the clinic had been mostly washed away. Immediately he thought that his insurance would cover all that, but didn't know about the Subaru. Tammy interrupted his thoughts. "Norm, you have a generator, don't you?"

"Yup, a Honda."

"Big enough to power a couple commercial freezers and refrigerators?"

"Should be."

"Good. We'll bring it over after we clean out all your food; going to be a parcel of mouths to feed, and I figure this is the best place to handle it. We'll need that generator to keep things from spoiling."

Here he was worried about insurance coverage when Tammy'd lost her entire house and everything in it, yet she was planning how to feed the town! Chagrinned, he looked back out to the boat. "Looks like Jimmy and Rusty," he said. They went out on the deck and waved.

"Town needs you bad, Doc," Jimmy yelled over the wind, arriving at what was left of the deck stairs a few feet above the boat. "Kin you git down alright?"

"Think so." Norm squeezed Tammy's shoulder and gave her a peck on the lips. "We'll get the generator when we can." Tammy nodded and Norm turned around to climb down backwards. He hung down from the last step as Jimmy maneuvered the boat underneath him.

"Got you covered," Rusty said, and caught Norm as he let go.

"So, what's up?" Norm asked, as Jimmy pulled away from the Club.

Rusty said, "Hypothermia, wounds of all sorts, one fellow thought he had a broken leg, a lady lost her oxygen tanks and was wheezing bad, and that's just with the people who were able to get to the fire station."

"First stop is Tiny's," Jimmy said. "Ralph's aboard, and Tiny says he's in bad shape." Jimmy steered the boat down Main Street to the *Never Been Beat.* Tiny came out and hoisted Norm up as Rusty and Jimmy held on to the side. Five minutes later, Norm returned to the boat.

"How's he doing?" Jimmy asked.

"Severe hypothermia. Got to get him to the hospital, but he won't leave until we look for Craig first on the island. I promised we would." The three men clustered behind the windshield as the boat headed out to the Gulf, hitting the waves head-on. The flurries continued.

Jimmy handed Norm the binoculars, saying, "Don't look like there's much of an island out there no more."

"You can say that again!" Norm said. "No house, just a chimney top. Some trees, mostly cedar showing red where their tops were busted, and...slow down a minute would you, Jimmy." Norm braced himself as best he could to steady the binoculars. "There's something dark in the top of one of the trees. Might be Craig."

Jimmy speeded up, the boat jumping and diving into the wind. After a few more minutes, Norm asked him to slow down again. "Yeah, it's him alright! Sweet Jesus, he must be freezing!"

When they arrived at the oak tree, Craig was a few feet above the water, mumbling and clawing at his sweater; it looked like he was trying to take it off. Rusty and Norm pulled him down onto a blanket. "Help me get all his clothes off, Rusty," Norm said, taking Craig's pulse. "Jesus," he said, "Hurry!" Norm started to strip.

They were going with the wind now, surfing the waves. "What the hell you doing, Norm!" Jimmy asked.

Naked except for his briefs, Norm lay down and hugged Craig. "Cover us up, Rusty. Got to warm him best way I can, or he won't make it! Has anyone radioed for ambulances?" Norm asked, as Rusty tucked in the blankets. Rusty looked at Jimmy who shrugged.

"Your radio work?" Rusty asked.

"Did before the storm hit."

Rusty turned it on and flipped through the frequencies. He chose one Jimmy didn't recognize and picked up the microphone. "May day, may day! This is an emergency, over." Nothing but static. Rusty tried again. On the third try, he was answered.

"This is Blimp Station Thirteen. Ensign Pulver here, over."

Jimmy's head snapped around; Rusty's eyes met his.

"Ensign, this is Rusty in Crescent Beach, over."

"Yes, Sergeant, hear you loud and clear, over."
Jimmy's eyes narrowed.

"We have an emergency here. Situation critical: town is covered in water, surge of maybe fourteen feet. People seriously injured with many still missing, gas leaking all over town. Contact Captain Smathers on your direct line. Tell him we need ambulances, dry clothes and blankets, emergency shelters set up in Perry. School buses or whatever to evacuate. Personnel to secure the area. Contact the Red Cross and all other emergency organizations in the area. We need immediate response. Is that clear? Over."

"Yes, Sergeant! Over."

"For the next few hours you can reach me at frequency 166.666. Got that? Over."

"Ten-four, Sergeant. Over."

"Over and out." Rusty put the mic away. Jimmy was poker-faced, but it was pretty obvious what he was thinking. "Crystal was wrong," Rusty said. Jimmy turned to concentrate on the waves.

"Rusty," came Norm's muffled voice. "Try rubbing Craig's feet to get the circulation going. I've got his hands in my crotch; they're like ice—he's about frozen to death!" Rusty worked on Craig until they arrived at the *Never Been Beat* where Rusty and Tiny managed to lower Ralph into the boat. Jimmy continued down Main Street, passing the fire truck being towed by a skidder. There was still over two feet of water at the cattle gap. When it became too shallow for the motor, Rusty towed the boat until they reached pavement. There was a good-sized crowd hovering around a bonfire and a few people laying on the ground to the side of the highway, covered in blankets. A Highway Patrol cruiser was parked up the road, its lights flashing. Sirens soon pierced the air and two ambulances led by a Perry police car came into sight. Rusty walk up to the state trooper who, mic in hand, was standing outside his cruiser. Jimmy watched them as they talked and saw the trooper nod several times before saluting Rusty.

When Rusty returned to the boat, Jimmy disdainfully held out both hands. "You got your handcuffs, officer?" He spat off to the side, shaking his head. "You're real good, you know that, Rusty? You make a damn good sleazebag," he added. "Had us all believing you was a real nice guy; played me and the whole town like a bunch of fools."

The ambulances pulled up. Rusty yelled to bring stretchers, then turned back to Jimmy. "No time for that now, Jimmy; give me a hand, we got to get Craig and Ralph here to Perry," Rusty said, climbing into the boat. He began to unwrap Norm and Craig. As Norm dressed, Jimmy, lips tight and eyes like ice, helped Rusty lift Craig out of the boat.

CHAPTER THIRTY-FIVE

Jimmy was right; when the wind began to die down, the water left almost as quickly as it came in, creating a dangerous current for those going house to house looking for survivors. The more the water flowed back out to the Gulf, the more devastating the scene became. The mobile homes and doublewides were hardest hit—gutted, leaning, tipped over, split in half, shredded like someone had gone wild with a gigantic can opener. Carport roofs had caved in on pickup trucks, scattered cars and trucks were buried in mud and seaweed, huge slabs of concrete had been uplifted from Main Street, trees and power poles were snapped in half. Grotesque sculptures of twisted PVC waterlines stuck up out of the ground, ripped porch screens flapped back and forth, capsized boats were left high and dry, docks had disappeared along with most of the boathouses. The entire town was covered by a thick carpet of tons of marsh grass and silt.

Rusty and Jimmy had agreed to work together, that it was more important to help the people of the town than anything else, and they had been motoring back and forth, hardly saying a word, ferrying people to the firehouse which was now above water. Several people were still unaccounted for, among them the ninety year old mayor who lived towards the point, past Tammy's. Rusty and Jimmy volunteered to go look for her.

Jimmy carefully cruised down Main Street, dodging the flotsam. To their left, only a few of the fish houses were still standing. They passed Big John's concrete block ice house, the single remnant of his store.

"People going to be digging out for weeks," Jimmy said, shaking his head. "That is, if they got anything to dig out."

"What's that?" Rusty asked, pointing at something swimming.

"Big moccasin?" Jimmy took a closer look. "Or, maybe small dog?" Jimmy turned towards it.

"I'll be damned! Dachshund; must be one of Maybelline's. Slow down, Jimmy, and I'll grab it." Rusty pulled it into the boat and detached the leash still fastened to its collar. The dog shook, beginning with his head and ending with its tail. Rusty lifted the tail. "Eeney or Miney." He looked at Jimmy. "You seen Maybelline anywhere?" Jimmy shook his head. "Guess we'd better head to her house after the mayor's."

They had to walk the last block to the mayor's house in a foot of water: it didn't look good. A tremendous slab of concrete had been uplifted from the street and had tumbled into the front wall. They carefully went inside. The floor tilted, a few old upholstered chairs and a couch in the living room were helter-skelter, a bookcase was tipped over and little china plates and bricabrac were stuck at odd angles in the mud. They entered the bedroom at the rear of the house. Lying face down in the mud, still dressed in her nightgown, was the mayor. Jimmy knelt beside her and gently stroked her matted and muddied gray hair. "Alot of Crescent Beach history here in this old gal. Town's going to miss her."

They silently carried the mayor back to the boat; she didn't weigh much. Jimmy washed off the muck as best he could before they lay her gently down in the stern where they covered her with a blanket. When the dachshund began to sniff around, Rusty picked the dog up. Jimmy started the Yamaha and they idled towards Maybelline's a couple of blocks away. With the wind down, they could hear sirens off in the distance.

"After this one, I'm going to take the boat back. Water's going to be too shallow and I don't want her high and dry like Charley is now," Jimmy said.

Jimmy approached Maybelline's with dread: it was the lowest house in town. They waded inside, passing through the living room into the bedroom. Nothing except scattered wet furniture, more knickknacks, clothes and bedding, and the ubiquitous mud.

"Maybe she made it out okay," Rusty said, as he left the room and led the way to the kitchen. He stopped in the doorway. "Guess not."

Maybelline was huddled on top of the refrigerator, staring straight ahead, two leashes still clenched in her hands. One of the dogs was down in the mud, the other two, attached to leashes, lay on top of the stove. Jimmy and Rusty lowered her and closed her eyes.

"Must have been terrified," Jimmy said, "trapped and watching the water rising up with no where to go." Rusty didn't say anything. Jimmy shook his head. "God acts in mysterious ways," he added.

When Maybelline and the dead dogs were in the boat, the dachshund went berserk. It began to howl and whine and thrash around in Rusty's arms. It didn't calm down for the entire trip back to the firehouse. Several men rushed out to help them with the bodies. They placed them next to two others.

"Who are they?" Rusty asked.

One of the men, whom Rusty recognized as the fire truck driver, said, "Tourist fishermen. Were staying in one of Tammy's cabins. All them cabins took it hard," he added.

"You were damn lucky you woke up when you did, Rusty," Jimmy said, climbing back into his boat. "Lucky for you, unlucky for me," he added. "Reckon I'll be heading home now afore all the water goes out and leaves me sitting on Main street."

"Mind if I come with you?" Rusty asked.

Jimmy gave him a long, sarcastic look. "What, you think I'm going to run off or something!'"

"Nope. Just want to give you something."

"Suit yourself."

Jimmy reversed away from the stationhouse and headed for home. They passed the *Stingray*, still wedged into the trees, but tilting badly on its keel now that the water had dropped. No one was on board; Beau had been deemed fit enough by Norm to go home and Charley was helping Norm out at the highway.

Eyes straight ahead, motor tilted up and heading for his dock, Jimmy said, "Imagine you was bugged when we was talking out on the Club's deck after the race."

"Yup, I was."

"So, you probably got what you was after?"

"Yup, I did."

"You bugged now?"

"Not really."

They approached the dock. The water was rushing out like someone had pulled the plug in a bathtub; Jimmy had to make two passes before they could grab hold of the pilings. Once the boat was secure Jimmy turned to look at Rusty. "Not really?"

Rusty climbed out of the boat with the dachshund under an arm. He extended a hand to pull Jimmy up, but it was ignored. When both were on the dock, Jimmy repeated, "'Not really.' What do you mean by that?"

Rusty put the dog down and unstrapped his life vest. He handed it to Jimmy, saying, "Here."

Jimmy took it and rolled his eyes. "Geez, thanks. What do I need this for? This'll do me a lot of good, rotting in a prison somewhere. Maybe I kin use it as a pillow."

"Take a look inside."

Jimmy unfolded it. "So?" he said, looking back at Rusty. Rusty reached over and opened the hidden compartment with the Velcro opening disguised as the heavy threads of a seam.

"Check it out."

Jimmy reached in and pulled out the recording device. "I'll be; clever, that," he said, looking again at the pouch area, then at the bug. "Must be waterproof."

"Yup, and it's got our conversation and a bunch of other stuff on it. Actually, it's got everything I thought incriminating or useful for the last month. But, as far as I'm concerned, it got lost in the storm. If I were you, I'd smash it, then drop it into one of those redfish holes you showed me."

Jimmy stood there speechless, then jumped down in the boat. Opening a tool compartment, he pulled out a hammer and smashed the bug on the edge of the dock. He put the flattened bug in his pocket and the hammer back in the compartment. He extended his hand up to Rusty. Rusty pulled him up.

"Why'd you give it to me?" Jimmy asked.

"Guess it's because I have to live with myself. Just didn't seem right, what I was doing; went kind of across the grain."

"Seems Crystal was right after all."

"Halfway, maybe. Say goodbye to her for me, would you? Don't think I could quite look her in the eye right about now."

"Will do."

"What are you going to do with her?" Rusty asked, looking down at the dog. Jimmy picked her up.

"I'll find her a home."

Rusty reached out, wondering if Jimmy would shake his hand. He did. "Well, maybe see you again, sometime. Take care of yourself, Jimmy."

"What about all your fish."

"I imagine they're some folks in town who are going to need it a lot more than me."

Jimmy nodded. Rusty began to walk away. Jimmy called out to him. "Hey, Rusty!" Rusty turned. "Did you really race against Junior?"

Rusty smiled. "Yup, sure did; but seems like a couple lifetimes ago."

CHAPTER THIRTY-SIX

Norm was sitting at his desk dueling with Huey with a pencil, tapping the parakeet's beak, trying to keep him away from the paperwork. When the parakeet hopped over to nibble on a corner of the insurance form, Norm shooed him away with the palm of his hand. "Go on Huey or I'll put you back in your cage." Huey flew up and landed on Norm's shoulder, chattering excitedly in his ear. Norm went back to filling out the form. What a pain, he thought.

The clinic was a complete loss; at least it had been cleaned up, as well as the roof of the house tarped. But that was it. It was impossible to get a builder or an electrician; it wasn't just Crescent Beach, but the whole Nature Coast had been hit—Dekle Beach, Keaton Beach, Steinhatchee, Horseshoe Beach, Suwannee, Cedar Key, and farther down. It was a builder's bonanza, a chance to cash in on FEMA as well as the insurance companies; builders were flocking in from all over Florida and south Georgia. The Perry motels were overflowing, and you couldn't buy a generator within five hundred miles. And not all the so-called builders were reputable either. There were those who slapped a magnetic sign on their pickup and talked a good game, but they were

dubbers with no real experience. With all the federal
disaster money being spread around, bills were being
outrageously padded. For those without insurance, they
either rolled up their sleeves or threw their hands up in
the air, ready to sell and move out of town.

The cleanup had been going on for close to three
weeks with the incessant beeping of frontend loaders
filling dump trucks with debris to go to the landfill a
couple miles out of town. Houses and trailers were still
being hoed out and pressure-washed, the mud in some
had been over three feet thick. Piles of ruined personal
possessions, yards and yards of carpet and rugs, busted
furniture, stained couches were in the yards, wreckers
were towing out cars and trucks, Ma Bell trucks scurried here and there, and generators were still supply-
ing a good portion of the electricity. Many families
were living in small campers brought in by the federal
government.

Tammy and her birds had moved in for the foresee-
able future; she was way too busy serving food to the
town to even begin thinking about building a new house,
even if she could afford to. It, along with most of her
possessions, had been lost. The mess was being cleaned
up by the same local fishermen who had cleaned up his
clinic and tarped the roof; they had lost their boats in
the storm and needed the work. At least his septic system was on line again so that they didn't have to queue
up with the others in front of stinking porta-potties.

He hadn't realized how much of a bachelor he'd
become, how different it was having a woman around
full time again. He'd go look for something in its usual place, but it had disappeared. He'd find out later
that Tammy had efficiently tucked it away someplace,
resulting in less clutter, but which also played havoc
with his mind. He wasn't allowed to keep his tooth-
brush and open tube of toothpaste out on the sink. No

more stacks of medical magazines by the toilet, or shirts
and pants left draped over chairs. Pots and pans were
promptly put away, no more leaving dishes stacked in
the drainer for days. The clean sheets once a week was
a nice change and somehow Tammy also found the time
to clean house and sweep up after the birds who were
always making a mess. So far he had done all the cooking when they ate at home; Tammy was too involved with
cooking, serving, and organizing the volunteeers at the
Club. The last thing she wanted to look at was another
stove. If she got hungry, she opted for crunchy peanut
butter on saltines.

Norm suddenly looked at his watch. "Damn! I'm
late, Huey," he said, immediately throwing down the
pencil and putting a finger up to the parakeet's breast.
Huey hopped on and Norm put him in his cage. The
green cockatiel across the room made a ruckus. "Settle
down, Henrietta. Tammy'll be taking you out when she
gets back." Norm quickly loaded up with quarters and
put a partial bottle of Jack Daniels into a rucksack. First
poker night in a month; about time, he thought, as he
headed out the door and down the stairs to Beau's.

Charley's Mustang along with Jimmy's new white Ford
pickup and Ralph's little Toyota pickup were parked in
the street in front of Beau's. Beau's Caddy had been replaced by a rent-a-car that was parked under the house;
it looked out of place. Norm didn't bother knocking
and went straight to the bar where he made himself a
drink before sitting down at the long dining room table.
Piles of quarters and the usual assortment of drinks were
on the table. "Mr. Mayor," he said, nodding to Beau,
"Gentlemen," he said to the others. Charley appeared
to have just won a hand.

"Where you been, Doc?" Charley asked, raking in a
pile of quarters.

"Filling out insurance forms."

Craig rolled his eyes. "Never seen so much paper-work. And the adjustors don't believe me when I tell them everything I had out on the island. And I can't show them what's not there."

"They shoulda been around when the water gone out," Charley said. "Ain't never seen nothing like that afore, and prob'ly never will agin; mud flats and oyster bars as fur as the eye kin see."

"You boys don't know what paperwork is," Beau add-ed. "All the rules, regulations, and requirements from FEMA are a nightmare. And as newly appointed Mayor, it falls on me to read and interpret them all. I'll tell you one thing and you can mark my words: if we accept their money with their conditions, then this town's going to become a far different place."

"Have to build eighteen feet above sea level for start-ers," Ralph put in.

"Eighteen foot up! Heck, half the town's people is too durn old to climb up that high. And who's gon-na carry up their groceries?" Tiny asked, shuffling the cards. "Me and Charley about got my place back togeth-er and it's a'staying put down on the ground where it belongs. They's a'calling that storm the 'storm of the century' now, so I figure we got another hundrid years afore the next one."

"Can happen any time, Tiny," Jimmy said.

"Maybe, but if'n you go a'raising them double-wides up eighteen foot like some of the people is planning to do, what's the wind going to do with 'em being up so high?"

"You got the *Ray* squared away, Charley?" Norm asked.

"Yep, all shipshape."

"Love that boat!" Beau interjected.

Ralph said, "Big John's just listed his property with me today. Said he doesn't have the money to even think of rebuilding. He's got a job at a fish house in Apalachicola and is going to move the whole fam…" Ralph was interrupted by barking and the sound of toenails skidding and scraping on Beau's oak floor. A dachshund with Skillet scrambling after it came running out of the bedroom. They banged into the table as they made the turn into the kitchen. Quarters went flying as Jimmy and Charley expertly caught their beers before they tipped over. Tiny, deck of cards in hand, wasn't so lucky.

"Dangnation!" Tiny exclaimed, quickly picking up his bottle.

"Paper towels on the counter," Beau said, before lowering his voice to Skillet. "Skillet, you and Miney take it easy! You come over here and say hello to your doctor. C'mon now!"

Norm put his hand out and Skillet, tail wagging, came up for a pat. The shaved areas were almost fully grown in and he looked almost up to weight. "How's my star patient, huh Skillet?" Skillet's tail wagged faster in reply.

"How'd you figure out it was Miney, Jimmy?" Tiny asked.

"Tammy knew," he said, snapping his fingers. Miney immediately came over.

"Dang if'n she don't look good! You got her on a diet?" Charley asked.

"Dry food and water. No more scraps. She's a good girl."

"Going to keep her?" Norm asked.

"Imagine. Grandyoung'uns love her to death. Won't let me get rid of her."

"Hear anything from Rusty, Jimmy?" Tiny asked.

"Nope, and don't expect to."

"Now weren't that the craziest thing: him being a statey," Charley said, shaking his head. "Why do you think he told us he was a road contractor and all?"

"Maybe he thought people wouldn't associate with him, sit around and drink beers and shoot the bull like regular folk," Beau said. "Other than maybe Norm here, would you have hung around with him if you knew he were a state trooper?"

"You saying we're outlaws?"

"No, Jimmy. I'm just saying I don't think you'd have been too comfortable knowing that; that's all."

"Got a point," Jimmy agreed.

"Where's Virginia? Helping at the Club?" Norm asked.

"Yeah, Tammy roped her into both shifts." Beau looked at his watch. "About time for the second." He looked round the table. "Enough chit chat; what say we play some poker." Tiny began to deal.

Over at the Crescent Club, the line started at the door and extended all the way down the new stairway to where the pool table used to be. Inside, the women were almost ready to serve. Tables that had been pushed together along the far wall opposite the bar had been replenished with plates and bowls of fried mullet, okra, swamp cabbage, french fries, mustard greens, cole slaw, hush puppies, and wild hog. Virginia and Tammy placed the final pitchers of tea along side thermoses of coffee and a multitude of pies and pastries on the bar. No alcohol was permitted during the meals. Everyone was welcome, including the construction workers from out of town, and no one was ever charged, although there was an enclosed box at the head of the bar for donations. It was a prodigious effort by the ladies of the town, church-going or not, but Tammy was the linchpin: absolutely no one worked as hard as she did and without her there wasn't a chance in hell it could have been pulled off, day after day.

Virginia and Tammy took their positions behind the line of tables. Sarah, the reverend's wife, stood between them. She started chatting with Virginia as Tammy, accustomed to being excluded by the church ladies, wearily turned to look out over Crescent Beach. Here it was, just before seven in the evening, she thought, and still plenty of hustle and bustle going on. More rubble was being carried to the landfill, open now around the clock. She could see two men leveling up pressure treated posts, another operating a cement mixer, and others wheel-barrowing mortar to masons laying block. She looked over towards the creek. Tiny's boat was in, as well as a half-dozen birddog and crab boats. The few fishermen going out these days were very generous, like with the mullet tonight. And the Piggly Wiggly grocery store in Perry! They had been terrific, donating what they said was produce too old to sell, even though most of it looked farm fresh. And they delivered all the way out here! Her mood swiftly changed when she saw the void on the edge of the creek where Big John's store should be. The concrete block icehouse, minus the compressor on top, was all that was left standing. Word had it that Big John and his family were moving out of town. And they weren't alone.

Tammy sighed and looked at the clock on the wall. Seven on the nose. She went to open the front door. People began to shuffle in, the noise in the bar quickly increasing ten fold. Tammy returned to her spot behind the tables, picking up a big spoon, ready to serve golden brown hushpuppies. Sarah, in her long somber skirt, surprised her when she began speaking to her.

"Tammy, I want to say that the Reverend and I, all the people of the church for that matter, want to thank you for what you've done. Your hard work and sacrifice and generosity have touched us all. You may not attend church, but I've come to believe that God sometimes puts the spirit of the church in a person; I believe you're such a person. I am proud to live in the same town with you."

Tammy didn't know what to say. She saw Virginia smiling at her from behind Sarah's shoulder.

"Will Dr. Norm be eating here tonight?" Sarah asked.

"No, he's having dinner with Beau," Tammy answered, wondering what Sarah would think if she knew that Norm was probably into his second of several Jack Daniels and playing poker.

"That's too bad. I was hoping I could invite you two to dinner at our house sometime next week."

The invitation about floored Tammy. She stumbled over her reply. "That would be nice...that is, I'm sure Norm would, er, we would, love to come." Wait until Norm hears about this!

"There is one thing, though..."

"What's that?"

"We allow no alcohol in our home."

Tammy smiled.

"Not a problem, Sarah. Sweet tea would be just fine."

ℰPILOGUE

TALLAHASSEE TIMES
Wednesday
August 1, 1998

As was reported in the TIMES ten days ago, two ama-
teur archaeologists, scuba diving in a remote flooded sinkhole
near the Wacissa River west of Perry, discovered a man's skel-
eton wrapped in chains and concrete blocks. Two bullet holes
were found, one in the victim's head and the other in his right
hand. Through a lead provided by retired State Trooper
Rusty McMillan of Crescent Beach, the remains have been
identified as those of Jose Arias, also known as El Espantoso,
a drug trafficker from Miami with ties to a Colombian cartel.

Forensic experts believe the body had been in the sinkhole
for at least several years and authorities are attributing the
death to a gangland killing. State Police Captain Smathers
told the TIMES, "Dental records from Miami have positively
confirmed the identification of this man. This was an execu-
tion, plain and simple, within the ranks of a notorious drug
ring operating out of Miami. We are not going to pursue this
case. The state of Florida is better off without this criminal."

In related drug trafficking news, it has been announced
that the Department of Defense has closed Blimp Station
Number Thirteen. Established in 1978 outside of Crescent
Beach, the blimp station was used in aerial surveillance of the
Big Bend area of northern Florida. Citing continual down-
time of the blimp due to weather and mechanical difficulties
along with a drastic drop in smuggling activities in the area,
a spokesman from the Department of Defense said that the
facility would be sold to a local LP gas company.

Facts About The Storm Of The Century
March 13 & 14, 1993

1. Also known as the No Name Storm, the Storm From Nowhere, and the Superstorm of 1993.
2. 26 States affected.
3. 235 people in over 100 boats rescued by U.S. Coast Guard.
4. 200' freighter Fantastico sank 70 miles off Fort Myers, Fla., with 7 of the 10 crew members perishing.
5. 147' freighter Miss Beholding ran aground off Key West.
6. In Florida, 59,000 cloud to ground lightning strikes as the storm moved onshore.
7. Florida had a 12 foot storm surge on sections of the Gulf Coast, 47 lives lost, 11 confirmed tornadoes, 18,000 homes damaged, 21 out of 61 counties declared federal disaster areas.
8. Damage exceeded 1.6 billion dollars in Florida.
9. More died from drowning than in Hurricanes Hugo and Andrew combined.
10. Snow reported as far south as the Gulf Coast of northern Florida: 4" in the Florida Panhandle.
11. Coastal flood warnings from Virginia Beach to Rhode Island.
12. Record low pressures in Worcester, Ma., Wilmington, Del., Washington D.C., Richmond, Va., Asheville, N.C., Raleigh, N.C., Columbia, S.C.
13. 3 million customers lost electricity.
14. Blizzard warnings from North Carolina to New Brunswick.
15. More water fell as snow than flows past the mouth of the Missisippi River in 40 days.

16. 8.7 billion dollars worth of damage in U.S.
17. Over one billion dollars worth of damage in Cuba.
18. Maximum winds over 130 miles per hour.
19. Most widespread disruption of air travel in the history of aviation.
20. Every airport from Halifax, Nova Scotia, to Atlanta, Georgia, was closed for some time.
21. Snowfall accumulation exceeding 40" was observed in at least seven states (Maryland, New York, North Carolina, Pennsylvania, Tennessee, Vermont, West Virginia).
22. Maximum snowfall amounts: Mount Mitchell in North Carolina—50" and Mount LeConte, Tennessee—60".
23. 17" snowfall at Birmingham, Alabama, was greatest recorded for any day, any month, any season.
24. 4 states set all time records for deepest snow (Georgia, North Carolina, Tennessee, Maryland).
25. Boone, North Carolina, had 21' high snowdrifts.
26. Estimated that the snowfall impacted the lives of over 90 million people.
27. Numerous record low temperatures: Birmingham, Alabama, recorded 2 degrees Fahrenheit.
28. Total of 318 people perished during the storm.
29. Affected at least 26 states and much of eastern Canada.
30. Last event of storm, Sunday March 14: 586' freighter Gold Bond Conveyor sank in the North Atlantic in 90mph winds and 100' waves. Entire crew of 33 perished.

*Sources:

1. *1993 Storm of the Century-Wikepedia, the Free Enclycopedia* (Internet)

2. *Superstorm-Storm of the Century-1993-History* (Internet)
3. *Superstorm 1993: 20 Years Ago This Week-weather.com* (Internet)
4. *The Storm of the Century-1993-Dixie County's Worst Disaster* ("Dixie County Advocate")

ABOUT THE AUTHOR

David Mather began visiting the Big Bend area of Florida's gulf coast in 1999, becoming a resident in 2006. The area and its people inspired *Crescent Beach*. He has written two earlier novels based on his experience in southern Chile while serving in the Peace Corps.

Made in the USA
Columbia, SC
13 November 2022

71032786R00233